A Demigoddess' Guide to Inter-Dimensional In-Laws

JaCol Publishing Inc.

Copyright 2019 © by JaCol Publishing Inc.

Illustrations Copyright © 2018 by
JaCol Publishing Inc.
FIRST PRINTING

March 2019
All rights reserved

JaCol Publishing Inc.
195 Murica Aisle
Irvine, CA 92614
818-510-2898
Editor-in-Chief: Randall Andrews
Managing Editor: Jessica Collins
www.jacolpublishing.com

ISBN:

Cover Art: Katie Ketchum

Acknowledgement

Being chronically ill can be lonely and hard work. But because of these people I"m able to do amazing things. Without them my life would be boring and much quieter. I'd be able to write to my heart's content without interruption and be totally without love, fun and care, so boring; my amazing husband Graeme, my kids and grandkids Caitlin, Savannah, Meagan , Nathanial, Sprout, Lauren, Aaron, Elijah and Lentil, Leah - the real one and her tribe, my in-laws, my bestie Jen Jen, Dave and kids, and soul mate Trace aka Irica, Mickey, Lyndall, Sue, Paul aka inspiration for Sam, Kirsten and their tribe, Tamie, Simon and Alastair, Tash, Michael, Eve and kid Max plus dog Max, my amazing Aunt Anne-Marie, and too many others to mention.

A huge thank you as always to my editor Randall Andrews, whom without my stories would suck, and to my cover artist, Katie Ketchum, who gives me that flavour of art. Also, to the usual living better and at all through modern chemistry, podcasts especially Joe Rogan's, Bunnings and garage sales. I've said it before and I'll say it again, this:
"We become what we repeatedly do. Don't be an arsehole. Oh and to all the Sim City people who left our club, screw you guys. I left too. Ha".

Contents

Chapter 1: Bye, Bye Birdy, Bye, Bye
Meeting room, UPA Mother Ship, Outer Syrian Galaxy

Shayne's waistline expanded faster than the universe. Her belly hung over the cushion several inches from the long table. She cursed whoever deemed middle aged pregnancy, upcoming nuptials, and demigod duties a great idea.

I'm trying so hard keeping up with this shit. Mother fuckers, wind it up quicker. I've got serious resting on the agenda. These cankles do not shrink themselves.

Annu's feathered friend shifted on her seat at the opposite end. "I know it seems I've spoken for a while but it's been difficult getting us all together and there are many aspects of your membership to cover before......anyway. The UPA's access extends well beyond this universe and Demigods like yourselves into unimaginable places. In a way we're a resource centre for higher beings and members with access to restricted places, information and special artifacts that are sometimes required for particular missions. I've sent a list of our protocols, regulations, and other important information...."

My brain hurts. Everywhere I go, I'm forced to learn. It's one important thing after the other. What's her name again? She's a walking, talking bird. But blue not yellow and more hard work than my pet budgie Birdy at five. The one I forgot to feed. Birdy it is.

Aside from three more like-bird beings, an assortment of weird creatures around the table altered Shayne's normal department.

Shayne twisted the communication band on her wrist; it pinched her skin. "Isn't Maybe-Marge's idea a bit antiquated? Shouldn't it be holographic or something? I'm so tired and blah. This is going on forever."

Oh my fucking gods. Any bigger and I'll have a planet named after me.

Annu rolled his shoulders and inhaled. "It's a trial system and it works for the most part. Maybe we should just go, you look uncomfortable."

Ah, right? He usually loves this shit, what gives? If he's horny he's shit out of luck. That's what got me in this mess.

Shayne's poked her gut in and out. "Nah. We'll only have to come back again another time. I want to break free. I want to break free. I want to break free from your thighs, you're so self-satisfied, I don't neeeed, oh wait, that's a bit naughty."

People groaned, moaned, and raised their voices.

Annu's eye twitched, he gripped her arm rest. "My love, please, don't. If we leave now they'll be time for me to help set up tables and check on Zeke's mother."

I'm getting De ja vu and a stitch. It must suck having a mum you love and she's dying. I can't even imagine what that's like. Why did mine hate me so much she left after I was born?

Rejection weaved a tea cosy over Shayne's brain, she picked the seams. "Yeah, yeah, yeah. I've heard that before. Just like family time and the magical, mystical date night. You, me, a fire and a good show. It's all bloody bullshit, mate. I'm not, having, the time of my life…. And I owe it all to youoooooh."

Birdy's chirp flipped Shayne's hormone switch. "My, my, my. Surely all that jiggling isn't good for the babies. May I proceed and stick to the point?"

Is that a jab at my recent lack of exercise? Is she calling me fat? I'll kill her. Shit. What if my gargantuan mass turns Annu off too now? Great. Fuck.

Shayne heated, cooled, heated, cooled and heated. "I'm guessing you all think I'm a talentless hack then? Nice. Thanks a lot."

Annu released her thigh and gritted his teeth. "Ah, sweetie. Calm down. Again, wrong crowd, wrong conclusion to jump to."

Chocolate withdrawal and swollen ankles over rode rational. "Oh. So they don't think I'm a whale?"

Annu stiffened and flushed. "Shay, how would I know? That's not the point, come one, let's just go. We've got friends at home."

That kind of means they probably do then. He didn't say no. He feels that way too. He doesn't want to be seen in pubic, I mean public with me.

Shayne collected crumbs of self-dignity. "Yeah well, I can't believe I'm saying this but no, we're staying until Birdy's finished. Remember, responsibility, duty and all that shit. No matter how long, long, long, long it takes for our good karma to arrive." Her prior life of couch surfing, debt dodging, chocolate eating and wallowing twinkled in a galaxy far, far, far, away.

Annu twisted in his seat, sweat beaded across his forehead. "Okay, great."

For once things are looking up and problems are manageable. Now to prepare for impending mother hood only version 2.0 and finding out what's going on with my man. I'm pulling testicle hairs getting information out of him in that regard.

Birdy's chirp cheese grated Shayne's patience. "I don't mean to interrupt but my name is not Birdy, it's Ankor. May I continue?"

The babies shifted, a foot jabbed into her ribs.

Shayne stuck her fingers under and pushed. "You two are trouble already. I'm sorry, Birdy, I'm an arsehole with no attention span whatever."

Maybe I'll be pregnant forever. I'll never see my whooha or feet again.

Birdy's shrill re-diverted Shayne's focus. "Right. You both arrived via a wormhole, did you send a ship separately?"

Shit, missed all that. Wake up, Australia, Tasmania is floating away.

Shayne shifted between numb butt cheeks. "No, why?"

The lion beside Birdy purred rather than spoke. "To collect the remaining Igigi from Marduk and return them here for protection. Unless you wormhole a craft with you?"

I don't know what he's talking about but he's so cute and warm and fluffy. Somehow I don't think he'd appreciate the compliment.

Shayne imagined cuddled up with him on cold days. "Ah, again no. Remind me who they are again?"

Annu nodded and raised a finger. "They're a race believed wiped out millennia ago until the UPA recently found some on Marduk where they'd hidden waiting for the return of their prophet Jazekial."

An elbow lodged under Shayne's diaphragm. "Oh yeah, that's right, one of my maternal, hormonal, empathetic decisions. Why are we doing it and not some transport company?"

Annu avoided eye contact, his scent drove Shayne nuts. "The Annunaki may have found them there too. You know the score, it's our job. We both forgot even though we suggested it." He nodded at Birdy. "We'll arrange transport ASAP. Are we done?"

Jacob better come back soon, I tell you. There's lots he needs to be doing. Fuck. Did I remember to grab extra linen? Oh and towels. Shit. Too much to do.

Indigestion bubbled in Shayne's gut, breakfast returned in a burp and fart. "My bad. I felt sorry for them. Man, they are patient people. I get annoyed waiting for microwave popcorn. For fuck's sake. Sadly, we're prepared for arseholes like the Annu-Knuckle-Heads. In fact, I'm writing a blog about it. Or I will when I get time. Instead of sending someone else, I'll pick them up on my way home from wherever I'm off next."

Will someone clone me a few hundred times? Then I wouldn't need a stupid assistant on the world's longest holiday.

Annu yawned and blocked the light. "A joint baby shower for you and the Prime Minister of Nexus, then pick up Ryan and Joey. And you're meant to supply the food for said party. Another good reason to leave soon."

Baby brain sucks. But once they're born I can't blame that anymore. I better come up with a better excuse for stupid and lazy.

Shayne's gut gurgled, she clenched. "Oh. I ate that fucking food. I thought you just really loved me when you went shopping. Shit. I'll have to pick up Ryan and Joey somewhere along the line. Which makes two more to protect when my powers aren't as reliable. Maybe you're right about leaving now?"

Responsibility beat Shayne to death and picked at her bones.

Annu massaged her nape, no grief for her demise in sight. "Of course I am. I know, you need some rest. We both do. I swear it's happening after the wedding. You'll get your date nights and then some."

Images of a chocolate, chocolate hulk invaded her mind.

Shayne relaxed into the chair. "Fuck yeah. That's what I'm talking about. All right you sold me. Sorry Birdy, we're cutting this short."

Mmmmm, I'm smothered in chocolate. Mmm, chocolate.

Birdy's shrill burst Shayne's brown bubble. "Not yet. These interruptions are pushing us away from the matters at hand. Shayne, while on Marduk, kindly obtain any information available regarding the rumoured Annunaki. An idea of their numbers from a direct source is imperative in our understanding their threat to Enlil's upcoming ascension."

A chocolate paradise circled the drain pipe and clumped.

Annu's eye twitched, he blinked, lots. "No. I'll go. She's not up to interrogations and I'm not endangering her. I'm taking care of it. What else must we know?"

I'm loving his caring side and all but he's giving me the shits. I'm losing control of myself here and fuck it, he's being kinda selfish.

Shayne shook off worry. "All right Mr. Over-flipping-protective. I'm pregnant not dying and perfectly capable of a simple pick up job. Hey, why are we involved with the Igloo guys too? Oh, you better give me a good description so I don't bring back the wrong people. Not that it's happened before."

Okay, once. Please don't be scary, although I am hanging for a decent horror movie. That DNA inheritance or whatever one sucked. What's wrong with critics?

Annu's tone sliced like a knife, he rose. "I'm just supporting you and there's more important things to do than talk."

Birdy glared and Annu sat. "Even we know precious little about them other than they're somehow repellant to at least the Annunkai and Enlil. A back up plan I pray we won't require. From memory, the Lexicon only mentions them and a sword of great power they crafted. We have this item in our secured area. As to the Igigi I believe they're around six feet tall, luminous orange skin and pale blonde hair. Their soft spoken and extremely polite.

Annu, I've tried speaking to you privately to no avail. I'm sorry, despite your assurances there's no chance Enlil can or will ascend, the gravity of the situation dictates we not rely on your word alone and it seems a just protocol. We've been unable to contact Lexicon's protector Jacob. This is highly unusual and concerning given it contains the essential incantation for said ascension."

There's a subtext I feel and don't see. If only my head cleared and my brain handled more.

Shayne's sixth sense fizzled and popped. "You mean Jacob? Don't worry, he's on holidays. Everything's fine, it must be a glitch. Enlil, can't get the book. Unless I'm wrong this one really might be as easy as letting time lapse."

Damn Zeke and Annu monopolising the book of late. I'd catch up and know more about him. Maybe. Fuck it.

Annu flinched and pushed back. "See, it's all fine. We'll catch up later."

Birdy motioned downwards. "Not this time. Enough of the deterrents, something's not right. Jacob's not on holidays or whatever that means without the Lexicon. You and the book are his duties. They're intrinsically linked. Without him there is no protection around it. Anyone with any power can locate it. Oh Gods, has Jacob been kidnapped? Is that why you're being strange? Is he in danger?"

Anytime someone mentions Enlil and Jacob, he gets weird. Fuck, do we really know each other?

Annu perched on the edge of his seat, flames grew, the room heated. "No, nothing like that. I don't know why you can't get through but I'm personally telling you he and the book are fine."

Shayne plonked, the chair creaked. "Honey, calm down. What's with you?"

Birdy's temple pulsed, her cheeks fluttered. "I want to believe you, yet I can't help feeling something's not right. We won't take chances. You know the stakes."

The creeps swept across Shayne, she shivered and faced Annu. "What don't I know?"

Annu licked his lips, flames spread down his arms. "I, I, he's fine. He's due back tomorrow, it's private family business. We'll talk about it later."

This is way beyond weird. This is brain tumour territory.

Birdy cocked her head and blinked. "I don't know what else to, this is, oh dear. It's a mess."

Tension crackled and intensified, the air thickened.

What the literal fuck? I'm so over this being late to the party shit.

The hand of doom choked Shayne. "Annu, I'm freaking out here."

The lion's teddy bear status abated, sharp teeth lined fuzzy muzzle. "We'll organise teams to search for him immediately."

The other birds and lions shuffled.

Shayne's patience got up and left. "Actually fuck later. What gives?"

Annu scraped the chair on the floor, sweat dripped from his temples. "Everyone stop. There's nothing wrong for the hundredth time. Leave it."

Birds cleared her throat and fluffed. "Out of respect and hope, you've a few hours to sort out your personal life, confirm details of Jacob and the lexicon or we'll take custody of the book and both of you, at least until Enlil's date passes. If something untoward's happened to Jacob however, there will be grave consequences. Gods or not, you'll not jeopardise any life. Alas, I fear this may be the shortest membership in our history. Annu, may I speak to you alone before you leave?"

I haven't sacrificed, suffered and learned getting this far to screw it up and be in hell not heaven anyway. When will this get easier? We're good people with good intentions and shit.

Shayne jabbed and growled. "With all due respect, fuck off, Birdy. No one's having a word or anything else until I'm done with my fiancé."

Like we need another headache. It's me that's supposed to fuck up. Not him. Shit.

Birdy's chin dropped, puffed her chest and left the room in a trail of feathers. "As you wish."

The others followed and mumbled amongst themselves.

Shayne grabbed Annu's arm. "You've got some 'splaining to do, Lucy. Have we and I use that figuratively, fucked up again or what?"

Annu combed fingers through his hair. "Well, oh, flark it. Yep. But keep your voice down. They can't know. I'm sure it's fixable and I don't want them losing faith in us."

Anxiety thrust Shayne's chest in a vice, she opened a wormhole. "Yeah well, I think that ships sailed away. Who'd have thought having everything I wanted would be more difficult than having nothing?"

I should have. One way or another my past will continue to bite me.

Chapter 2: A Monkey chased a weasel
Transport depot, Enki Island

A mental lump grew from where the first metaphorical shoe landed on Annu's head, the other dangled over a fresh spot. The truth in Ankor's telepathic messages formed into a big, ugly buzzard and ate Annu's good intentions.

Forgive me, I just can't seem to find the time to tell her I'm related to evil while she's pregnant and fragile when it can wait. Okay, there's more to it but I'm not there yet either.

The PFD engines escalated Annu's pulse, he followed Shayne into the ship.

Guilt consumed Annu and filmed over emotions. "I still think Erin, Rosie, or myself should come with you too. Unexpected things happen sometimes, it's inevitable no matter what we do."

And you're out of my sight and protection. It scares the shit out of me.

Shayne wobbled into the cargo hold and stood akimbo. "Well, I don't and if I hadn't committed to bringing Maybe-Marge to the party I'd go alone. I wish I'd gotten out of seeing her too though. Everyone can get fucked. No offence Maybe-Marge."

Marguerite paced before the flight deck. "Some taken anyway. I'm not happy about this detour you've thrown in last minute. The communication band's haven't been tested that far, and I have to be back this afternoon for other matters."

Shayne glanced at Marguerite and frowned. "Then fucking stay here too. Jesus."

Shit. I've totally flarked it up, again. I'm the cause of the crankiness. If we can just get through this, we'll be fine.

Marguerite snorted and stomped into the cabin. "I didn't say I didn't want to go, only that unexpected trips inconvenience me. There's no need for rudeness."

Annu reached Shayne in two steps and hugged. "Shay, don't take it out on her. She's been a good friend to you."

Shayne wriggled out of his embrace, her skin chilled. "For future reference you suck at lying. I'm such a dumb arse. How'd I miss this? Now I'm worrying about anti-Jacob as well. What kind of moron's un-create someone while trying to fix their first fuck ups. Fuck, fuck, shit. They can have the fucking Lexicon, It's nothing but trouble but they aren't getting us. How do we bring Jacob back? We are aren't we?"

Annu massaged her lower back. "Of course. Zeke and I are searching for answers, which unfortunately is taking longer than expected to figure out."

Without coming back to 'he who shall not be named' and I'm not opening that can of worms. Is it a good or bad thing he's stopped messaging me? My sanity demands good.

A swig from his hip flask warmed his belly and dulled the mayhem.

Shayne swayed and rolled her eyes. "Which, again stop when they take the fucking book. What the hell do we do then? Do we give up? We could find whoever wrote it and grill them for answers."

I wish we ran away sometimes. All right, a lot of times.

Beeps from the flight cabin preceded the engine firing.

Annu's heart palpitated, another swig released control. "I'm not sure but doesn't matter because I'm not letting that happen. It will all sort out. It has before. A few times, in fact."

There's a possibility I drink too much, it is only 11 a.m. Another problem for another day. Sober sucks.

Shayne rocked on her heels, the extra weight unbalanced her. "This is why you and Zeke have been obsessed with the book instead of helping me?"

Annu grabbed her and righted her. "Yes. I hoped we'd have him back before this weekend…."

I'm such a flarking arsehole. I'll fix this. I just need a little time.

Shayne hugged herself, her belly wriggled. "And you wouldn't have to tell me at all? Jesus, this is bad. We unmade someone."

I won't let my children down. I won't screw up again.

Annu rubbed her arms, tired painted him red. "I'm sorry. After finally fixing what happened, we found out you were pregnant. We had Erin's wedding right after that and brought ours forward. Everything steam rolled from there. Your health hasn't been good, there's a lot our plate and nowhere is private anymore. There's no space and time for anything else. Zeke's mother's declining health only adds to the tension in the house. I didn't want to tip it all over the edge. Especially after we'd done the right thing for this to happen."

Shayne's sigh wavered his faith in their continued success. "Fuck, fuck, fuck. Then what's with all the over-protectiveness and paranoia? And what the hell's your deal with Enlil? You have a fucking seizure each time he's bought up."

Flark. Flark. Flark. The less I want it said the more it's spoken. I'll tell her when the time's right. Like after marriage and a few more kids.

Annu's chest tightened, his ribs ached. "He's a bad God who's caused a great deal of death and pain. He scares even me."

Marguerite yelled from the next cabin. "Can we please leave?"

Shayne rolled her eyes and patted her belly. "Look. I better go before she has a conniption and I'm at my limit today. I'll see you when I get back with at least two extras."

Annu kissed her head and inhaled coconut. "Are you all right?"

Fatigue lined Shayne's cheeks and added more remorse. "Yeah.Shit happens."

Nothing better happen to you or my kids. There'll be hell to pay.

"We'll be careful. Stay in touch. Are sure you can't take Sam with you?"

Shayne waddled and paused in the doorway. "Yep. I'm sure. You're stuck with him. It's about time you got to know each other."

Annu back-stepped to the outer door. "I hope you appreciate the fact you've got people to invite. All my family is dead. I've got an ex-girlfriend and GI-Ang coming on my side."

Shayne's mouth dropped, her eyes blazed. "What the fuck? Leah's your ex-girlfriend? You're mentioning this now?"

Oh shit. I'm now King Idiot. Might be time to staple my damned mouth shut.

Heat flushed Annu's face. "Ah, only in the loosest sense of the term. More an ah, um, friend who, flark. I don't know."

Annu jumped outside and closed the door, the engine whirred.

In the passenger window Shayne dragged her hand across her throat. "You're so fucking dead."

The PFD flew into the sky and with it a brief reprieve from justified torment.

Someone tapped Annu's shoulder and took a year off his life span. "Who the f —?"

Zeke raised his palms. "It's me, Annu. Testy much?"

Annu breathed stress and exhaled torment. "Sorry. Lucky you came by. You're just the person I need to see."

Zeke's smile softened Annu's angst. "You remembered then? Finally."

What'd I forget?

Annu swallowed a lump of self-induced disappointment. "If you mean going through the book, yes I did. We're on a tight deadline. It's at home; I'll walk back with you."

Flark. Sam's up there. I might put it off for a while.

Zeke's expression sagged, dark clouds filled his sky. "Of course you'd think that. No. I meant the flying lesson you swore you'd give me today. Right now, in fact. I flarking knew it. You just want my powers with the book and all when it suits you, not because I'm your son. Screw you, Annu. I'm going to a party instead."

Oh Gods I don't have to worry about his safety here. He could be killed, kidnapped or who knows what if he's too far out of my sight. Too many bad things I can't control.

Paternal failure sliced Annu, blood pooled at his feet. "Flark, Zeke. I'm sorry. It's not like that at all. I do want to just hang out with you and things are crazy at the moment. I'm sorry, but I don't have time to check out your friends or the party venue before you'd leave. I won't allow you to put yourself in danger for so called friends with possible ulterior motives. You're staying here."

Testosterone dripped from Zeke's pores. "For flark's sake. Not everyone's an enemy. My friends like me for who I am and not for being your son."

Is he right? Am I jumping to conclusions? Don't panic. Keep calm. I've got this.

Annu's grip on his wits loosened, at present each encounter with a loved one ended in sufferance. "Of course there are people who'll friend you for all the right reasons, you're a great kid but don't be pig-headed and put yourself in possible danger's way until I'm sure it's safe. Is this about a girl?"

Seven and a half feet of irate teenager cast a formative shadow. "No, it's not about anyone else. For flark's sake. What kind of life is this? It's so unfair. I have rights too. I'm not a performing monkey. I'm going to the party whether you take me or not."

I can't tell him we both suck at it, he's not ready. Flark. This is making things worse.

Annu considered increasing the level of self-medication to the exit. "No you are not and no I am not taking you. I'll compromise by shifting a few things around in the next few hours to give you a quick lesson."

Ang had a communicator under his nose. "Hey Annu. How are things?"

Zeke's upper half engulfed in blue plasma, he pushed past. "I hate you sometimes. Neither of you understand me, and you're keeping me from those who do. You can't stop me doing what I want. I'll show you."

Annu bounced off the door frame. "Flarking hell. Take it easy, boy. No need for the drama. Come back here and let's talk about it."

Ang's frown joined the day's collective mood. "It's a good morning, I see. How's it all going?"

Duty wore a path upon Annu's back. "Oh wonderful of course. Every flarking minute with my son, particularly at the moment, is pure joy. No matter what I do, think, or assume I do the wrong thing. It's exhausting."

Sam shifted from behind Ang with his arms crossed and chest puffed. "You and I need to talk."

Annu raised his arms and left the ground. "Shit. Sorry. Must go I left something on at the house."

This day is just perfect. Maybe I should free my father. Might be less painful. Or not.

Chapter 3: The wicked bitch of the North

Marduk however many light years and headaches from Orion

Achievement of emotional intelligence eluded Shayne, she paddled in an ocean of woe. The PFD dangled between the swamp and muddy bank.

Everything will be fine. Fucking super fine. One damned day. Not today by the looks of it but in the future.

A cut on Shayne's arm healed slow, she brushed off a semi-dry cupcake. "Well, that's fucked our way home. Jesus, Maybe-Marge. Talk about a major brain freeze. What the hell, woman?"

Smoke poured from the engine, black goop oozed into the water. Left over decorations, presents and food littered the area.

Breath, keep calm. Think of the babies.

Maybe-Marge's usual placid demeanour sank beside the ship. "Today's a total disaster. Something bad happens every time I'm with you. For goodness sake. Why didn't I stay on Orion?"

What's her issue? Maybe she banged her head before the crash? What do I know? We all have our problems and she's not mine. The dodgy communications are likely the exact reason the Igloo's would hide in this place.

Crumbs stuck to the roof of Shayne's mouth, pain niggled her abdomen. "You know, I'm thinking the exact same thing."

MM's hair corkscrewed around her face. "You stay here and look for those Igloo people on your own. This is all your fault.

You'll have to wormhole me home because as I predicted the communicators aren't working."

That's my name for them Mrs Cranky McCrankerson so don't use it.

"Oh will I now. How about you get fucked and wait until it's a better time. While you're busting to get back to your comfy office chair, the Igloo's are battling to stay alive. I'm sure they'd appreciate a fucking house let alone a chair. You were flying not me; I didn't freak out and lose my facilities."

I hope that pain's stress related and not something wrong with the babies. The ship prevented any physical damage to us but self-healing's been slow lately, what if…? No. Don't think that way.

MM's jabbed her comm and tapped a foot. "I completely disagree. It's entirely your fault. You emotionally unloaded on me right before we entered the outer barrier."

Exhaustion niggled, Shayne's lower back spasmed. "You know what, get fucked. Actually, perhaps not getting fucked is your problem. I thought you were my friend not just work colleague and I needed to vent. That's what friends do and we spend a lot of time together. More than with my actual best friend who's currently at my place decorating for the wedding."

The ship's nose disappeared, mud extinguished the smoke.

Maybe-Marge smoothed her hair, crazy dripped from her forehead. "Yes of course. How could I forget? It's all you've talked of for the last few weeks. Anyway, this is getting us nowhere. Please, take me home now."

Three suns lowered, clouds swept across the orange sky.

It's a shitty situation. We're both out of sorts. Don't take it personally.

Shayne muffled anger for future good will. "I'm sorry you didn't get the memo. I'm reserving my powers for the Igloo's which only I'm allowed to call them. So suck it."

No 'Welcome to Marduk you are here' sign or a tourist information guide popped up, Shayne's sense of direction searched for a better home.

Marguerite's features twisted, venom tainted her words. "Shayne, sometimes I think you're not as vacant and idiotic as you appear. You like being oblivious because it negates responsibility and care. The heat is off you. You don't have too much of yourself invested, don't care too much or don't push yourself too hard. If anyone saw how smart you really were they'd expect more from you. More than you want to deliver. I'm not sure if it's a travesty or a blessing."

Okay. No concussion or stress. She's just a bitch. Apart from the hurt and ouch, I'm going to fucking kill her. This is like the worst day of my life. If she thinks she can out bitchy me, she's got another think coming. Friend or not. I'm fine with having only two.

Truth plucked Shayne's confidence feathers. "Is that fucking right. Listen here. Maybe your and Annu's horoscopes are cheating on or fucking each other, I don't know or care, but if you keep this up you'll be an ice sculpture in that muck over there in five minutes. Get a fucking grip."

Maybe-Marge's chest heaved, her colour drained. "I'm sorry Shayne. I didn't meant that. I'm not sure what came over me. It's all a bit much. I guess I panicked."

Calm, think. There's other things to focus on. Don't prove her right.

Shayne walked to the treed area ahead. "I'll overlook it this time. But if you ever speak to me like that again you'll not only know exactly what came over you, and you'll be really unhappy with it."

Fuck you, fuck you very, very muuuuch. We hate what you do and we hate your whole crew and please don't stay in touch.

Maybe-Marge lumbered, her irritation spread like fungus. "Where are you going? Shouldn't one of us stay near the ship?"

Trees stretched for miles with no sign of civilisation from her five-foot viewpoint.

I know what they look like, I should have asked where they hang out. Next time.

Shayne stood on tip toes and craned her neck. "What the fuck for? It's not coming back."

Maybe-Marge wrung her hands and fidgeted. "Will you at least contact Annu and organise another form of travel?"

Shayne's energy waned, she trudged ahead. "For fuck's sake. There's no need yet and we ahead of schedule."

The suns didn't illuminate the forest's unseen and unknown dangers.

MM offered Shayne a flask. "Stay hydrated then. I guess I don't have a choice. I'm sorry. I'm not coping well. I'll help you look and fasten things along."

Left, right, front or back. Tree, tree, rock, bush.

Shayne chose front and drank, her mouth unglued. "Thank you. I appreciate it."

Maybe-Marge froze mid-step; dazed, her lips trembled. "Ah, ah, ah. Yes. No. No. Please."

Shayne waved and clicked in her face. "Hey. Hello? You all right in there or what?"

Is this what a conniption looks like? I can't believe people are more freaked out than me. Who'd have thought it?

MM's eyes widened, she delivered a box of crazy to her own front door. "Yes. I won't. I—"

Shayne kicked MM in the shins. "Hey. Snap out of it. We don't have time for a breakdown unless it's mine."

MM shook herself and blinked. "I, I, I, yes. I'm fine."

Shayne stepped into an unmistakable pile, it sucked up her shoe. "That's just fucking disgusting. You might want to tell your face that, you look like what I'm standing in. When we get home go to a doctor. I think something's wrong with your brain."

What the fuck is? Hope she gets over it sooner rather than later. I've got enough to deal with.

MM glanced over Shayne into the forest. "No need for vulgarity. The crash disconcerted me that's all. I'm fine."

Squish, plop, squish, plop, Shayne dodged another dung heap. "Righto."

MM faced left and pointed. "We should go in this direction. I thought I saw smoke or something."

Shayne raised her foot, goop dripped. "That's a good reason to—"

A small figure darted between the trees metres ahead at regular intervals.

Shayne flinched and clutched her chest. "The fuck? Please don't be something that eats us."

MM clutched Shayne's sleeve. "What's wrong? What is it? Are we in danger?"

The figure poked out from behind a trunk, a orange skinned female darted back again.

Shayne detached MM, relief accompanied the walk in her direction. "Don't be scared, I'm here to bring you to safety."

The girl emerged from the tree and hesitated, her features cleared. "I don't believe you. Leave us alone."

Holy fucking shit. No way.

Shayne's heart skipped, her chin dropped. "Irica? Is that you?"

It can't be.

The girl immersed with the forest, late afternoon shrouded vision.

Shayne's hips ached, tired beat against her will. "Wait. I'm here to help you."

MM plodded in short strides, her gloom contagious. "It's getting dark and dangerous. We should help ourselves."

My further personal and spiritual development dictates my decisions instead of emotions since fucking Jacob up. Maybe Enki will look kindly upon me and fix what we did for us. Hey, hang on. Ryan's great with directions. I'll swap him with MM and try contacting Annu.

One of the babies hiccup'd, Shayne's belly bounced. "No. I told you. Look. I'm getting my son, he's good with directions. He's at my place on Earth. You can stay there until someone gets you later."

MM squeezed Shayne's forearm. "I'm not staying on Earth either. It takes too long to arrange a way back without you. What kind of solution is that?"

I'm too tired for this fucking shit. It's the day that never ends. It goes on and on my friends.

Shayne's care factor lagged, she slapped MM's hand. "Listen fuckarse. For the hundredth time I don't have the energy to send you home plus the Igloo's and my son. I'm not an intergalactic travel agent. I'm trying here. Cut me some slack."

MM flapped her arms and towered over Shayne. "Then get your son and some supplies at least. We'll head in the other way, where I suggested hours ago. I'm sure there are places to hide or some civilisation."

I'm going to punch you in your squished-up face soon. Why didn't I realise how horrible you could be until now? Am I that desperate for company?

Shayne swirled her arm, *open wormhole to my kitchen on Earth*, and half popped through in the middle of the room. "Sorry I'm—"

Ryan stood beside a medium-height, grey-haired, well-dressed woman.

Shayne stepped onto the floor and flipped her hands. "Ah son. What the fuck?" *Where's Joey? And who is this? Are you inviting her to the wedding? You were meant to let me know last week if you wanted anyone else to come."*

Oh. Shit, don't forget to send Annu a message.

Shayne concentrated, her head thudded, the connection wavered, the wormhole shrunk. "Shit."

Ryan lacked enthusiasm as if deflated. "I'll tell you later. This is ah, Sally."

Sally walked around the wormhole, returned to Shayne, and waved. "Hello. My goodness. That's quite, ah, incredible isn't it."

Shayne's limbs ached, her mind dulled. "Yeah. Awesome. And hi you too. Ryan what the fuck?"

This Sally woman faced Ryan and nodded. "Perhaps you should. It might be easier to digest."

Ryan shuffled, his red eyes pained Shayne. "She say's she's your mother."

Shayne's legs gave way, she slid to the floor. "Sorry, what the fuck did you say? Why are you messing with me in my condition?"

Ryan's arms appeared under her shoulders, he lifted her onto a chair. "I'm not. She says she's your mum. She contacted me yesterday."

Bees nested in Shayne's eyes, a fuzzy halo blurred vision. "Wh, wh, how? Why? Now?"

This-Sally rested her handbag on the table. "It's a long story dear, but I'd heard you were getting married and I took the chance to see you. Make up for lost time. I know it's a surprise but I don't wish to waste any more time."

My mother? Her? After all this time? I've lived nearly fifty— shit erase, all my life and now she's here? Wanting me? What do I do? What if she doesn't like me? And let's face it that's bound to happen about fifteen minutes into our relationship. Fuck, shit, fuck, shit.

Chapter 4: DNA Dissension
Enki Island, Enki, Orion

Zeke buckled under the weight of an under-appreciated, under-valued, under-accepted, dynamic God in the making.

Seems my powers are emotion based, which sucks as I'm not an emotional guy. Much. I bet there's a section about it in the book I haven't gotten to yet. But I will. Once I get past the time, space stuff. That's fascinating. I understand it better every day, it's like a part of me and no one's taking it.

With his back pack over a shoulder, Zeke exited the house via the laundry room. "Especially not because of their flarkups. And how dare Annu assume a girl's involved? As if I can't make my own decisions. Flarking heck. There is, but that's beside the point and Paige is a woman not a child. Who's Annu kidding? As if he's someone to aspire to. Ever since he escaped from that place on Earth he's been different and secretive. Hell, for that matter he hasn't been a father since I arrived on their doorstep."

Late afternoon dulled the landscape, PFD's zipped back and forth from the mountain top. Noise exploded from the house, footsteps quickened Zeke's pulse.

Shayne's male friend exited the back door, nodded at Zeke and headed into the side garden.

I'm not putting up with all the wedding shit a moment longer either.

Zeke kicked tufts of grass along the path and the rear forest. "I'll make a name for myself, no one will ever mess with me again and Paige will fall in love. Win, win, win."

Trees surrounded Zeke, forest noises comforted him.

Erin came from behind bushes and ruined inner peace. "Hey kiddo. Are you okay? I'm here if you'd like to talk about stuff."

Frustration tingled Zeke's skin, blue plasma flowed down his arms. "Why? Because I'm not old enough to figure things out myself? I'm not a flarking child, Erin. You and everyone else can stop treating me like one. I'm sick of it."

Erin blushed and looked away. "Sorry, Zeke. I don't mean it that way at all. I've been where you are, well not exactly but I know it's a tough time of your life. Believe me, I've slammed my share of doors because of my parents not that I'd admit it to my mother. I just meant I understand and I'm here for you."

Compassion unhinged Zeke's pride wagon, he hitched the wheel up. "You've got no idea what my life's like. You don't live with them and you're mother isn't dying. In fact, she can't seem to die. You're not the irrelevant object they bring out when they want to. No, damn it. I'm my own person and Demigod."

I maybe should have thought about getting some food before I left the house. I can't go back now so hungry it is.

Erin's patient smile wavered Zeke's control. "You're quite right. I don't know. However, I'm willing to listen and try to understand. That's something. So, please, as your-almost-sister, I'm asking you not to go to the party. It only makes things worse while proving the exact opposite of what you wanted. Don't make trouble, there's enough other people who do that out there. Come back inside and join us for dinner instead. We're a family."

Owl's hoots, animals scurried, and anger built.

Teenage insanity severed the link between Zeke's brain and mouth. "Listen, you're only out here from some misguided sense of duty, not because you really care about me so drop the act. Yeah, we share our respective parents but that doesn't mean anything. Don't bother calling me. I'm not going back there anytime soon." Zeke ran off, the backpack thumped into his ribs. "Screw all of you."

Erin's pleas didn't activate his conscience enough to stop. A red blaze sliced across the tree tops in the house's direction.

Zeke scurried through bushes. "Are you kidding me Annu? I've been gone for like five flarking minutes. Over protective much?"

The good-him wanted to go home, the bad one drove him into the elevator.

At the bottom of the mountain, he shivered in the night air. "And I forgot a jacket. Might write a list next time."

The external lights in the protectors' compound flickered on and illuminated the area.

Zeke's last outdoor adventure during the invasion returned, fear rattled courage.

I roughed it by force then, not choice. Erin's not just being nice, she cares. Annu and Shayne kind of sometimes might make me feel wanted. I don't know what's wrong with me sometimes.

Regret beat upon Zeke, his confidence waned. "I'd make it home in bed before anyone realised or cared. I'm being an idiot."

The communicator buzzed, Paige flashed across the screen:

'Hey Zeke. Wondering how far away you are? You promised me a dance and a surprise. The party's starting and Isaac's waiting to meet you.'

Lust overrode rationale, tingled his nether regions and moved Zeke's fingers:

'I'm on my way. I'll message when I'm closer. You'll get your dance and then some.'

Zeke headed for the docking bay and pressed against the wall. "This day's going to end a flark load better than it started."

Day staff filed out and the minimum night staff milled around the entrance. In the meantime it left the bay unstaffed for a few minutes.

Yes. I perfectly timed it.

Zeke slipped around the corner, entered the hanger and selected the first PFD. His heart fluttered, his butt hole constricted.

It's either now or never. If I get caught he'll throttle me. If I at least get laid first, I'm good.

Inside the flight deck, Zeke on the pilot's seat and dropped the bag on the ground.

Zeke hesitated over the buttons. "I've never flown by myself before. Which do I press first? Blue, blue, red? Shit, shit. Shit. Orange, red, green?"

Common sense smacked him upside the head. "Stop. I'm never getting anywhere if I panic the second I try."

The answer cleared, tap, tap, tap, the PFD's engine whirred to life; the hanger roof opened and revealed a star filled sky.

Zeke held his breath and selected elevation. "Here goes nothing or everything."

The ship shuddered and rose; the edge of the roof opened, he caught the side, metal crunched metal.

Zeke's hands shook, his guts flipped. "Okay. Breathe, breathe, breathe."

The craft popped into open sky and faced Yebu. The first cliff before the ocean showed on radar not far ahead.

A swipe of the tablet and an hour's flight to Yebu overwhelmed Zeke. "I totally forgot I had to fly over water. It looks like the ocean goes on forever. It never seemed this big or far away before. Maybe it's because Annu's been with me?"

No. That's not it, and I'm here now. Keep going.

The unknown swallowed Zeke, he gripped the steering shaft.

Don't look down and I'm all good.

An air pocket shook the PFD, the backpack opened and the book thumped onto the floor.

Zeke leaned and replaced it, satisfaction hugged. "I'm the man, baby, and here I come. Tonight's going to be amazing. Might even be two first's for me."

Chapter 5: Hell's Bells
Hell Dimension, Gamede

Even with once infinite power and isolation, Enlil, suffered at the hands of his greatest foe, mortals. The portal room walls constricted, the figure in the mirror blurred.

I'm not missing another ascension; it's not happening again. Not this close. Alhalso you Enki. Alhalso you. No matter what you throw at me, I'll send it back tenfold.

Enlil wriggled a mental worm in the woman's ear, the frame shook. "Alhalso. Stupid, stupid, meat sack. Of all the places and beings, you're there with them. I'll kill you, yours and probably even a few work colleagues for the enjoyment of it."

The stupid bitch. She had one thing to take care of and she nearly messed it up.

The woman shrank into herself, a green tinge stained her cheeks.

Blood trickled down her lobe. *'I'm sorry. I didn't know and nor could I do anything about it. You don't know what she's like. Please. I'll convince her to take us home somehow. Give me another chance.'*

Enlil released the frame and crossed his arms. "You're fortunate there's a portal on the east side of the planet in a group of caves. For now. Go and do not think about crossing me. I expect you there post haste. Under no circumstances bring one of those Igigi with you if you find them."

And of all the beings to pop back up again too. It's not a coincidence. Patience, think about this and reconfigure. All isn't lost yet. It's a minor bump. Although I'll still rip her to shreds the first chance I get and use her bones as toothpicks.

The portal room lightened, failure retreated into the shadows.

Her pitifulness and overindulgence angered him. *"Yes, my lord. I'm sorry. I —"*

Enlil broke the connection and headed for the secret door. "And I don't care. Alhalso off."

Now, to deal with the other many problems that I can't ignore any longer.

Coast clear, Enlil entered an outer chamber, removed the medallion from his neck, inserted it in a symbol and closed the room. "Annu, you'll have no choice but to answer me soon."

Something shuffled in the corner, fear turned Enlil and soured his gut.

Abbaddon, his newest general blocked the door way. "Your Grace, I'm sorry to disturb you."

Enlil doubled in size, horns popped in concentric lines all over, fangs filled his mouth. "What is it? Are you following me? Did Ralf send you too?"

Abbaddon backed up, hit the wall and protected his chest. "No, nothing like that. I swear. It's about the war; we've lost the Gamede borders, Gresk, the outer rings and all demons protecting them."

Anger erected barriers around Enlil's fear. "I didn't think they'd get this far. Dammit to here. Triple the numbers and this time ensure the men are incorruptible."

Abbaddon's drone eliminated patience. "The thing about that is, ah, you made those demons in your image and therefore they're evil too. Which kind of means they're, we're, prone to taking the easiest alternatives. Ralf also offers them whatever they want and follows through with it. Which you stopped doing some time ago."

I don't have the power to make more, fight Ralf and his followers off, and survive the incarnation process. If I use any more power there won't be a release.

Engulfed, Enlil lifted Abbaddon by the throat. "Yes, okay, I've had a few off millions of years, yet after I gave you all life and places to satiate your twisted desires you desert me so easily. Dissension is the appreciation I receive. I will not forget this."

Abbaddon's skin cracked and peeled, burnt flesh excited Enlil. "I—ah—I. You're incredibly powerful and mighty, my Lord. You never have to prove anything to me or your loyal subjects. I, I, I meant no offence. Please don't kill me. I'm only reporting what I heard for your benefit. I promise. I want to help you. I'm on your side."

Enlil dropped Abbaddon, the smell of crackle faltered his logic. "Humph. We'll see. "

If I wasn't running out of suitable replacements or sources of same you'd be lunch. It's difficult being the smartest being in creation. Why am I hungry? I've never eaten pork or anything for that matter. It's beginning.

"Yes my Lord." Abbaddon brushed off charred flesh. "I hope I haven't ruined my chance of going with you, my Lord?"

Yes but so has everyone else for the last kazillion years. I'll destroy this place and everything in it including you, you fucking piece of shit. But for now, I'll play the game.

Enlil faced the other way. "Of course not."

Apprehension and panic scented Abbaddon. "Lord, you're not going to like this either, but it's believed the Elder Gods offered Ralf assistance in exchange for their freedom and that he's close to releasing them. Given your last encounter didn't go well I thought you'd want to know. Also, Ralf has a dead or alive capture order out for you and the medallion."

Anyone with power can let them out. I'm too weak to fight a bunch of demons if they alone get in here. With the medallion and the Elders' I'm screwed. I must stop him. Or do I hide us both? More problems.

Panic cold cocked Enlil and dampened his flames. "Do not take notice, it's a ploy. He's not powerful enough. Stick with what you know and deploy another army."

Perhaps I should start thinking and making decisions with a clear head instead of furious? I hate feeling this way. I'm at someone's mercy, out of control.

Abbaddon spoke through gaped teeth. "Perhaps try negotiating with Ralf again?"

Enlil cracked him across the face. "No, you imbecile. It's well past that point. Just mind your own business and do what I asked. You know, you've never got anything positive to say and it's pissing me off. alhalso off, and leave me alone."

Abbaddon's jaw crunched, spit and blood spurted. "Yes, my Lord. I'll muster more troops from ….somewhere."

The ground grumbled, the sky groaned, fires from Ralf's army burned in the distance.

Enlil's chest tightened, the urge to breath frightened him. "No, no, no, no. No. I'm not doing this again. Give me strength."

Chapter 6: Blood Ties and Lies
Enki Island, Orion

Annu avoided the source of female laughter down the hallway and slipped into his office. Johnny's neigh triggered memories of bygone bachelor days, sleep in's and alcohol dazes; his life now a contrast of epic proportions.

It's been ages since I rode you, boy. I save my riding for Shay these days. Back then I had nothing but time. I drank, screwed, looked for treasure and the secrets to my past. I don't miss that. Hell, didn't I get more than I bargained for?

Annu bee-lined for the mini fridge and grabbed one of three premixed rum. "Gods' damnit, Zeke. You little shit, there were six this morning."

The similarities between them both troubled and humbled him.

Annu downed the drink before the past rooted, finished another on route to his desk and shuffled wedding stuff aside for the Lexicon. "Damn. It's probably in Zeke's room. Hopefully with him and my other drinks if he knows what's good for him."

What are the chances I'll make it out of here and back without getting roped into anything in Shayne's absence? Slim to flark all yet worth the risk.

Full can in hand, Annu lingered in the doorway. An oestrogen-free hall encouraged him to Zeke's room. Cackles and giggles from the kitchen quickened his pace.

Annu entered the Dead Zone. Unwashed underwear combined with testosterone assaulted him and didn't leave a name or number. "Flarking hell, boy. The washing machine is just next door. What is that flarking smell?"

Masses of detritus sans a smart arse son concerned Annu. "Please don't be a complete dumb arse like your father. Flark. You wouldn't take the book with you right? Please don't tell me it's in the hands of a hormonal-fuelled kid on his way to a party I don't know where, right before we're forced to give it up? Please? Or I'm flarked. No getting Jacob back. No finding a way to hide us from he who shall not be named in the future, stripped of my Godly status and on probation. Not happening."

Two fingers picked up the edges and poked for the Lexicon. Aside of a few lewd pictures and empty rum cans, no book incited doubt.

Annu punched in Zeke's number, it rang out. "Flark, flark, flark."

He messaged two of Zeke's known friends.

Ding, ding.

Maxe: 'Sorry. Haven't seen him for a while. He's been hanging out with these other people.'

Gav: 'Haven't seen him but spoke yesterday. Mentioned a party.'

The truth pained Annu with the intensity of a dentist's drill. "Son of a bitch. This is all I need. Shit. Whoever picked you up and flew you there is in a world of hurt too."

The hallway communicator wailed, Annu staved self-combustion and answered via his wrist. "Zeke's regained his facilities or Shayne's forgotten something?"

I hope and pray. Though why I bother I have no idea. May as well ask for a good day while I'm at it.

Tom, the supervisor of security from the transport hanger, filled the screen. "My Grace, Annu. I'm sorry to bother you."

What the flark's up now? I should have brought more alcohol home with me. "It's fine, Tom. What's the problem?"

Tom's troubled demeanour lowered Annu's confidence. "It's Zeke, my Lord. While I didn't personally witness it, I believe he's taken a PFD off the island without permission."

Great, just flarking great. This day gets better and fucking better. Now all I need is an anal probe and I'm set.

Annu plonked on the edge of Zeke's bed. "Are you sure it's him and no one else?"

I say with complete lack of faith.

Tom licked his lips and lowered his voice. "He dropped his school ID right next to where craft five is parked along with his communicator opened onto a map of Yebu. The duty officer witnessed his exit from the docking bay. He did some damage on the way out."

Yep. He's an idiot like me at that age. Sometimes the apple doesn't fall off the tree, sometimes it's still flarking attached. Bring on that probe.

"Then I guess there's no doubt. I'm sorry, Tom, I'll repair the damage."

Tom's frown merged into his wrinkles. "I understand your time is limited. Would you like me or another protector to bring him home, my Lord?"

Sober arrived and ruined the rest of Annu's day. "No thanks. He's my responsibility, I'll retrieve him. Besides, I doubt he'll get too far and if he does, it might teach him a lesson. I ask you keep this incident between us, please Tom. This needn't to go any further."

How embarrassing? I'll beat him with the damned book on the way home. My fatherly skills need serious work. Adding to the list.

Tom's smile suggested duty instead of pleasure. "Yes, my Lord. I'm sure he'll see sense and return soon. When and if he does in your absence, I'll inform you immediately."

What time does the inn close? Next step is stilling the stuff myself. Though I'm not sure that's a great idea given how much I already drink.

Annu directed frustration into his feet and burned the carpet. "Thank you."

Tom nodded and ended the connection.

Zeke's comm rang several times and went to a message service. "Zeke, unless you get back here within the next half an hour you're in big, big, big trouble. Oh, and in case you can't tell it's your father."

Annu tossed between more alcohol and calling Shayne.

Drink first. It'll calm my nerves before she yells at me for being over protective again.

In the hallway, Erin and Rosie exited the kitchen, ribbons hung from their arms.

Erin's smile widened, an assortment of odd jobs flashed across her eyes. "Hi Annu. Great timing. May you please help us put decorations up?"

Annu concentrated on the floor and pointed ahead. "Sorry, Ah, can't talk. Busy. Busy. Back later."

Much, much later.

Erin's eye roll and pout mimicked her mother. "Oh, okay. Fair enough then. Even though it's your wedding. It's not that hard."

The fuss-free office called, Annu's brain glazed. "Are you taking your mother's place while she's gone? Why do we need decorations? Or table settings? We're just saying I do and shit."

Erin raised an eyebrow and cocked her head. "So it looks pretty for your special day. Are you helping or not?"

The past and present collided into a ball of confusion. Wedded bliss, more kids and responsibilities weakened Annu's grip.

Erin moved side to side. "Are you okay?"

Last time there was three of us, me, Jaid and Irica. Holy shit, I'm getting married, again. Me. Maybe I'm not so hard to live with and be around. Irica, you'd laugh if you saw me. You probably have been the whole time. When you're not frowning at my decisions and berating me. I never thought in a millions years you'd not be at my next wedding or hold my kids. I miss you woman. Don't suppose you'll just appear and tell me how to get Jacob back and stop messing things up?

"Annu?"

Inside the office, Annu plonked on a bar stool. "Flark. Shit. I'm happily in love with another woman and voluntarily spending literal eternity with her. We're having twins. Flark. Can I do this without completely screwing things up?"

Yes, she makes my life worth it. I'm a lucky man. I'm telling her about Enlil when she gets home and we'll deal with it together. If only we controlled the level of craziness around us.

Annu called Shayne and again went to messages. "Shay, I know you're pissy but give me a call to check in. You two should be on your way home by now and have reception. I love you so much and I'll make it up to you."

The likeliness of Zeke's whereabouts smothered Annu with a dread pillow. "For flark's sake. I'm coming to get you and flark; I didn't ask where the party was because you weren't meant to go. Call me."

The communicator shrilled inches from Annu's ear, Lin, the feline UPA member waited for a connection.

"So not answering. There's little point."

Lin drifted from the screen; a male Peace Officer replaced him.

Annu's intestines formed a rope and lassoed his heart. "Oh Gods, no. What now?"

A patrician nose lead to thin, pursed lips. "Sir, Lieutenant Grimmett from the coastal office. How are you this evening?"

Annu's heart readied to leave via his rib cage. "I'm about to have a damned coronary or throw this comm into space. What's wrong?"

Please don't let anyone be dead. I can't fix that yet.

Grimmett frowned and shook his head. "No. It's your son, sir. Zeke, I believe. Peace Officers reported him flying over the coast and past Yebu a little over ten minutes ago. They're awaiting orders to pull him over and arrest him. However, given our desire to continue our good working relationship, I opted to contact you personally first. Are you aware he's not only unlicensed but not approved for solo flight? The penalties are usually quite high, not just for the child, but also the parent. I'll assist in this if I'm able but cannot guarantee they'll be no punishment."

Thank Gods he's not hurt. Zeke's now promoted to senior dumb arse.

"Yes I am, and I'm sorry. He took the craft without my knowledge but go easy on him. My son's mother's quite ill, there have been a lot of changes going on and......." A memory returned too late. *Oh shit. That explains it.* "And we missed his birthday."

I'm the worst father in existence. I've just started and I already suck. Least I've got a rough idea where you are and there's time to change my methods.

Grimmett's coldness bristled Annu hackles. "I'll keep this in mind, trust this will not occur again and you'll enforce your parental responsibilities."

Ow. Ouch. Judgmental flarker.

Annu smoothed them down for a worthier foe. "No, it won't. Believe me. And yes I will."

A premature hangover further dulled his care; a message from the Grand Counsel sharpened them:

'Grand Counsellor Marguerite has not returned from her trip with our Goddess due back an hour ago. Please confirm all is in order at your earliest convenience. If we do not receive your advice within the next half hour we are required to send search parties. We look forward to hearing from you. Regards, Devon.'

Every possible reason for Shay's lack of contact bombarded Annu. "Shit. Why aren't you answering? Even really pissed off at me you'd call by now. At the very least to remind me of something. Which one of my family angry at me do I find first? Shay. I know Zeke's alive and just being an arsehole."

The rest of the bottle swished the sides of Annu's frustration. He drank his way outside and tossed the empty.

When we get home I'm having a long shower, a bigger drink, and sleep.

Sam rested against the fence near the path's end, righteousness soaked his armpits. "You're not flying away this time."

Chapter 7: Bossy Bitches not Britches
Marduk many light years from Orion and a good sleep

Screams from the wormhole reconfigured Shayne's brain. "Ah shit. I can't leave her alone for one fucking minute."

This-Sally clutched her handbag and frowned. "It doesn't sound like everything is all right in there."

Maybe-Marge, the Igloo's, screams and shots behind me and perhaps my mother in the kitchen. My mother. After all this fucking time. Shit. Shit. Shit. What am I doing? This is nuts. Why is she here? Do I look crazy or like I've done okay for myself?

Ryan oozed depression, concern un-dazed Shayne. "What's going on in there? Is it safe for us?"

Shayne motioned to the wormhole. "As much as anyplace I am is. Either way, make up your mind stat. I don't know when I'll be back here. What's going on with you?"

Ryan stood at the precipice and squished his face. "Um, I'm not sure about this. There's nothing wrong."

Stress to the right, danger on the left and a bunch of other problems everywhere else.

Shayne prayed and shoved Ryan in. "Too bad and stay low to the ground."

This-Sally waited at the kitchen door. "I hoped our first meeting we'd get to know each other and catch up. This isn't what I had in mind."

I'm bringing her into danger but if someone finds out about her they might take her for the wrong reasons anyway. What the fuck? This is shit.

Zing, zing, zing. Boom, shriek, gasp.

Bits of wood and crap showered Shayne's back. "Yeah, well, me either, not that I've thought about it much."

One push, TS merged into the wormhole, Shayne jumped in and closed it behind her.

Ryan lay on his belly and covered his head. "This is a fine way to end a shitty day. Does this sort of stuff happen much when you're around?"

Oh the sad, sad, pathetic truth of my existence.

Pain dashed across Shayne lower stomach, she clenched her abs. "With surprising regularity my son. It's part and parcel of the godliness you aspire to. So, Joey?"

Ryan faced the trees and stiffened. "I said I don't want to talk about him. What are you doing here that you required my involved?"

I can't push or he'll get super pissy at me and won't tell me a damned thing.

TS huddled against a trunk, her green pallor matched leaves. "I don't ever want to do that again."

The pain lingered, Shayne slowed breathed and massaged her belly. "Sorry but that'll only happen if you stay here forever and I'm guessing that doesn't work for you. I need you to find north Ryan. That always seems a much requested direction." Projectiles hurtled across the tree tops and exploded meters away, everyone jumped. "Unless it's that way."

MM scrabbled on hands and knees the other direction, her manner grew teeth. "Shayne, It's dangerous and we don't have means to protect ourselves other than you and a few guns in the ship at the bottom of a swamp. I insist you hide us in the caves north of here as I've suggested until actual help not family members arrive. Lest you be responsible for the death of yet another Grand Counsellor."

See, I knew north was important. What a fine fucking mess this is turning into. I'm not yet capable of solo missions with extras. How humiliating? And I'm not even touching on the maternal rejection shit hammering me.

TS tucked up her legs and blubbered. "What? We'll die? You've killed people? I don't want to die, send me home."

The shots ceased, Shayne rocked, rolled, huffed and puffed into a seated position. "Listen you two, we all die someday. The lucky ones anyway. Get a grip, I'll keep you safe. North Ryan, where is it?"

Mine's being prolonged as a form of torture.

TS uncurled and shuffled closer to the tree. "I'm not dying on a different planet."

MM stopped and stared into the forest. "I'm trying. Yes. Please. I need, I need more time. I, I, I said that."

Will everyone stop being so fucking emotional and weird today? Seriously. I'm the one who should cry.

Shayne withheld punching her in the nose. "Ignoring your crazy for the moment. Right. Ryan, hello?"

Late afternoon and lack of local knowledge dampened Shayne's spirit.

Where the fuck is Irica's look alike and the rest of them?

Ryan took forlorn and ran for it. "I don't care anyway. You figure it out and leave me here to die."

Shayne slapped his arm, her tricep jiggled. "Quit it. You do so care and even if you don't, I sure as fuck do. If you're not going to tell me what's wrong stop moping about it and help."

Ryan's cheeks flushed, he spoke to his chest. "Joey and I broke up. He thinks I'm obsessed about not being like the rest of you and I've changed."

MM returned from the inattentive. "For flark's sake, Shayne. Stop messing around or when we return my report will reflect your non-compliance."

Shayne's love world shattered, shock redirected attention. "What? You and Joey have been together since high school. You're my golden go to couple. Like all Hollywood marriages for the first year. Fuck. My faith in relationships comes from you guys. Wh—"

Boom, boom, boom.

Ryan wriggled a finger in his ear and pointed. "Not again. Mum, come on. That way."

The ground rocked, Shayne fell onto her side. "Jesus H Christ. It'll be the fucking Annu-Knuckle-Heads, son's of bitches after the Igloo's."

Big time decision sacrifice here. Special beings require saving and so do the people with me. When you can't be with the ones you love, love the ones you're with.

TS's sobs and MM's brain spazz's cemented Shayne's decision.

Shayne covered the group in a protective aura, her energy ebbed. "Follow me and stay close together."

Fuck I can't keep this up for too long and wormhole. Fuck it.

MM's shoulders lowered and emphasised her exhale. "Thank the Gods you've come to your senses. All it takes is a decent amount of fire power."

Shayne's low crawl created a path. "Yeah, yeah, yeah. You and I are talking about whatever bug is up your arse first chance we get."

Tension in the group eased, in single file they reached a set of caves, Shayne's mind requested a holiday.

Time to admit defeat and get this train back on the tracks. Annu will probably be in his office at the protectors' compound and not at home where everyone including Sam is. I'll go there.

The hateful shroud fell from MM's shoulder. "It's best we move further in to search for communications and food."

Shayne lowered the protection, exhaustion plagued her. "Yeah, no need. I'm getting help and sending you home. Here is no longer your problem."

TS clutched her bag and shuffled. "Thank the Lord in heaven."

MM's moods switched faster than Shayne's. "Oh. I, ah, for completions sake shouldn't we check if those people are here first?"

What the fuck? Now you care about them?

Shayne rubbed the bridge of her nose and swirled, light appeared. "I'll do that. You get yourself some medical attention."

MM shifted further in, paused and bunched her skirt in her hand. "Yes, yes, perhaps I, ah, will."

Disconcertion accompanied a window to Annu's empty, dark office rather than a wormhole.

The external complications removed the grounding for Shayne's fine assurances. "Damn it to hell, no quick going home for you guys. You're here as long as I am."

MM's compliance unsettled Shayne. "I understand; it's not your fault. you've done the best you can."

Okay, did I enter an alternate dimension?

Ryan steadied her by elbow and concern. "Easy, Mum. Are you all right?"

Shayne faked cohesion with a smile. "Crap, of course it couldn't be that easy. I'm perfectly okay. You'd be amazed what I achieve when not completely lucid. Apparently, I've over done it a tad."

Plus I'm fucking old, pregnant and a demigod.

Ryan swapped roles with Shayne. "Well rest sometimes, Mum. It's not just you you're affecting anymore."

"All right, I got it. Duly noted." Shayne directed the window to Ang's office next door. "Hey, bloke. Where's Annu? He's not in his office."

Ang looked up from his desk and spluttered coffee. "For flark's sake, woman. You know I hate it when you do that. It scares the shit out of me."

Normally I'd laugh. I'm too damned over it.

The edges of both worlds blurred, Shayne held harder. "Sorry. Where's Annu?"

"I'm not sure. He left a while ago to get Zeke and wasn't at home when I called before."

Shayne's hope split and fled in different directions. "Shit, I don't have the energy to look for them. Listen, tell him we're okay but something happened to the ship, there's definitely Annu-Knuckle-Heads on Marduk and I need help killing them."

Ang nodded and wiped up the coffee spill. "Yep. Onto it."

A girl's voice diverted Shayne back to the cave. "You cannot stay in here. It's dangerous. People have entered and never come out again. Please, follow me right now."

Fucking finally.

Shayne half turned and lost her legs. "Ouch. Thank fuck you're all right. Don't worry about us, I take care of that."

Sometimes. Occasionally. Shit. You're an almost identical, younger version of Irica. It's weird but good.

Irica-Girl dripped panic, her breath rapid, she pointed outside. "Please. Listen. Before the Annunkai find us or the caves eat you."

TS slumped against rock, her handbag hit her knees. "I'm never going home am I?"

Ryan's cloud of doom lifted, he stared and sidled up to the girl. "Ah hello. I'm Ryan. Pleased to meet you and thanks for the warning. I completely agree."

It's been years since he's liked another person. Is he over Joey so fast? Surely not. Yep, everyone's nuts but me.

Relief put Shayne onto her feet. "Relax, I'm a Demigoddess, I've got some skills. Hey, you more than resemble an old friend of mine, Irica. I'm Shayne, what's your name?"

Irica-Girl frowned, she tugged at her top. "Izzy. Please, we'll talk about this later."

MM paled and licked her lips. "No. We're safer in here not out in the open with a complete stranger that someone else is trying to kill."

Shayne rested against a wall, the weight of her stomach quadrupled. "And you're back to dramatic. They are the whole reason we're here remember. You stay if you want to."

MM's bitch re-poked its head, her lips pursed. "Shayne, don't even think about it. You've only got her word to go on. There'r other people at stake too."

TS looked the girl over. "She's right. We don't know she's not here to hurt us."

Ryan stood in front of Izzy. "She's not like that. I took you on face value."

A mini love story. How sweet. And not appropriate. I mean who falls for someone in such a traumatic.......oh wait. Right. Moving on.

Shayne waddled to the entrance. "You know what; I'm only taking your words too. So shut up. This feels right and I'm an expert."

Outside the cave an eight foot plus silver skinned being pointed a weapon at the group. "Give me the girl."

Two more, a female and two males guarded the cave's opening.

Shayne protected her belly. "Seems I'm no fucking expect whatsoever."

Chapter 8: DNA Distractions
Enki Island; Protectors Compound, & Badlands, Yebu, Orion

Sam's a jack arse. Like I'd stand there, listen to ranting and not fly off. What does Shay see in that guy? He had his chance and lost it. No mere mortal satisfies my woman. Screw him. I am a great fiancé; I'm just working out the delicate balance between truth and omission for the greater good.

Annu leaned across Ang's desk. "Have you sent those ships yet? I need one to collect my jackarse son before I go to Marduk. Flark, is there anyone or anything which doesn't require my immediate attention?"

Ang crossed his legs and raised an eyebrow. "No, there's none available but I'm waiting for some to come in the next half hour or so before I send more out. Plus I'm transferring staff around so you've got back up. You know, if you two quit bugging me I'd get more work done."

Annu's persistence irritated himself. "Did she say if she needed me urgently or can I make a diversion first?"

I recant my prior, lunatic acceptance of our crazy lives. Out with the new and improved back in old and boring. Mundane life never looked so good.

Ang focused on a desk computer. "As I said, no. Shayne literally popped in and out. Though she did mention something about knuckle heads or what not. What's going on with Zeke?"

Who? Flark. Probably the Annunaki. Shit.

Annu pushed off the desk and paced. "He stole a ship and flew to Yebu for a party. Yet somehow I'm the one in trouble with the Coastal and mainland Peace Offices. If I don't go soon it'll get worse."

Annu's wrist comm vibrated, he fought throwing it against the wall and burning it. "Evening officer. What's he done now?"

The officer's gruffness confirmed another official reprimand. "Good evening, sir. I'm Captain Max of the Illiac Peace Office. May we speak for a moment?"

Annu braced himself for more recrimination. "Sure if it means you'll tell me I've won barter coins or something."

Once upon a time I'd have him for speaking to me like that. Oh how times have changed.

Max heightened fear and dismissed frivolity. "May I confirm you've spoken to your security men and Coastal Peace Office regarding your son before I continue?"

Annu's ears rang; control of his environment hurtled further away. "Yes. Yes I have. Just tell me what's going on."

"Zeke's flown PFD into the badlands, which you are aware, is out of our jurisdiction for several reasons."

Apple, tree, apple, tree. We'll start a new orchard soon. I'm done with this shit.

Annu poised above the end icon. "Yeah, it's a work in progress but I'm coming. My deepest apologies. I'm about to leave and make him serve hard time. This won't go unpunished."

By both of us one way or another. He needn't know about anything else going on in my family.

Will intertwined his fingers. "There's something else, not long after he entered the ship plummeted from the sky. We're not positive, though it's likely Zeke was inside when it crashed. We have no way knowing if he's alive or not without risking the safety of my men in unguarded territory."

No, no, no, no, no. Zeke's fine. Just fine. I can't. I won't.

Panic drilled through Annu's temple and into his brain. "Flark. Shit. Damn. I, I, I'll go there right away. Thank, thank you." The call ended with Annu's comprehension. "Flark man. Zeke's crashed in the Badlands. Shayne has to wait a little longer."

Ang bounced off his chair and banged a knee on the desk. "Hell. I'll gather some men and come too."

I should have gone earlier and stopped him. I assumed he'd come to his senses. Now it might be too late and it's my fault. I'm the worst father ever.

Annu tensed, guilt laboured his decision making. "No. This is mine to sort out."

Please, please, please let him be okay. I don't know what I'll do if you aren't. I should have been more patient.

The clouded night sky complimented Annu's gloom, he shot into the air.

Enki, if you want me to stay on your side make sure my kid's alive.

Ankor's image projected inside his mind. *"Annu. I haven't heard from you. I'm past concerned. I believed you'd have the book to us or get Jacob back well before now. What is going on?"*

Annu's sanity reached its limit, the island and ocean passed in a blur. "For flark's sake. Not even caring right now."

Past Yebu's coast line, he hovered on the Badlands border. Black smoke delivered fresh anguish.

"He's tough like me, I'm sure he's fine. Even if he is hurt I'll heal him."

The ship's nose wedged into the ground, banged up panels on all sides and branches of trees projected from the craft's underside.

Annu followed smoke and landed at the crash site. "So far I suck at parenting. What if I mess up with the twins too? What if? No. Don't."

A fire roared in the engine bay yet no dead kid in the vicinity tore his soul in half.

Annu ripped the door off and jumped in, his heart lodged in his throat. "Zeke? Where are you son? Are you all right?"

Blood drops on the floor; seat and controls alarmed him, his breath caught.

A section of the roof fell; Annu tossed it aside and removed debris. "Zeke? You're not in trouble anymore. I'm worried about you. Answer me."

And that flarking book. And your step mother. And I don't have enough alcohol. And this is getting all too hard.

Minus Zeke plus parental anxiety equalled zero peace of mind. Bad signal prevented calls and accepted messages.

You're not in here. Where are you? Are you okay?

Near the door Annu's boot crunched, pieces of Zeke's communicator nestled in the dirt. "Flark. Shit. He's definitely not getting his messages then."

Annu exited the craft and held a breath. "Think man. Where would he go? Would he have walked there? Has someone else found him? Where do I start? Do a few sweeps over and hopefully spot him? I'm so kicking his arse. Hopefully Shayne's home by the time we are and there's one less mission. I'd even put up with Sam and decorate shit I don't care about for some good luck."

The wrist comm showed a notification from GC member Laci:

'Annu just following up. Any news on GC Marguerite's E.T.A?'

He pounded frustration into a reply: *'Problem with ship but both fine. Will return later than expected. I'm sure she'll contact you when she's in range.'*

I shouldn't get any more messages from them now at least.

The forest closed in, cold invaded Annu's brain and chilled him. "This doesn't feel like a good thing coming."

Enlil's presence wedged Annu between stone and an impossible place. *'Good tidings my boy. You failed to answer me and I've taken drastic action to ensure your compliance. Bring the Lexicon to the caves on the other side of the island and enter the portal at the end. If you don't you'll never see Shayne or your unborn children again.'*

It's not possible. She's safe. He's putting me on.

Doubt drove Annu to the edge of self-destruction. *'You don't have them. You won't fool me. '*

I will not believe you unless I hear from her myself and it's not until the ships arrive.

Evil slicked oil along Annu's mind. *'You'll soon see it's no trick. There are portals on other planets including Marduk. I'm feeling generous given your current situation, you've got two hours.'*

Annu's blood boiled; the animal inside yearned for freedom. *'I'll see you soon when I kill you for this. Don't lay one finger on her.'*

'If I do, it's all on you. Like when you lost your first wife—Jaid wasn't it? '

The truth in Enlil's statement upended Annu, he clung to hope. *'I'll be there and you'll be sorry'*

Find Zeke, the book and get my family back. The alternative isn't worth thinking about. The world will end if something happens to them. I swear to you Enki and Enlil, I'll kill both you bastards myself. I'm done playing.

Chapter 9: Son of a bastard
Badlands, Yebu, Orion

In a dark forest void of the niceties on Enki, Zeke wiped dried blood from his arm. "Mental note, allow for taller trees, lack of experience and shitty focus."

If I can't get a lift home after the party, I'll just stay there. I'm eighteen, a man who evaded those Peace Officers. They've got no idea I was even there.

The moon's shadow turned trees into long limbed monsters, their branches waited to drag Zeke inside a wooden grave.

The heebie-jeebies strangled Zeke; he pulled up his jacket's collar. "Don't be silly. Men aren't scared of trees. I might read a few incarnations out which screw with Shayne and Annu a little. They'll come running back full of hugs and apologies."

A screech from the woods allowed fear entry.

Keep moving. Nothing here. If I don't see it, it doesn't see me.

Zeke's bladder tingled, he peed behind a tree. "I should have saved both rums for the party instead of—"

Men's voices zipped Zeke's mouth and pants. He ducked around and hugged the trunk.

Boots crunched on sticks and leaves.

A man sounded like he chewed gravel. "I hate going out here this late. Whenever we do something goes wrong for us. I'm starting to think this place is cursed."

Shit. Please go straight past me. Don't make me hurt you.

The other man's high pitch sliced the air. "You always look at the negatives. We're not cursed for flark's sake. We've done pretty well a number of times. Quit your whining."

A bug the size of Zeke's shoe buzzed around his head, he swiped at it.

The gravelled man groaned. "Tell that to your prosthetic leg and fake eye thanks to the goddess woman. I still have nightmares about it."

Do they mean Shayne? Who else leaves such a lasting impression? When was she here and why?

Branches crunched and snapped. "Shut up, Jude, or I'll jam my foot up your arse. You'll scare all the wildlife and we swore we'd never mentioned her again."

Buzz, buzz, chomp, chomp.

The bug biopsied Zeke's cheek. "Flark, fuck, shit, crap."

Footsteps stopped metres from the tree.

The one legged man glanced in his direction. "Who's out there?"

Shit. I'm in trouble here.

Zeke slapped a hand over his mouth. *Idiot.*

The bug circled Zeke's nose, paused at his forehead, jabbed and buzzed.

Zeke swapped hands and rubbed the bite. "Ouch. You mother flarker."

The one eye-one leg man smacked the other man's shoulder. "Jude, check that out."

Zeke flattened against the trunk and stepped to the other side.

Shit, shit, shit. I'm never getting to this party.

Jude walked around the trunk. "I don't see anything. Must be an animal."

Zeke shuffled ahead of him in the opposite direction.

Irritation soaked the man's response. "Well? What's taking so long?"

Zeke tripped and banged his head on a branch. "For flark's sake."

Jude appeared in front and smiled. "My mistake. It's a kid."

Panic stuck in Zeke's throat, he ran two steps. "Oh crap."

Jude grabbed Zeke's backpack and pulled. "Where do you think you're going? You don't look like you're from around here."

Rum, courage and bravado trickled down Zeke's back. "Leave me alone."

Mel hobbled on a synthesised prosthetic leg, a patch covered one eye. "Apart from making a monumental error in judgment what's a nice boy like you doing in a shit hole like this? What's in the bag?"

Jude removed Zeke's back pack and dropped it onto his foot. "Flark. You bastard thing. What you got in here?"

Show no fear or I'm toast. Be a man not a boy.

Zeke steeled and mustered his power. "None of your damned business. Let me go."

Okay. Great. I can't do it on demand yet. Should I mention who my father is? No, I can do this on my own.

Jude rifled through the bag, removed the rum can and skulled it. "I needed that."

One handed, Jude tossed the empty and removed the Lexicon. "This looks interesting and as if it's worth something." Fat fingers flicked the pages. "I don't understand a word of it. What is this about?"

Stop touching my book. What do I do? I'm actually kind of scared.

Words glued to Zeke's tongue, his lips numbed. "I....ah....I, ah."

Mel smacked Zeke upside the head. "Can't you speak in full sentences, you idiot? That why you're out here? Your parents dropped you off and told you to go for a long, long walk then flew away? I don't blame them."

Pain exploded across Zeke's skull, his temples thumped. "I talk fine, you flark arse. Why'd you hit me?"

Mel's sneer filled Zeke with dread, he gripped Zeke's shoulder. "To recalibrate your brain and it must have worked. You're talking properly. Now, make this easy. Other than being an incredibly rare paper leafed book, why do you have it? What's special about it?"

Annu and Shayne will have my head. Both are scarier than these two. I've got to keep it together before it's too late.

Zeke struggled in Mel's grasp. "It's just a book, it's not worth anything. Leave me alone and let me go. I'm nobody."

Mel squeezed, dug his fingers in and twisted. "Hell no. This is the highlight of our evening. Pass it here, Jude. I haven't seen one like this in a very, long time."

I'm going to pummel you when I get the chance. Any second now.

Venom dripped from Zeke's tongue. "Don't hurt yourself trying to figure it out, arsehole. It's not made for dumb arses."

Come on powers. Help me out.

Mel's other hand connected with Zeke's skull. "Shut up, smart arse."

Whack, Zeke's brain jiggled, he chomped his tongue.

Anytime's good. Please.

Fresh layers of pain painted Zeke's head. "Stop flarking doing that, cockhead."

Mel motioned to Jude. "You'll live. Get over it. Jude, the book."

Jude thrust it at Mel and tipped the back pack upside down. "Here. What do you think?"

The back pack's contents spilled onto the ground; hair gel, a toothbrush, three prophylactics and Zeke's dignity.

Great. Embarrassment adding to this flarked up situation.

Mel weighed the book in his hand. "Damn heavy. It's a keeper."

Jude looked up and picked his nose. "How much do you think we'll get?"

Mel flicked Zeke's ear and released him in favour of the book. "Don't go far. Not sure yet."

Jude captors scrunched his nose and kicked aside the bag's contents. "It doesn't make any sense to me."

Zeke dove at the empty bag and collected his stuff. "Give it back and stop trashing my things."

Mel pointed at the prophylactics and cackled. "Now we know why you're out here. Sorry kid, I don't think you're going to make what I assume was a special night for you. You're going to be flarked by us instead."

Ah no. Just flarking no. First chance I get, I'm running for it and never speaking of this again.

Disgust interrupted Zeke's fear. "Ah flark no. I'm not like that. Drunk sweaty ugly men are definitely not my thing. You two pervs keep to yourselves."

I kick Mel in the nuts, grab the book, run through Jude and keep going.

Jude recoiled and blinked. "What? We're not like that either. He meant, never mind. Where are you from, kid? You look kinda familiar but I can't figure out why."

Now I believe Annu would have been out here a time or two. That's logical.

Zeke moved closer and slung the backpack over his shoulder. "Forget it. I'm sure you struggle balancing a glass and talking let alone thinking too hard." He grabbed at the Lexicon Mel, held and missed. "Give it to me."

Now what do I do?

Mel flipped the pages, they shimmered. "Well, look at that. You're holding out on us boy. I might not be able to read it but if you can you're still useful."

Don't tell them. Grab it and go.

Zeke's energy surged, plasma protected him, he sparkled. "Not for you, I won't. I follow no one's orders. I warned you. Give me the book and let me go or you'll regret the day you were born."

About time.

Zeke's energy waned, the plasma absorbed into his skin. "Fuck, flark, shit."

Mel's smirk and clenched fist sent shivers across Zeke's kidneys. "You were saying?"

Jude slapped himself on the cheek. "Stop, Mel. I just remembered who he looks like."

Zeke's powers strengthened, his confidence grew. "Now you're getting it."

Chapter 10: Godzillafucked
Marduk

SilverDude drove the final nail into the trip's coffin, Shayne dug another grave.

I know this whole day's gone to shit but hang in there babies. If there's any real chance of danger we're out. I've got this. I'm not conceding defeat.

Shayne stood in front of the weapon, her aura covered her bottom half, Ryan, MM, Izzy and TS. "There's no way you're getting her. So you and your friends back the fuck up."

This is just fucked. Frankenfucked. Actually worse. Godzillafucked. Or FrankenGodzillafucked. That might be too far. Nah, it's not.

SilverDude squinted and retracted his chin. "Pardon? What did you say?"

The SilverDudette's frown made a vast improvement. "What language are you speaking, woman?"

Shayne's ankles tightened, she rolled them, fluid drained. "English, mother fuckers. Learn it and fuck off. Geez, how do I soar like a pterodactyl when I'm surrounded by Dodos."

I need water and to put my feet up soon. As in six hours ago.

The two male SD's mumbled to each other and shrugged.

SliverDude groaned and jabbed the weapon. "I don't understand you. Stop talking and give us the girl."

Shayne's patience frayed, fatigue poked holes in it. "Fuck off means go away. Far, far away and make it snappy. I'm tired."

MM plastered against the opposite wall. "Oh gods help us. We're getting deeper into trouble. Shayne, please be reasonable. This isn't our fight."

TS hugged her knees and trembled. "No, no, no, no."

At least they're keeping busy. It beats getting in the way. Though I'm over MM being negative Nelly and weird. She keeps up and she's un-invited to the reception. Won't matter as TS fills her spot. If she recovers mentally in time. Shit, I'll have to change the names on the table cards. Crap and—.

Ryan's screech rang the diva alarm. "I came for a wedding. A family gathering. Now I'm on another planet with aliens who want to kill each other and apparently us, the bride is held at gunpoint and could drop her bundle at any moment and I don't understand how this happened when I left home this morning. I'm glad I don't have powers. You all can keep this shit to yourselves."

How did my son become a bigger drama queen than me?

"Duh. I happened but calm down Ryan. For fuck's sake, I'm fine. I got this. There's ages until their due." Shayne crossed her arms and scoffed icicles. "Actually Maybe-Marge, every fight is ours and god's are against us here. Or former gods I should say. Right, SilverDude? You're Annuknucklehead? Punished for being complete arseholes whose reputations are dodgier than mine. Your reputations are worse than mine."

Screw him and all.

SliverDude pointed the gun centimetres from Shayne's forehead. "My name's Anshar. Not Annuknucklehead. With child or not, I will kill you, witch woman. Get out of the way."

Shayne flicked ice and gave him the bird. "I said no. You leave before I kill you. Or why don't you come get her?"

Speaking of which why haven't they grabbed her and why hasn't he just shot me yet? I fucking would have. Mmm.

The other SD's shifted to FSD's side, their weapons aimed at Ryan.

SD's scoff didn't instill confidence. "Don't make me shoot you in front of your son."

Motherfuckers messed with the wrong mother. And not fucker. In this case my bite is way worse than my bark.

Shayne protected Ryan and froze a ring around them. "Try it. I dare you. I double dare you, mother fucker. You know, I should watch more Samuel L. Jackson movies. That man can mother fucker like no other."

The protective aura shifted from MM and TS.

Shit, shit, shit. If I put it up again, I'll lose it all together.

SilverDude's nostrils flared, anger flashed across his face. "You're not an Igigi. Why do you care about her? Where are your powers from? How do you know about us?"

TS squealed and collapsed in a heap. "Oh god."

MM walked towards Shayne, her features twisted. "I…yes….no. I tried that."

I'm not yet perfect at multitasking. I'll deal with you two nut cases after this migraine.

The babies shifted sides; Shayne massaged a foot from under ribs. "None ya, as in none of your business where my powers are from. You can't touch her or you'd have done it. Which means you're screwed. You fuck off and leave her, her people, and us alone. I won't ask again."

I should have gotten more food and a fucking bed from the ship before it sank.

Ryan tugged Shayne's sleeve. "Jesus mum, really? She's amazing and all but can you not sacrifice yourself before dinner? Please?"

Shit yeah. I temporarily forgot. I've got to worry about you all too. Back to fake it until I make it.

Shayne aura dwindled more, her blood sugar dropped. "Oooh. Steady. I don't have a choice, son."

Ryan rubbed her arms. "I'm not leaving you then."

Always the faithful boy; bless him. I hope the next will be the same.

Shayne cocked her head and wiggled her fingers. "Vamoose. Get lost. Scram. Off you fuck. Bugger off. Arebaturkey. Adiosi. So long, suckers. Look, I can go on or do I need to spell it out with one more finger you giant moron?"

SD stepped towards the entrance; lips pursed "We won't leave without her. You best mind your own affairs witch."

Shayne froze the gun and tapped—it shattered. "Ha. Good luck. Then, it's a stand-off. You're not coming in and I'm not coming out. Stop calling me a witch or I'll freeze you next."

Silverdude aimed the gun higher. "Witch."

Izzy came around Shayne and stopped short of SD's reach. "No. Please don't hurt them. I'll come with you."

Shayne's brain fizzled, her control of the situation popped. "Ah for fuck's sake. No you aren't. Just settle down super girl. I'm protecting you here. It's what I do."

Ryan smiled and oozed adoration. "You're so noble Izzy."

SD lathered confused like shampoo. "I don't care about any of this. No more parlour tricks."

Hang in there, I have to protect them. I can do this. I've fought and killed them twice before.

Shayne's protection left the others and drifted back to her. "They're not tricks, arsehole."

The other SilverDude aimed at the TS. "There are other ways to do things."

Just do it before I miss another opportunity.

Shayne kicked his shin and re-covered herself, Ryan, TS and MM. "For fuck's sake. I can't take my eyes off you for two seconds."

The shot struck the roof further down; rock's tumbled from all sides and blocked further entrance into the cave.

Energy drained from Shayne quicker than breakfast, she wobbled, and her belly ached.

Hanging on, hanging on, hanging on. Must stay focused. Enki, please protect the babies and the innocents, which I'm aware probably doesn't include me.

Dust sullied vision, Shayne cleared her eyes. "Stay here and take care of those three."

Ryan huffed and puffed his way Izzy. "Oh, ah. Okay."

Shayne kept low and swiped SD's knee, one touch froze him.

Behind FrozenDude, she touched the female and one male on the calves. "Annunakicypoles, you bastards."

Air cleared, Shayne's breath dragged, she patted her belly. "Nearly there."

The last unfrozen SD lunged at her. "Who are you?"

Enough of this. Time to call in the big guns.

"Stop right there." Shayne pointed an iced finger. "Maybe you've heard of my fiancé Annu whose mother is Great Goddess Ann, his father's unknown, or Ki, he's my father."

Even though he's in some super-duper heaven, he's got my back.

The unfrozen SD lowered his gun and frowned. "If you're one of us, why are you opposing us? Especially when you're marrying Enlil's son and he'll be your father in law. He spoke excitedly of your impending birth and nuptials."

Shock knocked Shayne into next week and a good chunk of another four months. "Sorry, he's what the fuck?"

Smugness twisted SD's mouth. "Oh, my. It appears you weren't aware. Enlil is Annu's father. It's your turn for surprise. You'll give me the girl of course."

Shayne shot streams of ice and froze him solid. "Guess again, fucker."

She grabbed a rock and smashed in his face.

My darling, future husband has known who his father is for weeks. That's his big, nasty secret and why he's acting so weird. When we get out of here I'll fucking kill him. Twice.

Chapter 11: A Begotten Son
The Badlands, Yebu, Orion

Above the forest, fates habit of dumping shit on Annu aided an epic bad mood. "He'll flarking rue the day he created me. As for you Ann, when next we speak you've got explaining to do. What kind of father does this?"

Losing my shit achieves nothing but more pain. All hope is not lost yet. There's time and the means for me to end this once and for all. I won't pay the ultimate price for my arrogance and pride like my father. I will be a better husband, father and God if it kills me. It's just another test. Which, how many of those does one man need? Don't answer that.

Shay and Zeke's level of help importance escalated, switched and flipped.

A cool breeze offered a metaphorical shovel; he blocked the wrist comm from wind.

Ang answered in the transport depot, a flurry of activity muted him. "Hey. You saved me a call. Where are you? Those UPA people, the GC, Peace Officers and your visitors from Earth are looking for you. You obviously aren't with Shay yet."

Oh shit, if she's with him, she knows. I'm so flarking dead. I'm never hearing the end of this. My own damned fault again.

Annu's power dipped, he shuddered down. "What the flark?" he lifted and settled halfway. "Close to total disaster and complete melt down. Can you check with those ships on Marduk if Shay's there right now?"

"Shay, are you all right? Where are you?"

Ang walked outside into the dark. "Not yet, they're in the no contact zone for at least another couple of hours. What's happened? Weren't you getting Zeke and going there? Talk to me."

Annu's limbs tingled, he drifted meters down. "Flarking shit. Someone's messing with me too. Listen, long story short, I'm in deep shit, and I should not have gotten out of bed this morning. Shay may be in terrible danger, and I need Zeke and the Lexicon to save her. Before I go ballistic do you have a way to track them both?"

The screen backlight Ang. "Flark man. Zeke maybe as he's on Orion, Shayne no. Sorry. Will you tell me what's going on?"

The fluctuations abated; each second elevated Annu's family's danger and his concern.

Marguerite can take care of herself. Did Shay pick up Ryan? Erin may know but I don't have time to contact her. Shit. Breath. Get help where I can.

Annu swatted pride and clenched control. "I…he… flark, just, it has to do with my father. I'll explain later. Please for now, where's Zeke?"

Ang typed on the computer, his concern reassured Annu. "Geez. Sorry man. We lost his signal after he entered the badlands and it hasn't connected again so he's still there somewhere. That's all I get. Anything else I can help with?"

The tingle returned, Annu plummeted several metres feet first. "Shit, shit, shit, shit, shit."

Tree tops approached, he twirled and stopped short of impalement.

Again the sensation dwindled, Annu righted himself and flew further in. "I do not need this shit right now. Or any time for that matter. Come on my boy. Let me know where you are."

Will he really hurt her? It's not worth risking it.

Annu searched in hundred metre circles, on the next rotation a one legged/one armed man and another with smoke from his head tossed stuff into an old PFD.

I never thought I'd be glad to see those two flarkers.

Annu slowed and landed before the men. "You have twenty seconds to answer me, have you seen a kid who looks like me through here recently?"

Mel clutched his chest and leapt. "Flarking heck. Annu. Who? Ah, the boy."

Jude's eyes widened, he brushed soot from his hair. "Oh yeah. Well. Look, we didn't know who he was until right before he left and set me on fire. But we didn't lay a finger on him. Don't hurt us."

Relief scraped a layer off Annu's anxiety, he half ignited. "Where did he go? Did he have a book with him?"

Mel swallowed and sucked his bottom lip. "Hey don't get mad at us. It was a completely accidental meeting. I've got no idea where he went."

Annu's growl drove birds from the trees and animals from the ground. "Did he have a book?"

Time's ticking away here. Why's there always flarking obstacles. I'm over it.

Jude paled; black sweat ran down his cheeks. "Yeah he did have a book. He's welcome to it. He didn't tell us where he was going. Please don't hurt us. You're family have inflicted enough punishment on us for six lifetimes."

Good point, Shayne, me and Zeke. But you flarkers deserve it.

"Tell me something useful and I may consider it. Do you know of any parties in this place on tonight?"

Mel's shoulders rose to his ears. "Just the one that weird Isaac guy's having with some other weirdos."

Annu's brain imploded across his skull. "Great. Flarking great. There's never a shortage of bad guys. Is there a factory somewhere that spits them out? Isaac? Why is that name familiar?"

The Enlilian's. I might just put my head in the oven and set it to disintegrate.

Mel shrugged; his chin disappeared into his neck. "I don't know but he's been yapping to anyone who'd listen all week that some Enlil person's coming to the party and we're all going to die. Blah, blah, blah. Like we haven't heard that before."

No. This is messing everything up. Who is this guy? Why didn't Enlil mention him? Some nasty surprise perhaps? Yet another test?

Annu bottled rage and held the lid down. "Where's this place? What's Isaac look like?"

Jude missed half his beard, he pointed a shaky finger. "About two k's east from the Better's Inn. It's a big old stone place with a bunch of open fields around it. Black hair, black eyes, always wears a black hat and with a face no one's mother would love. Can we go now?"

Annu raised his arms, leapt up and remained land bound. "Yeah."

Mel's bad breath wafted. "Well, that's a son of a bitch."

Annu gritted angst and grabbed Mel by the collar. "Give me the flight codes. I'm taking your ship."

Mel nodded and slobbered. "Ah. Yeah okay."

Jude handed a data chip from his pocket to Annu. "Sometimes it takes a few go's to start but it will get you there. For what it's worth I hope you get your kid back, and we never see any of you ever again."

The craft's pilot side door dangled from the hinge half open. Annu punched a hole in the it and ripped it off. "The feelings mutual."

Inside the flight deck Annu inserted the chip and entered the destination. "I've had glimpses of those magical things people call good days. I don't think I'm destined for any soon."

The ship rose into the sky, Annu grappled the steering shaft. *'Enlil. There's a problem and I need more time.'*

'You've got five extra minutes.'

"I see generosity runs in the family then.'

Chapter 12: The Enemy of my Enemy is an arsehole
Marduk and Gamede (Hell)

Shayne erected an ice barrier across the cave's entrance and fanned herself. "I can't believe this. He outright kept this from me and other people knew. I'm a fucking idiot. They're all laughing at me."

Our entire relationship is basically based a bunch of bullshit, smoke and mirrors. Neither of us have any fucking idea what we're doing so we're just smiling and waving while inside we struggling to adult or person. Fuck. I don't know anymore.

Ryan patted Shayne's shoulder from a meter away. "Given the magnitude of said information I know it won't have been an easy decision for Annu. Not with shit like this going on constantly."

The heat from Shayne's anger formed cracks across the surface.

Shayne kicked, stomped and glared. "Why are you taking his side? That's really unfair. You're my son which means you automatically agree with me not him. Or is this a man thing? I should have known."

Ryan's grimace incited infanticide, on an adult. "Mum, be reasonable. He's a rational man and I'm sure he had a good reason. Sit down, take a few deep breaths and calm down. The babies need you, we need you. You're no good like this."

Like what reasons exactly? I will still accept a brain tumour and retrograde amnesia.

Shayne perched a flat edged rock, her back ache hung around longer than her first sexual encounter. "I'll do at least one of those things before I kill someone."

Izzy bent and spoke to Shayne's belly. "Hello, sweet souls. I won't let anything happen to you."

Funny, I'd normally want to punch someone's face in for doing that.

A warm buzz energised Shayne, her furor lessened. "I hope they're still sweet when they're born. I'll put you on the list of baby sisters if you like."

TS's hair stood on end, her clothes matched the shabby state of her face. She wandered in circles. "Are you sure we're safe? When are we going home? To Earth I mean. Far, far away from here. I'm never leaving my house again."

Fucking drama queen. We haven't even had a proper conversation. This is mental.

MM bit her nails, blood trickled down a finger, and she mumbled gibberish.

Okay. This is too fucking hard. No. Old me thought that way. New me gets to suffer. Yippee.

Shayne levered off the rock, a speck of adrenaline kept her upright. "Yes you are for fuck's sake and I'll get you on that fucking ship if it kills me, wherever that shall be. Meantime, the other Igloos are left alone. I'm guessing the remaining Annuknucklehead's are after them full force now. All right, I'm going to get them too. Jesus those dweebs went so nuts over you

Izzy. Why are these guys so scared and why do you look like my dead friend? When she was alive of course not dead."

Idiot.

Ryan flung his arms and snorted. "Great. Two seconds after a major near death experience you're right back into it trying to get yourself killed. You can you please just take it easy for a while."

Izzy brushed his hand, Ryan relaxed. "It's who she is and you must accept it," she faced Shayne, "Back in our older's day, we were created by Enki to stop Enlil and the Annunaki from getting too far. Though, during our long time apart they've devised other ways of dispatching us as you've seen. Irica is, was, my grandmother. I only met her once."

The information clunked together, Shayne's mind and pride hurt. "Wow. Just wow. Hey, so she had a kid at some point?"

Something to keep in mind for another moment. Birdy said Enlil needed Annu and the book to get out. Thank fuck he can't get either and his time's running out. We won't need Izzy and the others as back up. They can live normal, fear free lives. Lucky fuckers.

TS smoothed her hair and clothes. "This is such a crazy situation. I'm not sure how you deal with it all and aren't crazy, er."

Not well sometimes and fuck knows.

Shivers run up Shayne's calves and circled her knees. "It once involved a large amount of weed and chocolate. These days, not so much. It's a lonely job being awesome.

No wonder Annu freaked out. Enlil's fucked up. But why didn't he trust me with this? Doesn't he truly love me or think I'll handle it? Not that he's off the hook in any way.

Izzy emitted calm and comforted Shayne. "I shall assist you."

"No way short stuff. Just point me in their direction. And to maybe some food and water. Ryan, may you please stay here with Izzy and Sally-Possible-Mum. Maybe-Marge can do whatever the fuck floats her nutty boat. I'll be back before you know but I really, and I mean fucking really need your non-magical help here."

Izzy's softness refilled Shayne's hope for humanity and herself. "You have a valid point and I cannot argue with it."

Ryan drank in Izzy and slurped. "Yes I'll stay, mum. Though I'm not calling them what you do. It's weird. You better make this up to me and I'll worry the entire time."

Shayne stood on tip toes and scruffed his hair. "I promise we'll spend some actual, normal time together soon. Ish. Earlier if you want to baby sit."

Izzy wandered to the other side. "I will for sure."

Ryan strode steps behind her. "Yeah, yeah, I've heard that before."

Heartburn flamed Shayne's oesophagus, she clenched her teeth.

Are you kidding me? I haven't eaten for hours. Or peed. Or well, anything nice really.

TS rose and dampened her rude. "Thank goodness. This nightmare will be over soon."

Shayne wandered to the middle of the cave. "For some of us. Can't say the same about my beloved however. Are you coming Maybe-Marge or what?"

"I'm not coming outside with you but you're coming with me to the portal on the other side of that rock wall." MM produced a gun from her robes and grabbed Izzy by the scruff. "As soon as your son clears the way."

Shayne's sense of reality shattered, she questioned her over tired imagination. "What the fuck? That wasn't an option. What are you doing? Put her down."

Either she or I have totally lost our marbles. Fuck, I should have watched her closer.

Izzy squealed, kicked and missed. "Why are you doing this? Let me go."

Ryan lunged, MM lifted Izzy higher, his hands twitched. "Please, if this is a joke it's not funny. Friends don't do this kind of thing. Unless maybe at Schoolies."

Shit, shit, shit, shit. Snap to it.

Shayne's safety and trust in her entourage demolished. "Maybe-Marge, everything is all right. Put the gun down and I'll send you home via wormhole right now. Just calm, relax, breath. I'm sure you're entitled to stress leave."

If she is, I fucking am. I'm seriously going to study hostage negotiations. It's ridiculous how often I'd use such skills.

MM darkened, her pupils large, her actions deliberate. "Shayne, shut the hell up. Boy, I'll shoot your mother first. Move those rocks." MM shot centimetres from Ryan's feet, he leapt. "Get to it."

Shayne's maternal protection attacked, her blood warmed. "Don't speak to my son like that. So help me, I'll kill you with my bare hands and throw you in the portal."

MM's cheeks glowed, she struck Izzy. "You won't risk their lives. I said move, boy."

Izzy scratched and gouged MM's arm, her courage inspired. "You're just as evil as the Annunaki."

Shayne wanted to punch the triumph right off MM's face. "Do as she says Ryan, for now. Have you been a treacherous bitch the whole time?"

How fucking stupid am I? What's with planetary leaders these days?

Ryan stumbled over, knelt and tossed rocks aside. "You may as well give up. Mum will kick your arse first chance she gets."

Shayne's attempted aura failed, anger put the pieces together, and she undid her wrist band and waved it. "You designed these new fucking communicators to weaken us for this reason. Why? Enlil is evil, I don't understand."

She hurt me and my babies. Of all the horrible, cruel things to do. You beat Annu omitting the truth. Pretending to be my friend tops the list. Why do people seem to hate me so? I'm fucking loveable. Most of the time. If you get me on the right day and all.

MM's true self reflected in her contorted features. "Oh for goodness sake. Yes, for on Orion but I didn't anticipate coming here. You're meant to be in hell from the portal on Orion and I at a Counsel dinner. Luckily it's had enough effect to rectify my mistake."

Instead of disappointment and sadness, disgust arrived.

Shayne tossed the band and hit MM between the eyes. "You mother fucking, cock sucking, duplicitous, cold hearted piece of shit. All this time. Man is your karma gonna be the biggest, baddest bitch ever."

MM recoiled and rubbed a red mark. "If that's it, I've achieved more than I thought. I've had enough of your vulgarity. My relationship with Enlil is none of your business."

Shayne slowed her breath and cleared her head. "Aha. Whatever major loser. You fuck stick."

Distract her and get the gun, then fucking kill her like twenty-five times.

MM dug the weapon into Izzy's temple. "Stay where you are. Don't come any closer. It if matters, I initially rejected him."

Izzy whimpered, tears streaked her cheeks. "It's okay. Protect yourself and the others.

Shayne's heart lodged in her throat, the babies flipped and took uncomfortable to new heights. "Yeah of course your feeling bad changes everything. Bitch, now I'll rip your fucking head off and toss it into the portal before you."

Whatever humanity dwelled within MM evaporated. "If you move another centimetre, I'll kill them and making you dig out the cave."

Check and......

Shayne's powers lagged, she emptied her verbal arsenal. "Fuck that little mouse because I'm a god damned Albatross. MM was a witch, a sneaky little bitch. But fuck that little mouse because I'm an Albatross."

MM shot a ring around Ryan. "Fuck you, Shayne."

Mate to you. Fuck. I never was good at chess.

Shayne slumped and digested failure. "Leave them alone and I'll do whatever you want."

Chapter 13: It's my party and I'll die if I don't want to
Badlands, Yebu, Orion

Annu landed behind a shed on the other side of the property. Noise from the yard before a beaten down house raised Annu's concern.

Despite concentration, curse words and avid devotion none of his powers worked.

It's never too early to retire and take up golf or whatever bored people do. I'll be a stay at home father. Shayne and the others can carry on without me. I'm too old for this shit.

Controls released, Annu wiped angst from his forehead. "I'll wring their damn necks and make them wish they'd never thought of this hair brained scheme."

Out of the ship and into cool air, sobriety delivered fatigue.

Lactic acid built in Annu's thighs, self-preservation burned in his veins. "If and that's a big if, I make it to the flarking house. I swear I'll nail that flarking book to the wall and build a safe around it. Including retina scanning plus fingerprints and a shit test to get in."

The music—new age rock, crash and awful, heavy metal loudened each stride.

A headache beat its way around Annu's skull. "I can do this without powers. It's a few drunk guys to toss around, grab my kid, kick his arse on way home, save Shayne, go to bed and never wake up. Easy."

Walk in the mother flarking park.

Around the house's side Annu hid behind a heater and peeked over the top of a fence.

Rather than occupied by a nutcase spouting to a few misfortunate souls, dozens of lights and lucid people surrounded Zeke on a pedestal chained with the book beside a stringy older man in a black cloak and a restrained goat.

Fatherly pride bubbled in Annu's gut. "Flark me. That's my boy. Look at him go. We don't do things by halves in the family. He wanted to be centre of attention."

Armed men surrounded the entries, exits and stage; the crowd included weapons baring persons of both sexes.

Annu emptied the first flask and started the second. "Maybe appealing to their saner sides will work?"

Zeke recited a passage from the Lexicon, a purple haze emanated from the book and swirled above; sparks trickled from Zeke's lower half.

Arms poised, the cloaked man nodded. "Good. Continue."

That must be Isaac. Of course.

Zeke read faster and glanced at Isaac.

Annu rolled his shoulders and cracked his neck. "At least he has the good grace to appear concerned."

Obstacles magnified by a kazillion, Annu's self-confidence circled the drain.

Isaac rose above the podium, his arms spread. "Rejoice in the power of the Gods."

Temporarily maybe, mother flarker, and believe me it'll hurt when I get it back.

The crowd's eyes widened, mouths opened, Zeke spoke louder and frowned.

Of all the places and parties my kid shouldn't go to he picked a flarking cult dedicated to releasing his evil grandfather, whom he is yet to find out about. He won't be happy either.

Annu snuck around the corner, crept and slipped into the crowd.

Zeke paused and faced Isaac. "Hey, I'm bored; I don't actually want to hurt my father so untie me. Can't we get back to the party?"

Annu weaved towards the podium. "Aw how flarking sweet of him."

Halfway there a surge of people pushed Annu back and sideways another few metres. "Move will you."

Isaac lowered beside Zeke and gripped his shoulder. "You'll stop when I say you'll stop. We're just getting started. When your father arrives and we sacrifice this goat, the real fun begins. Our Lord and saviour Enlil will be freed. Rejoice."

Oh flark me. What's with this rejoice shit?

The crowd cheered, waves of people rushed at the stage.

Annu's attempted ignition, his thumb flamed and pinky warmed. "Great. Just great."

Zeke's jaw dropped, the book wobbled. "What? You want to use my father to free who? Flark. You never wanted to be my friend did you?"

Shit. Please don't tell him before I do. Please. Please. Please.

Isaac's smile severed Annu's last shred of hope. "Your grandfather, Enlil. Smarts you got from your father not him. Why would a God in waiting be friends with a boy like you?"

Zeke lowered the book; he expressed a full range of emotion. "My grandfather? Really? How do you know?"

Annu shoved and pushed forwards, his chest vibrated. "Zeke, hang in there. I'm coming."

Oh flarking heck. You arsehole.

Zeke slapped his thigh and pushed his tongue under his lip. "Da, you're flarking kidding me. What are you doing here? Oh-my-Gods. Did you follow me or just remember my birthday? I can't go anywhere or do anything without you interfering. No, you didn't want me to find out about Enlil."

Annu rode a wave of disappointment toward the stage. "I'm ah-he, ah-look it's not the time to be mad at me. I'm here to save you from him."

Okay, I really, really must not keep shit to myself and focus more on my kids. From now on. And I need the book but flark. Now's not the time.

Zeke stomped, blue plasma surrounded his head. "I had this figured out without you. I take care of myself you know. Isaac's not a big problem. It's under control." Several gun laser's appeared on Zeke. "Oh. Scratch that."

Isaac cleared his throat and rubbed his hands. "It's about time you arrived." His clap rang across the stage. "Zeke, recite the incantation transferring his powers to me."

Zeke's voice cracked, the plasma fizzled. "No. You don't know what you're doing. I've seen the consequences of that sort of thing. You're nuts." The laser's doubled, Zeke swallowed hard. "Da."

Isaac smirked and gestured to Annu. "Wrong on all counts. Get him."

People submerged, a random hand stabbed a knife into his shoulder.

Jab, jab, two more stabs to the gut.

Annu threw punches and charged ahead, blood soaked his shirt. "Zeke. Don't listen to him. Zeke."

Zeke's scream muted, he struggled against the chains. "Da. I can't undo these."

Three men grabbed Annu and pulled him back.

Annu dragged them forward, copper tainted his tongue. "Touch him again and you're death will be legendary."

Keep moving, don't stop, he needs me, don't fail him.

Isaac cold cocked Zeke across the face. "Pick up the book and read."

Zeke's head whipped, he swayed, and red trickled from his nose. "No."

Annu launched over people, the first collapsed, separated and created a hole. He somersaulted between and stopped amidst feet.

Boots kicked, arms grabbed and knives jabbed.

Annu hugged a pair of legs, steadied and elbowed to his feet. "Flark off."

Crack.

Isaac whipped Zeke in the chin. "Read."

Zeke spat blood, his head hung, plasma dwindled. "No."

Whack.

Blood streamed through Annu's fingers, hands clawed and ripped. "Hang on kid. I'm...I'm coming."

Isaac spread his arms and palms up. "Use a chalice to collect his blood and bring him here. Now."

People blocked each direction, Annu's head buzzed, his pulse slowed.

A woman approached his side and collected a stream of Annu's blood in a bowl.

No, no, no. Not like this.

Annu's growl weakened him, he slapped at her. "I'll be back to kill you later."

The crowd drew inwards, body odour and righteousness enveloped him.

Annu shoved, pushed and kicked. pain exploded from a knife wound down his side. "What is it with you people and knives."

Arms lifted Annu onto a parade of hands.

Isaac's voice drifted. "Excellent. Quickly."

Finger's probed, desperation hugged Annu. "Zeke......run. Take...book out...of...here."

Please Enki. Help—.

Oblivion welcomed Annu with brand new fears.

Chapter 14: The Roof, the roof, the roof is on fire
Gamede

Bong, bong, bong.

Inside the clock on the wall struck twelve as a reminder of human time constraints.

Enlil's temple twitched, his lungs burned, his heart thudded to life. "For alhalso's sake. Salmu, salmu, salmu. It's one thing after another around this place."

Everyone's against me. No one sees where the future's headed without my input. I am the mighty Enlil. The woman may not be here but as long as Annu thought she was, it worked. Until now.

Boom, boom, boom.

Outside, Ralf's men batter-rammed the castle's front gates and on Orion, Annu laid lifeless in a pool blood, Enlil's grandson recited from the Lexicon. Power travelled from Annu to a man in black.

Boom, boom, boom.

Patience crumbled like last week's torture victim.

Enlil ripped the clock from the wall and tossed it. "Who the alhalso is this Isaac? I've never told anyone to sacrifice animals or play such terrible music. I mean really. What are the world's coming to? It's harder and harder to find good devotees. It's wasting precious time."

The clock broke into pieces, reformed and reattached to the wall.

I hate my eternal life sometimes. I really do.

Boom, boom, boom.

Abbaddon skulked in the hallway outside the door. "Ah, is my lord all right? Perhaps it's time to leave."

Enlil's temperature soared, the room heated, flames ran from him along the floor. "Do I alhalsoing look okay, you piece of my salmu? I'll decide if and when I go anywhere. What the alhalso are you doing here? Get out there and stop them."

Boom, boom, boom, crunch.

The gates buckled and the bottom half cracked.

Everything will burn and from the ashes I'll build new realms with a significant lack in the pitiful and pathetic. Stay strong, don't show weakness or they'll lose fear of me too and I can't have that.

Abbaddon stuttered sour breath, drool emphasised his words. "I'm sorry, my Lord. I, we, I tried. There's too many of them. I warned you."

Boom, boom, crack, crack, crack. The gates bowed, the locks broke and former minions stormed into the castle grounds.

Enlil's sanity developed more holes than a politician's memory; he strangled Abbaddon. "I don't want to look or hear you ever again. This is all your fault."

The demon's eye's bulged, goop poured from his nose and ears. "Please, please. My…my…lord—"

Abbaddon's head caved in, Enlil released and wiped his hands. "That feels a little better. Now, nice and calmly I'll put out another fire before I'm captured."

Clangs, bangs, and crashes erupted from the castle's entry door.

Demon shoulder's banged into stone and each other. "We're coming for you, Enlil."

A larger, spiked battering ram made its way to the front of the group.

In the mirror image, Enlil summoned an ethereal form, a black slick erupted from the stage's crevices and tentacles stretched across the stage. "Alhalsoing heck. Nothing like a bit of pressure. They find me, they find my secrets."

Thud, thud, thud.

The boy stomped, his voice broke. "Da. Annu. Wake up. There's something coming and I don't know what. Da. Come on."

Enlil's worm slid for Issac and widened. "At least someone shares said pressure."

With a hand on his chest, Isaac's roar strengthened Enlil. "It's beginning. He's blessed me. Boy, keep reading."

The worm's slick bubbled, Enlil's energy dipped. "Ah, you have no idea. You'll be sorry you wasted my time."

The boy dropped the book, plasma enveloped his torso. "No flarking way. I'd rather die, you flarking bastard. You'll pay for this."

In the right hands he'd be a great prodigy. There's great potential and he's at a malleable age. I'll consider not killing him later.

Isaac approached the boy and slapped him. "Not until I'm ready you insipid, twat."

Enlil's tentacles touched and consumed Isaac's feet. "Idiot. Waste of space and air. I'd say it so you could hear it if it didn't drain me more."

Isaac shifted a leg, it stayed in place. "Never panic in the face of darkness friends. This is a test of my strength and faith."

People mumbled, gasped, and clapped.

Annu stirred and rolled his head. "Ahhh."

Enlil climbed, squeezed and devoured Isaac. "When you get down here you're so screwed."

Thud, thud, thud, bang.

Chunks of stone tumbled; they made a small hole in the entry door.

I'm still not panicking, I've got this. All right, I may be a little concerned.

Isaac's scream's increased tension and drama. "Please, my Lord. I intended to send it all to you. I swear it."

Rows of people rushed for the exits, a handful climbed the stage.

Enlil surged electricity through the tentacles and constricted Isaac's chest. "You filthy liar. That's what your kind does and yet they're the blessed ones."

A dead Isaac slumped, the people on stage seized.

Enlil's energy decelerated, a forced breath burned his virgin lungs. "No, no, no. Damn."

Bang, bang, bang.

Zeke broke his chains, ran to Annu and shook him. "Da. Please wake up. I need you."

The boy's fatherly loyalty stung Enlil, his inabilities unnerved him. "Why has no one felt that way about me? Am I not worthy?"

The stolen powers travelled from Isaac back into Annu, he sat up and gasped.

Crack, crack, crack.

The entry doors opened, the demons entered his domain.

Bitterness jaded Enlil, he spat at the portal. "Neither of you deserve each other. This should be about me. In time he would have understood why I'm like this but it's too late. I gave you the chance Annu and you'll pay for dismissing me."

Remember the bigger picture. Stay focused.

Zeke collected the book and ran off the stage with Annu.

Enlil changed positions and searched for Shayne, another breath request terrified him. "Marguerite, why aren't you here yet and around that girl instead?"

The room ignited; everything in it, aside from the clock, burned or melted.

I can't stay here any longer. I have to leave, find a place to hide until things work out. If they find me they find my secrets. After I gather my wits and get drunk first.

Enlil lay where a couch once stood. "I'll have a little lie down. It's been a trying day. I'll unwind and reconfigure. Abbaddon get me a drink and make it a triple."

Abbaddon's bones hissed in the corner, demons infiltrated the lower levels.

Solitude accompanied Enlil's laugh. "Ah yeah. Guess not. I'll find another replacement. If there's anyone left. Mostly I bring this onto myself. But you'll never hear me admit it in public."

The second in charge, Malek, clambered in and glanced at his bosses remains. "My Lord, we must protect you. Why are you on the floor?"

I'm still not giving up. This is a temporary setback.

Enlil's mind fragmented, sane and insane blurred. "Yeah that sounds great. By the way, you're promoted to Captain. Gather as many men as you can and do not let them down here."

Great sacrifice always brings great rewards. This is that part of the process that's all.

Malek snorted snot and confusion. "Yes, my Lord."

Enlil rolled onto his side and tapped the floor. "It might be an idea to choose a new second in command just in case."

Malek sucked his bottom lip and paled. "Ah okay."

It sucks when there's no one to pray to except myself. I'm not sure that ever worked anyway. .

Chapter 15: Politics in Space
Marduk and Gamede

Trouble and bad guys followed Shayne like flies on shit; she dragged her feet to the blue light. "You call me stubborn. I've told you a dozen times to go back with the others. I'll handle this and don't need you to worry about."

And not even a shower gets rid of my attractive qualities.

Ryan remained beside Shayne and maintained eye contact with Izzy under MM's grasp. "Like hell. I'm not leaving any of you with her. You pick some odd associates mum. Where do you find these people?"

How apt my boy.

Power swept over Shayne's hands and disappeared. "Mmm, luck I think. It's the other story of my life. Apparently I need challenges. You're staying with me until we reach the room but do not go inside. Portals suck up everything in the vicinity."

Ryan's voice lowered, he finger combed his hair. "And what do we do in the meantime? What will you do with her? I suggest you hang around this amazing place and hypnotise some creature into killing her."

This isn't the first time I've been dragged to my alleged death. Though the first time I didn't have an audience. I should have my own fucking reality show. A beleaguered, misunderstood Demigoddess's adventures in Space. Something like that. It'd sell for sure.

Shayne hooked her arm through his, the babies moved in their sleep. "I flipping live on this shit. Relax. The stupid bitch has forgotten about my wormholes and stuff."

If it works and except when it suited her. It better open when I try or I'm gonna cry. Ha.

TS clutched her handbag to her chest. "What if your thingos fail again and she shoves you in? We're all left her to die."

Fucking needy much? Argh why can't I throw her in instead? My karma's fucked anyway.

Shayne's stomach ache waned, a bad mood waxed. "Is that thing your security blanket or are your brains in there?"

TS's frown disrupted Shayne's control. "What are you talking about?"

Irritation soaked into Shayne's bones, she ground her teeth. "Your hand bag. Is it made of gold? What's in it that's so important?"

TS's pissy tone intensified the awkwardness. "Is that relevant to the current situation? For a part god you're rather unorganised and lacking in real power."

Fucking hell. Is it me or is she a total fucking bitch? Do I blame the situation or are we just rubbing each other the wrong way? You know what, when I get home we're installing a moat filled with Salty Crocs, Jelly fish and a few sea snakes.

Shayne sucked patience dry and tossed the shell. "Forget it. Stay back here with Ryan. He'll make sure you're safe."

Light twinkled from the portal room, the ground trembled.

Ryan smoothed his tongue over his teeth. "Mum, that's well beyond my duties as the wedding usher. There are science fiction movies that start like this."

Tears streaked through dirt on TS's cheeks. "I've made a terrible mistake. I should have never looked for you. I want to go home."

You obviously thought being my mother was a mistake and too much hard work. You know, you've whined a lot but you've not made one attempt at getting to know me or supporting me. How did you just leave me and never check on me again until now?

Rejection disintegrated Shayne's focus. "Why'd you abandon me? Did I do something wrong? Did you forget where Nan and Pa lived? I may accept temporary insanity depending on the circumstances."

TS stopped crying and jutted her chin. "How can you possibly ask me that in this situation, one you put us in I might add? Are you insane? What kind of person starts a conversation like that while her family's in mortal danger instead of fixing things? Why bring all this up now? Or at all? Can't we just move past it? You're a grown woman not a child."

Ah ouch, ouch, ouch. Me, clearly. Duh.

Their fate often lay in the hands of magical lights with destinations unknown.

Ryan's sighs warmed Shayne's ear. "Um mum, you might want to leave it for a better day."

Shayne put on imaginary sunglasses and faced TS. "I'm sorry but no. I have to know. Being abandoned by your mother, the one person who's meant to love and protect you from birth is a defining moment. Please forgive me for being hurt about being dumped. I am an adult and as you said it was a long time ago, so what's the harm in telling me now? I won't hate you."

Anymore than I do already.

A draft shifted TS's hair, blonde and grey roots confused Shayne. "I don't think it's fair anyone holds a past mistake over me for the rest of my life. It was a difficult time and nobody understands what I went through."

Aha. Right. I remember you as a brunette in Nan and Pa's photos. Not a blonde.

Unease shifted ire, Shayne's yummy fluttered. "How long have you dyed your hair brown?"

This-Sally's cheeks flushed, she patted her head. "For fucks's sake. Years. Why does it matter? Will you just quit with the questions and get this over with."

The ground trembled and cleared Shayne's attention. "It's too late to start telling me what to do. Something's not right here and I'll figure out what it is."

MM yelled from the room's doorway. "Shayne get up here before I kill the girl."

Shayne slapped her cheek and hurried. "Stay here all right. This isn't over."

Or not. What's with this woman? She's less maternal than I am and that's fucked.

Izzy's determination shone brighter than the portal. "Don't do as she says. I'm not worth it."

Idiot. Focus. It's not about me.

Apprehension pinched Shayne's nipples and twisted. "As if. You're more than worthy. They've got nothing to do with this."

MM let off two blasts, recoil thrust her shoulder back. "I'm not taking any chances. Hurry up."

I've got control and you'll see it firsthand, bitch.

A shot grazed Ryan's side, he toppled into Shayne. "Shit. Shit. Mum."

Shayne steadied, faked calm and panicked for real. "Fuck, fuck. It's all right. A big scratch."

TS held the bag like life-support. "Please don't leave me here alone."

MM tightened the screws on their fucked status. "Next one's in his head."

Shayne jogged, cortisol hid pain and discomfort. "Like fuck bitch. You're also un-invited to the wedding and I'm keeping your present. Ryan stay behind me."

Ryan caught up and covered his wound. "Mum, don't do anything rash."

TS lagged beside Ryan. "You aren't like her at all. Please keep me safe."

Whatever. Fuck you too. I'm okay by the way thanks for asking. Fuck.

Shayne touched Ryan's hand. "It's okay. Have faith."

Ryan guided TS behind him. "I might shit myself soon."

Limited escape options echoed like their footsteps.

Resignation followed Shayne inside, the portal swirled in a corner. "Yeah, I'm not far behind you."

Here I go again. Hang in there babies. Please be okay.

MM dragged Izzy by the hair to it. "You two get by me. Shayne, you know what to do."

Ryan's fear brushed Shayne's arm. "Jesus fucking christ. This is next level shit."

TS's teeth chattered. "I'm not going over there."

MM lowered Izzy and shot Ryan in the foot. "Yes you are."

Ryan fell; blood soaked his shoe and painted the ground. "Ahhhhhhhh."

Shayne used her hand to seal the site. "No, no, no. Oh Gods. You fucking bitch."

TS ran to MM with her hands up. "Okay, okay. Don't hurt me too."

What the fuck? That's her fucking grandson.

MM lunged one handed for TS and shoved her into the portal. "Now you'll get in there."

Chapter 16: Parental Divorce

The incantation page in Zeke's pocket afforded some piece of mind, the book rested at his feet.

Enlil's my grandfather. If he's some magnificent, evil dude why did he intervene? Damned Annu. He's no right keeping this secret, it obviously affects me too. Maybe I'm too harsh. He did try saving me. Sort of. But so he should. Shit. I'm related to pure evil.

Zeke stretched self-assurance via his legs in the co-pilot's seat. "You're such a hypocrite, Annu. Another secret comes out you've hidden from me. Forget trusting you. You think I'm just a stupid kid who can't deal with anything. I'm my own man with my own destiny and you need to accept that."

Any second now he'll rip me to shreds. Well he can screw himself. If he hadn't come after me none of this would have happened. Shayne has her moments but she's not too bad. Plus she's carrying my siblings.

Annu cleared his throat and tapped the steering shaft. "Yeah I know I messed up with you and Shayne big time. When I found out I didn't handle it well and couldn't bring myself to tell anyone. It's not the kind of thing you blurt out over breakfast. Your mother being so ill didn't help things either."

Flark. Maybe he's sorry and does care? Or is he just talking himself out of trouble? I'm stuck with two emotionally crippled parents. Please don't let me turn out like him.

Confusion attacked Zeke's righteousness, he raised his defences. "If I'd done something like that I'd never hear the end of it."

Annu's rum tainted body odour soured the air. "Aha. Let's get back to what you have done shall we, stealing a ship, flying to a forbidden place and using your powers with the Lexicon to screw with me and Shayne. Right around when Enlil has a chance for freedom using one or both of those things. Look aside from all that, I'm new to this parent stuff and still learning. Give me a break."

He does have a point but I'll never admit it. I wonder if I'll ever hear from Paige again? I didn't see what happened to her. Did she fake her feelings too?

Zeke retrieved the book, calm washed over him. "I might not have done any of that if you hadn't forgotten my birthday and our flying lesson. I don't like being treated like a tool or asset. All our time together centres on the book."

Contrition lightened Annu's tone. "Yeah I agree with you there. I'm so flarking sorry, kid. We've had so much going on it slipped our minds. I promise we'll make it up to you when we're all home together. I totally understand why you went anyway. Please don't get angry at me again, but I need the book for a different mission. I'm dropping you home and leaving."

Disappointment shrouded Zeke, his confidence dipped. "Honestly, did you come and find me because you were worried or for the book?"

Annu slapped the control panel. "For flark's sake, boy. I went to get you and bigger shit happened on the way. I want to tell you what but you'll try stopping me."

This doesn't sound good at all.

Zeke scraped the middle of the barrel and plucked a tadpole. "Does this have to do with Enlil and Shayne, given she's not here and all?"

Annu's breath lifted his huge chest. "Yes it has everything to do with them."

I don't know how those two manage to get themselves into these situations but they do and then it becomes my problem. Do I get any recognition for it? No. This is why I have the page. I deserve better than this. Someone recognise my true worth and show all these other idiots.

Cosmic responsibility hampered Zeke. "Then you either tell me and take me with you or I use a spell to hide the book for safety."

The cabin temperature lowered, their surroundings blurred.

Anger embellished Annu's words. "Enlil has Shayne and if I don't bring the book to him he'll kill her."

All he'd read about Enlil returned, Zeke shivered. "Yeah to saving Shayne but you're not giving him the book. It's universal homicide."

Annu's shoulders raised to ear height, his jaw clenched. "He won't hand her over without it. I don't see what choice I have."

If you don't know there's a way around that you can't be forced to use it.

Zeke patted his pocket, fear lessened. "I'm coming with you."

Annu shook his head and scratched his beard. "No you're not going. I knew you'd do this. Don't make me worry about you too."

I'm scared and vulnerable without you. I clearly don't have great instincts or judgment when it comes to people yet.

Zeke opened the Lexicon towards Annu. "Okay. I'll stay home if you read this particular incantation."

Annu squinted, his lip spasm'd, he mumbled into his shirt. "It's the one for pausing time."

Frustration slammed the book shut. "Oh my Gods Annu. You're not even close. It's for turning water into wine. See this proves my point. You need me and I'm coming."

The craft's engine wound down and stopped, a pink light enveloped them.

A male boomed from the dash board communication system:

"Annu, under instruction from the Universal Protection Agency you are hereby detained for return to the mother ship for contravening a UPA covenant. If you do not comply, you'll be arrested. Please prepare for boarding."

A vein in Annu's neck pulsed. "You're flarking kidding me. I don't have time for this. No. No. No."

Disbelief over Zeke's parentage sat between them, his will to live nosedived. "What else did you do? I thought those guys liked you?"

Despite a succession of taps, punches, and pleas, the craft remained inert.

Annu's flames ignited the seat; he rose and patted out his pants. "Same reason you're not happy with me on a much bigger scale and it's not helping." Annu jabbed, flames trickled from his hand. "Stay here and bypass their locking system. I'll prevent them getting in. When I give you the word, take off."

Oh shit.

Annu entered the next section with Zeke's confidence; the stench of hot metal invaded the ship.

Pressure dulled Zeke's memory; his hand trembled over the controls. "Flarking hell. I only did this hours ago."

Bangs the next cabin's door rang through the craft.

Zeke slow breathed. "Red, blue, red, blue, green? Or blue, blue, red, green?"

Nothing changed. Metal crunched from outside, boom.

The outer door flew across the cabin and imbedded in the opposite wall.

Zeke burst from the seat and into the next section. "Flark."

Half a dozen armed lion-like beings entered via a shaft and captured Annu in an orange beam.

A powerless Annu pounded on the walls. "Put me down. You're making a huge mistake."

A blue feathered creature approached Zeke. "I am aware you're Annu's son. I'm sorry, you've done a wonderful job taking care of the Lexicon but please allow me to take care of it and join us."

Loyalty tugged at Zeke, he tightened his embrace on it. "I'm not giving it to anyone. You're wrong about my father. He knows what he's doing."

Why am I saying that when I know he's not. Do I want the book for the right reasons?

The bird lady's relaxed presence conflicted Zeke. "While it doesn't seem so, this is for his own good. We will do him no harm. I understand your reluctance and admire your veracity. I'll allow you to bring it onto the ship and place it in a special case. We'll return it as soon as it's safe to do so. I promise you."

Oh crap. I can't argue with that. Annu being with them works for now and keeps him out of trouble.

The lion beings transported Annu off the ship.

Zeke walked to the shaft and hesitated. "What about Shayne and the babies?"

Ankor gestured a feathered hand. "That situation I'm afraid is yet to be sorted out. Perhaps a clever boy like you will figure something."

Someone who appreciate my skills already.

Chapter 17: Missed it by that much
Universal Protection Agency Mother Ship
Orion's Upper Atmosphere

What Annu wanted and what he got seldom coincided. More often than not they acted like polar opposite magnets.

His escape attempts resembled a babies attempt at flying a PFD and time remained his biggest problem. "Let me out. You're making a massive mistake. He'll kill her."

How and when did doing the right thing become so wrong? How'd I screw this up?

Ankor flittered between two armed and serious Lyrons. "I'm so sorry, Annu. I've prayed for Shayne, unfortunately there's no other way of ensuring her safety at the cost of all creation. I deplore restraining you, yet you've left us no choice. We're not about to let you do the one thing you promised you wouldn't. Please don't hate me."

The Lyron's maintained eye contact with Annu. Another two guarded the doorway and an unknown number outside.

Annu's ire percolated, his boots melted into the floor. "If you let me out right now, I'll consider it. At least send someone to save her."

Where's Zeke and the book at? How do I get them both and out of here? Think man, think.

Kick, kick, punch, punch.

I said think not act. Work brain. Tick, tick, tick. The way out is currently lost on my dumb forlorn arse.

Slam, bash, crash.

Ankor clasped her fingers and lifted her chin. "We are not monsters Annu. We're looking into sending someone but we've no way of knowing what they'd face or a way to get them both out again. It's effectively a suicide mission. There's a lack of volunteers as you'd imagine."

This cannot be happening. Am I a bad person who deserves constant punishment and unhappiness? Tell what have I done and how I rectify it.

Eyon, a tall, pale, black haired being rocked on his heels. "We have no desire to cause you or Shayne personal distress and harm. We'll work for the next twelve hours to find another way; there's no guarantees."

He lied to me. I've got longer, though he could kill her anyway. Flark.

Bureaucracy destroyed Annu's present and future. "Whatever happens to her while she's down there I'll do to you. Speaking of which, what will?"

Feathers bunched between Ankor's eyes. "We're unsure. There's no record of anyone going there voluntarily nor escaping from there after death. It's futile to torture yourself with possibilities."

Annu's blood cooled, a sadness lodged in his throat. "Are you saying it's pointless to want to save my future wife from death?"

I wish I'd never spoken to you at the DSI facility. As soon as you mentioned him, and I spoke his name, my life became another kind of hell. Now the only light in my life will die without me. Again. And these bastards will let it happen. Well I flarking won't.

Ankor's lower lip quivered. "I, I don't know what to say or do. It's a terrible situation, one I wish hadn't happened. "

Annu concentrated power into his palms. "Not as much as you will when I get out of here. Get the flark away from me."

I feel four guards outside the door and others at each end of the hall.

Ankor steeled and avoided eye contact. "Please, you'll only make things worse. I'm truly sorry, Annu. I wish there was another way. "

Not me. Not anymore. You've made this easier.

Annu closed his eyes and relaxed. *'Zeke, where are you son? Please help me out.'*

Eyon broke Annu's concentration. "There's no point ruminating over this. You'll be given fluid and sustenance when required. If you require anything important ask the guards."

Annu dragged his nails down the glass and growled. "One way or another I'll get out of here and do what I have to. Not you or anyone else will stop me. You're only prolonging the inevitable."

Eyon's lack of fear bumped Annu's pride. "Greater power denotes great responsibility. Perhaps you've more of your father in you than we'd first believed. We won't allow that kind of scourge to destroy creation again."

Is he right? Am I doomed to repeat Enlil's mistakes? Did he suffer the same injustices at Enki's hands? What if they're all wrong and he's right?

Sorrow invaded Annu's soul, tears burned his eyes. "I'm not losing my family for a second time. Let me out and I won't rip your heads off and use them as bowling balls."

Flark it. Enki this is your last chance to prove me wrong and you right. Keep Shayne and the babies safe. I beg you Enki. Screw this up and it's all over for us. I'm done doing your dirty work.

Eyon's forehead tightened, his breath quickened. "Threatening harm upon a UPA member is punishable by expulsion and sometimes death. In this instance given the high emotions and difficult situation I shall over look this but don't push your luck."

Each jab at the tube softened it a little; Annu twisted his finger to make a hole. "Like I flarking care. Where's my son and the Lexicon?"

Eyon's red cheeks highlighted a pale face. "Both are safe and their whereabouts are not your concern. Whatever favour you had from all the good you two have done is hereby gone. Annu, you'd serve yourself well to spend this time reflecting and re-establishing your devotion to the creator rather than your own personal needs. Guards, watch him every second and do not let your attention waver. He's not to be trusted."

Ankor clasped Eyon's forearm. "Let's not escalate matters. Calm down before you say things you'll regret."

Eyon flipped Ankor's hand off. "Your soft nature will cause us trouble one day."

Annu's frustration spilled over. "Oh, I'll reflect all right."

On how I'll kill you on my way out just for fun.

Eyon strode from the room, guards repositioned around the capsule.

Ankor lingered and twirled her thumbs. "Annu, I know—"

Annu seared Shayne's name into the plastic. "Get out."

Chapter 18: Karma's a bitch but I'm worse
Marduk & Gamede

On the other side of the portal waited an evil future father-in-law and a pissed off possible-mother.

I bet after she fell in she finally dropped that stupid bag. Friending Maybe-Marge might be my worse decision yet. And that's saying something.

Vengeance operated the gears, Shayne steered. "This is putting another real dint in our future friendship. Not that there is one."

MM shielded her face and waved the gun. "Will you shut up? Get in there."

Snap. Goodbye arsehole. I probably should check on This-Sally anyway.

Ryan favoured his other leg and held Izzy. "Mum, Mum, don't do anything stupid. Mum."

Shayne hunched her shoulders, charged and collected MM around the middle. "It's on now, you fucking bitch. The world's better off without you."

MM's breasts suffocated Shayne. "Let me go you maniac."

Shayne pole drove MM into the portal and released. "Ryan….take care of —"

Oh crap, oh crap, oh crap, oh crap.

Ryan's yell disappeared in the starred tunnel, light exploded from everywhere. Instead of twists and turns like wormholes, it provided an almost direct route.

Shayne landed on her knees in sand. "I'm already rethinking my decision."

The smell of sulphur and overcooked meat blasted her. Dilapidated buildings covered one side of the landscape, desolate open plains the other.

Shayne rubbed her belly, pee trickled down her leg. "Is this what it's usually like?"

TS laid unconscious on the ground, sand drifted over her and her handbag.

It hasn't really been a good getting to know you trip. Well I suppose it has but not in a fucking nice way.

Disjointed screams and yells supplied theme music. In the distance smoke billowed into the sky, weapons boomed, evidence of recent battle scattered the landscape.

Pain ricocheted across Shayne's stomach, self-preservation pushed it aside. "Where the fuck are you, Maybe-Marge? I'll mess you up so bad Enlil won't recognise you. If he doesn't get to you first."

MM emerged from some rocks, tore out clumps of hair and screeched. "How could you do this? He'll find me. I don't belong here. I tried doing the right thing, and I didn't actually hurt anyone."

Hatred soured Shayne; she withheld scratching her eyes out. "I hope he fucking does. In fact, I'll help him. Hello Enlil, here's the stupid bitch you sent to bring me here. Come get her. I'll watch—"

Zap, zap, clump.

Izzy tumbled feet first out of a portal onto the ground; she rolled metres and stopped on her side. "Oh thank goodness."

It can't be, shit.

Shayne rubbed her eyes, surprise unglued them. "Izzy? What are you doing here? It's not safe. Please don't tell me Ryan's here too. Does no one listen to me?"

MM walked in circles and picked at her skin. "I…I….I…"

Izzy dusted herself off. "I couldn't let you sacrifice yourself and your children for me. It must be destiny you and I came across each other at this time. Ryan objected but stayed behind after I placed bandages on his foot and provided directions to my people."

Shayne's maternal side swelled and contracted. "Bless him. He's safer there without us. Before I get us out of here, I'm killing and maiming her first."

Wormholes better fucking work this time or look out.

Izzy squeezed Shayne's hand. "Will hurting Marguerite keep you on the path to spiritual enlightenment?"

Great. More pressure from the holy. She's like my walking conscious. Only prettier.

Sores on MM's arms weeped, her screams streaked the air with fear. "No, no, no, no, no, no, no."

She's still got to live with herself, if she makes it out.

A TS comatose lessened Shayne's problems.

Shayne's new, better self-evicted revenge. "All right. Fine. She's possibly suffered enough."

Izzy released her hand and hugged herself. "I knew you'd make the right decision. Can we leave now?"

The hairs on Shayne's arms and nape prickled. "Someone or thing is watching us."

The colour drained from MM, she covered her mouth. "Oh no. Please… I did…..no."

MM's recent nutty manner made sense. "Ah. She does that when Enlil's talking to her. I'm such a dumb arse sometimes. Looks like he's pissed off too. Sucks to be her.

A series of howls shifted Izzy closer. "Ah, how about now?"

The baby bump prevented Shayne climbing Izzy like a tree, she lead Izzy to a TS and squatted. "Yep. I'm on—"

Four hell hounds emerged from between buildings and headed for MM.

MM lifted a leg up and down. "Please… no….stop."

The hounds pounced on her and tore her to shreds. Her screams emptied Shayne's well. Blood sprayed, clothes ripped, muscles torn and bones crunched.

Izzy squealed and clung onto Shayne. "They're more horrific than they sound."

Shayne's aura protected Izzy and TS, she swirled for a wormhole. "Fuck this."

Not even a twinkle of light saved her sanity.

Swish, swish, swirl, swirl. Nada, nothing, zip.

Sweat dampened Shayne's back, she chewed her nails. "Shit. I hate it when that happens."

Stay calm. Don't lose it yet. Save it for something worthy. Bigger. Like what I don't know.

Izzy's strength wavered, she gulped in air. "Why isn't it working? How do we get out of here?"

Bad luck rained on Shayne's bravado, she raised an umbrella. "Stress, pregnancy, and possibly an outside source. Or this place."

The hounds bounded off and left pieces of MM in their wake.

TS roused and half sat up, her chin fell. "Where the hell are we? What were those things?"

My future guard dogs. They're effective and loyal.

Shayne pushed her back down one handed. "Go back to sleep," the other covered Izzy's eyes. "Don't look over that way."

This is an extreme version of how far people go when committed to doing the wrong thing, and what happens after they do.

Izzy exhaled and shifted Shayne's hands. "Thank Enki that's over. What happens without your powers?"

The babies turned, kicked and stretched, Shayne held her breath. "From experience, I've learned there are other ways to fight when I have no powers or back up. It happens. Though I've never tested myself in such a place. We'll need a portal out of here."

TS cuddled a retrieved handbag. "I'll give you everything I own to send me home."

At least she's holding that instead of a grudge.

Shayne leaned on her side and worked upwards. "Yeah I'm not sure I'd want it and you've made your feelings abundantly clear.

Sand's great for exfoliation. Have at it. Izzy do you know anything that helps?"

Izzy rubbed her eyes. "Dead or alive, there's plenty of ways to get into Hell. In fact it's easy. But, to my knowledge there's only two of getting and both nigh impossible. First be a pure soul and either Enki or someone else sacrifices themselves for you. Or the portal Enlil uses to ascend. As for live people being in a dead place, I have no idea but it won't be good."

Shayne's purity ended in 1985 at a Kiss concert, her relationship with Enki didn't suggest he'd do anything more than ignore her requests. "I'm pretty sure we won't find a tour guide who doesn't want to eat us."

I'm too tired to care right now.

TS kicked dust and a good attitude. "You're a complete mess. I wish I'd never found you. I've been a fool."

Hurt tolled upon the hellish day, sobs burned Shayne's chest. "I don't blame you. I'm useless. I've got no idea what to do. My own actions hurt people all the time."

Izzy's gasp and TS's yelp paused Shayne part woe.

A seven foot mixture of pig/hare on top and hippo on the bottom waited. "Excuse me, I'm Ralf. I believe we may assist each other."

Shayne flinched, her heart skipped, the babies kicked. "Unholy fucking shit, Ralf. What are you doing sneaking up on us? Don't you take another step."

Izzy wrapped around Shayne's arm. "Shayne. I'm scared."

TS thudded to the ground in a waft of dust.

She's making a habit out of this. The woman isn't built of strong stuff.

Shayne pushed Izzy behind her. "It's okay. I got you. Ralf?"

Ralf glanced between MM's remains and TS. "I know a way out of here."

The hole Annu made filled in again. "What's with people putting me in sardine cans? Knowing my luck those lumps of stress will turn into tumours. Big, nasty, mucky ones. Hell, it's easier than dealing with divine family disputes and Sam. Who'd think I'd look forward to actual hell."

A bell dinged, the guards raised their weapons, the door opened and Ankor flitted into the room.

What does she want now? I saved you from harm a couple of times and I get this in return. I know you're doing the right thing but it's for the wrong reasons. It's hard not to blame you for it instead of me.

She hovered ahead of the guards. "Please leave us for a moment."

The guards frowned, nodded, and exited.

Ankor reached the tube, her sigh fogged the glass. "I apologise for the lack of space but a larger one compromises the cylinders security. There's a darkness inside you which grows each day and it concerns me on a personal level. I know this isn't who you are. Normally, I'd keep my feelings to myself, since I returned from DSI on Earth, I've been plagued by dreams offering a different version of events leading up to you saving me. Much of it I don't want to relive but in them we'd became close and I told you Enlil was your father. Something in your eyes tells me these are not fiction but memories. "

One of the guards looked at them through a window and knocked his weapon against it.

Venom tainted Annu and buried care for others. "Whatever happened doesn't matter anymore. I'm done with everyone and the only God I'll ever rely on again is me. I told you to flark off so get out of here instead of torturing me with your bad feelings. Unless you like it?"

Ankor flinched as if he'd slapped her, her feathers fluttered. "Of course I don't. What alternative do we have? The second we let you out you'd go to hell."

The memories chinked Annu's armour, his human side stirred. "Damn right so you best do that."

Disappointment clouded Ankor and dulled her colour. "Again, you'll never know how this pains me. Pray for guidance and wisdom."

I can't let her make me question my decision and let emotions weigh in.

Annu rendered prayers useless as tits on a bull. "Then to feel better unlock this, fill me with rum, show me where the book and my son are. I'll go from there."

The door opened, the guards returned and stood either side of it.

Ankor's compassion dulled, her demeanour sagged. "Until next time Annu. Perhaps it's time you definitely relied on faith."

I'm an arsehole. But I can't be nice and save Shayne. It won't work.

Each second captured, equalled certain death, surrender breathed down Annu's neck. "Yeah, probably not. Hasn't done a flarking thing so far."

Ankor, and his confidence in her, exited, the doors sealed doom inside.

All right, there's not much left to try.

Acceptance of Annu's one option wore, stripped and flogged him. "Asking isn't taking sides or giving in. It doesn't change who I am."

"Enki, if going after Shay is right, please show me. Get me out of here or something."

A caged animal paced inside Annu, desperation thickened the capsule's air, and burnt rubber stung his nose.

"Enki? No time like the present to answer me."

A clock above the door counted down Shayne's fate, lava bubbled in Annu gut. The guards didn't blink, budge or care.

"Enki?"

Tic, tic, tic, tic.

"Fine. Screw you. Enlil, are you there?"

Ouch. That hurts.

A worm re-entered Annu's mind and slicked his thoughts. *"Yes. I'm listening."*

Don't give in. Be strong.

Humble tasted like onions with more gas. *"I'm bound by the UPA. They've the book as well."*

"What do you want from me? Why should I help you again?"

Annu's pulse raced, his brain hurt. *Take what you need from me to do so, send my wife home, and I'll come to you voluntarily. I'll do whatever you want."*

Darkness probed Annu for places to settle. *"Are you prepared for the consequences of your offer?"*

If I do this properly there won't be any. "Yes. Are you?"

A series of alarms tolled outside, a guard opened the door and they marched into the hallway.

Surprise coloured Annu happy. "That was flarking quick."

A block of light stopped the worm part way, Enlil's presence retreated. *"It wasn't me."*

Zeke burst in with a book sized lump under his jacket. "Da, we've got to be quick."

Annu slapped the tube, doom lifted, hope resurfaced. "Believe me, I will. It's so flarking good to see you."

"Enil the deal's off. I take it all back. Send my wife home before I come after you."

"Too late."

Annu's heart sank, fear nipped his bud.

Oh my darling what have I done? I'll make this right yet.

Zeke reached the control panel. "Yep. I bet it is. Remember that when we're home later and you want to punish me."

The tube unlocked and Annu's powers returned. "You're on son. Ah, free air. How I've missed thee. I thought you didn't agree with me."

That's one problem down. I don't want to hurt any of them. They're trying to do the right thing too.

Zeke waited beside the doorway. "We're not there yet. They're not getting the book and I still don't want you to go, but I don't want you locked up either. I'm hoping to change your mind before we get there."

Annu depressed the button and burst into the hallway. "Good luck. Which way?"

Zeke glanced both ways and shrugged. "Ah, left I think."

Beings of different descriptions poured in and out of rooms in a frenzy, and armed guards scanned the hallway.

Annu's sense of direction warped. "Right it is."

The Guards spotted them, raised their weapons and headed their way.

Zeke stumbled over his feet. "Oh crap. Already?"

Annu dragged Zeke into a nearby room and hand-welded the one door closed. "This is not good for my equilibrium."

Zeke glanced out a window. "Okay. It seems I'm not great with directions. I only thought about getting the book and you."

Bang, bang, bang.

Single minded just like his father.

Annu rolled his shoulders and cracked his neck. "A tip for both of us next time, have the actual escape route figured out first."

Come on brain. Work.

Guards rammed the door, the lights dimmed, and a large air vent in the roof offered a crammed solution.

A woman's voice rumbled through the door. "You're making things worse for yourselves. It's not too late to give up and resolve this peacefully."

We're at the hostage negotiation stage. That escalated quickly.

Bang, bang, slam.

A laser burned a small hole and a circle in the door.

Frustration lumps tripled, Annu pushed them down. "It was too late days ago."

Zeke searched either way, a frown creased his forehead. "What do we do Da?"

Say goodbye to a few layers of skin.

Warmth spread across Annu's chest. "We're going to elevate ourselves my boy. I'll push you into the vent up there and you pull me in. Given we're in space and you neither of us can breathe in it, we'll need a ship to get back to Orion."

An outside force penetrated his aura, Annu's energy lowered. *Oh fuck. I'm screwed.*

Chapter 20: The Devil's in the details
Gamede

Emotional imbalance and torment steamed out vents in the walls. Ralf's men's boots blocked sections of light and cast shadows.

Enlil's confidence in the hidden room beneath the portal disappeared. "Alhalso, alhalso, alhalso. I can't suck much out of him; I can't see the woman or anyone else. Shit."

A cupboard blocked the invisible door; a pile of bricks beside a hole in the corner supplied the sole exit.

The Elders' groans rippled along the floor and up his spine.

A constant requirement to breath and blood in veins terrified Enlil. "Like everything it's a matter of perspective. I'll still ascend and nothing will stop me."

Nothing better stop me. I won't survive humanity in this place.

Ancient powers please protect me. This room and I are invisible, out of sight, doesn't exist. You won't find me.

Blue mist emitted from the ground, swept around and filled covered exits.

Enlil's bones ached, hunger bothered him. "I can't wait until all this is Annu's problem and he finds out once I'm gone and he's in Gamede, he replaces me. That and a dead woman will teach him for ignoring me."

Noise from the hall outside dried Enlil's mouth, his stress level elevated to universal.

Still invisible. Move along. There's nothing to see here.

The eternal clock chimed through his brain.

A demon's grumble above Enlil's head reconfigured his heart rate . "Tear the place apart. He's here somewhere or we'd have found him."

The protection won't hold much longer. Do I dig my way out and find somewhere close to hide? If I do I may never get back here. Alive anyway.

Enlil's luck swung like a pendulum. "Flaming heck. I must decide before it's too late."

The Elders' swarmed Enlil's mind. *"Do you require our assistance again Enlil? It's not too late to ask as Ralf did. You're aware we do not play favourites."*

Enlil huddled in a corner. "Draw and quarter him. He's nothing, worthless. I made him from the dirt this castle stands on. He doesn't have the capabilities to pull this off without your help."

Why am I shitting myself then? Because I self-sabotage.

Unease drifted across the room. *"And used him to trap us in the dark beyond. Yet you're scared of him."*

I've got a big mouth sometimes. It says things I pay for later. Or now.

Enlil's dignity slipped from his grasp. *"Don't take it personally; it was a cocky time in my life. I'm sorry. Please help me instead. You'll have half access to my parents, my son, his family and half of everything."*

Screeches and screams surrounded their words. *"We'll consider it."*

This is the lowest I've ever gone. I can't go down further. Am I sure I want to do this? Is it worth this much proving Enki wrong?

Boom, boom, smash.

Yes, yes it is. "Please, hurry."

The Elders' tightened their grip on Enlil. *'We accept your offer upon delivery of your kin Enlil. While we may forgive your last deception upon freeing us, it won't happen again.'*

Enlil's mind wriggled free. *'That doesn't work for me.'*

"I can't do that. I need the woman for collateral myself. Just give me what I need and you'll get what you want."

"Not this time. We require the woman and your son first."

Physical ailments weakened Enlil. *"Fine. I'll bring them to you."*

"Don't delay."

Now to get out of here and find them without getting caught myself. This is not how I pictured this would go. But I've got control on my side.

Something pushed against the door, the cupboard shifted.

Enlil fumbled at the medallion, a blank space on his chest allowed dread entry. "Where is it?"

On hands and knees he searched the floor and came up empty.

Another shove and the cupboard toppled over.

Enlil wriggled into the hole and replaced stone behind him. "The joy from ascension will be even greater after all the trouble I've endured. I've got what's mine coming. The invasion aside, this is the closest I've gotten and a great sign. I'm not giving up."

Light escaped gaps in the bricks and lit the bottom half of the tunnel.

Demons stormed into the room and removed all Enlil's peace of mind.

Malek's voice stomped all over it. "Men, protect that necklace they found in the hall. Ralf may want it and keep looking."

Lucky I made him choose a second in charge though not for reasons of betrayal.

Enlil crawled over bugs, bone remnants, hopelessness and despair. "This is neither right nor fair. Enki's never suffered in his entire existence."

Dirt imbedded in his nails, dust filled his lungs.

More light flooded the tunnel and unnerved Enlil. "Hey, I think he's in here. Someone get around the other side of this. I'm going in after him."

Gas and a nugget exited Enlil's butthole, he quickened towards the exit still metres ahead.

Enlil's blood pumped, his muscles laboured, his breath jagged. "How do humans get around and do anything? It's ridiculous. This body may fail me before I'm captured."

I'm a rat trapped in its own cage by its own spawn. There's poetic justice there I don't want.

The demon behind got jammed in the entry. "Damn it. Pull me out."

Boot steps and noise above propelled Enlil to an unknown fate at the end. "Still under control. Each challenge presents its own solution. I must believe in myself."

Stone ground against stone, the exit's door shifted. Night streamed into the tunnel and two demons poked their heads in.

The biggest smiled and clapped. "Yep, we found him."

Enlil's heart pounded, he vomited in his mouth. "Okay solution, come at me."

Chapter 21: Let's not do the Time Warp again
The Gamede Psychiatric Hospital, Ardrossan, Adelaide

I wonder if there's like a social media for hell. Actually, that's all social media. I'm not friending anyone nor inviting them to the wedding.

Shayne's slap to Pig-Beast's chest recoiled up her arm. "Are you fucking serious? How? Take us there right now."

Pig-Beast licked snot from his tusks. "I, ah, yes. Do you realise you're in Gamede? The way out is via the ascension portal but you must hide until then and I know just the place."

Speaking of which if Enlil's my father in law, Enki's what to me? Apart from the creator of me and all of course. Damn now I'm voluntarily using my brain.

Their surroundings and vulnerable position begged several questions.

Shayne stepped back, her attempt at protection failed. "Hang on a minute, why the fuck are you trying to help us? Don't even think about eating me. I might look chunky at the moment but there's not much meat. Just lots of bone and grisly bits."

What would I taste like? Better than Maybe-Marge I'm sure. Gross. What a weirdo.

PB's breath matched his funky body odour. "Please don't insult me. It's complicated. I'm the leader of a rebellion against Enlil, your father-in-law. I've a vested interest in your survival. I won't let him ascend and you're part of that."

Shayne pegged her nose closed, her hunger abated. "Oh really? So, he's not popular here. I don't suppose there's another way out? That will be dangerous as hell. Literally."

Izzy's resemblance to Irica unnerved and comforted Shayne. "Hiding isn't such a terrible idea given our circumstances."

PB-fixed his attention on Izzy. "You're one of the Igigi. He's terrified of you. This is most fortuitous. Come."

I hate needing a dictionary to understand people. What the fuck?

Shayne's brain hurt, fatigue settled in. "I suppose you're right. It'll give us a chance to come up with something. Though, I don't trust you."

TS stirred, half sat up and froze. "Damn. It's still there and so am I."

Unfortunately. You're so flipping needy when you're awake.

PB's sigh raced Shayne's. "You have every reason not to, however I vow once Enlil's time's up I'll release you through the portal."

Thank fuck for that. How will he open it? I should be able to by then anyway. Ryan's on Marduk alone and unprotected, only until the ships arrive. Rosie, Erin and Sam will wonder where I am. How does time work here? Fuck, shit. I hate thinking so much in one day.

A device on PB's collar buzzed. "Ralf, he got away. We've lost several men."

The babies squirmed and stilled, scared barrelled Shayne from each direction. "Oh, fuck me. If he's out here too we're double fucked. Hiding it is."

Hush little ones. I'll protect you. I hope and fucking pray.

PB spoke to his lapel and motioned forwards. "I'm almost finished up. I'll head to the castle once I'm done."

Relief loosened Shayne's tension; she pulled TS onto her feet. "Come on woman. Let's do this."

PB lumbered along a dirt road, dismembered body parts created obstacles.

That's so fucking gross. I'd lose my lunch if I'd had any.

Izzy matched Shayne's pace. "Looks like things are working out anyway. This might not be so bad after all."

"I hope you're right. Though, let's keep on our toes. It's incredibly dangerous for us being here."

TS dragged along and trailed dust. "We're just friending all and sundry now are we?"

They approached rows of warehouses, a sign at the start—Torture Alley chilled, another on the first building—Reality Stars, intrigued.

That makes all kinds of sense. I fucking hate those ridiculous shows. Except Real Housewives of Hell might interest me. As long as I'm not the star of it.

Shayne slipped a freak out into her pocket. "Unless you come up with something better or go alone, shut up and walk."

TS stiffened and clutched her bag tighter. "Fine."

I'll pry that thing out of your cold, dead fingers if I have to. Whatever's so precious in there is bugging the shit out of me. Is there a building for liars?

They passed Politicians, Tax Offices, Parking Inspectors, Social Media trolls, School Bullies, Government Officials and lawyers.

Ha, more than one.

At the end, PB veered left and walked towards a brick wall with many doors.

PB waited in front of the middle one. "Hurry up."

Reluctance slowed Shayne, and dread matched her step for step. "I'm not sure about this."

TS slapped her bag. "Really? This you're worried about? Not being in hell or anything, but this tips your scales."

Shayne channelled wits from anyone greater and smarter. "Shut up or I'll set those hell hounds after you."

Drastic but necessary.

Izzy squeezed Shayne's arm. "Stay calm. Don't let her get to you."

TS pursed her lips and trembled.

The door grew larger the closer Shayne got, her blood pressure elevated. "Lucky for both of us you're here kid."

PB opened it; a plush forest on the other side lowered her fears. "As I said, I'll collect you when it's time."

Norsca deodorant quality, Alpine fresh air filled Shayne's lungs. "Thanks for making this whole adventure not so shitty."

Izzy followed Shayne inside. "It is pretty. I didn't think there'd be a place like this in hell."

TS's bag lowered, her shoulders dropped. "Oh. Well. Perhaps this won't be so terrible."

Shayne slowed her breath and re-grouped. "We'll have a chance to get to know each other while we wait."

Before I know it time will fly and we'll be home again. None the worse for wear save missing a fake friend.

TS's pallor resembled bird shit. "Oh…I….yes. Ah—"

Seems I've really screwed a chance at a relationship with her up.

The door closed behind them and everything went black. The forest, TS, Izzy and the babies disappeared.

I didn't even touch anything.

Despair turned Shayne in circles, her newfound assurance jumped off a building. "Hello? Where'd you go? Did I do something wrong?"

On the next rotation images formed and the scenery changed. No evil father-in-law, ancient god, collector, nor gravity embracing breasts instilled terror like the Adelaide Psychiatric Facility.

Dressed in faded medical scrubs plus a hospital arm band, eroded Shayne's sense of self. "Fuck, fuck, fuck, fuck, fuck, shit. Enki, please tell me this isn't real."

The Universe kicked Shayne in the back of the head and kneed her in the kidneys. An aching body further disrupted the pretend theory.

Panic pooled between Shayne's breasts. "It's not possible. I'm imaging it. No. No. No. It can't be. Please. I'm not really here. It's all in my head."

Patients milled around a dead garden further on and moved as if entranced.

A half smoked joint appeared in one hand, a lighter in the other.

Shayne inhaled sweet, heavy smoke and held it. "Okay. So it's a real nightmare? That's no kind of consolation. Ralf the bastard lied. Actually, he told the truth but I didn't listen. This is really fucked up and creepy. Lucky the weeds good."

Hold on. I've done this before. I made it out. I know I did.

The warm fuzzies trickled down her spine; she inhaled again, the ground thudded.

Shayne's held breath whooshed out. "Gods please no. You keep your joint if that's who I think it is."

A larger, meaner, uglier version of Nurse Rye rounded a corner and came after Shayne. "There you are."

A rotted version of Geoffrey from Ward 3 bounced along beside her. "Hi, Shayne."

Shit, shit, shit, shit, shit.

Pee trickled down Shayne's leg and into her sock. "You're pretend. A figment of my fucked-up imagination. You just don't know it yet."

Geoffrey jabbed, his finger fell onto the ground. "I found you. I told you I would."

Shayne dropped the joint, threw the lighter and backed up. "Fuck, this, shit. No. Just no. Both of you fuck off and leave me alone. I'm not doing this again. You won't beat me."

Demon Rye's grimace injected horror in Shayne's spine. "That's where you're wrong and you're finally getting your dues."

Shayne turned, fell and crawled backwards. *Protect myself. Aura go up.* "Fuck off, you evil bitch. I'm a Demigoddess. I'll freeze you and shatter the pieces."

Where are you powers when I need you? Is this...have I gone back? Did I never leave?

Demon Nurse Rye leaned and lifted Shayne up by the shirt. "Still no magic powers I see and you're smoking drugs again. No wonder you forgot your doctor's appointment. Extra punishment for you."

Fresh terror devoured Shayne like hot cake. "Someone, help me, please."

Demon Rye's claws gouged Shayne's flesh. "We'll help you all right. We'll remove that wickedness once and for all. "

Enki? Dad? Anne? Anyone please get me out of here.

Chapter 22: Derivative DNA
Orion's upper atmosphere in UPA Craft

Exam-like apprehension gripped Zeke; he scraped along the vent and dropped into the transport depot behind space ships. "Yes I am."

This is bat shit crazy, but it's kinda fun. Quality time at last. Albeit screwed up.

Annu's stress licked Zeke's toes; he approached the ship's pilot side door. "For the hundredth time, son, if Shayne, by some miracle, isn't home then I'm going alone. But don't worry, we're coming back sans Enlil. Now isn't the time for a rebellion or sacrifice."

Yells and bangs at the other end of the depot hurried Zeke, he followed Annu inside. "And, for the last time, they're after me too now. Besides, maybe it's best to not bring the Lexicon and hide it somewhere else."

And I need you. Plus If I don't go, you'll definitely screw up and we'll all die.

Alarms rang, stress and tension built.

Annu poised over the controls. "Mmm, which is the first one? Flark. You might be right. Please start reading it between now and then find a way for Shayne and me to get out again without it. I'm out of ideas, and I realise I'm acting on faith and the best case scenario. I have to."

Oh, shit. I didn't expect that. It's a compromise and he's listening.

Tap, tap, poke, poke. Nothing.

The ship beeped, whirred and stopped.

Worry water lapped over Zeke's seat, he lifted his feet. "Before I do, I'm searching for the machine's user manual before we're stuck here."

Ah why didn't I think about that when I flew over? Idiot. Too obsessed with Paige's tits.

Annu's cheeks reddened, he grumbled and groaned. "Damn it. Make it fast."

Smack, smack, bang.

The communication system roared music and dulled outside noise.

Zeke widened the page's view of the flight panel. "Try blue, blue, orange then red."

One hopes that's simple enough for him.

A man boomed from the speakers and instilled fresh urgency: "Attention all personnel, remain where you are and allow the guards access to your pods and stations. We have a highly dangerous escapee somewhere in the ship. If you see him and the boy he's with, do not engage but alert security at once."

Another international or inter-space dilemma. I'm glad I'm not a full God. It's way too hard. I can't think under this much stress. It's not easy stopping your father from making the biggest mistake of all time. He doesn't get it.

A siren blared from the cargo hold, Zeke's nerves twanged. "Flark. Come on, get us out of here or I'll fly."

Annu's slow responses dispelled Zeke's confidence in him. "Last time you crashed. So no and be patient. I'll work this out."

Bang, bang, bang.

The ship swayed and rose; the ceiling opened with freedom only meters away.

Shame burned Zeke's cheeks, embarrassment opened his mouth. "I know I screwed up but you don't have to keep reminding me. You don't like it if anyone does it to you either."

Slap, slap, mush, mush. Annu's hand smushed two at a time. "That's the first time I've mentioned it. Relax."

Zeke erupted in plasma and waited in the doorway. "Aha. It's blue, blue, orange and red."

Annu pursed his lips, flames licked his fingers. "Mmmm. I'm sure I tired that already."

Bang, bang, bang.

UPA guards appeared from nowhere and surrounded the ship's former parking bay.

Oh flarking heck. Stay there will you.

Zeke ran through the cabins and plasma-welded the outer door. "Please hold."

The engine roared, the landing ramp dropped to the ground, and the guards jumped out of the way.

Zeke returned to the flight deck and plonked into the chair. "You know, this is probably the worst birthday I've had overall. Seems like everyone's out to challenge me."

The ship exited the roof and drifted into Orion's upper atmosphere.

Self-satisfaction spread across Annu; he slumped into the seat. "See son. Told you I'd figure it out. Listen, I'm sorry it's like this. We'll make it up to you. I swear."

Zeke climbed a branch above stupid up the family tree. "Yeah, yeah. We'll see."

Annu veered towards Orion, everything on the floor rolled to the other side.

Zeke stopped the book between his feet and banged his shoulder into the window. "Ouch. I see where I get my flying skills from."

A pink glow across Annu's neck travelled down. "And your smart arse nature it seems." Annu released the steering shaft. "Flark. He's draining my powers again."

Clink, clink, clink. Boom.

An explosion from the rear slowed and shuddered the ship.

Zeke's compassion went down with his confidence. "You mean Enlil? Flark, why would you allow that? Why aren't we shooting back?"

First chance, I'll start writing it this stuff down. Not Shayne's version of it but actually doing it.

Annu's hands shook on the steering shaft. "For Shayne of course. I'd do the same for you. These guys are doing the right thing and I don't want to hurt them for it."

The almost silent space provided comfort and greater perspective.

Zeke scratched his chin, concern conflicted with hope. "They're not quitting either and I don't blame them. This is flarked up."

Annu's demeanour hardened, he clenched his jaw. "Yes, I'm aware and wish it happened to someone else. Anyone else will do."

Boom, boom, clang. Smoke and burnt metal streamed through the ship.

Zeke flicked through pages and stopped at protection. 'Please bless, protect and keep the ship from all kinds of harm without harming others."

Blue plasma encapsulated the ship.

Annu pulled the shaft right and smiled. "Well done, son. Good thinking."

Renewed confidence brushed off Zeke's self-doubt. "We all have our gifts. Maybe you'll start paying more attention to mine. Okay, now back to reading the book for you. How'd that happen?"

Lack of attention faltered the ship's protection.

Ping, ping, boom.

The ship tipped sideways and everything with it.

Zeke slipped off the seat and onto his knees, the book's corner jabbed his gut. "Ouch. Crap."

Annu cocked his eyebrow and retracted his chin. "You were saying? This is just ridiculous. How much more can one man take?"

Zeke grasped the book before it slid through the cabin. "Two men and yeah, yeah."

A fleet of larger UPA craft banked either side of them.

Ping, ping, ping.

Annu turned away from Orion, his worry wave crashed upon the shore. "I'm not bringing this shit with us. Flark it."

Boom, boom, boom.

This being a god shit is kind of hard. I might be hasty in my judgments.

The rear of the ship crunched, outer panels hurtled past the windows and fresh smoke filled the cabin.

Zeke bumped his head and read faster. "For flark's sake. Will this day ever end?"

Chapter 23: An eagle with broken wings
Gamede

Shayne regressed eighteen months, vomit filled her mouth, and terror eradicated reason. "Let me go. You can't treat me this way. I'm very powerful and I know the creator on a first name basis. Enki, Ghost Dad, please free me from this torment."

It's real. I'm actually here. I wasn't ever free. I just lost my bundle. Enki where are you? Ghost Dad?

Nurse Rye carried her to the front entrance, enormous breasts swallowed Shayne. "The more you move the more it hurts, your highness."

Blood warmed Shayne's side, worms of faith trickled through her fingers. "Put me down, you fucking bitch. I'm not a piñata. You need scaffolding for those things. I'll choke you with my pee soaked socks."

Nurse Rye thudded into the building, her stride efficient. "Sure you will. Keep going, it makes this all much better."

Shayne hung and bounced into hopelessness. "Fuck, fuck, fuck, fuck, fuck. And repeat. Please, I beg of you let me go."

Patients watched from the common room doorway, antiseptic and death steeped the walls.

Tears burned Shayne's eyes, her chest constricted. "Please one of you. Stop her. Help me."

A grey haired woman in shabby clothes slapped her cheek and scrambled after them. "I know this is just another of your tricks Enlil yet I must check."

Something about her drew Shayne in. "I don't know who you are but I'm fucking real. Please help me."

The woman jogged behind Rye and shook her head. "I've heard that before. What's your name? Where'd you come from?"

Whack.

Nurse-Rye spun and hit the woman with Shayne. "Shut up and get away from her."

Shayne's head swam, the collision rippled down her body. "For….the… stop."

Oh gods. I'm not dying like this. I don't deserve it.

The woman flew a few metres and hit the wall. "I know what you'll do to her. Leave her alone and take me instead."

Nurse-Rye continued onwards with the fly in her ointment removed. "I see stupid runs in the family, Sally."

What? Whose family? I can't keep up. Why does New-Sally care?

Shayne lifted her chin, pain stopped her halfway. "Please don't do this for me. How do you even know me?"

New-Sally looked past Shayne and stammered. "It's… ah, complicated. Where did you come from? Why now?" She kicked the back of Demon-Rye's knees. "I said put her down."

Nurse-Rye lowered Shayne and lunged at the New-Sally. "I said shut up."

Shayne's butt and hip hit the floor, her back spasmed. "Jesus fucking Christ. Like I needed that. Thank fuck I'm not pregnant right now. If I ever was."

Nurse Rye punched New-Sally in the guts and revealed mottled skin. "I'll be back to finish you later."

I'd get a weed whacker onto those babies before rot sets in.

Shayne shivered, her perilous position amplified. "For fuck's sake, you giant gorilla. Stop hurting her."

Nurse-Rye's smile shrank Shayne's un-possessed testicles. "I'll hurt one of you so choose which it is."

The hall lengthened and darkened.

Anguish choked Shayne, she loosened its grip. "Me. Leave her alone."

Brain, think of a way to save my own arse. Again. For like the millionth time in the past year. Real or fake I'm not giving in. I'm not the same person inside anymore.

The torture behind closed doors tightened it.

Medical staff pushed a gurney down the hallway, blood soaked a sheet, and an unattached arm fell at Shayne's feet.

Nurse Rye's breath brushed Shayne's ear. "Your smart arse mouth is about to get what's coming. Just like the rest of you."

Full blown crazy existed a blink away.

Annu, Zeke, Erin, Ryan, the babies. I'm getting married soon. It happened. Hang onto that.

Shayne bolted for the exit doors. "Not today, you fat fucking bitch."

Nurse-Rye appeared a metre in front of them, the door on her left opened. "The doctor will see you now."

Shayne stumbled and crawled away. "Shit. Fuck."

Nurse-Rye's shadow encompassed Shayne, she lifted her. "It's finally time to remove those delusions once and for all. You must accept you're sick and need fixing."

Acrid pee wet Shayne's pants. "No. Not like this."

Nurse-Rye carried Shayne into the room and retrained her on a medical bed. "The doctor will be in shortly."

Enki if you help me I'll devote all my spare time to starving orphans. I'll even travel and read to them or some shit. Enki I beg you. Please help me somehow. I promise and I know I have lots of times before but I'll stop swearing and eat less junk food and argue less with Zeke.

Sobs multiplied Shayne's dehydration. "You mother fucker. Wait until I'm out of here."

Nurse Rye waved a black liquid filled syringe. "Here's something to make you sleep, I mean scream."

A no teeth, sunken chested Doctor Unders, and a long, sharp probe filled the doorway. The woman's hips swayed "I'm sorry to keep you waiting Shayne. I promise you'll get all of my attention."

Saliva gummed in Shayne's mouth. "Fuck no."

Nurse Rye left the bedside and paused at the door. "I'll check on you later.

I'm stuck. There's no way out.

Blood dripped from Doctor Unders probe. "I warn you, this will hurt."

Shayne grabbed her sarcasm before it too escaped in her stead. "Even though you were a bit stuck up on Earth I never imagined you so, ah, fucked up."

Doctor Under's twirled a rusted scalpel. "It's all about fear. I'm merely a representation of your deepest nightmares."

Please, please, please someone help me. Enki? Where are you?

Chunks of breakfast covered Shayne and everything else. "Well I'm going to quit dreaming. I beg you. Stop."

Doctor Unders scratched the blade down Shayne's temple. "That doesn't sound much like begging."

Surprise softened Doctor Unders hatred; she cocked her head and dropped like a bag of shit.

In her place New-Sally held a blood encrusted hammer. "I'm sorry I took so long."

New-Sally dropped it, rushed to Shayne and untied the straps.

Relief ran down Shayne's cheeks, hope restored. "Thank you. Thank you. Thank you."

Thank you Enki you did hear me after all.

Shayne rubbed her wrists and slipped off the bed. "New-Sally, I owe you my life."

Confusion flashed across New-Sally's face. "Ah that's okay. Just Sally's fine though."

Shayne brushed off vomit, the smell roiled her stomach. "Well Just-Sally it is then."

Just-Sally's frown darkened in dim light. "I meant, never mind."

Shayne kicked Doctor Unders twice in the head. "Take that bitch. I better never see you again."

EDU's groan drove Shayne into the hallway.

Patients attacked an unconscious Demon Rye in a corner and blocked the exits.

Shayne's still un-swollen belly added more misery. "This is fucking creepy. I'm done with horror movies and I mean fucking done. And breakfast is off the menu for a while."

I didn't realise how much I miss you until you aren't here. I hope you're safe and you come back when I'm out of here.

Just-Sally crept along the wall to the front. "You're a strange woman, Shayne. Pray no one stops us."

Shayne gripped a hand rail and stuck to Just-Sally's heels. "Why are you in Hell and how do you know me?"

Staff entered the hallway, patients swarmed them.

Shayne shoved Just-Sally. "Screw this shit. Sorry to pry but you know. Might not get another chance."

Yes I did. Why lie about it?

Just-Sally spoke over her shoulder. "This isn't the place or time and it's complicated."

Frustration tickled Shayne's ribs. "I'm sick of hearing that. I want answers."

Just-Sally shoulders rose and fell. "Later."

An invisible wall raised between them, Shayne peered over the top. "Yeah okay. Whatever. What is this place?"

What's with secretive Sally's?

Just-Sally crept with her back to the wall. "This place is designed to break determined souls or hide them."

Patients pushed Shayne sideways and separated her from Just-Sally.

Shayne's heart left her chest and entered her throat. "Shit. Fuck. Hey, Just-Sally."

Distance and people muffled Just-Sally. "Shayne...."

Doctor Unders hollered from the other end. "I'm coming for you."

Shayne crawled amongst legs and stinky feet. "Like fuck."

Focus, focus, focus. I'm close. Don't give up.

Kicks in the arse and ribs slowed her, Shayne smacked into the solid surface and climbed, pain weakened her reserve.

Just-Sally jumped and waved metres from the exit. "Shayne. Here."

Shayne elbowed her way the last part and climbed Just-Sally's pants. "Thank fuck for that. I'm not losing you again."

A surge of patients bombarded the exit, the doors swung open. Fresh air dulled the stench and offered tainted freedom.

Just-Sally stuck close to the wall. "Ditto."

I don't want to know what's next. I want to go home. I may never help anyone again after this.

The rush cleared, Shayne preceded Just-Sally outside. "We made it."

Just-Sally patted Shayne's hand. "This isn't the end. Stay strong."

Bright light burned Shayne's eyes, she covered her eyes. "For fuck's sake."

The scenery altered again, Play School's theme blasted from an adjoining room. Saucepans rested on the bench aside a pile of vegetables, a leg of lamb defrosted in the sink.

Shayne stood in a replica kitchen from over twenty years ago. "You're not fucking kidding me."

Chapter 24: Blackholes and Butt Holes
Orion's upper atmosphere and Orion

Back in Orion's outer atmosphere, Zeke's protection waned as did Annu's adaptability. At some point his wrist comm came off and negated contact home.

Either good things don't happen to good people who do the right thing or good things don't happen to good people at all. There's little flarking reward and point to it.

On an upside, Annu's power and energy returned in slow increments. "Flark, flark, flark, flark. No pressure, son."

Zeke hyperventilated in the co-pilot seat. "I'm trying here. It's hard to concentrate given the circumstances."

The suns rise over one side of Orion prevented travel in their direction and set upon Annu's self-worth. "Start with the biggest problems; we're using our little fuel chasing these guys around with no end in sight."

Bunches of UPA fighters joined the other ships in their pursuit.

These guys are as relentless as bad guys. Which is usually a good thing.

Annu yanked the brake, flipped them ship sideways and reversed. "Hold on."

Guts, objects and the last of his care factor lurched; Pages crunched, tempers flared and shit unravelled.

Zeke hissed and clapped. "This one hides us while we check home and not waste time if she's not there."

Annu mentally hugged Zeke. "This is why you interpreting the book instead of us is a great idea. Not because we don't want to, well me anyway, but because you understand it. You light up when you read and everything becomes clear again."

How did a dumb arse have a smart kid? I should listen to him more.

Zeke's eyes moistened, he lowered the book. "Oh. I thought, shit."

The ship's protection ebbed from the rear into the cabin.

Annu converted annoyance to patience. "I should have told you that before. I'm only learning this father stuff and I'm sorry I screw it up sometimes."

Boom, boom, another panel flew past.

Zeke closed his eyes and sighed, the blue film returned. "For flark's sake. Thank you."

I should help him work on his focus.

'This is the hard part of all this. It's not all glory and controllable."

Zeke slapped the book. "Yeah, that's abundantly clear. Hey, repeat this after me and Enlil can't take any more of your powers and we're hidden."

The fleet of ships returned behind and beside them.

Wasted time frayed Annu's edges. "Flark yes. All right. Enlil can't take any more of your powers and we're hidden."

Zeke echoed through the flight deck, the words danced along Zeke's tongue. "Okay. Repeat after me Elohim, Yahweah and The

Source," the pages light up, a pink haze shrouded Zeke, "Cool. Physically, spiritually and mentally, bless, protect and keep me from all kinds of harm. Go Annu."

Oh my flarking Gods. Ala Kazzam would be simpler.

"Elohim, Yahweah and The Source, physically, spiritually and mentally, bless, protect and keep me from all kinds of harm."

Zeke's voice smoothed and deepened. "In all your glory, I ask you restore my power and eradicate the transfer between myself and Enlil. Blessed be all."

"In all your glory, I ask you restore my power and eradicate the transfer between myself and Enlil. Blessed be all."

Pink haze headed for Annu, entered via his feet and consumed.

Annu welcomed his former glory. "Thank flark for that. When I find out who wrote this they'll get a damned good talking to and a thank you."

Zing, zing, zing.

A parade of UPA ships popped up ahead, weapons armed and ready.

Annu clenched the steering shaft and his butt hole. "Oh flark."

The pink glow returned to the book. "It's just luck okay. They don't see us."

The fleet dispersed in different directions around them.

Annu's mind cleared, dread left the building. "Great. Two down and more dangling."

Zeke gripped the book to his chest. "Flarking heck. All right. There's a way to project yourself home. It might pay to get Erin too. I'll concentrate on this thing."

The half-baked plan sunk in the middle, the outside crumbled.

Annu selected auto and leaned back. "Involving Erin means she becomes another casualty. I'll visit Ang and find out both at once. How does it work?"

Zeke flipped pages and tutted. "You really need to read this yourself sometime anyway. Simple version, recite the same beginning as before, picture where you're going and say I project myself to Ang's office on Enki."

That's next on the list if we survive this.

Annu shallow breathed and drew his power inward. "Elohim, Yahweah and The Source, physically, spiritually and mentally, bless, protect and keep me from all kinds of harm; I project myself to Ang's office on Enki."

"You got it."

The air crackled, his hands tingled.

Annu's ethereal self drifted above his physical one, a silver cord connected them. "Flark, I should lose a few pounds and cut back on drinking."

Zeke crossed his arms and cocked his head. "Really, Da? Keep going."

Ang, Ang, Ang, Protectors Compound.

An unseen force tugged ethereal Annu, bright lights flashed; Ang's desk replaced the controls.

Ang stared at a communicator, his worry palpable. "Where the flark are they? Are they even together? I don't know how to hold everyone off any longer."

Guilt opened Annu's mouth without thought. "Sorry, guy. I'll make it up to you but you've answered one of my questions. Damnit."

Ang fell off the chair and slapped the desk. "For flark's sake. Will you two stop doing that to me? I want danger pay. Who does that?"

Annu silenced a chuckle and floated closer. "I'll get onto it. Sorry again."

Zeke's voice tickled his ear. "Ah da, hurry up. I've got an idea but we don't have long."

Shit. Always time demands. I never try this out for fun before I have to use it.

Annu clung to a finger of hope. "Listen, I'm okay, but I'm pretty sure Shayne's not. Have you heard from her or the ships?"

Ang's apprehension removed any mirth. "Ah no and no. Though I hadn't heard of any major catastrophes on Orion I thought you may be together by now. You owe me for putting up with that friend of Shayne's, twenty million calls from the GC, those UPA lot. They're camped up at your house and have the grounds under surveillance. We can't send any ships out without their say so. If they know we talked, I'm toast."

PFD engines roared from the transport bay and time as a construct sucked.

Annu's long for inebriation increased. "Funny ha ha flarker. You wish. Damn, I'd hoped and prayed. Anyway, I'll check in when I can. Stay there in case anything happens in our absence. Oh, and Zeke's with me."

The responsibility we have over everyone is crushing sometimes. Anything we do effects creation. I must think before I act more.

Ang hung his head and nodded. "All right. Same goes."

Zeke's tickle intensified, his irritation invaded Annu. "For flark's sake, man."

Annu tipped a finger. "Later. I'll have all this sorted out soon enough."

I flarking hope. Shit. Crap. It's a start.

Annu followed the silver cord to his physical self and laid back, the two halves reconnected. "You're worse than your step mother. What'd you find?"

"Get stuffed. There's a space wormhole four clicks to our right which leads to Marduk. Where exactly I do not know. What's your plan for when she's not there?"

Go to hell and ruin or give up everything to get her back.

Annu's neck tensed, his shoulders bit. "Let's do it."

"Only one problem."

"Of course there flarking is. What?"

Zeke sucked his bottom lip. "I can't keep us hidden and open the wormhole. I need more practice at that. You'll have to open it and fly."

I swear I will never let you down again.

Chapter 25: If I'm dying, I'm trying
Gamede

Six dings of the clock dissolved the present, past and future. A constant state of walking on egg shells and covered bruises wore Shayne down.

The bitter taste of acceptance and reluctance stained her tongue. "He'll walk in any minute expecting dinner on the table and I've barely started it. What have I been doing? I'm a stupid idiot and deserve whatever he dishes out."

Why didn't I set a reminder much earlier? I shouldn't have hung out with the kids so long. This is gonna hurt unless I make it quick smart.

Seven-year-old Ryan burst into the kitchen and encircled Shayne's legs. "Thank you for helping me with my homework, Mummy. Are you sure Daddy won't be mad?"

Last night's beating reminded Shayne of her stupidity each movement, breath and word. "You don't have to worry about that, my boy."

I hope that didn't damage my kidneys. Let alone my ovaries. Bastard. Thank God I'm not having more kids. How and when do I leave again? He always finds me.

The front door rattled open and slammed shut.

Shayne nudged Ryan towards the lounge room, the hair on her arms raised. "Off you go. Turn the TV up, sweet, until dinner's ready okay?"

Ryan's blonde head bobbed, innocence steeped each bounce. "You're the best."

Please don't let them hear. Please, please, please keep him away from them. How'd I get myself into this so deep?

Rod's snarled and chilled Shayne's core. "Why the fuck's my dinner still on the bench uncooked?"

I've done this to myself.

Rod's back hand rattled Shayne's teeth; his front hand wiped a year's memories.

Shayne's jaw clicked and her eyes watered. "I'm sorry. I'm so sorry. It's all my fault."

Old Spice, alcohol, and arrogance pulled Shayne by the ear to the bench. "You're not yet but you're gonna be, woman."

Shayne wiped blood from her mouth and scraped carrots into a pile. "I know, I know. I'm sorry but it's coming. You'll see. It won't take long. I swear."

Ryan ran into the kitchen, his concern almost undid Shayne. "Mummy are you okay? Oh hello, Daddy." He hugged Rod's middle. "I missed you today."

Rod's skill of being two separate people often stunned Shayne. "Did ya, buddy?" He scruffed Ryan's hair and scooped him up. "Let's go and play while your mother fixes dinner. She needs all the help she can get."

Shayne turned and tossed vegetables in a pot. "I'm fine, love. Off you go."

Ryan giggled his exit from the kitchen. "Bye, Mummy."

Erin's squeal of delight drove the knife deeper.

I can't, I won't keep doing this. Surely there's more out there? I don't deserve this. Do I?

Shayne slid meat from a bowl into a fry pan. "Don't forget to season it. Not just salt and pepper, garlic too. Two shakes of salt, one of pepper and a teaspoon of garlic."

A news report blasted from the lounge room, the kids quieted.

How many times do I have to be told? He's right. I'm an idiot. God I'm lucky the kids still love me.

Tears wiped, seasoning added, oil in the fry pan and vegetables simmered.

Order equalled no pain or suffering. Most of the time.

Rod lead Erin into the kitchen, his words clipped. "Mum, Daddy want's to know how long until dinner? He's asking once. What does that mean?"

Shayne jaw clicked back into place, the sink captivated her. "About ten minutes. Not long. I promise."

One day I'll get something right. Today's already not that day.

Rod's undertone promised two broken ribs and a possible nose. "Yeah, sure."

Movement between bushes paused self-deprecation.

Shayne stirred the pot and squinted. "What's out there?"

A person peeked around a bush and back again.

Something about them niggled rather than scared Shayne; the hot pan seared her forearm. "Oh hell. Probably one of his girlfriends. Great."

Gross that BBQ flesh smell. Just like when Annu burned me on the bum while fooling around. Huh? Who? Geez he hit me hard. I've lost my mind.

One handed Shayne turned on the cold tap and stuck the burn under. "Pay attention, idiot."

A brunette flashed between bushes and triggered a partial memory.

Shayne leaned closer and tapped the window. "I do know you. Fuck. Oh I swore. I never do that. He hates it. It's not worth the pain."

Bang.

Rod punched the kitchen door. "You said ten minutes fifteen minutes ago. What the hell are you doing? Sometimes I swear you like being beaten."

Shayne swallowed bile and gripped the bench. "I, I, I saw someone outside. I think we know them."

Please, please, please don't let the kids come in here and if you'd be so kind as to stop Rod hurting me I promise I'll be nicer to the Salvation Army Collectors.

Rod flipped between furious to curious. "Way to be vague woman. Friend of yours or not they shouldn't be in my yard without my permission." He grabbed a baseball bat by the fridge, disgust written across his forehead. "If it's a man you're fucking while I'm at work I'll kill both of you."

Shayne raised her hands and held onto hope for a better life. "No. It's a woman. I'd never do that to you. You know I wouldn't."

Rod hit the bat onto his palm. "We'll see. When I come back in here my dinner better be on the table. You hear me?"

I want to smash your fucking head in with that thing and watch you bleed out on the floor. "Yes. Yes I hear you."

Shit. Where did that come from? And I swore again. He's hit me in the head too many times.

Bat raised, Rod stormed into the back yard. "Whoever you are, you're gonna be sorry. Show yourself."

Preservation abdicated to fear, hopelessness raised walls around Shayne's heart. "I'm sorry whoever you are out there but it's me or you, and I'm sick of it being me."

A long lawn obscured the person and encumbered Rod's search.

Ryan scampered into the kitchen holding Erin's hand. "Mummy, where's Daddy?"

Shayne plastered a smile on her face. "He's outside, love."

Ryan glanced in the yard's direction. "Are you really okay? Daddy sounded mad."

The part of Shayne's heart reserved for her kids melted, the horror of her life lessened.

Shayne hugged them and sticky taped the pieces of her soul together. "I will be, baby. We're all going to be okay."

I have to stop this here and now. No more.

At arm's length, Shayne kissed their foreheads. "Ryan, do me a favour and take Erin next door to Sue's house for a while? Daddy and I need to talk. Nothing bad, just usual stuff."

Ryan's nod and stiff shoulders filled Shayne with pride. "Of course I will. Come on, sis."

Erin's curls glowed like her smile. "See you soon, Mum."

Those two are going to do okay despite me and jack arse out there.

"I love you guys."

Innocence exited the kitchen and out the front door.

Rod trekked through the yard and checked every bush, tree or container. The mysterious person either left or hid better than Houdini.

He swung the bat over his head. "I'm going to fucking kill you when I find you for making me do so much exercise."

Shayne clutched the hot fry pan and tipped the steak onto a plate. "I'm so fucking done."

The phone next to the cupboard startled her.

Shayne balanced the fry pan and answered. "Hello?"

"That you, Shayne? Is Rod free? It's Geoff from work."

Not for me to interrupt him without a whack in there ear he's not. I'm not sure I care anymore. If it weren't for the kids I'm not sure what I'd do to myself or him.

"Sure is. Hi Geoff. He's busy at the moment. Can I leave a message?"

Swing, swing, rant, rant.

"No worries mate. Tell him to go straight down Rendleshem instead of work, a shitter truck's jack knifed. He'll need twice as many tow ropes; it's stuck bad and be careful. After the rain we've had, the road's slippery and sometimes they'll end up tipping over on you instead of the tow truck."

That place is such pile of crap. I'm never living there.

Shayne scribbled on a nearby the notepad. "Aha. What time?"

Geoff droned and crackled. "About eight.

Thank God. I'll pack our stuff up and leave while he's gone.

Shayne drew big swirly tornado things on the paper. *Weird.* "Got it. I'll pass it on."

Phone replaced, Rod entered the back porch without the mysterious interloper.

The stranger, a dark hair middle aged woman waved behind the shed.

Oh my fucking God. I remember now. Dumb arse.

Shayne's mind woke, fear and terror waned. "That's Just-Sally. Oh thank fuck for that. I'm still in hell. Moron."

Rod's presence interfered with moving on. "Are you fucking demented? You will not speak like a sailor. You're showing the filthy tip rat you are."

Courage embraced Shayne, she twirled the pan. "Now listen here, fucker, things are changing. I'm not the crazy one here. I should have done this a long, long time ago."

Rod eyes widened, his face reddened. "What the fuck are you doing? Put that down."

Thunk, thunk, whack. Thunk.

Rod dropped onto the kitchen floor, groaned and passed out. Large, egg shaped lump formed on his forehead.

Whack. Whack. Lump, lump.

Shayne stomped a foot on his chest and twirled the fry pan. "Surprise, fucker. A new day has dawned. I'm leaving you and if you ever come after us, I'll kill you."

Just-Sally entered from the back porch. "I worried about you. He's a scary man."

Shayne kicked him five times in the nuts. "Thanks for reminding me this was all bull shit."

I better not forget the phone message. No need to be totally cruel.

She collected the note, a nearby stapler and attached it to a lump. "Good riddance, arsehole."

Just-Sally pushed up her sleeves and prodded him. "Fair enough. I don't blame you. He'll be out for a while."

Shayne stepped on and over him. "Believe me this arsehole was my biggest obstacle."

"Don't jinx yourself. Do you have a plan of any kind?"

One more kick and Shayne left the house. "It's more a collection of vague ideas, desperate measures and pathetic pleas than a plan."

Just-Sally sucked in air. "Oh God help us."

Seems both Sally's are prone to drama. Another similarity.

"Don't stress yet, it's two more options than I usually have."

Just-Sally slouched at Shayne's side. "Oh yippee. Thank God."

Sarcasm too. Nice.

The yard turned into an open field, the scroll mound a few meters away.

Shayne's first and greatest foe stood akimbo beside his cohorts. "This place is a fucked up version of this is your life."

Chapter 26: Another day, another planet, another problem
Enki Island, Enki, Orion & Marduk

The craft travelled down the starry tunnel, unlike Shayne created ones, everything stayed whole.

Annu gripped the steering column despite no control; he tucked his legs for extra support. "Well, before you came along I hated flying one of these things. Kind of ironic one of my powers is flying and I spend so much time in these. Then again irony can be a real bitch."

It's very pretty and puts things into perspective. I'm not sure if Enlil's recent silence is a blessing or a curse.

Planets whooshed by and the wormhole veered left. Like a canoe at a waterfall, the ship rocked on a tip and dove over.

Zeke dug his fingers into the arm rest. "I didn't know that yet I'm not surprised. It shows."

Right, left, up, down, down and up.

The wormhole spat them out in a planet's upper atmosphere, outside panels glowed red, the engine spluttered and died with chances at happiness.

The steering shaft shuddered, Annu lost grip. "This isn't good. Flark. Prepare for a really, really, really harsh landing."

Green tinged Zeke; he shallow breathed and curled up under the console. "Screw this."

The ship creaked, groaned and crunched.

My lord in heaven and all that shit, Ann, Irica, anyone else that might want to save my arse please do. I'll owe you one. Yeah right. As if.

Annu's teeth and mind vibrated. "We only have to make it through this part. Once we're close enough I'll fly us from there, as much as you hate that too. Consider this at least five flying lessons in one. A whole bunch of what not to do's."

The craft snapped, crackled and popped. Its rear tore and hurtled away, exposing them to the elements.

Oxygen diminished, Annu's lungs burned, the ship folded at the middle. "Flarking hell."

Zeke hunched and clutched the book. "It's hard to breath. Da, help me."

Screw this. I've got you kid. I note it takes a catastrophe before you ask.

Annu scooped up Zeke, hovered and protected them. "Hold on tight."

The craft's tip disintegrated in seconds, the remaining engine bay exploded.

Zeke squeezed Annu's middle and swallowed. "I'm scared. I don't want to die yet."

The book dug into Annu's gut, warm mushy feelings disrupted his masculinity. "Ah you'll be right. I've got you. The next's bits gonna hurt. No matter what don't let go."

Re-entering a planet via me is a new one on my list of things I never wanted to do. It's going back on there right after this.

Zeke echoed in the bubble. "This is flarked up. There's no way it'll suck more than—"

Just do it.

Annu flipped and bulleted through the atmosphere. "Flark......"

Zeke plasma field cooled the aura's air. "I stand corrected."

They broke out the other side into a clear, violet sky.

Annu paused above an equal coloured ocean. "Yeah, right then. Flark."

Zeke pushed off Annu, the teenager returned. "There wasn't any need to hold me so close you know."

Yeah, yeah, sure thing.

In the distance, laser fire above a forest and a case of the 'can't be flarked's' waltzed past.

I pray there's a time no one will want to kidnap, kill or maim my wife other than me. This is not what I envisaged when I planned to have a family. The first and this one. Oh and let's not forget things being easy. Not so flarking life or death every damned time.

Zeke's tap on the shoulder broke Annu's daze. "Hey. You okay?"

Annu rolled his neck and prepared. "Ready. May as well dive right in. My main objective if Shayne's not there fighting is the portal. Yours is finding somewhere safe near the protectors."

Zeke's neck and chest reddened, he turned away. "Oh right. So after all that I get shoved off with baby sitters while you take the book and risk everything. What do I have to do to prove myself? You know what? I'm not allowing the book out of my sight and definitely nowhere near Enlil. None of that has changed because I got you out."

I don't have enough time to memorise the incarnation for our use. Is he right? Can I fake it? Will he sense I'm lying and kill her? Flark.

Annu held Zeke and drifted towards the smoke. "You don't need to prove anything and have regardless several times over. I know you're right, but I'm not letting us get stuck in there and leaving you alone."

Zeke stiffened, his fight deflated. "Right. Of course. Me either but I just don't know what else to do."

The self-importance is strong in our genes. Used for either good or bad. I better work on that too.

They approached the shore, battle sounds grew closer.

Still no word from he who shall not be named. I best make up my mind fast. I'd kill for an alcohol induced coma.

Annu's pulse matched his speed. "Let's see what shit fest we're about to next encounter. Don't suppose you've got any rum stashed in your jacket?"

Zeke gave the short straw to Annu. "Ah no."

Worms crawled under his skin and burrowed in his joints. "Looks like we're both doing this sober then."

Chapter 27: A Fettered Mess
Gamede

One armed Sham-man, No-face-Banna, Iggy, Syrl and Hyl full of laser holes lined across the road. Mistakes of the pasts habit of reappearance tortured Shayne more than anything or one else.

Guess Iggy never made it. I can't say I'd blame them. I'd be pissed at me too. Who wants to go around looking like that and being big, fat losers? Screw scared. I'm tired and hungry. Probably a little gassy too. I've crossed the line from batshit to Godzillacrazy.

Sham-man's scars added to his charm. "I've waited for this moment. I knew you'd end up here. This is will be nice, slow and painful. You'll feel each cut until you die. I'll do it for eternity."

Shayne's flat belly disconcerted her, she balanced grief and despair. "Fuck."

Babies. I'm still not pregnant. I'd swap everything to have the babies back again. A respite's been nice and all but I'm never complaining about being pregnant again. But I have to make it through this before they can. Keep it together a bit longer.

Split-face-Banna slurped her words through half a tongue and little teeth. "Fuck indeed."

Brown blotches appeared on Shayne arms. "Gross. This is ridiculous and I'm hangry. Go fuck yourselves or each other. I don't care which."

What are they age spots? Nah I'm too young and vital. Not. Sometimes.

Goop dripped from Sham-man's lips, horns protruded from his skull. "I'd forgotten that smart arse mouth of yours. I'll take extra delight ripping out your tongue."

Shayne's first, middle and last line of defence jumped into action. "Jesus fucking Christ. You'd think being dead softens one up, but no. Show no fear. I'm nearly there. You guys should consider anger management therapy. Or any sort of therapy at all will help."

Iggy spun a spike lined axe; frozen chunks fell from his arms. "What's hangry?"

Shayne drew circles in the dirt and scrambled for ideas. "Angry and hungry. A bad combination. Worse because of this place. Kind of like funny pissy. That's when you can't take it out on the person you'd like to so you make funny but cranky jabs at your loved ones instead."

Sham-man stomped and motioned at Shayne. "I'd suppressed how irritating you were. Go get her. Move."

Shayne walked backwards. "Fuck, fuck, fuck."

Hyl lifted Shayne by the collar like he held shit. "Excellent."

Shayne erupted her upper half and froze Hyl's arm. "I need powers to stretch me a few inches so this stops happening. It's downright humiliating."

Hyl's fingers beat Shayne to the ground, he probed his part hand. "I can't believe you did that. You stupid twat."

Shayne crawled backwards and hit something solid; her gusto waned. "Shitty, shitty, fuck, fuck."

Split face-Banna knocked on Shayne's skull. "Even the dumb get lucky sometimes."

Defeat clung, seeped and wallowed. "Don't I know it."

I hate this fucking place. It sucks. It's a terrible idea.

Sham-man clasped his hands. "For someone who'd have to study to be considered stupid, you're gifted at getting yourself out of trouble. Too bad all your luck's gone now. No one saves you in here."

Maybe I'm looking at all this the wrong way. Instead of being negative its nice people care so much about me. I've clearly made an impact on them. They just have trouble showing their love.

Shayne's throat constricted, her heart skipped. "So you did miss me? I'm touched though I didn't get a birthday card from you. What's with that?"

Banna sniffed Shayne's hair and touched the spots on Shayne's arms. "Shut up. You're smelling dead. We don't have much time. Hours at most."

Huh? That's just fucking mean.

Concern maligned Shayne, the spots grew. "Ah, what do you mean?"

Sham-man slapped Shayne upside the head. "Silence. You're the most irritating, absurd creature I've encountered."

Shayne's ears rang, teeth rattled and brain swam. "I'm really getting sick of being told that too. You arseholes need a new routine. This one's getting old. I should be so yucky, yucky, yucky, yucky. I should be so yucky in looove."

Banna yanked a chunk of Shayne's hair. "Flark no. Give me a knife."

Shayne's hormones and patience passed their limits. "Fucking let me go, you deaf tone bitch. Insult me again and I'll fucking kill you myself this time."

Hyl heaved, he grabbed Shayne's forearm and twisted it. "I'll tear it out using my teeth."

This escalated quickly. They've really worked on their team buildings skills since the last time we met.

Sham-man pulled Hyl back. "Not so fast. We'll take her away from here before anyone else sees and we get pulled into that stupid war."

Aw. At least that's something nice. I'm kinda special.

Banna released Shayne's hair and kicked her in the hip. "All right. For the time being."

Shayne internalised agony, the skin on her hands sagged. "If you're going to torture me and shit, you can at least answer a few questions. I don't know how many times you've been in this position but it's damned helpful to know why you're going to die."

I've hurt worse than this when my autoimmune decides it wants to kill me. I'll save suffering for late night musings.

Iggy's half nose and frost bitten ears delivered no regret. "Live people cannot stay in hell for longer than twenty-four hours before they deteriorate and die. It's not a place for the living. If you die down here your soul's trapped."

Oh shit fuck. Man when shit happens to me it's not little, it's monumental. How do I get away from them and to the portal?

Shayne raised her smart arse shield. "Thanks for the heads up, Iggy baby. That's me fucked then. I've been here awhile and dead really doesn't work for me. I'm too busy for the rest of the week, month, and year in fact. By the way, I see the deep freeze did wonders for your complexion. Looks like you lost a few pounds too."

Ah, dick head. There's an important point in there.

Sham-man licked murky lips with a split tongue. "Bring her into the temple."

Not that fucking place. This shit's so last year.

Iggy entered the dank, dark temple mound in a trail of his flesh cubes.

Shayne's will to live attempted a last ditch approach. "We all know how this is will end. We'll fight; I'll kick your arse and kill you. So, you may as well let me go now." Inside, memories of their battle barrelled Shayne, her chest compressed. "How about now?"

So much pain and death. Most of it inflicted upon me.

Iggy and Sham-man walked past a crumpled body in the corner, Shayne's heart tore.

It's not her. Don't even try looking.

Split-Face-Banna's scoff enticed retaliation. "Stupid bitch."

Shayne twisted her lower half and kneed Banna in the hip. "Say that again you fucker. Definitely now."

They left the outer rooms and into the tunnel system.

Oh Gods. Which includes me in part and is no help at all. Or hey Jesus. I haven't tried him yet. 'Ah Jesus, I know I say your name in vane a lot but if you help I swear never do that again. I'll choose someone else to violate.'

Hyl dug his elbow into her back and ribs. "You're making it harder on yourself. Which is fine by us."

Shayne's fight and flight battled to the death. "You'll pay for this."

Sham-man veered left, Iggy went right. Each turn, doom thudded louder.

The pit-room ahead emaciated Shayne's good fortune. "Or now? Definitely, extremely, very much now."

A red glow—screeches and probable death excreted from the hole.

Now, now, now, now, now, now.

Sham-man stopped at the edge. "You'll experience what I did when you shoved me in. I hope you enjoy it just as much."

Banna and Hyl carried her to him and lowered.

Shayne shrugged and mustered salvation. "All right fuck arse. Have at it."

Sham-man's cackle sent it back again. "After a little pre death entertainment."

Oh God in heaven. I truly am Godzilla screwed and not in a good way.

****

The writing on Shayne's wall read 'you're fucked', her courage committed suicide. "Our time apart has changed us all. Some better than others but let's not continue old habits."

What the fuck am I saying? Who knows but what else is there?

Sham-man transformed into a tall, scaled beast. "I disagree."

Gulp. 'Enki? Jesus? Ghost dad? You there? No one's ever there when I need them.'

Shayne pulse raced, she scooted sideways. "Oh fuck."

Sham-man grabbed Banna, tore her in half and tossed the pieces. "Now you're scared."

"Sucked in again, bitch." Shayne brushed off goop and vomit-burped. "That smells and feels pretty real. Crap. Crap."

If I die here where will my babies go? Where are they now? I've regrets, many, many, regrets.

Iggy squealed from the door way and took off.

Hyl raised his hands and backed away. "I'm out. This is too much."

Sham-man squished him and scraped the bottom of his foot on the pit. "Weaklings."

Oh fuck.

Hyl juice sprinkled Shayne; the pit provided the nicest option.

Shayne delved deep and flung little ice balls. "Fuck you and the horse you fucked in on."

A giant tongue flicked, drool slopped. "Stupid woman."

I may as well be throwing Maybe-Marge toothpicks.

Shayne clung tighter to vitality than her last twenty bucks. "I'm starting to agree with you."

Fetid breath and rancid body odour churned Shayne's gut. "I'll eat and regurgitate you to make this meal last."

Throwing rocks is just plain idiotic. Next bright idea?

A talon scored Shayne's cheek, blood trickled, her breath shortened. "Trust me there's not enough of me to make anything decent. I'm like a Tic-tac or something."

Sham-man snapped Shayne's left arm. "Do shut up."

Pain eradicated Shayne, the limb dangled and the bone protruded. "You mother fucker."

Don't cry. Don't let him see me scared or hurt. Yeah fucking right. I don't care if he knows. I am scared. No actually terrified and badly hurt. Please someone tell Annu I love him and I fought to the end.

SM picked her up in two fingers and held her above the pit. "I'm glad you aren't giving up yet."

Do something, anything.

The world spun, stars flashed, a headache stabbed Shayne's temples. "I see you driving round town with the pearl I love and I'm like fuck youooo. I guess the change in my rocket wasn't enough, I'm like fuck youuuu. And fuck her tooooo."

Okay not that. Thank God no one else is here to complain.

Sham-man screeched, squealed and snapped his teeth. "Enough. Stop."

If I die I'm going on my terms and they're all coming with me.

"Fuck. Tough audience. I'll try another. At first when I see you cryiiii, it makes me smile…At first I felt Tad for a while…..but then I just smile, and it was fun for a whileeee."

Sham-man's intensity drooped, he slurped saliva. "I still cannot fathom how you, of all beings, killed me. And your determination is infuriating."

Another happy customer. He better leave a good review.

Shake, shake, shake.

Shayne's brain wobbled, agony circled the runway and landed. "It's a gift….more lives….than a cat."

Claws slashed her gut; Sham-Man dislocated Shayne's right shoulder. "What God in all hells created such a tortuous creature? When you die, I pray in great pain for you to go to heaven."

Shayne corralled his weakness and reigned it in. "Mother fucker. Neither of us are that lucky. If you threaten to kill someone, do it properly. Oh my God, Sally, look at her butt, it's so big. You like big butts and you cannot lie, your other brothers can't deny. When a girl walks in with bitty, bitty paste, and some icing on your face you get spun."

Sham-man dropped Shayne onto the ground and raised his foot. "What dastardly power is this? Stop it at once."

What once controlled her, now empowered.

Shayne rolled under his legs, movement marked pain's return. "Mine dipshit. I've paid my dues, time after time, I've done my penance and committed many crimes. This is about you by the way. And made mistakes, quite a few, you've had your share of pandas kicked in my face but you've come through."

Sham-man slapped his ears. "No, no, no."

Pain by old friend, he doesn't know how close you and I are.

"'Cause you're not a champion my not friend. But we'll keep fighting to the end." Shayne dragged to the pit's edge and peeked over. "My goodness. I bet you don't see that every day."

Sham-Man lowered his hands and frowned. "It's a trick. Part of your ploy."

Just-Sally held a laser weapon in the doorway and reinforced Shayne's belief in goodness. Pressure eased, confidence grew.

Shayne pointed into the pit. "There you go. So you're smarter than you look. Lucky it's not stupider than you look."

Steam erupted from Sham-Man's ears, he grabbed at her. "No more playing around. Time to die."

Just-Sally shot Sham-Man in the back, the recoil blew her sideways.

It sliced Demon SM across the chest, he stomped after Just-Sally.

Shayne's clutched Sham-Man's leg. "A little bit of Banna over there. A little bit of Hyl in the air, a little bit of sanity coming here, a little bit of fuck this on the stairs."

Sally collected the gun and re-aimed. "Get off her."

I don't care why she cares, just thank you whoever made her that way. Fucking thank you.

Sham-Man tossed Shayne across the room, she hurtled towards a wall.

Shayne flinched and rolled into it. "Oh Gods. Fuck. You arsehole."

Dust invaded Shayne's nose, eyes and mouth. Her vertebrae cracked and crunched.

Just-Sally blasted Sham-man in the knee, hip and shoulder. "Die for God's sake. Shayne are you all right?"

Shayne stumbled forward, her brain swam. "Not at all. Thank you so fucking much for coming again."

Sham-man reached Just-Sally, he whipped his tail. "You're dying first."

Just-Sally struck him in the gut with the gun. "I don't care what you do to me, just leave her alone."

The woman's avid consideration and outright compassion restored Shayne's faith in humanity.

Shayne rubbed it all over and soaked it in. "Listen, look after yourself. Run. Get out of here. I'm not worth dying for."

Just-Sally slipped around Sham-man's side and poked one of his wounds. "Yes you are and I should have realised long ago."

Sham-man's growl rippled, he swiped at her. "This is ridiculous."

Shayne threw chunks of rock, her hip tore, her shoulders tensed. "I said leave her alone arsehole."

Sound distorted, the air cooled, a creepy sensation swept across the room.

Sham-man halted and glanced at the door. "Ah, not now."

What's going on? Did he catch crazy from prolonged exposure to me? It's going around.

Just-Sally rushed to Shayne and checked her over. "Are you all right? I don't like this."

A hooded man with his face covered approached Sham-Man. "Enough. Leave her. She's mine."

Sham-man shrank to his usual size. "My Lord. Please this is my only chance."

The man's intense and precise speech unsettled Shayne. "I appreciate that and I will not repeat myself."

Who the fuck is this guy? He's got some authority. The local librarian? Why the creep factor then? Aside from the obvious. Why does he love me too?

Sham-Man smoothed his robes and nodded. "Understood."

Shayne wrapped the good arm around Just-Sally. "Not that I don't appreciate this undying devotion but why and who are you? If you want to kill me too, get in line."

The hooded man cleared his throat. "Now isn't the time. We must leave."

Shayne raised the broken one. "I'm not getting far until this heals and it's gonna be slow. You've got time."

The man clicked his fingers; they stood in a green field. "If I must."

Another click and Shayne's injuries disappeared. "Oh thank Gods in Heaven."

Still no babies but I think it's a good thing for the moment.

The man flinched and groaned. "Stop that."

Just-Sally got behind Shayne and trembled. "I know who he is and we're fucked as you put it."

This-Sally re-materialised, she swished her arms. "Where did you go?"

The man removed the hood and unhinged Shayne's rickety gate. "It's time we formally met. I'm Enlil."

The resemblance to Shayne's love disconcerted her, she plonked on her arse. "Ah shit. There really is no good here."

Chapter 28: Relative Unease
Marduk, however many hangovers from Orion

Flark, bastard. Please Shay be safe. You don't deserve this because of me and him. Damn him for putting my babies at risk too.

Annu's thrust energy like a sonic boom at the Silver Beings. "I'd rather deal with these dead relatives than the alternative. If I ever make it there."

The power encapsulated, sucked, and imploded them.

Plop, plop, plop, plop.

Arms, legs and torso's rained on Annu's parade. "That's disgusting."

The remnant protectors maintained a perimeter below, their numbers diminished each attack.

Another surge dipped Annu's vigor, he activated the communicator. "Eli, maintain at least 500metres wide area around you. Keep on guard for ground forces I don't see. Roger."

Eli's voice crackled, the wind dulled every second word. "Yes, our grace. A few of the beings left, maybe to grab more weapons, who knows. If so, despite you healing all our injured we're in trouble. There's only so much we can do with the ships weaponry destroyed. Roger."

The story of my long, long, pitiful life.

An unprepared season of regret arrived, unprepared Annu shivered. "I know. We'll get there. Just hang on a bit longer. Roger."

"Ro…ger."

"Who the flark was Roger?"

In a clearing after the forest Zeke stood next to Ryan and a group of orange, short humanoids.

Ah, these little people are the mighty Igigi. I hope they're more powerful than they appear.

Annu landed before them, time's whip scored his back. "Ryan. Nice to see you. Wish it wasn't like this. I'm glad you found those guys." He patted Zeke's back. "Thanks for doing it so fast too."

Zeke buried himself in the Lexicon. "Yeah, no big deal. That's what we came here for."

Feeling the love here, son.

The group gazed at Ryan with hopeful expressions.

Ryan exuded the opposite; he rubbed the back of his neck. "Man, am I glad to see you. By the way, they've mentioned a sword no longer in their possession which can hurt or kill sorry, your father. Is it worth telling the bad guys you're related? They might lay off."

Flarking UPA, not enough time or thought to get that bastard thing.

Annu's emotions numbed, he combed fingers through his hair and got stuck. "Not such a great idea. Could go either way, and my luck dictates I'd choose the wrong one. I'm sorry this shit happened kid. I'll tear Marguerite to pieces when I see her. Is it much further to the caves?"

I'm apologising all over the place lately.

Zeke's finger sped across pages. "Mmm, no. Maybe."

Flip, flip, tap, tap.

He won't let me take the book with or without him and I'm not risking her life further. Some point really soon we're going to clash and it won't end well.

Ryan pointed west and shrugged. "About twenty k's and another group of those guys away. Every time we're close they appear. Try not to worry about mum, you know she'll probably luck out somehow. I gotta tell you though Annu, she's pretty angry at you for finding out about Enlil like she did."

Flark. She knows and in precisely the worst possible way. I'll hear all about it for the next forever. I'm an arsehole.

The semi-bankrupt emotional bank opened its doors to shareholders.

Annu questioned all his motives and dismissed the answers. "Yeah. It wasn't my best move but I'm working on rectifying that. She'll always worry me, Ryan, I love her. She's my everything."

Ryan squished his face and smiled. "Aw. That's so fucking sweet. You deserve each other. You've always had my support."

Zeke's sass made its own comeback. "At worst she'll sing them to death. Thanks for noticing I'm here by the way. There's definitely only two ways out, a portal or a selfless sacrifice by someone. Any way I look at it, it's suicide or genocide."

Flarking hell. They're my options.

Annu stifled insanity with his lost wits. "Boy, how can I not realise you're right there when I came with you. Stop. If I go without the book he'll know and he'll kill her. So that's not happening."

Ryan and the Igigi wandered a few meters away.

Zeke stared at the ground, his Adam's apple jiggled. "I love Shayne and my unborn siblings but so far the book's been right on everything. It's not going with you but if I can hide it safely and I think I know how, I will."

Enki, you better have something up your sleeve. I am not raising my family in hell.

The choice scored across Annu's soul. "As much as I loathe it, you're right and so am I."

Zeke stuffed the book under his jacket and crossed his arms over it. "Mmm. Still doesn't solve the problem though."

"I'll work on that during the next few minutes I have left to think." Annu motioned to Ryan. "Tell your friends to stick close to each other and you. You take care of them even if you can't see me. Once we're there, under no circumstances separate or leave the caves again."

Late afternoon in the forest foreshadowed Annu's fate.

Ryan rejoined Annu and nudged him. "All right. Done. Are you okay?"

Zeke glowered at the rear in blue. "Are we leaving or what?"

To further complicate being there, what about this Sally turning up from out of the blue? Does he know her? Is this another of his game?

Annu wandered on and left the jab behind. "As well as I can be I guess. I wonder why Shay's mother showed up after, what, how long exactly?"

Ryan's clenched teeth and frown reminded Annu of Shayne's. "I don't really know if they've ever met. Apart from the whole giving birth to her part. Mum hates talking about it and I understood why. How does a parent just ignore their own kids and pretend like they don't have any? Mum doesn't know but I found out she has a half sister and brother her mother did raise. That would really hurt her."

Flarking bitch. I lost my first son and she neglects her daughter. Cruel, cruel, woman.

Annu swept aside vines and reserved the anger for later. "Maybe that woman's in the right place then. You're a good son Ryan."

Zeke sprung up at Annu's other side. "Is what you're talking about relevant to me because if it is should I know what's going on?"

Teenagers. Can't live with them, can't kill them. What do I do about the book?

Trees cracked in the distance, a bunch of protectors flew through the air and out of sight.

Annu ignited and faced Zeke. "Stay hidden and moving towards the caves. I'll be back soon."

He burst into the air and landed beside Eli.

A laser wound on Eli's side seeped. "Shit. You shouldn't be here with us."

Crumbled protector's bodies scattered the surroundings.

Two Annunaki stuck a device into the ground and pushed a button.

Crack, crack, boom.

The dirt exploded, concussion thrust Annu and Eli sidewards, distance between the enemies shortened.

More Protectors painted the landscape.

Challenges bitch slapped Annu and kicked him in the nuts. "Bastards are relentless. Shit. Eli?"

A tree trunk compressed Eli, blood trickled from his mouth. Dirt sullied vision and death had eradicated assistance.

Annu's chest compressed his heart. "Me and my shadow."

Crack, crack, boom.

The air rippled and swirled.

Debris bounced off his aura, his power dipped.

Annu ascended metres above the trees, dread circled with him. "Zeke? Ryan? Where the flark are you? If I don't see you soon, I'm going anyway even though I don't want to. Come on."

Enlil's worm invaded Annu's mind, a triumphant beat to his words. *I have your woman beside me. Would you like to say hello?*

Chapter 29: The Fat Lady Sings
Hell, hell, hell

Enlil's attractiveness conflicted with the hammer of doom he wielded. "I'd been under the impression it was difficult to keep you quiet. It appears not."

Come on woman. Snap out of it. Your and the babies lives are at stake.

Shayne's fucked-up life-semi-death nose dived. "Well, it's not every day I meet the devil or whatever in person. I guess it's a little underwhelming. I'm not sure what I expected."

Liar, liar, you're pants will soon be on fire.

Enlil's voice combined warm honey and gravel, he re-classified parents-in-law from hell. "Where's the woman who brought you here?"

Shayne faked bravado and farted denial. "You mean Maybe-Marge? Your dogs ripped that bitch to bits and spat out the bones. I hope something similar happens to you if you don't let me go."

Just-Sally tensed, cold fingers brushed Shayne's skin. "Be very careful. Do not make him angry."

Shit, shit, fuck, shit. Enki come on. Really? I mean really? This is taking the whole testing thing to a stupid level.

Loneliness, hatred, and desperation steeped from Enlil. "Which explains why I didn't receive a wedding invitation." He growled and glared at Just-Sally. "You'll pay for your interference woman."

Blood from a cut on his forehead trickled down his cheek and lessened Shayne's fear.

He's bleeding, he's human. Yeah, scary as fuck and powerful as hell but there are chinks in his armour. Like PigBeast Ralf. The lying mother fucker. All is not lost. Yet.

Just-Sally inhaled, her hands shook. "It was worth it. I'd do it again."

TS woke and touched the ground, her teeth rotted, and her cheeks sunken. "Where am I now? What's am I like this? What did you do to me?" TS looked at Just-Sally. "Oh shit. It's you."

Just-Sally's fear capsized. "Janet? Why are you here with her? What did you do?"

Apparently there already is the Real Housewives from Hell here. In another place and time, I'd laugh.

Shayne welcomed the distraction. "All right. Enough. How do you know each other and me? Something fishy's going on around here."

Enlil's smile belied the hatred in his tone. "If it's the truth you want, you'll choke on it. The woman you call Just Sally is the real, biological mother who abandoned you at birth, one of the biggest sins and I have no fucking idea who that one is. Now move. It's not safe."

Smack, smack, smack.

Shayne drowned not choked on waves of shock and despair. A combination best dealt with chocolate and foot massages, not hell.

"No. No fucking way. You're full of shit. I don't believe you." She cocked her head at the Sally's. "He's lying right?"

It's all been bullshit? Who's my mother? Somebody is full of shit.

Just-Sally swallowed and licked her lips. "He's right, Shayne. I am and I made a horrible mistake I've paid for ever since. Janet is a former prison roommate who I assume is pretending to be me now that you're famous. She'll be after money."

TS backed up and shook her head. "She's the liar. I'm your real mother."

Shayne dry retched air dragged through her lungs. "Oh my Gods and Enki. This is fucked up. You two are fucked in the head. I don't even know what to think right now. Fuck."

No, no, no. This is all too much.

Enlil winced and dragged Shayne by the arm. "Don't say his name again. Move or you'll suffer worse."

Shayne flopped and flapped. "I can't see how that's possible. I'm going to rip your faces off. I tried and cared. What the fuck does this all mean for me now?"

Just-Sally trailed them with her hands clenched. "I'm so very sorry. I'll get you out of this somehow. I'm truly sorry for what I did. I was young and stupid and confused."

The thud of Shayne's heart echoed in her chest. "How? You two deserve to die down here, but I don't."

TS skulked from fear not guilt. "Not for trying to make a better life for myself I don't. You're not leaving me alone."

Tears from Shayne's eyes and heart blurred vision. "How cold hearted are you? Did you know Just-Sally had died?"

This is the worst torture anyone could wield against me. She faked being my mother, the bitch, and the real one is in hell. What the fuck did she do other than give up on me to get in this shit hole? Do I even care?

TS looked everywhere else. "I, I, I thought it wouldn't hurt anyone and I needed money bad but I sure as heck didn't expect to end up here because of it."

Enlil's growl chilled Shayne. He tugged her by the jacket. "Enough of this rubbish."

A bomb exploded close by, annoyance formed a second skin over Shayne.

Close gunfire and the smell of burnt metal paled Enlil, he released her.

Shayne rubbed the burn he left and gave him two fingers. "Ha, ha. They're coming to get you. Sucked in fucker. By the way you're off the Christmas card list too."

Boom, boom, boom.

Fear flashed across Enlil's face. "Damn. Not now. Curse you all."

Dirt, metal and rock rained, Shayne shielded her head. "Shit. Don't get me too."

Piles of debris offered the lone protection and cover, she slipped behind him.

Enlil turned left, right and stopped. "Which way?"

I'm fucking you up before I die. Then your brother and I need a big talk.

Shayne dragged both Sally's behind a rock pile. "This in no way constitutes forgiveness so don't mistake that."

Boom, boom, boom.

Enlil flopped to the ground and crawled towards her. "Help me, if you don't you'll be sorry."

Shayne pulled loose threads from Enlil's sanity. "I see the signs, you're truly fucked. It doesn't feel good does it?"

A group of demons rounded a corner and headed for Enlil.

Shayne shoved both Sally's in the other direction. "Fucking get out of here."

Enlil jogged past and into some building debris.

Someone grabbed Shayne from behind, lifted and slung her over his shoulder.

Shayne beat a goat like demon in the back spikes sliced her hands. "Fuck, really? Put me down, you bastard. You fucking stink."

Two half-headed demons collected a Sally each and went right.

Shayne kneed his chest and struggled. "Put me down. I'm not part of this and let the other two women go."

The demon grunted and vibrated his chest.

Enlil bolted from the direction he'd come from with PigBeastRalf on his heels.

The enemy of my enemy is my enemy and all that shit but it doesn't help me.

Shayne flopped around the corner, her escape options as fucked as her state of mind. "I don't even know what's going on anymore but I'm exhausted."

Past the next building the landscape changed into dirt roads and battle fields.

Amongst throws of hideous creatures and no sense of direction, Shayne released her woes. "Is this the real life, or is this just fantasy? Caught in a landslide, no escape from realty. Open your pies, look up to the supplies and pee."

I'm completely nuts, but I think I like it. Sorry babies. Mum's evicted from sanityville. It was bound to happen soon anyhow.

Prickled hands prodded Shayne, the demon grunted. "Stop making that infernal noise."

Disorientation threatened Shayne's lucidity. "No. I'm just a poor girl, I need shit loads of sympathy. Because I used to be a little high, a big bit low, anyway the farts blow."

Chapter 30: Baptism by Fire
Marduk & Hell

Another missile soared over the tree tops and landed mid forest. Wildlife scattered, trees fell and isolated Zeke.

Zeke's hearing dulled, the book slipped. "For flark's sake. Doing the right thing sucks. I wish I'd stayed home and never gotten powers. I don't want to die and I don't have enough control over my powers to use them properly."

It's not my fault, I only have so much time and it's always occupied by other stuff. Where's Paige now? Has she thought of me? Almost definitely after that display but not positively.

Solitude drew the trees closer, shadows longer and courage shorter. Sound amplified, fear used Zeke as a door mat.

His protection waxed and waned. "Flarking hell. Annu? Ryan? How many hero wannabe's are scared of the dark? Probably one."

The lexicon flapped its cover and hummed.

Zeke smoothed the leather. "You're a pain in my arse and sadly my best friend. I know what he's thinking and I'm torn. Am I'm strong enough to stop him? What if I'm wrong?"

Touch allowed clarity and realisation.

Yes, yes I am. The caves are close. I'm sorry Shayne but if he's not going without it, he's not going.

Most of Zeke ached for an alternative, he rested against a trunk. "Where the flark do I hide you no one, including my father will look?"

The answer neither surprised nor concerned him.

Of course. You nitwit. Should have thought of that before.

Zeke concentrated, a small, personal dimension opened above his open hand.

He placed the Lexicon inside and closed it. "Now there's no chance of him or anyone else getting it."

I'm not looking forward to what he's going to do when he finds that out.

Branches crunched, Zeke un-welcomed the break in solitude.

A deep voice drove him to hide. "They're not too far ahead. Once you've got them sufficiently restrained, get the male human to lead them back to base. We'll need all our resources for after our Lord's release. I'll fetch the boy. Watch out for Annu, lead the fight towards the portal."

All right, Da's not hurt. If I go the other way, I'll bump into the Igigi and Ryan. I must get there before the Annunaki find them and protect them because I can't fight these guys myself.

The magnitude of Zeke's situation floored him, he froze.

Or just stay hidden until all this is over. What am I thinking? I'm still a kid. Not a man.

A woman moved to the trees nearby. "Yes, Gilgamesh. After so long, we're close. Our time's coming. We're free of this place."

Air thickened, sweat soaked his shirt and panic moved closer.

Please, please, please don't see me yet. I'm not ready to deal without help. I totally should have trained physically with Shayne and Annu before demanding I'm part of things.

A pit burned the bottom of Zeke's stomach.

"Don't be complacent or rest your guard until it's over. There'll be plenty of time then."

Shit, flark, fuck.

Zeke splayed onto the ground and whiffed his armpits.

I might start showering more often.

The woman's voice and footsteps drifted away. "Of course."

Sticks broke next to Zeke's hiding space. "I know you're here boy. Don't be scared, I won't hurt you."

Panic ascended Zeke's testicles and shortened his life span. Blue plasma trickled across his hands and left.

Shit. Shit. Shit. Come on powers or a miracle. Protect me, keep me hidden. Please.

Rethinking the whole scenario. I'm important too. This is beyond me.

A male Annunaki peered over the trunk. "There you are. Pleased to meet you, I'm Gilgamesh. I don't want to hurt you."

Zeke's heart skipped, he perched on his haunches. "Why? What do you want?"

Any attempt to grab me and I run. Even though he'll follow me. Stick to the plan except I forget which one I'm working on.

The man sat on the trunk and blocked the light. "Despite what you've been told we're not the bad guys. Enlil, your grandfather deserves freedom. Imagine what it's like being imprisoned by your own brother for unjust reasons and prevented from your true destiny. Families are complicated, yet, you're able to rectify this by ensuring Annu and the Lexicon reach the caves in time. He won't listen to us. When Enlil's free you'll be the powerful and worshipped god you're designed for. Not babysitting lesser beings and being a spectator."

That's not what I expected him to say. I'd be safe but do I want that? I never wanted any of this for that matter. I'm glad I hid the book but I might suffer for it anyway.

Zeke half rose and aimed a blue hand. "I'm not stupid and I've done my own research on all of you. I don't trust you."

Giglamesh's skin shone, a halo encircled his head. "But you trust your father? How many times has he lied to you? Boy, evil is a subjective term, one you've much to learn about along with perspective. You think Enki hasn't killed or taken many more loved ones away from their families? And for no just cause or reason. Followers of Enki have lied to themselves and others. Ask yourself, what will saving the Igigi and stopping Annu do for you grandson of Enlil? They're capable of destroying your entire genetic history. We want your father to go willingly and do what he should, not be distracted. He doesn't understand the truth and freedom to come. Show him. Bring your whole family together as they should be. You're the clear headed one."

He's right on many levels. I don't know what's real or true anymore. I only take Annu's word for things. Enki's taking my mother away. Maybe Enlil can save her. Annu's been wrong before. Big time wrong.

Confusion disrupted Zeke's huff, he crossed his arms. "How do I know you're telling me the truth? You've killed a lot of people since our arrival."

Gilgamesh patted his knee. "We aren't trying to hurt them, we're protecting our future. Son, join us and as an act of good faith, you'll see they're supervised rather than killed until after Enlil's release. You'll also maintain control over the book."

This might work if I don't have to produce it first.

Zeke swallowed bites of betrayal. "What do you want me to do?"

Gilgamesh shifted to the side, light fell on Zeke. "Tell your father you'll protect the Igigi while he's gone so he enters the portal with the book right now."

Ah, *this is the exact opposite of what I had figured out.*

Chapter 31: The Sacrificial Lamb Roast
Hell, hell and more hell

Life and time took meaning with your mortality in question Sane walls crumbled into dust at Enlil's feet. Down the side of a building he wriggled inside a crevice.

Scrapes, cuts, bruises and torn muscles concreted Enlil's hatred of humanity. "I won't stay in this vessel. This treatment is not worthy of a God like me."

The Elders' entered Enlil's mind and slicked down throat. *"It appears you're incapable of completing your end of the deal and your reign, in your self-created hell is over. We're coming for you."*

Vultures of defeat circled Enlil like a vulture and picked his cadaver. "No, no, no, no. Not yet. Not yet. Not yet."

Demons stomped past inches from him.

Enlil's legs weakened, he gasped and slumped. "I can't keep this level of intensity up."

There's not enough left in me to fight them. I need more. Much more.

The other demons continued forward past the building. The last one carried the wretched woman in his arms, her belly flat.

Where the alhalso did they go? They were the main reason not to give up yet. I'll make her get them back. New, innocent, unborn life will get me the rest of the way.

She looked up, squinted and pointed in his direction. "Hey, that looks like fuckface. Hello, fuckface. I see you. Ha. Sucked in again."

The demon looked over his shoulder and turned halfway. "Who are you talking about now?"

Butthole clenched, chest tight, Enlil shrank against cement and drew on reserves. *Invisible, invisible, invisible.*

The woman clawed his chalkboards. "Not you this time, moron. Enlileo. The big bad dude around here you're looking for."

Enlil's verve swerved, he gritted his teeth. "For hate's sake."

Invisible, invisible, invisible. For a little longer.

The demon wandered over and peered at the crevice. His weapon hung from his belt. "Nice try, no-one in there."

Yes. Just a little closer and it's mine.

The demon turned, the woman squeezed the demon's groin and punched him in the chin.

He let her go and doubled over. "Ahhhhhhh."

The woman headed in the same direction as the others. "Screw this and all. I fucking hate this place. How the fuck do I find Just-Sally? I'll die before I leave here at this rate. Stupid, stupid, horrible place. And what the fuck is that smell all the time?"

Enlil lunged, grabbed the weapon, killed the demon and sated his anguish.

She paused at a junction and looked both ways. "Right. And?"

He approached from behind and used a choke hold with the weapon at her temple. "You're right about one thing at least. You'll die here."

The woman clawed, bit and kicked. "Let me go. Help. Someone. Rape, fire. Help."

Enlil's arm muffled her; an iota of peace soothed him. He dragged her into an alley between buildings.

If the payoff wasn't so huge I'd have given in by now. She's quite a weapon in the right hands. Not sure I'd set her upon anyone though. No one deserves that.

At a crossroads, blood trickled from bite marks, dirt gritted Enlil's eyes. "I'm still too far from the castle."

Her slobber dribbled down his arm. "Mfphngodhd."

Enlil tightened his hold, the biting returned. "Women are by far the most idiotic, non sensical, irrational creatures Enki ever created. Capable of great love and great hate. Weapons of mass distraction."

Will she be the death of me? Is she another torment from my brother?

The woman freed her mouth and licked her lips. "Being stalked is a real bitch isn't it? The hot shoes on the other hot foot now. Bad toys, bad toys, what you gonna poo. What you gonna poo when they come for you. Big, chunky ones I bet."

Enlil gathered himself before he drifted, physically removed her mouth and bound her hands. "Oh for the love of...... me."

The act lagged his energy and gumption.

Totally worth it.

She probed skin in its former location, her pupils dilated, her fear shone. "Mmm."

At the next building Enlil entered through a side door and hid behind upturned cupboards.

The woman's stunned expression lifted his spirits. "Mmmmmmdmdmd."

Will anyone care that sacrifice pains me when I'm left with no choice?

The door opened and closed, someone shuffled around.

Enlil's heart thudded, he shoved Shayne down. "One sound and you're literal history."

The person walked towards the cupboards, more dead female hormones tingled his senses.

Anger half rose Enlil and raised his pulse. "Get the fuck away from us."

A roughed up Sally dragged a leg, her stubbornness confounded him. "For the last time. Take me instead."

The woman climbed the cupboard, pointed at her face and swished her arms. "Mmm."

Ire consumed Enlil, he kicked the cupboard aside. "You're worth nothing. I'm done with you."

Sally's resolve strengthened the closer she got. "I don't care anymore. Do what you must."

Desperation forced rationale, Enlil talked himself off the ledge.

Wait, don't use the last of it on her. Calm down or I'll give myself away. I've got to get back to the portal yet. Leave her to the others.

Loud noise outside undid his work, Enlil grasped the woman. "For hate's sake."

She struggled out of his grasp and at Sally. "Mdmdmmdmdmd."

Sally raised her chin and hands in repose. "I'm sorry, Shayne. I should have done this long ago. Dear father who art in heaven, hallowed be thy name."

Agony ripped Enlil's souls, his guts burned, his skin crawled, his ears bled. "No. Stop. Don't do this."

"Art in heaven, hallowed by thy name. They kingdom come, thy will be done, on Earth as it is in Heaven, give us this day our daily bread and forgive us our trespasses and we forgive those."

Enlil's eardrums popped, his head roared, his eyes and palms bled. "No, no, no. Stop. Please. I beg you."

Sally's words dismantled all equilibrium. "Who trespass against us. For thyne is the kingdom forever and ever in all its glory amen. Lord in heaven please hear my prayer. I pray you save my daughter Shayne from this place and I shall remain in her stead. I repent my past mistakes and I'm truly sorry for my actions. I should never have abandoned my daughter with my parents for them to raise her. Nor should I have waited so long to do something about it, but here I am. I beg you, my lord, most humbly. Our father who art in heaven, hallowed me thy name."

Bright light enveloped the woman and raised her off the floor.

Enlil's soul purged his pitiful self. "I beg of thee Brother, please no more. Set me free from this misery."

The woman's mouth returned, her hands freed, she glowed. "Thank you so much but please save yourself and Izzy. Please Enki keep them safe too."

The light enveloped Sally and ruined Enlil, he collapsed onto concrete.

It flashed, blinked, disappeared and took both women.

Enlil shivered, the pain abated in fragments, fresh anger in its place. "You'll pay extra for this brother. Setting me up to fail. You knew all along, planned it that way. No one but me sees your darkness. That's changing."

Arms scooped Enlil up and onto his feet.

No, no, no, no.

Two demons on either side, front and rear, prevented further escape.

Enlil's mind swayed, his knees wobbled. "Let…..me….go."

Ralf patted his belly and crossed his arms over it. "I told you I'd get you but you've always underestimated me. Never mind you've plenty of time to figure it out. I'm so glad I'll watch you suffer for the next few hours while your opportunity comes and goes. You'll love the special friend I found for you too. Then when reality hits, oh the joy we'll have."

The Igigi girl trembled at the arms of a demon.

Enlil's acceptance fought delusion. *I might actually be ruined this time. No greater torture exists than being human.*

Chapter 32: Holy Moly Guacamole
First Level of Heaven

Sally disappeared amongst white clouds. "I love you. I hope I see you again one day."

Soft, warm and fluffy cuddled Shayne, every part of her, hummed and cheered. Happiness reigned first place, peace eased all her woes.

Shayne floated onto a gold path surrounded by lush gardens. Cute animals scurried from shrub to bush, trees laden with fruit invited despite no hunger.

For the first time in ages and I'm no longer tired or sore or angry. Oh shit. Fork. That's right.

Shayne's belly hummed and vibrated. "Fork it. I'm in heaven. No wonder I feel so flicking alive, I'm dead instead of saved. Ship, flick, ship. I had plans for later and I won't flicking get married. Again. But this time for the right kind a wrong reasons."

What the flick? Oh yeah. Duh. Probably can't swear here. But if I was going to get in trouble for it, I'd have by now. Surely.

The path glimmered in either direction and into the distance.

Shayne turned in a circle and flung her arms. "Now what do I do? Where's the eternal supply of chocolate waiting for me? Or foot massages by Idris Elba and Thor?"

Two figures formed down the path and walked Shayne's way.

When closer, their features cleared, Shayne melted into a puddle of joy. "Nan and Pa, I've missed you so much."

Nan hugged Shayne's side. "And we've missed you too, sweetheart. You've overcome a great deal of adversity and pain to be where you are. We're so proud of you."

Thank you, thank you, thank you.

Emotion flooded Shayne, her happiness dyked the deluge. "I'm sorry I've screwed up a lot. I've really tried being a good person like you taught me but people make it hard sometimes. I guess it's too late now. We're together again though."

The kids, the babies, what will happen to them? Annu will be devastated and destroy everything.

Pa wrapped arm around and patted her belly. "Oh kiddo, you're not dead, this is just a quick visit. You're much too hard on yourself. Our lives are for learning, loving and experiencing. Despite a rough start you've kicked in your heels and gave them what for. You're amazing. I'm rooting for you."

Shayne soaked in their grandparental goodliness. "Thank you two so much for giving me the best possible life you could. I want you to know Sally's the reason I'm here and not a total screw up. Please don't leave me yet."

They twinkled and shimmered, Nan squeezed Shayne's side. "We know. There's more important things you must do while here. Remember even when you can't see us, we're around. I love you."

Pa scuffed Shayne's hair and kissed her cheek. "Love you kid."

Shayne stored their collective love for future, dark moments. "Ah, okay. I love you two too.".

Ki linked Irica's arm in the crook of his, plus an older, crisper version of Enlil and Annu walked on Irica's other side.

He carried a perfect red rose and sparkled like diamonds, a golden aura completed the awe.

Butterflies flittered in Shayne's gut; another tsunami of happy swept her shores. "Oh Enki. My flicking Gods literally."

Close, nearly flicked up already.

Enki waved and slowed his pace. "It's nice to see you. We'll speak in a moment after you catch up child."

He reminds me of a nice school principal, if they resembled Santa and created something from nothing. Oh gods. Shut up.

Irica and Ki reached Shayne first.

Irica's embrace warmed Shayne's cockles. She eyed the bump, the babies hiccupped. "Shayne, Ashera, it's good to see you. You look wonderful."

Shayne inhaled lime and oranges. "We've missed you so flicking much. I'm so sorry Sham-man killed you. It's flicking not fair. We didn't even get time to know each other. I'm not a total lick after all. There's a tonne of stuff I'd have driven you crazy since then. Oh and I met your granddaughter. I didn't even flicking know you had children."

And again. My cursing knows no bounds.

Irica's stroke of Shayne's hand removed her fears. "No, no. It all happened for a reason. It's neither of your faults. I always knew my destiny and I'd lived a long, long life beforehand. Fear not dear girl I will return one day and you'll learn all about my past."

Excitement altered Shayne's focus. "Really? When? How? Can you come to the wedding? Annu will flip his ship."

Irica's smile calmed Shayne. "Not exactly. All in good time, my girl. You've lost none of your spark. Make sure you keep Annu on his toes. It's good for him. By the way, Jazekial must yield the sword," she brushed Shayne's cheek, "Never change and never give in," and faded into gold dust.

Shayne grasped at floating specks. "I won't. I wish we had more time."

She may not blame me but I still feel responsible. Who's the Jaz guy again?

Ki clasped his hands, his eyes sparkled. "My dear daughter, I wish it were in better circumstances. However, any is better than none. You look well and you're doing a wonderful job. I'm likewise proud of you and your accomplishments. While you're here, may I request you just call me father or Ki?"

Shucks.

Shayne's cheeks warmed, she scratched her ear. "Aw. Thanks, ghost dad. Maybe. Any chance you'll pop in more often? Like for the wedding? One of you surely? Or answer me from time to time?"

Will we ever get to the hug stage or are we doomed to live awkward city?

Ki's version of affection concluded with a pat on the back. "I do hear you, except it isn't my place to fix things for you. I'll definitely try and pop in. Remember this is your journey and you're more than capable of discovering solutions to big problems. You just need to believe in yourself like we do."

Yeah, I guess I've gotten us this far. Mmmm, maybe. Don't over think it.

Back patted, feathers fluffed and the ver back in her verve, Shayne drowned in goodness. "Ah, ah, okay. Thank you."

Ki raised his hand and lowered it again, he'd reached his affection limit. "There's evil and difficult times ahead Ashera. The darkest ever foretold. Sacrifices must be made. No matter what you think, it's not over yet, it's only beginning. You'll require all the help, faith and courage you muster for the next chapter."

A shadow drifted over the area, the love sucked from the air.

Shayne shivered and rubbed her arms. "Oh goody. Thanks for that. So, the nice stuff you said was softening me up for the blow?"

Confusion clouded Ki's expression. "Why would I do so? I only say what I mean."

Awkward City it is.

Shayne shrugged and fake smiled. "Just kidding. All good ghost... dad, Ki. Any tips?"

Ki opened, closed, open, closed and opened his mouth. "Don't delay. Rely on your faith and inner strength. Take care, my child."

Frustration bypassed past peace and calm.

"Mmm. Aha. Great. All right. Thanks again."

Ki's own fake smile tickled Shayne. "I bid you farewell and leave you in the Creator's arms."

Shayne gave him the thumbs up. "Righto then. See you next time."

Ki walked a few steps and disappeared.

Enki handed the rose to Shayne, he smelt like Christmas, hugs and chocolate. "Ashera, we finally speak in person without being overheard or interrupted."

I'm alone, face to face with God and now I'm not sure what to say. Ship. Think of something.

The gate between Shayne's brain and mouth closed. "Where were the babies while I was in hell? Why do we men have nipples? And what's the go with Platypus's? Did you make a mistake? Why did you give us periods? Did you hate women that day or what? Oh, Elon Musk and Donald Trump. What the flip dude? Why bring me here?"

Enki's chuckle removed cares, concerns, and childhood trauma. "Dear child. Even though I created you, you still surprise me with what comes out of your mouth."

Shayne showered in his mirth and goodness. "Maybe I'm your challenge. I'm certainly everyone elses. Come on big guy, spill."

Enki gestured to a gold park bench behind them. "Firstly the babies opted to return to our nursery. It was their choice. Second, Gamede is out of my sight and domain. Unless a soul is sacrificed or prays directly to me. You're strength and sheer determination compelled me to warn you the situation with Enlil is about to get much worse. Combined with other things going on in the background like free will and a bleak, unknown future awaits.

Everything rests upon choices all parties make. I do want you to know and remember when the time comes to always have faith, even when it seems there's no logical reason to. I love you child and you're protected from the worst kinds of harm. Keep hold of that spark inside you at all times."

Shayne shifted closer and drank in serenity. "If I wasn't here I'd have a migraine after that. I appreciate the heads up. Look, I met him and he's a real pick not to mention intense. Rest assured Annu's not going to help him in anyway. He won't get out so there's no worry there."

Nutmeg and a dash of redemption wafted her way. "My brother's hatred and anger saddens me constantly. I'd give almost anything for him to be the loving God he's capable of."

We all have flicked up family relationships.

Shayne swung pain free legs. "I don't suppose there's a joint around here?"

Enki's smirk welcomed dimples and hugs. "I'm afraid not. You'll also require the sword possessed by the UPA, and as Irica advised it must be wielded by Jazekial. Along with the Igigi around the portal should weaken him enough to restrain and or kill him. The closer he is to the portal and ascension, the stronger he'll be. Under no circumstances trust him."

Shayne's brain beat against her skull. "For flips sake. Is this advice for just in case or what? Oh yeah, you can't tell me."

Enki massaged the back of her neck in slow circles. "At present it's not a concern but it will be if Annu, the Lexicon or its creator Zeke, are anywhere near the portal."

Shayne's brain slowed and surged again. "Wait a minute. You mean Zeke wrote the book? How is that possible? It's really old, we only just got it and he's a kid."

Enki exuded kindness she lacked. "Yes he did and it's not the focus here."

Admonishment curtailed Shayne's parade. "Yeah true. Another sorry. A big, fat one though."

Enki's honeyed tone removed her deepest fears. "It's nearly time for you to leave. As thank's I'll answer a few of your questions. And, where shall I return you?"

I'm in Heaven and still no cupcakes and unicorns. Not one flicking chocolate bar either.

Reluctance stuck Shayne to the bench. "Home. I need to talk to Annu and come up with something. We always do. Now, back to the nipple thing for starters."

Chapter 33: Love lies bleeding
Marduk & Gamede

Annu swerved Annunaki air strikes with the caves in his sights. "Flarking hell. I'm sorry, Ryan, I'll come back for you guys. I hope and pray. I'm leaving you in their hands."

The unknown whereabouts of the Igigi further tortured Annu.

Zeke doesn't seem restrained or hurt, what do they want with him? I can't get close enough without risking hurting him too. They're right near the book and I'm flarked without it or Zeke. I don't do faking stuff well, look how lying turned out and I'll need whatever else is in there to face Enlil

Annunaki and Zeke pressed a path through forest towards the caves. A mammoth pile of problems twisted his reasoning.

Annu flew adjacent and a little ahead. "Hormones, testosterone and good intentions are a deadly mix."

At the end of the trees, they grouped around Zeke and obscured him.

The hills above the caves came into view, a low pitched hum and bells came from unseen places.

Annu's intestines looped around his spleen. "Flark, flark, flark. I don't, I can't, flarking heck."

Self-hatred pulled each side in a tug of war.

He flew with the rational part of him gone. "Please forgive me. This is the shittiest, flarking decision to make."

An explosion preceded yells below, louder hums and bells less than a kilometre away ruined Annu's mental health.

Salvation found someone better to deal with. "Did he cause that and or is he hurt? Does he need me? Will everyone stop messing with me?"

Gods in the heavens, Ann, please protect him in my place.

Zeke sped between trees, his aura dwindled. "Flark........."

Annunaki trailed him by mere trunks, their intent palpable.

Zeke threw dull plasma balls, they fizzled a meter from him. "I said no. Flark off. Stay away from him."

Annu's pulse rose and fell more times than he counted. "Thank flark for small favours. He isn't on their side. But, will he meet me there?"

Crack, crack, wail.

A laser whip cracked Zeke on the back of his legs, he dropped onto his face.

Two Annunaki restrained him against a massive tree trunk.

One pointed a gun between Zeke's eyes; the other bent his little finger in the wrong way, the one next to it also broken.

Crack, crack, wail.

This isn't happening. Don't make me choose.

Blood oozed from damaged knuckles, Zeke's shoulders slouched. "Do what you want. I'm not giving in. Flark you and Enlil. No one's getting the book."

Crack, crack, snap, howl.

Annu agonised between his loved ones. "I don't… what do I."

Pain filled screeches decided for instead.

Annu annihilated the beings and landed by the tree. "Shit kid. You know how to get my attention. What were you doing with them anyway?"

Zeke nursed his damaged hand, his chest sank. "They wanted me to help them. Filled me full of bullshit. I'm so over all this."

Annu healed Zeke and licked dry lips. "You're a good person, Zeke."

"Thanks, but I'm not sure that's worth much right now. Go, get Shayne."

Ask him, ask him, ask him. He'll hate me, hate me, hate me.

The words stuck to Annu's tongue. "There's a lot of times I agree with you. Son, I need the book."

Zeke sucked his bottom lip and jogged ahead. "There's a problem there and a solution. You'll hate me when I tell you what I've done."

Flark, flark, flark. If Shay didn't need me I'd have given up by now.

The hum vibrated from the ground and up his legs, each bell toll chipped off a chunk of his worth.

Annu freak out simmered, his flames heightened. "Nothing you say or do will ever make me hate my own child. What is it?"

The lack of a lump in Zeke's jacket dampened them.

Zeke's chin quivered, he shifted out of arms reach. "The book's gone, gone. You can't take it."

The bottom fell out of Annu's world. Everything it hinged upon went down the shit shoot.

Annu wobbled, hunched and swayed. "She's dead. I've wasted time and had no other back up."

Zeke shifted closer and reached at Annu. "I'm sorry it was the only safe way. But, I'm coming with you to help instead. Even though I don't want to."

All I see is my family dead. All I care about is them. Please get out of the way. Please.

Annu's conscious beat on his back door and rattled the knob. "All right. I, I, you did the right thing."

How does Shayne pretend convincingly? I suddenly require such a skill.

Zeke's nervousness reflected in a stammer. "You might want to tell yourself that. We're nearly there."

They rounded some dirt mounds and reached the caves.

"Hear me boy, your woman's dead. Your kids are dead. Soon everyone you've ever known or loved will be dead. And they'll suffer to their last breaths."

Annu dropped to his knees and covered his face. "Oh Gods no."

Everything blurred, stars danced behind his eyes, anguish bifurcated him.

Zeke touched his shoulder. "Shit, Da. Are you all right? Do you hate me?"

Two males and a female Annunaki emerged from the dirt mounds with their aimed weapons.

Annu snapped, he barrelled into the caves and allowed common sense to lead past piles of rocks into a tunnel. Light exploded from a room further down, the ground rippled

Annu's roar accompanied a jump into the vortex with hatred held tight.

Chapter 34: Wedding Interruptus
Enki Island, Orion

Nothing on Orion, Earth or Shayne's luscious rear yard compared with Heaven's beauty and perfection. A horde of beings in the garden further trashed residual tranquility.

Suck it up, sunshine. Real life's back. Now to catch up.

A hot bath, joint and food called Shayne. "Argh. Get in line. Where's Annu?"

Manash, the Junior Grand Counsellor reached her first. "Thank the Gods you are safe. Where have you been? Has Marguerite gone to the office?"

Shayne crossed her fingers behind her back. "I'm sorry, dude. She was very severely and dramatically killed. I'm sad as fuck about it. Anyway, long story short, you're in charge."

It's best not telling him or anyone shoe Maybe-Marge really was. Why add more complications? Though, they need a better political system.

Manash slapped his forehead, his eyes widened. "Dead? I don't understand. How did this happen? That's terrible. We must prepare her remains for burial."

Shayne stepped around him and patted his chest, the babies stretched. "Ah, yeah. That might be a little tough and an open casket's out of the question. If it makes you feel better start a support group for grieving council members or a Go Fund Me. Oh, and we'll kick in for funeral costs of course."

Erin, Rosie, and Sam on the back verandah provided an oasis in a people desert.

Finally time to spend time with you guys. Any second Annu will run out, scoop me up and all will be right with the world. Right after I blast him. Hours of foot massages may assuage me.

Banked by lion beings Birdy blocked the path. "Shayne, where's Annu and the Lexicon?"

Huh?

Oblivious tickled Shayne's chin. "Ah isn't he inside? Look, if he hasn't given you the book yet, it's for good reason. I'll tell you before he does, speaking from experience Enlil's no threat and his minutes are numbered. And I now know Enlil's, Annu's, dad. No thanks to you."

Birdy's chest feathers fluffed, the colour faded. "Good Gods, no he's not here. You aren't aware of what's happened and he's there for no reason without you. What a mess. You must fix this."

Why am I getting a bad, bad, feeling. Crap, crap, crap. Don't tell me, just don't.

Shayne's senses heightened, her relaxation plan obliterated. "All right. You seem to know where he is, the least you can do is catch me up."

Birdy's determination stilted, she stared at bushes. "He's in Gamede Shayne, Hell."

Shock punched Shayne in the chest. "Why? How'd he know I was there? Fuck, fuck, fuck. We're meant to get married soon. Stress is not a wedding present. Why does the universe hate me?"

Birdy clucked and shuffled. "Enlil contacted Annu somehow and said he had you, while he didn't for a time I expect. Nothing stopped Annu coming after you and Gods know we tried to."

The magnitude of Annu's feelings expressed in action floored her. Two unexpected sacrifices on Shayne's behalf in short succession blew her little mind.

Unconditional love removed the baggage around Shayne's hidden heart. "He jeopardised everything for me. He cares about me in ways I'd never imagined and now everything's all fucked up. That's just cosmically mean. Wait, so you knew where I was and didn't do anything about it?"

Enki, this is a low ball and you neglected to pass on a few details under the guise of free will. For the greater good I'm sure. Fuck it. I'd like a few minutes to absorb this shit.

A patch of feathers on Birdy's arm fell out. "It's a complicated situation and we'll discuss that later. Regardless of why Annu's incredible sacrifice will result in all our deaths. Shayne, you must go back and stop this before it's too late."

Pertinence deflated Shayne's elation. "Way to put a dampener on my love fire. Let me get some shit together and I'll go. But I want it noted that I don't like you or the way you do things. I'm not doing this for you at all, it's for everyone else."

Birdy shifted aside and nodded. "I understand. Please, I implore you, move quickly."

I want to pluck her. It's one thing to hate on bad guys but how do I hate on good guys I don't like?

Erin pushed aside people and reached her mother. "Oh my cookies, Mum. Were you really in hell? That's probably why all my mental messages rebounded. I was worried. Calming everyone down while not knowing how you were sucked."

Not a part of Shayne existed without pain or complaint. "Yes unfortunately and I'm going back of course because it was so much fun the first time. I appreciate your help, sweet."

Fair skin emphasised dark bags under Rosie's eyes. "Thank God you're all right. I got really stressed out. There's so much left to do. Did I hear you say you're going again?"

Shayne hugged Rosie and relished their time honoured bond. "Aha, weddings on hold for a while. Please hold down the fort again until I come back."

Erin cleared people off the path. "Everybody move and give her some room please."

Sam's biceps and shoulders bulged; a vein pulsed in his neck. "I'm glad you're okay but you're always in too much danger. We need to talk about this wedding and your role here."

Rosie slapped Sam's arm, her strike bounced off. "For fuck's sake, Sam. Not now."

Fuck my life. Seriously. Have a one night stand and impregnate that shit.

By the back verandah, Shayne's ankles swelled, her calves tightened. "Yeah Sam, come on, dude."

The lion being's growl at the bottom of the stairs reminded Shayne of an old poem, Fuzzy-Wuzzy. "There are actual, urgent matters requiring your immediate attention and unless we approve your plan of action, we'll arrest you in Annu's stead."

Shayne's irritation grew longer than her consideration. "Like fuck you will. What are you a library monitor on acid? What's the penalty for really overdue books, death?"

Birdy touched the Fuzzy-Wuzzy's paw. "Eyron, both of you, please, let's not escalate unnecessary aggression in the wrong places."

Shayne stomped, dust flew up her nose. "You didn't come after me either because you didn't want to. I know where we stand so fuck off and let me do what I do."

Mother fucker, cock suckering, bastards.

Rosie clutched Sam's arm and nodded at Erin. "We'll leave you guys to it. This is way over our heads."

Shayne's not so cheery, cheer squad deserted. "Thanks for that."

Birdy fluffed and puffed. "Shayne, I'm not sure you understand the gravity of the situation. Annu bought the Lexicon with him to Gamede as collateral. Zeke's likely with him."

Anymore rides on the emotional roller coaster and Shayne qualified for a lifetime supply of free tickets.

I want valium. Lots and lots of valium. With a vodka chaser.

Shayne plonked on a step and squished personal space. "Jesus Christ and all the apostrophes. Why didn't you say that to start off with? Shit, shit, shit, fuck."

Fuzzy-Wuzzy doubled Shayne's membership. "It's irrelevant why Annu went and the only thing that matters is stopping Enlil. Our only option is you. Get up and go."

Shayne ground her teeth and rose. "I'm fucking going all right. I just wanted a few seconds to work shit out, and it's not irrelevant, dumb arse. He doesn't break rules for the heck of it, except for his family. He has more loyalty in his little finger than your entire furriness."

Birdy dropped more feathers. "Annu's right where Enlil wants him. I know we have no right asking you, but we truly don't have any other choice."

Shayne dismissed the back handed compliment as stress. "Right. In return you collect Ryan, Izzy and the Igigi from Marduk. There's a bunch of Annuknuckleheads trying to kill them. Your information was right on that."

When I crave chicken again, you're on the fucking menu. And you get no more help from me after this dilemma.

Birdy's eyes narrowed, she whispered. "Ah, yes. We assumed you'd ask this. We'll ensure they're returned safely. Sorry for the pressure but soon the ascension process begins, planets shift, strange things happen and the event brings its own mayhem."

Shayne arched her back, her feet disappeared. "I want their sword you've got now. Actually, forget picking up Ryan etc. It's quicker if I wormhole to Marduk and bring the Igigi with me. Oh joy of joys."

Images of the fake mental hospital and Sham-Man demotivated Shayne and chinked her rescuer armour.

Birdy brushed off loose feathers. "As you wish. Eyon, retrieve it and escort Shayne on her journey."

Fuzzy-Wuzzy's nose twitched. "Yes, of course."

Shayne channelled her best ha, di, ha, ha look. "Good. Get to it."

I'll make him like me somehow.

Birdy's colour brightened, her demeanour lifted. "Thank you. I'll pray for your safe return."

A mental list of supplies formed in Shayne's mind, food made number one. "Aha. You do that."

Ang jogged through the side gate. "Did Annu find you? Are the others okay? The ships I sent should arrive on Marduk shortly."

Torment made a macramé pot holder from Shayne's intestines. "Yes but no but I'm not sure. As usual nothing went to plan and is a mess. I'll fill you in soon but I'll need your help too. Oh, please make sure the barriers are up over Enki and Yebu."

Sam tumbled out the back door with his testosterone intact. "Are you all right, miss? I'm here if you need."

Shayne dismissed the damsel in distress. "I'm as good as I'm gonna get for the time being. Thanks anyway. I take care of myself these days."

A tall, thin, long legged, attractive brunette ambled into the backyard with a wrapped parcel. "Hi. I'm looking for Shayne or Annu."

She's so not coming to the wedding. I'll look like Princess Fiona near her.

Sam fell out the doorway and landed on his knee. "Shit. Who's she?"

Fuzzy-Wuzzy purred, the air stilled. "Hello there."

Rosie giggled behind Sam. "You right there, Sam? See something you like?"

Sam stared, his chin dropped, he blubbered. "I don't know what you're talking about."

But he can't like her. He's always had a crush on me. What happened to that? Some Orion version of a Victoria's Secret model comes along and pushes me out. I can't compete with her.

Shayne's confidence plummeted faster than stocks in Emu farms. "Someone put a bag or something over her head and get her some full sized clothes."

The girl's smile illuminated the yard, her legs glowed. "I'm Leah. I'd like to drop my wedding present off early and help."

Shayne wrapped the last of self-respect around her shoulders. "Like fuck you are."

Chapter 35: The Loaded Apple Tree
Gamede

Intense heat and hatred completed Annu's life long search for his father's location. "She's not dead, she's not. I won't believe it until I see it."

'I'm here Enlil and I'm coming for you.'

First impressions indicated a primal battle of wits waited at the end. Clouds grumbled, lightening cracked, and animal sounds created gloom.

Keep it together, this is the worst place and time to lose my shit. Or is it the best? I don't flarking know anymore.

A sense of belonging unnerved Annu, darkness yearned for release. His flames fanned higher and hotter. "I'm not flarking staying and giving in. Stay focused man."

Smoke billowed around a castle in the distance; body parts littered the immediate area. A bright, large container full of floating beings on the far side provided an unusual feature.

"What going on down here? Did Shay cause this?"

'Shay, do you hear me? Are you all right?'

Annu readied for takeoff. "She's survived worse. But this is pretty flarking bad."

Legs first, Zeke dropped from mid air and bounced off Annu's aura. "Flark."

Annu ducked from reflex. "Shit, Zeke. Why did you follow me? It's suicide."

Zeke scrambled to his feet. "I'm not letting you screw things up."

The clouds rumbled louder, lightening struck in several places.

Funnily messing up a lot is strong in our DNA, which doesn't bode well for this time.

Annu's concerns built a subdivision and sold lots. "Of all the stupid things to do. Now I'm worried about you too. Please, if you only listen to me once, find somewhere to hide and stay there."

Zeke's aura crackled and hissed. "Like hell I will. I'm the only one keeping your head straight and I'm not dying early because I stayed behind."

Man I love the confidence he has in me. Little shit. He's not thinking. He'll get hurt or worse. I guess he's safer at my side. Calm down or I won't find Shayne and we'll all die.

Annu swam in panic and wore fear floaties. "Shit, shit, shit. Why didn't you just stay home and not go to the party like I asked you? If you had, you wouldn't be in this place. Do you realise that? Unless you found another way you're stuck too."

"Come on Shay, answer me."

Proximity cleared and Enlil reverberated in Annu's mind. *"You finally made it, shame it's too late. The dead can't talk."*

"Keep pushing me and see what happens. Where are you?"

Annu grappled voluntary defeat, his testicles shrank. "I don't care about the consequences, I'll enjoy killing him."

"Head straight north, land in the area behind the castle and make it quick."

Diminished flames pushed deeper Annu into the lake of angst. "Stop taking my powers, you bastard."

The surroundings blurred, his breath quickened and brain fuzzed.

Zeke smacked Annu's bicep, his voice broke. "Hey. Snap out of it. I need you here. Stop answering him back. You're making it worse for yourself and we fixed him doing that remember? It must be something else."

Then what? Think, calm down, breath. He's right. My son's smarter than me. I should admit it, listen to him and move on.

Moonlight shone on the wrist comm's screen, a blue dot flashed beside its camera.

Annu exhaled slow, ripped it off and into pieces. "Shit. Flarking Marguerite. If I ever see her again, she's dead."

Zeke's neck muscles relaxed. "Yeah, well, I wouldn't worry about that right now."

Is Gamede a nightmare because you're away from your loved ones and Enki? What else makes it a terrifying place for mortals and gods alike?

Annu rose metres, circled and landed. "You're right again. Keep making a habit of it and I'll be taking lessons from you. We must head north and we're faced south. On an upside, son, if we're stuck here the heating's cheap and there'd be plenty of BBQ's."

Zeke's thick facial hair and reason cemented changes from boy to man. "I can't believe you're joking right now. Where are we going? I can't hear inside your head you know."

We're flying whether he likes it or not.

Their lost years tainted the current, Annu embraced the remains. "Ah sorry, kid. To his castle and flying is the fastest option."

Zeke strode on strong legs. "Yeah, all right. Before we do, I just realised. You can kill Enlil anywhere but nowhere near the portal. Not that it matters without the incantation but better be doubly sure. You get him away from there while I'll free Shayne. Or the other way around."

Common sense prevailed and brushed off a layer of worry.

Annu coveted Zeke's adaptability and hugged his shoulder. "I'm so glad someone got brains. That's brilliant."

And I didn't die saying that. Lesson learnt.

Zeke struggled out, his cheeks glowed. "Yeah, ah, all right. I told you, you needed me. Finding where they are in the castle without giving ourselves away and losing the upper hand may be the difficult part."

On a path before building ruins lay a torn up, dissected body in a red. An embroidered GC, MC above the pocket fizzled Annu's hatred.

Former, wasted respect peculated it. "You flarking twat. Well, someone saved me the trouble but given Shayne came here with her, this is either really good or really bad."

"Shay? Please answer me and end my misery."

Zeke's current habituation of rightness promoted him to Senior Plan Developer. "Da, focus, we're wasting—"

Hideous creatures erupted from the side of a building further on and stormed their way.

Zeke's plasma evaporated, he clutched Annu's forearm. "Ah, crap. Do something."

Annu's eruption failed, "What's flarking up now?" In the middle of the road he waved. "Wait, wait, wait. I'm Enlil's son. We're with him."

They slowed; a green, scaled beast faced the others and mumbled.

Zeke regressed from man to boy and back again, he patted his jacket. "Shit cakes. Of course, I want it when it's gone."

The green beast lumbered over, a stumped tail thumped the ground.

Part transition, Annu thrust an arm before Zeke. "Get behind me and be ready."

Zeke held it and swallowed. "Okay. Sounds good to me."

A small device similar to Marguerite's wrist comm dangled from the beasts arm. "We know who you are and you're right on time. Find your father and bring him to us."

For flark's sake, Enlil designed those for her. Flark. What's this idiot talking about? Why must every good thing in my life be countered with something undeniably worse?

Stacked odds barraged the border around Annu's faith. "What? Why don't you know where he is? Why are you all pissed at him?"

The beast spat, its tail swished black dust. "He betrayed us and will die before he ascends. Given he needs you, he'll do what you ask."

Zeke tutted and paced. "Is there anyone, anywhere, who doesn't want to kill a member or members of our family? There's more of them who want to than don't want to."

"I'm hearing you." Annu's flight or flight mingled. "What about the woman with him?"

We'll soon find if my confidence exceeds my abilities without powers.

The green beast exuded Shayne-induced-frustration. "We're not sure at present and almost past caring. She's ah, a difficult and annoying creature. Please take her out of here post haste."

Annu's pieces drifted back together, his internal torment lowered. "It will be my pleasure. In the meantime I'm not doing a flarking thing for you other than dissection."

More creatures spilled onto the road, the green beast's arm raised. They charged; bodies and weapons separated Annu from Zeke.

Zeke's wail focused Annu's ire. "Oh, Da, Da, Da."

Annu cracked his neck and drained his wits. "This fighting shit's getting old fast."

Chapter 36: The Scooby-Don't Gang
Orion, Marduk & Hell

The improvised, semi-reluctant, back, back, back up team of Erin, Fuzzy-Wuzzy and Sam assembled on the porch.

The UPA craft shot into the distance, Fuzzy-Wuzzy stayed behind.

Shayne gave it two middle fingers and an air kick, the sword clunked into her shin. "Don't come back real soon. Buzz kills."

Despite a bruise jewel's in the hilt glimmered in moonlight, energy tingled up her leg.

I hope you're as magical and killable as you are pretty.

Leah in all her perfection picked flowers and destroyed Shayne's esteem. "You're garden is amazing."

Sam gazed at her in extended, male peripheral. "You're amazing."

A full stomach and quick shower restored Shayne's humanity and guaranteed Leah's continued existence. "Oh for fuck's sake."

Erin crossed her arms and shivered. "Mum, please tell me it's warmer on this other planet."

Shayne shifted the sword to the other side. "I'm sorry, love. I don't remember, I had impending death keeping me warm. Grab a jumper."

In all of history I doubt there's ever been more fucked up gods than Annu and I. I'd be worried if mortals fared even better than us.

Erin's screwed up nose suggested petulance. "That covers the weather; will it stop me getting killed too?"

The babies rotated bounces on Shayne's trampoline aka bladder. "If Enlil made it, it will. I'm so not peeing for the millionth time before I go."

Sam stuck his hands in his pockets. "You left the probable dying part out of your sales pitch. I don't see why my non magic self is going. What good am I?"

A troubled mind exhausted Shayne; she dragged the sword toward Sam. "Because you're carrying this pain in the arse, it's really fucking heavy. And help if there's any damage to the planet in the meantime. Which there may be. I promise you're all safe and won't die unless I kill you."

Sam fake smiled and touched the hilt. "Yeah, yeah. Funny lady. So just like the old days I'm the heavy object carrier?"

Fuzzy-Wuzzy yanked it his way. "I'll carry the sword. It's not for inferior, Earthling hands."

Right, the whole male, pissing contest thing is universal. For fuck's sake.

Shayne stuck an arm between. "Fine, whatever. Let Fuzzy Wuzzy have it if he's cranky about it."

Sam gripped and pulled. "I'm not inferior to some furry, talking, arsehole lion. I'll carry it."

Erin flipped her palms up. "Really Sam? Now, of all times?"

Fuzzy-Wuzzy tugged, his muzzle twitched. "No you won't."

Shayne's patience kettle boiled over. "Don't start this being total dicks, all right. I'm not fucking having it. Time to put your muscles where your mouths are and cooperate or stay behind."

Fuzzy-Wuzzy blinked in succession and straightened his whiskers. "I, ah, I don't have to listen to you. I have my own mission."

There's a diva in every bunch. Seriously, next dilemma I'll have a team that's at least fifty percent on my side.

Leah ambled along, the flowers twirled. "I'll stay here if you like and help out."

Sam's tongue protruded, he let go. "No need to be snappy, miss. I don't care that much about it. It's a good idea if I stay to keep her, I mean Rosie, company. She might need me."

Fuck. If he stays, how do I teach him for liking someone young, gorgeous and spectacular? Even though I've never and won't reciprocate said feelings. There's no legit reason for me to come up with. Damn it.

Due to low numbers, Shayne canned friendicide and idioticide. "Fine. Fuzzy-Wuzzy carries the sword and Macho man saves the ladies. Are we all good now?"

Erin shook her head and tapped a foot. "May we get this over with? You're the one who's meant to get married soon not me."

Shayne swirled her hand, *Marduk, Marduk, Marduk. Near the caves,* and opened a wormhole. "Yeah, we'll see."

Ang carried arm full's of weapons up the path and stopped beside Fuzzy-Wuzzy. "I thought we'd better be safe than sorry."

Fuck, I forgot about him. I'm terrible at that.

Shayne scratched an imaginary itch. "Great idea. You're first in."

Ang peered into the vortex. "Are you sure it's safe?"

Shove, wave goodbye, next. "Yep."

Fuzzy-Wuzzy hesitated at the precipice. "I, ah."

Is it bad I want him to disappear as much as I want his help?

Shove, wave goodbye, next. "Keep the momentum going. I know you're all excited about our arrival."

Erin clasped Shayne's hand. "Together?"

Shayne nodded, entered and soaked in the silence. "You first. I want to stay here for a lot longer."

The tunnel narrowed, sound returned and peace shattered.

Shayne's feet touched dirt, she closed the wormhole. "And here we go."

The portal caves on the right forced memories of the last visit.

Ang collected weapons from the ground. "Interesting experience."

Fuzzy-Wuzzy hunched and dry retched masculinity. "I'm never, ever, doing that again. That's ridiculous."

Erin's sarcasm blossomed, she peered into the caves. "Chicken. Where's all your pee and vinegar now?"

Pride swept over Shayne, she squeezed Erin's waist. "Miss Experience right here. Thank you darling girl for coming."

Erin shifted them away from the entrance. "I'm not looking forward to going in there."

Enki, protect me and mine and keep us from all harm. Which is a tall order.

Shayne's top crept up; she tugged it and apprehension down. "No time like the present. Fuzzy-Wuzzy, are you ready?"

He steadied against a large boulder. "For the millionth time, my name is Eyron."

Shayne clapped and rubbed her hands. "Aha."

Ang carried the guns to the cave entrance. "I'm still coming."

Shayne's ankles ached, her fingers swelled, pregnant complicated everything. "You're a fucking legend, mate. The less time we spend in there the better. This must be quick."

Ang raised an eyebrow and clicked his fingers. "Ah, yeah. Okay."

Fuck, I miss Annu. I can't wait to see him even in Hell. Our get together locations suck.

Erin whispered in Shayne's ear. "What aren't you telling me?"

The whole truth glued her tongue. "We just can't stay long."

Please make this end quickly and before Erin suffers any effects at all from being in Hell.

Fuzzy-Wuzzy wiped his mouth and balanced the sword. "I've never been treated so—"

Yells from the forest preceded broken sticks and someone running.

Shayne erupted her aura; blood rushed to her head, goosebumps covered her arms. "Everyone good should be gone. Who's this to fuck things up?"

The sword shone in Fuzzy-Wuzzy's hand. "Surprise is a constant factor when around you."

Ang dropped his bundle bar one and aimed it at the forest. "I hope I brought enough guns."

And I hope I bought enough blind luck to cover everyone.

Shayne's aura pushed them aside. "I'm the biggest one you'll ever need."

A figure ran into the opening and towards the caves.

Wind removed dust from their face, recognition slammed Shayne.

Ryan opened his arms and quickened. "Mum? It's so good to see you."

Shayne met him halfway. "Thank the Gods you're alive. Why didn't you go with the others?"

Ryan held her at arm's length and relaxed. "I wasn't going anywhere until you got out and I'm so glad you're okay. Are we going home now?"

Shayne clung to hope like the last square of chocolate. "Aw, you so sweet. You know I'm harder to kill than tax debt. I'm sorry, Ryan, you've missed a few things. I'm going back."

I've said that like fifty times. I should have put out a newsletter. And this shit comes at a time when my hardest decision should be something borrowed or blue and recovering from a hangover. Mother fuckers. Enlil is a literal mother fucker because he fucked Annu's mother. Which is gross. And I'm left with a nasty image.

"Why?" His sigh brushed Shayne's forehead. "Annu went after you. Where's he?"

Fluid built around her ankles, Shayne flexed and un-flexed her calves. "Short version is we missed each other and he's still in there. May I ask where the Igigi or the Annunaki are?"

Ryan shoulders raised and tensed. "The Protectors left with what they believe are most of the Annunaki and some Igigi. Except for Izzy, whom I hope you did see. The others stayed with me. I understand their language now. It's really weird."

Shit. I can't leave my kids here unguarded. Fuck, fuck, fuck.

The suns dipped, a larger planet appeared behind them, Shayne's nape hair rose. "It's starting. I'm sorry, we have to go."

Erin hugged Ryan and picked leaves from his head. "I didn't realise it was you. No more complaining you miss all the interesting stuff. You're smack bang in it."

Ryan's concern bled over Shayne. "Shit. Sis, you're here too? This is worse than I thought."

A low pitched grind vibrated the ground, rocks tumbled, wildlife screeched. Clouds blocked half the light.

Shayne's pulse fluttered, her belly tightened and contracted. "No it's not. Everything's fine. Just fine. Come on."

This is the absolute worst time for Braxton Hicks but completely understandable given my stress levels.

Colour drained from Ryan's cheeks into his neck. "When will the creepy stuff end?"

Erin hooked her arm in Shayne's. "Not until we finish it. I'm terrified but not leaving you, mum. You're not doing anything like this alone again."

Ryan's hand across her lower back trembled. "I second that. I never thought I'd say this after how you were back then, but you've really turned your life around. In the universal, godly, fucked up type way of yours. You still don't do things by halves and it beats picking you up off the floor."

They do love me. I didn't completely screw things or them up. I'm not as useless as I think I am or was.

The wound on Shayne's soul closed another centimetre, tears burned her eyes. "Thank you both so much. I love you buckets."

Erin paused and tapped her chin. "Which reminds me, you like owe me about sixty bucks from—"

Bells tolled, the ground trembled, the sky darkened, and inevitable arrived.

Hope past its expiry date, Shayne hugged the kids. "Son, I need those other Igigi stat."

Chapter 37: Deadly Deception
Gamede

Gratitude boosted Annu from anguish; he strangled a creature from behind. "Zeke? Zeke? Where are you now?"

Tremors unsettled ground, bells tolled from unseen places, the moon shifted sideways and Annu worried no longer.

Tusks in the gut winded him and released the being.

Annu hunched, drew in his fists and sucker punched the assailant. "Shit. I should have paid attention. Powers have rusted my techniques. Not that I have trained much of late besides watching Earth's, cage fighters on that TV thing."

An invisible conveyer belt ejected creatures at regular intervals, some died but lots more replaced them.

Meters away, Zeke bobbed and punched a horned one in the head. "Da, Da. I'm all right. You watch out."

Annu plunged his hand into a chest. "What's Ralf want with Enlil, and where are they?"

The creature collapsed, its head lolled.

Annu retracted, goop dripped onto his shoe. "Flark. Bit much. Never mind."

Speak of the Devil and he arrived. *"You have to help me. I'll slit her throat if you don't hurry."*

"Enlil, you're so full of shit. I know you don't have her and your creations are after you. You're on your own, we're out of here. Never, ever and I do truly mean that, contact me or mine again."

Creatures smashed Annu sideways, his arm twisted behind him. "For flark's sake. This is unproductive."

It seems good things don't happen to good people. Unless, I'm not a good person at all.

Zeke dodged sets of hands and shoved a rat-dog thing. "Da, I can't get closer."

"You won't let me die; it's not in you and against your better interests."

Jab, jab, jab.

Strikes in Annu's abdomen expelled his lungs, his guts lurched. "You….stay….there…then."

Thump, thump.

White light exploded from Annu's temples, his head thudded. "Flark."

Talons grabbed, tore and shredded his arms.

Annu clung to consciousness; he punched the creature in the groin. "This is a shitty way to find out I'm incredibly out of shape. Fat arse, lazy, disgrace of a God."

I admit it's time for better eating and less drinking or I stay this way.

The force of six pregnant, angry women fell into Annu. "Mph."

Annu's head bounced off the ground, his brain swished. "This…is…not…going…well."

Outside sound dulled, inside sound reverberated. A brick plonked at the base of his skull and fogged thought.

The weight on Annu eased, he gulped air and wiped sweat from his eyes. "Flark."

An arm grabbed and heaved, Zeke blurred. "I can't leave you alone for five minutes. What would you do without me?"

Annu's legs wobbled, he clutched Zeke and his dignity. "No need to humiliate me further, son. Just taken by surprise that's all."

Zeke surged plasma and cleared a barrier. "Sorry. Did you find out anything before you killed the last one or did he get you first?"

Annu's equilibrium unequalled, awareness dribbled back. "Nothing pleasant or helpful. Hey, why do you have some powers?"

Zeke dodged a fist and faced Annu. "If you fight hard enough against it, focus, and are angry enough, that helps. I think I saw the box controlling the devices but getting to it's hard. Though, it's occurred to me we're looking at this situation all wrong. These lot may save us effort and pain."

An empty flask complicated their complications.

Annoyance peppered Annu's tongue. "That's good to know now. In what way is this not flarked? This isn't a joke, it's serious."

Zeke flinched, his Adams apple jiggled. "I do realise that. Enlil should know Shayne's whereabouts and they've already got him. So we either let them take us to him or you shoot off, get him and deliver him to them. So don't kill him until after you find out she's okay? It doesn't matter what they do, they can't ascend anyway. Literally, who knows, jumping into the portal regardless might send us home."

Damn. I didn't think of that. Again he's taught me something.

Annu's arrogance dropped a few rungs, he softened his defences. "I'm sorry. Again. And thank you again. That'll work."

Bang. Bang. Smack.

A punch to the face and Zeke's nose spread, blood splattered, he chomped his lip. "Flhindd."

Annu's pressure valve blasted a hole through his ceiling, his hands flamed. "For flark's sake. I'm done with this."

A demon clamped something upon Annu's wrist, his enthusiasm plummeted.

Annu turned and raised a fist. "You flarking."

Zeke clutched Annu's arm and shook his head. "No. Just go with it."

Surrender goes against everything I am but I'm sure it will all be fine. Just flarking fine. Like cut glass and razor blades in your morning coffee. Mother flarking, twat waffles.

Annu's submission bellied inner struggle. "Yeah. I'll add another tumour to the pile."

Horned hands restrained his other wrists; strong arms lifted and carried him.

Zeke raised his hands and spat. "I give up. Please don't hurt me anymore."

Shit, I almost believe him.

The demon carrying him out weighed Annu a thousand fold. "Shut up."

Annu lolled his head and closed an eye. "Where are you taking us? Where's my son?"

The creature exemplified dead puppies and broken dreams. "To your father where you'll be reunited before ascension."

Annu's heart palpitated, insane lumped beside panic. "Why does Ralf even care about that? He's not a God. I ask without actually wanting an answer."

They passed piles of rusted metal, bones, and trees. Unkempt garden beds surrounded boarded up buildings, large dogs wandered on bones for legs.

Mould lined the creature's teeth; death lingered in its breath. "He'll release the Elders and replace Enlil using both of you."

Don't panic. There's no way this Ralf will succeed. Keep your cool.

Sureness wrapped a comfort blanket around Annu. "Ah, you best tell him he's shit out of luck. Ascensions are for Gods not inhuman beings with delusions of grandeur. Trust Enlil to make such a mess."

The creature snorted snot. "Enlil created Ralf as the original demon from his own blood. So he's like you and can ascend."

Shock evicted confidence and moved on in to Crazy Town.

Annu's stomach churned, he slapped its arm. "You're flarking kidding me? No freaking way. It's not true."

No, no, no, no, no. Flarking no.

Off beat drums loudened; a castle came into view.

The creature raised a matted eyebrow. "You'll see for yourself soon enough."

All manner of beings in various states of decomposition staggered, wailed and moaned.

Annu's grip on reality dripped like wax. "Oh shit."

Bright light peaked from behind two lined planets, the bells tolled sharper.

Ethereal tentacles plunged into Annu's core. *"Son of Enlil, there's something you don't know which changes everything."*

Panic stormed Annu's mind, personal space evaporated. *"Who the flark is this?"*

"We're the Elders they speak of. Unrestrained, our power knows no bounds. In the right hands, your hands, we'll make this universe right again."

Annu's anger chilled, creation's existence laid in him. "This is flarked. Got any rum?"

"Ah no. Flark off. I've got enough problems."

The creature grimaced and continued on. "Not for you."

A thick, dark, bleak foreign substance penetrated Annu's brain. *"The darkness in you calls; it yearns for truth and justice. We will give you all you desire if you release us first. Enki will reign no more."*

Faltered faith surrendered mental protection. "Get me alcohol and we'll see."

Chapter 38: The end is high, nigh and low
Gamede

Irony and Murphy's Law out ranked Karma in cosmic's 'Fuck You' department. Outside the castle grounds in an outbuilding reserved for the worst souls, Enlil's nerves prickled.

Metal restraints dug into Enlil's wrists and ankles, the skin beneath bruised and bloodied. "I want to scream, purge, yell or give up. This heart is faulty; it'll burst right out of my chest."

All right, I'm not quite where I want and losing my godliness by the second I've been in worse situations and survived. This time is no different. It'll only make my release sweeter.

Will to fight fell and festered each unwelcome breath.

The torturer poised a brand over Enlil's abdomen. "You're hardly in a position to bargain."

Enlil's thoughts danced like puppeteers without a puppet. "Release me and you'll suffer less than the others. I've always been good to you. Remember the day after I created you and you first tortured someone. You found your calling because of me."

A group watched in the doorway, their enthusiasm rose with Enlil's suffering.

The brand seared soft, belly flesh, hair singed. "Now you're getting a close and personal view of my abilities. How ironic?"

Burned circles resembled human naval's, yet another reminder his former perfection and godliness slipped away.

Enlil's anus opened and closed, foul air emitted from it. "You're only solidifying your permanent death. Don't believe Ralf's lies."

The crowd's cheers stripped him and evoked weakness.

Why me? This treatment isn't fair or just. Is it my growing human biology making me feel pathetic and weak? Why do I care that they're judging me and consider me inferior? I'm doomed forever and it's not my fault.

The torturer twirled a red, hot rod, shivered and stabbed Enlil's side. "He's delivered thus far where you never did."

Enlil's muscles tensed, senses heightened, nerve endings roared. "No, no, no. I beg you stop. I'm your creator."

The torturer held it centimetres from Enlil's side. "I'm eternally grateful for that."

Heat built anticipation; a tremor shifted the bed closer.

It lanced below Enlil's ribs, he bucked, and warm water trickled down his cheeks. "No. I don't, no, no, no."

Spikes on the bed pierced his back, the room blurred, death crept along his spine.

I must hold on a little longer, the suffering will pass.

The stench of his own burnt flesh nauseated him.

New emotions bombarded Enlil, his pulse slowed. "Stop. I can't take anymore. You're killing me."

Claps and cheers boomed into the room, aloneness amongst company depressed him.

Stop showing fear, it makes it worse.

The demon's features twisted. "It's too late for pleas. We've got time and you to kill."

Humanity tipped Enlil upside down and shook. "You need me alive."

Don't give up, don't give up, don't give up.

Imminent defeat tasted metallic and ulcerated his tongue.

The demon's laugh emptied Enlil's reserves. "Did you ever imagine your creations turning on you, our creator, because you intended on doing the same thing to us?"

Lightening cracked, thunder roared and time passed. The demon audience showed confidence and freedom he lacked.

Don't give up, don't give up, don't give up.

Tremors bounced Enlil and drove the spikes deeper. "Alhalso......."

The torturer stumbled and upended the brand. It hit his foot. "Blastard thing."

Pain choked Enlil's laugh, his breath dragged through his lungs. "Serves.... you.... right."

The torturer selected a bigger one and heated it. "You won't find any joy soon."

A bull demon carried Annu over his shoulder into the room. Another dragged an unconscious grandson in by the arms.

Enlil's sufferance eased, his tolerance level shifted to one. "About time."

The torturer lowered the rod and frowned. "Who're they? Why are you bringing them in here?"

He deposited Annu against the wall, Annu groaned. "They're his son and grandson."

Torturer gestured to Annu and Zeke. "And why are they here?"

Zeke half roused. "Wh, wh, wh."

Annu opened his left eye, looked around and closed it.

He's awake and he'll save me but I don't see the book. I hope Ralf doesn't have it.

The bull demon's shrug blocked out moonlight. "Ralf wants you to prepare and watch them until it's time. He's releasing the Elders soon."

Terror bear hugged Enlil; his chest tightened. "No. No. The fool. He'll kill us all."

Annu's right eye opened, flames flashed across his chest. Out of eye sight, he drew a line across his throat with his finger.

Yes, yes, I know.you hate me. I return the feelings but you serve a purpose. For now.

The torturer clicked his forked tongue. "All right. Leave them there and close the door behind you."

Enlil moved his wrist, the restraint tightened, pain rocked him. "Grr."

Bull demon grunted and stomped out the door. "See you there."

The torturer returned to the fire and brand. "The family who bleeds together stays together."

Enlil struggled and arched his back. "Do something, for fuck's sake."

The torturer paused mid stab, fire consumed from him. He screamed, slapped at his cheeks and crumbled into a heap.

Annu stood in his place, his eyes pools of ire. "Your life depends on your answer, where's Shayne?"

Little does he know underneath his darkness lies inherent faith in the good. Such people usually assume others tell the truth despite how many times they've lied.

Enlil mouth dried, his cauterised wounds burned. "Nice to meet you too, son. She's near the portal. I'll show you where."

Annu's boots blackened the concrete. "I knew it wouldn't be easy. Give me a reason not to kill you."

I'm not giving you the bigger reason yet because I'm running out of tricks. I'm holding off until I have to.

Confidence restored Enlil's enthusiasm and diminished pain. "You won't find her without me. Where's the book?"

Annu glanced at Zeke, his flames heightened. "You'll get it when I get her."

For Alhonso's sake. He's as stubborn as I am and much more irritating.

Enlil nodded to his wrists, his head thudded. "Get me out of here plus stop the Elders being released and you've got a deal."

Annu's lip twitched, he melted the restraints. "I'm requesting a DNA test after this. I have big reservations about accepting you as my father. I don't care about anything but Shayne so don't push your luck."

Circulation returned to Enlil's arms, he massaged the abrasions. "Damn you're pig headed. You will care as all this affects you in ways you don't know yet."

Zeke erupted in a blue energy, climbed the wall and stumbled over. "Da. Stop right now. Why are you letting him go? If he's told you about Shayne, kill him."

Ah families. They're the best. I have not missed having one.

Rain fell on Enlil's hope desert. "Back off, son, it's complicated and over your head. It's about time for a family reunion."

Chapter 39: The Grandfather Clause
Gamede

Thunder roared and lightening cracked outside the window.

Not so long ago I went to a party to get a girl. Now I'm in this place with no end in sight. Why didn't I stay home?

Zeke moved between a rock and a hard place. "Annu, Da, do not let undo another restraint. Have you lost your damned mind? There's no scenario where freeing him makes sense."

Has this place made him go nuts? He isn't thinking, he'll kill us.

Annu's jaw clenched his jaw. "Stop panicking. It's only for a short time until I've got Shay. I'm not spending hours looking while she's alone out there. Look at him, he's no threat."

Welts and pus covered Enlil's bare, bulged gut, his hair thinned. "For fuck's sake. Now you're just irritating. Boy, you don't understand what's going on. Back up and mind your business. Leave this to the adults."

There's no respect for me as a man anywhere. I won't let them distract me. There's too much at stake.

A fraction of compassion lanced Zeke's passion, rationale squashed it. "Neither of you underestimate me. Annu, no matter what, don't trust him. He may seem like a tired, beaten up old man and not an evil beast but come on. The book and all we've learned about him more than indicates not just caution but destruction. Look how he's flarked you around already without his full power.

I bet he doesn't even know where she is at all. Is she even here? Was she ever?"

A sixteenth of the last three planets showed, divine light pierced the first.

Annu's stomp cracked the concrete, he loomed over Enlil. "Well, is he right?"

Enlil switched between human and beast. "Of course I had her, and she's in danger out there alone. Especially when Ralf releases the Elders. We all are. It's him you must stop."

The pit of Zeke's stomach churned, he encapsulated Enlil in plasma. "You're full of shit."

Annu combed fingers through his hair and unravelled. "Flark. I can't risk it. You, Shay and the babies are all I have."

Guilt fizzled Zeke's control. "I, I, I. Shit. All right. But his hands stay tied up."

The plasma ball popped, spikes on the bed impaled Enlil's back, he screamed. "Oh Hells. Get me off this thing."

Panic heightened Zeke's powers and clouded focus. "I'm sorry. I didn't mean to hurt him."

Or did I? Am I full of hatred like Enlil and don't realise?

Annu positioned Enlil onto his side, blood pooled. "All right. I understand you think you're doing what's right but sometimes the lines are blurred and this is one of them. Please Zeke, help me out here?"

Zeke undid the last restraint and twisted Enlil's hand behind his back. "As soon as you've got Shay, he's history. And don't expect me to be nice. I've no compunction about killing him myself after all the shit he's pulled."

Rounds of lightening illuminated outside, divine light entered the next planet.

I need to make some choices quick but have no idea what ones.

Enlil's pained tone tripled Zeke's confusion. "You cannot kill me without affecting everything. It's not just about your woman's safety. There's another incantation and if Ralf gets out, everyone's screwed either way. Not only that, if I die here, you two are permanently stuck in my place."

The walls inhaled and exhaled, time slowed.

Zeke released him and leaned against a wall, his heart ached. "Oh shit. Shit. Da, this is such a mess. I do not want to die. I don't want Shayne and the babies to die either. Him, however, he can die."

Surprise shadowed Annu; he stumbled and gripped the bedside. "I flarking knew it would be impossible to succeed. The damned universe is against me. I'll wring your neck for this. You kept that to yourself until the last minute. Flark, flark, flark."

The ground groaned and cracked.

Enlil wriggled to the bed's edge. "For good reason. Now, move."

Annu's eye twitched, he burned a leg strap. "Don't forget arsehole that you're part free subject to my whim."

Doom clouds invaded Zeke's sky, desperation cleared a path.

Flark. I know what I must do and I don't really like it. Isn't doing the right thing like that?

Zeke's rushed to the exit. "I'm sorry Da; I'll make it up to you when this is over. What I'm about to do makes the most sense."

Annu cocked his head and half turned. "What? Wait, Zeke. What are you—"

Zeke slammed the door and welded the edges. "I've no choice. I pray you'll understand when I let you out later. However, I do expect a punishment a fraction severer than grounding, but I'll live. We all will."

Creatures busied between castle gates and the main entrance.

Zeke immersed in darkness. "Stopping the Elders escape is number one, and then to find their incantation."

Tremors rocked the ground and created several crevices, orange lava bubbled around the edges.

The back of Zeke's head banged into the door, his neck jarred. "Are you kidding me?"

The tremors increased, a crevice headed his way and devoured all in its path.

Zeke climbed the door, jiggled the handle, kicked, and punched it. "Ah da. We got a problem."

Releasing Enlil probably isn't a great idea either but screw dying.

The crevice reached meters ahead, panic consumed Zeke. "Da. It's a really big problem."

Thick steel muffled Annu, the building shook; the ground shifted and deposited Zeke on his butt.

Zeke's ribs jabbed into his lungs, debris imbedded in his hands. "Flark."

The crevice reached the building. Crack, crack, crack.

Stone bricks tumbled, a corner dipped into lava.

Oh hell no.

Zeke wobbled and yank the door. "Da? Da? Are you okay? Answer me."

I'm out of ideas and scared shitless.

Red rain dirtied vision and muted sound. The ground beneath exploded and broke open.

Zeke somersaulted, his knee cracked into his nose. "Fjdoddod."

Orange lava streamed from the crevice and separated into limbs.

Zeke's hope grew legs and ran; he backed up into half a stone wall. "It's true. Oh shit. I'm flarked. We're all flarked."

Ah I made a massive mistake coming here even without the book.

Giant feet provided a platform for a lower half, torso, shoulders, a neck and a fiery crown embellished head.

The orange being's footsteps created craters. It leaned, picked up a handful of creatures and ate them.

Pee soaked Zeke's pants, he hunched. "This is all my fault. I should have done so much more. I'm useless. I've fixed nothing, I've made it worse and I'm alone. I'm a fool for ever thinking I had this worked out, could save everyone. If I live, I've so much to learn. I'm sorry, I failed."

More orange beings emerged from the lava, the divine light widened.

A dead Isaac staggered from behind a pile of stones, his smile all sharp teeth. "I never did get to say happy birthday."

Repentance marched single file down Zeke's spine. "No. No. Just no."

Isaac lunged and collected Zeke around the neck. "Happy birthday."

Chapter 40: Out of the frying pan into Hell
No prizes for guessing where

Earth quakes, bells, fate and lights destroyed the evening plans of procrastination and food consumption.

An ice wall separated Shayne, the others and a bunch of dead things. "This shit gets weirder every fucking moment. What's next? Wait, scratch that. I don't want to know."

Fuzzy-Wuzzy fuffed and flapped. "Hurry up. Must you talk about nothing incessantly?"

Shayne last nerve boomeranged off stone and hit her in the eye. "Has anyone ever told you how much fun you are to be around? Even more than a Tax Office employee and I love them so."

Fuzzy-Wuzzy's growl accompanied a chill up her spine. "Please, for the love of the gods, say something useful or be quiet."

Shayne filed his mood in the 'don't give a fuck' drawer. "That's one problem taken care of. Time for the next. All of you gather further in the back in the opposite direction to where I'm going. Got it?"

Erin's pupils dilated, her cheeks flushed. "Mum, you'll need all the help you can get. No way am I not going. I told you that."

I hate that she's right about this. Hate, hate, hate it.

Shayne patted Erin's shoulder. "Love, our last mission was to Mary Poppinsville in comparison. This one's flat out the first Saw movie and maybe two sequels. I don't want to jeopardise you guys. I know it hasn't worked yet but try sending messages to Enki somehow. I can't believe I'm going to Hell again. It has to be some sort of fucked up record."

Ryan's concern invited doubt to a doubtless plan. "And do we just sit here and look pretty or what? I feel useless, again."

The heebie-jeebies climbed Shayne's leg. "Yep. That's it and stay safe in my absence. Too bad we didn't get time to rally up the other Igigi."

Erin rubbed her arms, tears welled. "All right. Maybe. Heck Mum. This sucks."

In so, so many ways. And then some.

The inevitable doom's flight reached the terminal and readied for departure.

Shayne embarked with a discount ticket. "I know. I totally agree. Ang, Fuzzy-Wuzzy, time for another of those portal jumps you love."

Ang slipped a third gun into his jacket. "I'm starting to like this."

Will his weapons make any effect on the already dead?

Fuzzy-Wuzzy threatened Shayne's kill no friend's policy. "My name is Eyron. Please remember it. If you can."

Shayne's moodiness outranked his, her hackles raised. "You've earned yourself first in line for bait Fuzzy. Keep going and you're the only one."

I'm not fucking around anymore. People better start paying attention.

A hum preceded tremors across the ground and up the walls, rocks tumbled.

The first hint of fear crossed Fuzzy-Wuzzy, he clutched the sword. "No need for nastiness."

He entered the tunnels and darkness.

Shayne mustered enthusiasm, the babies turned. "Sorry my darlings. We're at it again."

Ang nodded at the tunnel. "You know, this takes Best Man duties to a whole new level."

"We'll make it up to you." Shayne kissed Erin's cheek, her soul ached. "It's okay, baby. I'll be back soon. I promise."

Or die trying. I'll make everything okay again. I have to.

Erin swiped at it and looked away. "You better."

Ryan kissed Shayne's head and rubbed her belly. "See you all soon."

Shayne faced the tunnels, her feet concrete blocks. "This is great. Just fucking great. Other brides to be are dealing with hung-over fiancées who've spent too much money on strippers. But no, what am I doing? I'm going somewhere I'll probably die at least and smell bad at most. My favourite kind pre-wedding activity. Not. Next visit Enki you've got explaining to do."

Inside the dark closed in, her kidneys chilled.

Enki fucking help us, please. I'm using my free will to beg you Enki to help us. Please. And keep Izzy safe wherever she is. Do not let this be our end.

Further down the light intensified and cemented Shayne's fate. She clutched her wits and pushed on.

Ang waited in the doorway. "You okay?"

Looks like fucking grumpy Fuzzy-Wuzzy already jumped in He'll be sorry he went first.

Shayne followed him inside and to the portal swirling in the corner. "Yeah. Super fucking okay. Link your arm into mine, it might lessen the impact. Oh how I wish it lead to Jamaica or some island."

Ang bent and poised an arm, his neck cricked. "Me too. I'll hold onto you instead."

With his hands on her shoulders Shayne walked in, memories of last time returned along the starry path.

At its end, shoes touched sand and denial died.

Shayne licked her lips, heat sucked all moisture. "You know the list of people to rescue grows by the second. Now it includes us."

Ang dropped onto his feet and exhaled. "That's a real trip. Not sure whether it's a good one or otherwise yet."

Fuzzy-Wuzzy hugged his knees, the sword rested at his feet. "I, I, I, I, I, yuck."

I should feel bad about him being sick but I don't.

Shayne did a three sixty and stopped halfway. "Mmmmm. Still no map. Bugger."

Bright orange beings destroyed everything reachable in the distance, clouds cleared, planets appeared larger and closer.

Disbelief dribbled out Shayne's mouth. "What the fuck's happened since I've been gone? The place has gone to…here. Jesus Christ. Who'd thunk it could get worse? This is so, so, so, not good."

Something red protruded from dirt on the right, recognition heightened Shayne's anger.

A tug released Fake-Sally's beloved handbag, Shayne opened it. All identification therein showed her true name and address. "I fucking knew it, bitch. You went all out on this one."

A copy of Shayne's original birth certificate lay between two unpaid bills and a hand drawn map to her house on Earth.

Rejection beat a path to her heart; Shayne double locked the door and tossed the key. "You'll have no more of my time and thoughts. We're done."

Ang stroked her back. "That sucks. I'm sorry she did that to you."

"Me too but never mind. Moving on and far away."

Shayne closed her eyes and slipped the certificate into her pocket. *Annu my love I'm here now, again. If you haven't seen him yet be wary of Enlil. He's full of shit but it doesn't matter because I've got something which can end all this. Where are you?*"

Annu's voice broke chips of worry off her shoulders. *"Shay? Thank flark. What do you mean now and again?*"

Chapter 41: No respect for our Elders and No rest for the Wicked
Gamede

Concern peeled from Annu, light drove back darkness and his universe survived another day.

Annu fist pumped himself. *"Shay, stay there. Do not risk yours or the babies' lives again. I'll come down to you but have to find Zeke first. I repeat, stay where you are. I love you very much. We're nearly there, we'll just ride it out until the time passes and come up with a way out."*

Behind abandoned pits of torture, Annu dangled Enlil over a crevice, lava licked his hair. "You flarking lying, piece of shit. Being nearly human and all, I'd kill you now, but then I can't kill you again when I discover more of your lies."

Shayne's love provided music to Annu's soul. *"Ah. Done. If I come across Zeke I'll message. I can't wait to see you. I love you shit loads too. There's so much to talk about. Oh and if you see a blonde orange skinned girl let me know too. Please."*

"I, ah, I, okay. We'll talk about everything later."

"At least they'll be one because of us."

"We're not there yet my love."

"Yeah, don't I know it."

Shayne's music reached critical mass in Annu's brain. *Enough, time to focus on where I am.*

He waved Enlil across the surface. "Right, where were we?"

Enlil spluttered and reached. "Without her you'd never have helped me. Since we found each other you've shown no regard or care. I did what I had to. You'd do the same. Once you give into the darkness and see where it takes you. As my son, you're entitled to rule this place if I bequeath it. You can start again."

I don't want to believe you but something tells me he's not lying about this stuck here shit.

Annu's skin prickled, raw power probed his protection. He reinforced his borders. "No thanks. It clearly didn't work out well for you and it's too damned hot. This woman who pretended to be Shayne's mother is that your doing?"

The Elders guarded the castles surrounds and left mayhem in their wake.

Shayne played a non requested encore. *"I will. Have you missed me?"*

Annu tossed roses on the stage and left his seat in the front row. *"Of course. We'll talk soon my love. Chat later."*

Lava singed Enlil's hair; he clenched his abs and spluttered. "No. It was that woman's stupid idea and she's likely dead. Shayne's real mother sacrificed herself to release her ages ago. I had no idea she'd come back again. I beg you my son, stop. Kill me or not, I can't take anymore."

The BBQ'd smell deterred Annu; he flicked Enlil like shit off his shoe. "Did you ever stop when someone begged you? What about draining my powers and trying to kill my family? You should at least suffer some."

Focusing on the bigger picture is the only thing stopping me killing you despite everything. Karma is rarely fair.

Enlil whipped side to side, spit and tears dribbled down his forehead. "I can't fight Ralf if I'm unconscious."

"Yes and I can't wait. By the way, you still owe me a date night."

A fraction of regret slowed Annu's anger. "How did you and Ann even meet let alone conceive me?"

"I'm pretty sure this counts. When we're together there's you, me and a nice big fire. Isn't that exactly what you wanted?"

"Smart arse. Have you left yet? Please tell me the books nowhere near you or him?"

And here we go again. Another concert. If I answer back, this continues until next month. If I don't, I'll hear about it for triple that. I'll make it up to her later.

Enlil coughed blood, his eyes bulged. "Of all the Annunaki she captivated me with an innate joy, deeper understanding. She had a way with the other gods and the humans. I watched for a long time before I approached her. When I finally did, that was the beginning of the end and it led me here. Wretched women bring nothing but pain, suffering, and trouble. To cement her guilt the bitch has refused to answer me since."

Flarking one sided, blinded, arrogant piece of shit. His perspective's skewed.

Fury flowed through Annu; he dropped Enlil onto the ground. "I dare you to ever call her that again. At any time have you realised you self-sabotage? You've brought this all on yourself."

Enlil's spine cracked, his head bounced. "All right, all right. Enough."

The gateway between levels of hell and heaven opened. Souls in the well froze in place and dismissed former stress returned in spades.

"Honey? Hello? Aren't you talking to me anymore?"

Oh my flarking Gods.

"Yes, it's just hard to talk….give me a few minutes."

Light pierced another planet and illuminated their hiding spot.

Annu drifted towards an unseen harbour, he steered for safer shores. "Why am I messing around with you? I'm done."

Enlil gasped for air and Annu's leg. "Stop, wait. You need me to show you the right parts in the Lexicon to stop them."

Their luck with twisted fate stayed Annu. "I'm too old and it's too late for horse shit. What else you got that stops me leaving you?"

Enlil rolled onto his side and clutched Annu's ankle. "You don't know their weakness. It's not just here that's affected. Even the heavens where your mother, wife and son are will suffer."

No. Don't buy into it. Deception is what he does. He's proven that.

Jaid flashed across Annu's mind and sliced his soul.

He choked renewed grief with common sense. "You know what? I'm really starting to hate you. You're really getting on my nerves. By the way, we didn't bring the book. Get up and walk flarker."

Enlil had the bad grace to appear offended. "You lied. I don't believe it. How dare you?"

Annu's patience packed up and walked out. "Yep. Sucks being lied to doesn't it. Where's this other incantation?"

Now the tables have turned flarker. We're finally getting somewhere.

Enlil avoided eye contact, he lumbered along. "The one time I had it briefly in my possession I made a copy. Just in case."

Annu prayed for an, as yet received, quick resolution. "Where is it?"

Enlil squished his face and coughed. "On Ralf's scalp. That's why I demanded the book."

Universe comes together; again, universe explodes, again.

Annu engulfed and rose. "For the love of Enki and all things holy. You're a piece of work."

Enlil flinched, lesions appeared on his skin, and he blubbered. "No, no, no. Stop. Don't talk like that."

A pity party rained on Annu's parade, he lowered. "Fine. Thanks for the heads up but you're not going anywhere near him or the portal. Or dying for that matter. That's all I flarking need. No tricks. Got it?"

Enlil's demeanour lifted. "Yes, of course. I'll do no such thing."

An Elder glanced in their direction and peered. He motioned to another and pointed.

Getting into a fight with them will prolong getting out of here.

Annu dragged Enlil by the shoulders into the dark. "Aha I'm sure. What's the deal with me taking your place if you're dead or gone?"

Enlil's expression darkened, his eyes shone. "Because of your cursed DNA, you'll or yours shall become the leader of hell and subject to the same restrictions as I. It's divine law and punishment. Undeserved mind you."

Annu crunched a pile of dried, human bones. "Then my bad luck is keeping you alive until I find a loop hole."

Enlil's colour drained, his lips cracked. "You still won't do anything. You can't."

This is just flarked up. Who comes up with shit like this? Oh how I rue the day I decided to find my father.

Annu bit his tongue and tasted sufferance. "What's the special sword Shayne's brought and this Izzy girl she's after?"

Enlil shrank into himself, rocks clunked his head. "The sword is here with Shayne? Keep it and the girl away from me."

Ah, another glimmer of fear. So the sword and the Igigi really do affect him. Handy to know.

Annu helped Enlil onto his feet. "First lesson about humans. That shitting yourself feeling is fear. Get used to it. There's much more to come."

"Change of plans my love. You'll have to come to me and risk your life again, with the sword and whatever else you've got. Try finding Zeke on the way and prepare yourself. Long story short, I've got Enlil, we can't kill him, Ralf released the Elders and has the incantation."

"Oh, that's who they are. What the fuck? Are you serious? Well that's just great, fucking great."

Annu lead Enlil by the elbow. "As part of your punishment you can listen to Shayne rant and sing."

An Elder walked onto the road and stopped. "There you are. We gave you the chance to join us and you refused. Now's your penance."

Chapter 42: This is some bullshit
Fourth level of hell, hell

I cannot fathom any logical reason Annu needs Enlil alive except for daddy issues. Fuck we all have some of those but they don't take us to hell. You know what Enki; I'm questioning why you gave us powers, fuck loads of responsibly and no clue. We're not qualified for this shit. We haven't even finished the Certificate 1 in DipShit yet.

Hells and heaven's levels overlapped, a bone crunching drop existed in-between.

Shayne rolled from the edge onto her back. Despair became her go to snack. "We're fucked. There's four more levels from here to the first. Enlil might ascend; Ralf might too, if anyone lasts long enough. In short we're fucked. Godzillafucked too."

Creatures and human souls jumped into the abyss in escape of The Elders, who renovated Hell. What splattered bodies didn't cover, lava and destruction did.

Shayne pushed onto her elbows. "Did you hear me? I said we're fucked."

The sword stayed in Fuzzy-Wuzzy's grasp, a cumbersome reminder of their duty. Since their arrival he'd faded alongside his manners.

Lion-Guard's white muzzle and whiskers twitched. "Vulgarity is your response to everything. We'll climb them. Simple."

He's sucking the fun right out of this trip and there wasn't much to start with.

An elder smashed a chunk off the second level's edge, it tumbled into the next.

Save the odd hiccup the babies stayed still. "Well duh. I figured that much. Come on then before all Hell really does break loose. I'm not giving birth here. Way too much redecorating."

Lord knows I hate that shit.

Ang perched on his haunches, weapons ready. "I must say, Shayne, things are never boring when you're around. But, I'm not making a habit of it."

A lump clogged Shayne's throat, her allergy to early death flared. "Damned right and don't forget it. You know, I need this shit like a hole in the head. There's a hole in my head, dear Liza dear Liza, there's a hole in my head, dear Liza, a hole."

Shayne levered up and stood, blood pressure dipped, her brain sloshed. "Oh blah. I took a trip without leaving the farm."

An arm supported her back; Ang's breath brushed her nape. "Are you all right? This isn't really the best place for a pregnant goddess. Can we do this without you?"

The dizziness abated, Shayne slowed her breath and righted. "I fucking wish but no. That's the story of my life. Or death. Whatever shall be. The sooner this is over the better."

Something banged and scraped on their right.

Fuzzy-Wuzzy climbed the rocky edge, the sword hung at his side. "I'm not waiting anymore."

Shayne's enthusiasm level equalled her care factor, nil. "Yes. Geez. Grumpy and bossy. Are you married?"

Fuzzy-Wuzzy adjusted his position and slotted his foot into a wedge. "That's none of your concern."

"So, that's a no then."

Ang knelt beside the opening and offered his knee. "I'll give you a boost and go after you. That way if you've got any issues I'm there."

His kindness softened Shayne's apathy, she shrugged off woe. "Thanks. I do appreciate it but for both our sakes let's pray that doesn't happen. I'd take you and two layers out too if I fall these days."

Ang patted his leg and guided her up. "I've still got plenty of weight over you. There's no time like the present."

Shayne wobbled, a chunk of his hair steadied her. "Shit. Sorry."

Ang shrieked, squeezed her thigh and hissed. "It's okay. I wanted a haircut."

Again my humungous weight is a burden. Geez. Embarrassing.

Shayne picked a path of least resistance, dirt clumps plonked onto her head. "What the…?"

Fuzzy-Wuzzy hit the three quarter mark and reached for the next rock ledge. "Don't come up until I make sure it's safe. It's harder than it looks."

That's kind of nice. Maybe he isn't such an Ahole after all.

Shayne cleared her eyes. "Thank you. Good idea. Appreciate it."

An Elder dropped demons four levels above, they headed for Lion-Guard.

Shayne's heart skipped, she clutched her chest. "Hey, shit. Look out."

Fuzzy-Wuzzy looked down not up, two demons clunked into him, he lost grip. "No, no, no, no."

He groped at rock, it crumbled, his grip failed, the sword slipped from its sheath.

Do something woman. Don't watch him fall and die first or lose the sword.

Shayne surrounded him plus the sword in a bubble. "Try to relax. It won't hurt you. I'll take you to the top."

Ang came up behind and scared her. "Can you do that for us too?"

Oh my fucking God. Like I needed that. Not.

The spots on Shayne's skin returned, her energy lagged. "Not if I want to make it anywhere else. I'll try something else."

Fuzzy-Wuzzy flailed and recoiled off objects. "I don't like this."

Shayne drifted him away from the wall and up. "Yeah, well, we all have problems. This is like fucking life and death Jenga."

Ang climbed around and beside her. "There's always a catch with this god stuff isn't there?"

Don't focus on how high it is and how far away the top is. Just go and do it.

Shayne's brain ached, her control wavered. "Yep. Just shh for a—"

Metres from the next level, blonde hair and orange skin distracted Shayne. "Shit. Izzy."

The bubble burst, the sword and Lion-Guard dropped like all Shayne's dreams.

Ang leaned over the edge. "Eyron? Eyron? Damn it."

Shayne rested against the wall and fried scrambled wits. "Shit, shit, shit, shit, fuck. Passion fingers here fuck's everything she touches. Hey, Fuzzy-Wuzzy?"

The sword shimmered two levels down, near the well of souls. Creatures, demons and debris obscured the way.

Izzy waved and cupped her hands, her words dulled. "Shayne, thank the Gods. I'll come to you."

My faith in you Enki is restored. Thank you.

Shayne flipped her away. "No, stay there and hide, I'm coming to you. All right?"

Ang peered over her shoulder. "She's the kid you mentioned. How'd she survive this long?"

Fatigue weighed Shayne's back, her fingers swelled. "I'm guessing whatever terrifies The Elders and Enlil about her kept her safe. Which is good because those guys are probably our only weapon of consequence against them."

Izzy's concern resonated across the cavern. "Please be safe. I'll pray for you."

Shayne motioned forwards. "Yeah, yeah. Go kid. Catch you soon."

Ang rolled his neck and sighed. "So, sword then, Eyron?"

The Elder stomped the edge of the wall.

Crack, crack, crack.

Shayne's hand and foot ledges collapsed; a dirt slide hurtled Shayne two levels down and into the ground.

Dirt filled her mouth, panic choked her pleas. "Dhddd."

Chapter 43: Plain out of flarks
Gamede

Humankind's familial history oft showed blood relatives provided comfort, love and support to each other. For Annu's godly alternative, they delivered pain, devastation and death. No fluffy toys, hugs or good wishes waited for him this visit.

Our first father son getting to know you session's been considerably taxing. First impressions were definitely right, he's exactly who everyone thinks he is. I cannot let my guard slip even when he's vulnerable. Which has been the entire time thus far.

Fingers swiped at Enlil and scooped up piles of dirt. "Your time's up nephew."

Enlil crawled towards Annu, terror heavier his expression. "Fuck, it's Taturus. Son, please, save me."

Nothing like testing a faulty relationship early on.

Annu grabbed Enlil and zipped the other way. "Here we go."

The souls of loved ones dangled over a literal pit.

Enlil clutched handfuls of Annu's jacket, his breath laboured. "Thank you, thank you, thank you. You won't regret this."

Combined foul body odour soured the close experience.

We both could use a few showers and less close contact.

Several kilometres from Taturus, Annu turned down an alley and deposited Enlil against a wall.

Cuts, scrapes and deeper wounds painted Enlil. "What the fuck was that? Warn me before you do that again."

Patricide licked Annu's soles. "Not likely. Don't get comfortable. He'll find us any second. What are their weaknesses?"

Dogs howled, demons roared, souls screamed. The entire place replicated all Annu's worst boyhood nightmares.

Annu rattled Enlil by the shoulders. "What…are…their…weaknesses?"

Red spit dribbled down Enlil's chin, his eyes wept. "There's an unprotected patch behind their left ear which connects with their power. It must be pierced with a, or the, sword. The level of force determines if they die or are under your control. When five are disabled the others surrender. They must be incarcerated before the ascension as there's no controlling them after. There's ancient, powerful chains hidden in the portal room to restrain them with."

I knew it wouldn't be easy. It never is. I may as well accept that fact now.

Around the corner, Annu's pulse matched his heart rate. "Right. Sounds easy. Piece of cake. One question, how the flark do I get up there?"

Taturus headed for them, each step covered great distance. "There's nowhere to hide we won't find you, Son of Enlil. You're all owed your dues but Enlil's first."

Three Elders climbed the gateway from hell to heaven's first level; light beings flew around the opening and blasted weapons.

The whereabouts of the others remained unknown.

"Shay, I hate to rush you but what's the ETA on you and the sword of destiny? Situation's normal, totally flarked up and I need it like you need chocolate."

Annu considered surrender and mental breakdown. "For Flark's sake. Where're the others?"

Despite being in the same place with combined powers, Annu and his family members scattered the realm with risk of dismemberment.

"Zeke, I'm okay and the crevice didn't get us. I'm sorry things are screwed up between us right now but it's my fault not yours. Listen, the Elders are looking for you us too. Hide if you aren't already. I love you and I'm proud of you."

Enlil's eyes closed, his tongue swelled. "You'll find out soon enough. If the Elders are after you, they won't stop until you're dead. You best have a well thought out plan in place like I did or it's your fault if we die."

Surely punching his face in won't kill him? Right?

Doubt twisted Annu's intestines; he punched the wall beside Enlil. "Don't kid yourself. This is all on you not me. I don't suppose you'll share how you managed it. Did you climb them one by one using your favourite sword?"

Enlil's sneer hinted at the darkness beneath. "Foolish boy. This isn't a game. You've no idea what Gods you're playing with. They're the main reason I created Ralf. Even though the sword destroys Ralf, he's able to wield it and be around the Igigi without side effects. I also created a number of demons specifically to distract them. Which I clearly cannot do now."

Paternal disappointment assaulted Annu, he bunched Enlil's shirt. "That's completely unhelpful. Flarker, before you get too cocky, this entire situation and place exists from your arrogance and stupidity. You succeeded at nothing more than making a miserable place to wallow in."

Fire shrank in Enlil's eyes, he pushed Annu. "You've no right judging me in Godly matters. Look where all your power and righteousness have gotten you. Thus far when things have gotten out of hand it's been because of your lack of attention. You've reacted to such events with no control and forethought. Your own arrogance in fact, thinking you were in control and your actions had no consequences bought you here where you'll be punished for eternity too."

Annu's bones cooled, his flames dwindled. "I came here because you flarking told me you had Shayne. That's the only reason."

Enlil molded smug like clay. "And what's the lie you told yourself for keeping my identity secret after you'd found out and smashed the mirror so Shayne couldn't see me in the portal room? You're like me; you just don't know it yet."

The bastard is right. Why didn't I just tell Shay the truth from the start? What if even after I've done the right things, been the right person and god I still end up like him? No, hang on. It's not over yet and I'm not giving into the evil within.

Annu smashed Enlil's handmade pot. "I'm nothing like you. When this ends only one of us is making it out of here."

The ground vibrated, the building shook, the roof lifted and divine light streamed in.

Enlil's Adam's apple jiggled. "Prove it."

A peripheral orange glow preceded a new face. "Surprise."

Annu clutched Enlil and shot into the air. "Crap, shit, flark. That didn't take long."

Surprise plastered the Elder, it jumped. "You get back here."

Annu flew behind the castle, his butt hole puckered, an ulcer burned in his gut. "All this shock isn't good for my general well being."

Enlil slumped against Annu's chest. "I thought I asked you to warn me next time."

The Elder followed and almost kept pace, it yelled over its shoulder. "Taurus, Artison, here."

Annu rose to the sky's limit and circled. "Yeah, you did but the answer was no."

In a few breaths, Annu's lungs adapted to thicker air.

Enlil wriggled, his breath stank. "Why are we just hovering?"

The Elder streamed lava from its fingers. "This is adding to the degree of torture you'll suffer soon, Son of Enlil. Give him up and we'll ease off on you."

The key to ending this is Ralf. With him dead and ascension off the table, everyone calms the flark down. Except us.

The flow stopped short of Annu's heels, he lifted his legs and drifted sideways. "Because, jack arse, I'm looking for someplace to hide to get my shit together and kill these bastards."

Taurus and another Elder joined their friend.

"Ah, Shay. Any moment now would be great. I'm out of options."

Zeke ran past the dilapidated buildings, they'd left.

Annu's blood pressure lapped his pulse. "Ah, shit."

Taurus followed Annu's line of sight and turned.

Annu's hope folded into an origami swan and burst into flames. "Shit, flark, shit, flark. Things get even more challenging."

"Shay, for flark's sake. Answer me, are you all right?"

Death for real pursued Shayne like after Christmas extra kilos. She clawed, raked and dug upwards. "Bmdmdmd."

Air, air, air, air. I can't breathe. Oh gods. Oh gods. Oh gods.

No baby movement elevated Shayne's anxiety to stellar.

Muck imbedded in her nails, the ends of her fingers shredded.

Keep going, I'm nearly at the surface. I'll be all right. All this will be a forgotten nightmare.

Terror burned her lungs, Shayne spat and breathed more dirt. "Ddoind."

"Shay? For God's sake woman, answer me."

I'm not close; I'm still too far away. I'm going to die in this fucked up way. Why didn't I watch the second Kill Bill movie more?

Layers of bone fragments, squishy things and bugs fought Shayne's determination.

Shayne's diaphragm compressed and spasmed. "Ddohdn."

Tears muddied her cheeks, fatigue weakened her progress.

Enki, please, help, help, help. God Fuckshit, you save me too.

Snot blocked her nose and dribbled down her throat.

Panic wrestled Shayne in a cage; something sharp sliced the top off a finger, her nerve endings fired.

I'll die in a ready-made grave. There's no way out and no more people willing to sacrifice themselves to save me. Fuck it. I wish I wasn't such an arsehole most of the time and I didn't whine about everything. For Fuck's sake. I'm giving up again which is my usual solution to things.

Shayne twisted panic's nipples, kneed it in the groin and clawed.

"Annu, I'm buried alive and suffocating. Help."

Shayne's shoulder knotted and spasmed down her flank.

A lifetime of bad decisions and empty promises lessened her confidence in destiny.

"Holy flarking Enki woman. Why didn't you say so? Where are you?"

Relief loosened death's mental embrace.

"That's a really good question and I should have thought about it. A few levels down under a fuck load of dirt. So hurry. Please."

Shayne's reserves wrote an IOU, she tunnelled around her head.

"I'm coming. Hang—"

Creepy crawlies wriggled a path in the dirt and brushed her hand, Shayne recoiled.

"Hang what? Hurry."

Time dragged, her movements staggered, Shayne's heart beats slowed.

Images of dead, decayed and rotted bodies soured her mind; a copper taste overwhelmed her.

"Honey, are you there? I'm scared."

Bony fingers tickled her spine and ruined faith.

I hate this and nothing's working. Useless will kill me, I probably deserve it. I'm a waste of space, the best thing I can do for the universe is let go. They need a worthy goddess.

Shayne stopped digging, responsibility sloughed off, acceptance delivered peace. Pain and fatigue eased, an invisible force hugged her.

The babies wriggled and refocused Shayne, guilt flushed her chest.

I'm doing it again. Damn it. I always give up. I have faith when I want it but I never truly surrender to it. All the faith I have in the bad succeeding, I should have in the good succeeding. I'm doing incredible things just not for long enough. As powerful as all the evil fuckers are, we're more so, otherwise the entire creation would be in permanent hell. Maybe I'm not such a dumb arse after all. Maybe-Marge might be right on some things. Still not sad she's dead.

Shayne surged energy outwards.

Whoosh, dirt billowed, shifted and constricted further. Disappointed almost buried determination.

Doesn't matter, it happens. Not giving up.

Shayne scooped harder, the ground rumbled and vibrated, the dirt around her loosened.

I don't care why, it's a win.

Hands blocked trickles of light, grabbed Shayne's and yanked.

Oh thank you Enki. I really mean it. From now on I swear I'll have more respect not just for life in general but cosmically too.

Gratitude dulled muscle pain and boosted Shayne's ascent.

She fell at Fuzzy-Wuzzy's feet and gulped air. "Thank you so fucking much. I take back all the bad things I thought about you and didn't say."

A pile of sliced up demon dogs littered the ground.

Fuzzy-Wuzzy's matted, bloody fur and a bleak demeanour deflated Shayne. "Are you all right? You're lucky I saw where you fell."

The poor bastard had to fight to save me. Hey, where the fuck's Annu?

Shayne finger scooped removed dirt from her mouth. "Not at all and I don't think I ever will be again. We totally should have our own reality show. Not that I'm ungrateful but what took you so long?"

Fuzzy-Fuzzy lifted and steadied Shayne. "That's a yes then. You were pretty far down," he motioned to the dog bits, "and they slowed me."

The mental hospital on their right regressed Shayne to childhood, pee dribbled down her leg. "For fuck's sake. I want my Mummy. If I had a live one."

Decomposed patients staggered and moaned, random limbs fell. Shayne's reality fractured, her brain fuzzed.

Lion-Guard gestured, his words dulled. "Shayne? Hello?

Demonic hyenas guarded the hospital grounds. A renewed Nurse Rye and Doctor Unders talked in the middle.

Remember good's as strong. Right? Right? Fuck going back there again. It needs burning for starters.

Fuzzy-Wuzzy waved and shook Shayne. "Hello. Did you leave your brain in the dirt? Now isn't the time to lose what little there is."

Shayne stroked his fuzzy arm, her crazy eased. "You're funny. Not. Hey, if you don't already, you should totally touch yourself when you're stressed out. You're like a big teddy bear and rather comforting."

Oh that came out weird. I never had a teddy bear, it's not too late.

Fuzzy-Wuzzy flicked her off and cleared his throat. "Woman, when this is over, it would be my greatest pleasure to never see or speak to you again."

Shayne filed offence in the drawer above his moods. "Right back at you. So, cranky pants, where's the sword? Or Annu? Or Ang? Or Izzy? I'm ready to finish this shit. Our only objective is to ensure no one fucking ascends. The rest we'll try fixing after."

Where is Annu? Why didn't he save me and why did he stop talking? Is he in trouble again?

Fuzzy-Wuzzy pointed to the hospital. "I dropped the sword on the way down in there and I haven't been able to get past those dog things to retrieve it. I've not seen Ang nor the Igigi you described. Time's running out."

Bad luck dictated Shayne's existence; she picked clods from her hair. "Of course it did and of course it is. Well, your comforting side's gone. You know, I'm the one who should be pissy here. My future husband's the fucking anti-Christ and his son is the anti-anti—"

A massive orange leg tore through the fourth levels sky and obliterated the mental hospital. The other foot landed metres away.

Shayne's luck worm turned. "Oh shit. I forgot about those fuckers. They have some good points after all."

Fuzzy-Wuzzy yelped and led Shayne back. "If you keep this up I'll end our non friendship sooner than I first thought."

"I'm fine with that."

Chapter 45: Well that's flarked it
Gamede

Everything in sight burned, smoked and smouldered.

"Shay, if you're okay, get up here with that flarking sword. This shit's getting out of hand."

Annu flung black holes, wormholes and arseholes at Tarturus, all dissolved on impact. "Well this is shit. I'm getting nowhere. Nothing works. Everything I do enhances him and drains me. I can't stop one and there's eight more. Zeke, for flark's sake get out of here."

Everywhere I flarking look there are problems and no solutions. Time to make some.

"Ah, working on it. About time you answered me. I was worried and you could say please. It's not like I'm having a good time either."

Heat from Tarturus sucked moisture from the air, tension crackled.

Annu's eye twitched, his brain farted. *"Please."*

Zeke darted between Tarturus's legs and thrust plasma. "No. They're taking you to the portal because you didn't listen to me."

Shame niggled Annu's arrogance. "Don't keep reminding me. This is mine to deal with, get away and save yourself."

Tarturus swiped Zeke, Enlil swung inert in his free hand. "Pitiful child. You cannot hurt me. I, however, can and will hurt you and you'll suffer incredibly in the few seconds you'll live."

Our familial last name should be Clusterflark.

Zeke hovered off the ground and blasted plasma. "Yeah, you were all trapped until like five minutes ago. The odds are we'll make it happen again so enjoy it while you can."

Annu's ears rang, he zipped and sapped around the elder's head. "Leave him alone you bastard. Listen, Zeke, quit being stubborn and hide. I've got this covered."

The sweet spot of destruction on Tarturus' neck flashed past, two more Elders approached.

Zeke plasma lassoed Tarturus's legs. "I don't need your self-preserving help. You're screwing things up. You, go hide or whatever. Even with Ralf out of the picture they'll destroy heaven and I won't let them."

Tarturus split it in one step, leaned and grabbed at Zeke. "Wretched being, stop these infuriating games. I'll smoosh you regardless."

Zeke slid under his grasp, cockiness fit like a new coat. "Good luck. Others tried and failed. I'll find a way to kill you all."

I admire his tenacity despite it probably causing of his death. Now I wish he'd listen to me.

Annu's paternal guilt built, nothing in his life worked. "For flark's sake. The stress of you risking yourself is worse than planning the wedding."

Zeke zipped around Tarturus's ankle in a blue haze.

Tarturus clomped and clapped. "Arggghhhh."

Annu scooped up Zeke and flew to the sky's limit. "Listen, there's not much time. I could be chopping Ralf's head off yet I'm stopping you getting killed instead."

Zeke struggled out of Annu's hold. "What? Why? Likewise. I might not agree with you but I don't want you dying in the process. Which is delaying me from reaching him first."

This is ridiculous. Why is he so damned stubborn? Don't answer that.

Annu herded and corralled patience. "Son, the other incantation is on Ralf's head."

Zeke drooped, paled and blinked. "That's…oh gods, flarked up. Let's get him then?"

The Divine light increased and widened, the first section of the doorway opened; nothing prohibited entry between lower heaven and hell.

All those innocent souls including my loves ones will perish without our help. I won't let them suffer.

Each progression towards ascension burnt the wick faster, the vice of responsibility tightened.

Annu relished the closeness to Zeke despite the circumstances. "I can't let Enlil die either remember. Or we're double screwed. Find Shayne while I deal with the Ralf part and it's then truly, absolutely no longer a concern. Unless you get the book back from where ever you put it and please don't."

Zeke made space and gripped Annu's arm. "No chance of that. It's safe. You haven't made a dent on him yet?"

Tarturus grew taller and raised his arms. "You'll never escape. It's only a matter of grasp."

Pay attention idiot. I really must work on my multitasking.

Annu drifted across the sky out of reach. "With the sword, the three of us might bring them down once ascensions out of the equation. Ralf's number one."

Zeke's head dropped to his chest. "I'm sorry Da. I've been an arse."

Swat, swat.

Annu hurtled backwards and somersaulted mid air. "What….the…flark…………"

Zeke flew the other way, his shriek trailed. "Da—"

Annu hit solid and slid into Tartarus' hand, lava encapsulated him in a ball. "Oh shit."

I'm tired of constantly fighting hate filled beings.

A broken laugh chilled Annu, the elder's smile stretched. "Finally. I told you I'd get you."

Annu emptied his arsenal, lava remained his prison. "This is flarked."

Tartarus walked to Zeke hunched on the ground. "Boy, I have your father and grandfather. There's nothing left for you but to die with them."

Zeke groaned and clutched his stomach, his arm hung out of position. "Let, let him, let him go."

Damn it kid stop protecting me and save yourself. I'm not losing you for any reason.

Annu's mind exploded, helplessness overwhelmed him. "Zeke for the love of the Gods shut up. Tartarus, leave him be. You've got me and Enlil, you don't need him."

Tarturus shook Annu like a can of paint. "Silence. I'm sick of hearing you."

Blood rushed from his head to his feet. "I know how Shayne's piggy bank feels. Flark. That sucked."

Tarturus loomed over Zeke and poised his fingers as if to flick. "Quiet or I'll do it again. Now boy, I wonder what noises you'll make when your brains squish out your ears."

Annu's guts tipped, fear doubled the nausea. "Jesus, flark, fuck, Zeke. Run."

Zeke's face twisted, he crawled backwards. "I can't, I'm hurt bad."

Tartarus picked Zeke up and swung him. "Not yet you're not."

"Enki, flarking help me now, if you do nothing else save my kid. Or you'll be the one who not just suffers but dies."

Two women elders jogged over and vibrated the ground.

One brushed Tarturus' arm. "Ralf's ordered not to kill them. You're to bring them to the portal instead."

That's something and they'll take me there. But Enlil and Zeke too. Flark. Next idea.

Tartarus straightened and glanced at Zeke. "Isis, Origi, how much longer will we keep this facade?"

What?

The female on the left spoke through gritted teeth. "Until he opens the portal as agreed."

Tartarus' sigh raised Annu. "Incorrect, we only require his head and the medallion. I'm finished playing with him. Though," he glanced at Annu, "I can't kill these three before then."

A stay in their death sentence lowered Annu's blood pressure.

Wait, what medallion?

The female considered Annu and Enlil. "What three? I see only two."

Tarturus raised his empty hand. "No. Not again."

Annu relaxed against the bubble wall. "Yep. That's my boy."

Now to reserve my energy for my escape.

Chapter 46: Arrested development
Second level, Hell

Concern for Annu budged the chip on Zeke's shoulder.

The cut on his chest seeped, he removed one of Isaac's leftover barbs. "As far as anyone else knows, I got away from Isaac on purpose not because of a horde of deserting creatures."

Said father's capture conflicted with duty. Ralf's skull likewise blew holes in the comfort the Lexicon's safety supplied and Zeke's faith in success.

My plan's gone to shit. I can't take much more. Maybe I'm not half the man I thought. I want to go home. Back to sleeping late, pimples and crushes on girls. Nothing scarier than a few rums and laughs with friends.

A safe distance from victimless torture chambers, implements best not left to the imagination covered most of the immediate area.

Loneliness warped Zeke's mind, his echo amplified solitude. "I'm about over narrow escapes. The flarker nearly got me as well as Annu. How the flark did he manage that to start with? Which, let's face it, doesn't bode well for me long term. For now, I'm free in one sense but I can't save everyone at once."

Blood faded on surfaces like the pieces of his previous existence. An irate desperation underwrote Zeke's past, present and future. The more he ran from it, the closer it got.

Zeke limped past disposed bodies and rested against an unlit fire pit. "Aside from Shayne I'm all that's left to fight. If she's even alive. Oh Gods, what if she and the babies are dead already? They didn't deserve any of this either. I never got to know them or be a big brother."

Anguish ripped Zeke to mental pieces. A dislocated arm dangled, a deep wound on his side, cuts, bumps and bruises covered the physical side.

All combined, the injuries delivered a brutal reality.

Fires raged in the distance and self confidence waned.

Despite Shayne and Annu's flaws no matter what they don't quit. If I learn and take anything from them, let it be that.

Zeke's thoughts muddied, his throat dried. "This makes everything worse. What the flark do I do? There's no one to ask or tell me what's right."

Demonic dogs howled and barrelled past the pits.

Slouched onto his side, hot needles jabbed Zeke's ribs and jabbed his shoulder joint. "Shit, shit, shit. I need a drink or several."

The temperature soared, the air thickened.

A twinkle of peace lightened Zeke. "I won't give up just because it's hard and I might die. That's the righteous thing to do. Enough of this bullshit. Stop wasting time and get to it or fail at great cost. This is what being a Demigod and man is about too. Ma didn't raise a quitter."

Fresh focus and adrenaline cleared some confusion.

I've got this. I believe in myself and my abilities.

Layers of defeat dropped from Zeke, he clutched the source of power and channelled it outwards.

Zeke's shoulder raised and cracked into place, the side wound sealed, the others lessened.

Brown spots on his skin and an energy lag remained. "What are they from?"

Do I want to know? Is it relevant?

Zeke slapped his leg and followed a different path out of chamber. "Annu will be okay for now. I don't require the sword to kill Ralf and he's the biggest threat. Wish I'd practiced with my powers more before now but never mind. I'll get to the castle first arrive and ambush Ralf. I should gain control of the Elders at the same time. Then I'll go from there. All set."

Wait, I best destroy Ralf's head in the process for extra insurance.

Bones cracked under his feet; Zeke entered a dead forest near the Well of Souls.

Elders protected the castle kilometres away on the other side.

The hair on Zeke's nape rose. "If only I flew or turned invisible."

One of Enlil's bombshells slammed Zeke, his heart pounded, doubt returned. "Flark, flark, flark. It doesn't matter what I do if Da or Enlil die in the meantime." *Don't think about that. Keep going. Over thinking brings more problems.* "What a flarked up family we are. This isn't a realm I'd want to live in."

I want out of here and the sooner the better. I never wanted any of this to start with.

Faceless demons with exaggerated movements and terrified expressions stumbled down a road. Decay, desolation and hunger saturated the air.

Zeke's aura half erupted, he veered and jogged in time with his heartbeat. "It's not good when evil is scared. I'll have nightmares for months."

The creatures passed and left a trail of foul goop. Divine light strengthened, protection around the Well of Souls flickered and failed; all external entrances to hell and heaven closed.

An Elder smashed into the well's side and scattered souls.

The light being's screams above shattered Zeke. "You flarking bastard. Stop that."

Zeke's sped through trees, branches scratched his arms.

The Elder collected some souls and threw them into Gamede; the light being's descended further into the darkness.

I'm too—

A solid force struck Zeke's back and hurtled him forwards.

Rock smashed Zeke's nose, his bottom teeth pierced his lip, and blood filled his mouth. "Whdfge?"

Crack, crack, crack.

Zeke's ribs crunched, his breath drew, his vision blurred. "You mother flarker."

Get up before it kills you, stupid.

Isaac wavered, blood dripped from a solid steel mace in his left hand. "I bet you thought you were free and clear. You're wrong again and the perfect present to give Ralf in return for my freedom."

The side of Isaac's head remained caved in where Zeke struck him earlier.

Panic chomped Zeke in two bites. "No, no, no. For flark's sake."

Isaac's grin emptied Zeke's hope. "Yes, yes, yes and time's a wasting."

It's all been for nothing.

Chapter 47: Never kid a kidder

Gamede

The castle in view righted all the wrongs and elevated Enlil to hopeful. He closed his eyes and groaned at intervals.

All the muck ups and being almost human will be worth it if my son and grandson don't ruin things for me.

In their merged bubble, Annu's persistence deterred joy, a physical symbol of Enlil's lone weakness and greatest regret. "Why did he mention a medallion? What aren't you telling me now? Flark."

Enlil lolled his head and dribbled. "I, I, I don't, know where are we?"

Annu shook his shoulder, flames singed through his shirt. "Yeah right. Like I'd believe you. Answer me flark arse."

Enlil eyes opened, he clenched, and pain threatened his facade. "It's, no, use, wasting….energy."

Annu squinted and shifted aside, he seeped ire. "You better pray he doesn't find Zeke. Flark. There's a way out, I know there is. I thought this was my bad luck but I'm pretty sure this is all because of you. You're a magnet for flarked up shit."

This is might be harder than I thought. For the love of me. Why does anyone want children? Does Annu have an off switch? Or anything similar and where is it?

Enlil embraced control, hidden knowledge enabled success. "You know nothing about me. I'd worry about yourself."

Annu engulfed, a wave of energy drove them apart. "I'm not doing this. Get us out of here."

The bubble's temperature soared, moisture and air evaporated.

Enlil's body cracked and crunched, he blistered. "Heck. Stop, you're killing me."

Tartarus opened his hand and smacked the top. "Enough. Tell the boy to come out."

Light closed Enlil's eyes, burned skin tightened and cracked. "Please just fucking do it. I can't take anymore. I'll die."

I really can't. Damn this feeble form. Ah yes, it already is.

Annu's stubbornness knew no bounds. "No. Go flark yourself. If you want him you find him."

Cold over rode heat, shivers induced further pain.

Enlil clung to determination like a mother does a child. "For alhalso's sake. Think about what you're doing."

Ralf's call of return to the Elders and the higher bell's kicked in Enlil's last efforts.

Tarturus huffed cold air and closed his hand. "He'll pay for your arrogance too."

Pain dulled, the shivers eased, awareness drifted. "I, I, I, don't feel right. What's happening to me?"

I must hold on longer but it's so hard. I'm close and Annu's slipping it out of my control.

Annu frowned and examined Enlil's leg. "All right. That one's scared and you're hurt badly. You probably don't deserve this but it's more about me than you. Not that you'll understand that either."

Purple energy entered Enlil, absorption cleared the bodily upheaval.

Two by two, Enlil's injuries healed, his disposition repositioned. "I didn't know you could do that. I no longer wish to tear myself apart."

Annu clicked his tongue and rolled his eyes, he removed his hand. "You're as dramatic as Shayne. Though that's where the similarities end. I want to kill her way less than you."

A strange sensation overwhelmed Enlil, he neither wanted to kill nor maim Annu. Feelings of hatred found temporary respite.

Warmth filled his heart, the shell around it fractured. "What's happening now? Am I dying? What did you do to me?"

Annu's smirk confused Enlil, his scoffed tripled it. "Nothing's wrong with you. It's another human emotion for you to freak out about, gratitude. People usually say—"

The world dropped from under them, Enlil tumbled in air.

Tarturus stumbled backwards. "Not you lot too."

Ground approached, Enlil flailed and readied for impact. "Help, help, help."

All that planning for—

Arms scooped Enlil from beneath and upwards. The search for redemption stalled.

Enlil's heart beat hurt his chest, he clutched Annu. "What took you so long? What happened?"

Elders' legs blocked the view and disturbed orientation.

Annu's massive chest expanded. "And you're back to arsehole. No thanks necessary. All in a day's work around here. The big guy dropped us and we're about to find out why."

Enlil stiffened; worms crawled under his skim "Why are you flying so close to him? I have a really bad feeling about this. Get away from them."

If he doesn't capture us again how do I get to the castle away from Annu? The good part of him is stronger than I realised.

Tarturus and two female elders paused on an invisible line.

Annu whipped around the side. "Because anything that scares them is useful. Just, sssh. I'm sick of hearing you."

An urge to jump attacked Enlil, he patted a bald patch. "Listen to me, it's suicide. Go after Ralf instead."

I'm getting desperate here and I despite that.

Annu landed before the Elders and near a female Igigi. "Hi, you must be Izzy."

Enlil ducked behind Annu away from both foes. "Oh salmu. This is cruel."

The female relaxed, her smile radiated. "Thank the Gods. Annu, I'm Izzy. I don't like starting off things this way yet I wonder why you've kept the dark one alive considering. I must admit he doesn't exactly look how I thought."

How do I get rid of her? I can't kill her.

The crook of Annu's arm constituted a great peek hole. "Yeah, bit of a technicality with killing him. I'm waiting on Shayne and the sword. Hop on. We'll chat somewhere safer. Face their way and try keep them back on route. "

The bigger picture fell off the wall and shattered Enlil. Pieces of the wood embedded his existence.

This is cruel, cruel, cruel torment. I'm running for it. What are the chances I'll make it there and not get caught a metre away?

Enlil smacked Annu's back and walked two steps. "Ah no. I need this like a hole in the head. And I've enough of those. Not to mention Ralf's getting closer."

The Elders near, Annu's hand on his neck and a well lit sky calculated his odds at zero.

Annu's sigh bumped Enlil, his hold tightened. "Yeah, this is all about you and your terrible time of things. Oh woe is you. Do shut up."

Izzy stood on Annu's foot and encircled his waist. "I've never done this before."

The precessional equinox quickened, each planet's appearance drew his end near.

Enlil shuddered, fresh skin bubbled, his soul twisted. "For alhalso's sake. At least make the torture quick."

Annu peeled Enlil off his back and shot into the sky. "Yeah, yeah, yeah. Not so tough now are you."

Sudden movement dropped Enlil's gut; he vomited in his mouth, their surrounds flashed. "I'm, I'm, I'm, salmo."

Izzy's hand brushed Enlil's, sparks zapped him. "Wow, wow, wow."

Enlil's oomph drained, he clawed and slipped along Annu's side. "Get away from me."

The castle disappeared behind them. Pressure mounted, hilled and peaked.

Annu tipped, clutched his arm and pulled. "Geez you're hard work." He hovered above the forest and faced Izzy. "Sorry this is a quick chat, but for reasons I'll explain later we can't kill flarkface here for now. I'll hide you someplace so you make sure he goes nowhere while I'm busy."

Certain failure crushed Enlil, sweat and snot alternated down his chin. "No way. I'm done with this."

I'm forced to show my hand too early. I pray I don't suffer for doing so.

Chapter 48: Fucklesticks

Hell

The Elder left the sardine-canned mental hospital for not yet, destroyed buildings. A sense of accomplishment lifted Shayne despite lack of involvement.

I've never been happier to see something ruined. Now if it had been the Tax Office I'd be doing star jumps.

Shayne's pace quickened, still babies negated elation. "We better sift through that mess quick smart. Where the fuck did Ang go?"

Fuzzy-Wuzzy smoothed his nose with a paw. "I still don't know. We'll start in the middle where I saw it fall."

Shayne "Good idea. Hey, did I tell you about my magic boobs?"

Fuzzy-Wuzzy dug with front paws or sorted debris. "Will you just look for the sword?"

He has every right being stressed. I'm only trying to lighten the mood.

Fewer scary, supernatural creatures comforted and concerned Shayne. "They disappear when I lie down. Ha. Times are grim. We're on a whim. No time to waste, I'll eat some paste."

Fuzzy-Wuzzy frowned, whiskers twitched. "Please do not sing again. My ears are recovering."

Mmmm. Moving on.

The enormity of the situation pinged Shayne between the eyes, she tossed mush covered bricks. "Fine. It was rap by the way not singing. It only gets shittier from here. Fucking Enlil, the arsehole. This is all his fault. I've said this before and I'll say it again, this."

Marks on Shayne's skin darkened, lightening struck and fractured the Well of Souls.

Shayne's focus split, her soul wept. "If this keeps up my Nan, Pa, Just Sally, Irica and kazillions of others are in danger. That shouldn't happen when you're already dead. We can't let them suffer anymore."

I love you all so much. I promise we'll make things right no matter what it takes. I'll make sure you won't have a reason to yell at me next time we see each other.

Fuzzy-Wuzzy rested on his haunches and extracted the sword's hilt. "Yes. I've got it."

Relief eased Shayne's internal anguish. "Fuck yeah. About time something went right. Let's do this."

Fuzzy-Wuzzy retrieved half a sword, he slumped on his butt. "Oh for poop's sake." He placed it besides him, delved in and removed three separate pieces. "This is not good. Not good at all. It's a disaster. I must stop hanging around you."

The air stilled, continued bad luck had no place in their live future.

All right. More time and help is needed. One hurdle over, another one appears in its place.

Panic fought faith, Shayne shallow breathed. "You almost swore. Things must be bad. The sword will be fine. I'm sure it will still work. Let's not lose our shit yet. Right. Okay. Please. Fuck."

A doom cloud covered Fuzzy-Wuzzy, he gathered the pieces. "Which part of that's not good sounded like it would? To be perfectly clear, no, it will not work unless all together. As originally intended."

Shit, shit, shit, shit, shit. And shit.

Panic won round one, went back for seconds and tagged devastation.

Shayne held the pieces together. "Fuck, fuck, fuck. This thing was vital. Enki if you dump us in a world of shit the least you could do is give us the means to solve it. Aside from my dumb arse. Is there any glue? What if we hold it like this? Or this? They may not notice."

Fuzzy-Wuzzy nuzzled Shayne's shoulder and purred. "Sometimes situations get worse before better. It's always darkest before the dawn. Which is why we rely on faith. In fact, it's so strong that it's the only reason I'd sit next to you anywhere."

I'm focusing on the kindness and not the jab.

Hope sat beside confidence on a high shelf.

Shayne stood on tip toes and reached. "Sometime's life is a box of chocolates fate replaced with laxatives and you're out of toilet paper. But I appreciate the sentiment. Looks like I better find some newspaper."

A dark, lonely, endless void consumed them if they failed.

Fuzzy-Wuzzy's nuzzling ceased, the purr died. "I have no idea what you're talking about half the time. Come on, if we can't stop this, we can do a shit load of damage in the meantime."

I'm starting to like him again. Now how do I tell my loving fiancé our chance at success is a kid's toy?

Shayne smoothed her tongue over her teeth and gagged. "Jesus fucking Christ. Someone get me a toothbrush stat. Wait, maybe bad breath will knock someone out."

A whip cracked, her hair rose, her skin prickled.

Fuzzy-Wuzzy inspected a triangle of light. "What's that?"

Flashes blinded Shayne's dark adjusted eyes. "Ah ow. Shit."

Crack, crack, thump.

A dozen bodies tumbled from air and landed metres away.

Shayne clutched her belly, her aura protective engaged. "Who the fuck are these lot?"

Fuzzy-Wuzzy's hiss flattened her arm hair, his ears pricked. "Be ready."

In the middle of orange people, Ryan assisted Erin onto her feet. "Thank goodness. We had no idea where we'd end up or if we'd have to look for you."

Shayne sucked her bottom lip. "I guess you found the Igigi then. I'd hoped in a way you wouldn't and stayed there."

Erin tutted, frowned and brushed herself off. "I told you I had that covered. I can control my powers."

I'm glad and sad at the same time. Nice to see they listen to me. Not.

Erin's tattered clothes suggested a rough time on Marduk in her absence. "You're not alone there. After you left everything went crazy. It felt like it forever and we barely made it."

Peaked didn't become Ryan. "For once in her life she's not exaggerating. This is the second planet in like two days and neither have been fun. Wait until you hear the shit we've seen and experienced." He faced the group behind him. "Follow us, stay close."

Responsibility curdled concern; Shayne fumbled the sword pieces like rosary beads. "Fuck. Okay then. Welcome to hell, please stay behind me in an orderly fashion."

Erin raised panic to new heights, she hyperventilated. "Shit mum. Are you serious? How did you manage to break it? What will you do now?"

Be strong and confident. It will rub off.

Ryan's eyes watered, a childhood facial tic returned. "Please tell me you've got something up your sleeve? Mum? Please?"

Fuzzy-Wuzzy pounced off on all fours towards an opening up to the next levels. "I'll do this myself."

A metre on and pain swept across Shayne's lower back, a nerve pinched. "This is sort of like Donkey Kong. Of course I have another plan."

I'm not showing I'm hurting. There are bigger problems.

Shayne drifted above it and soldiered on. "I do not, in any way shape or form have another clue. Not that I had one to start off with, which is why I had put all our hope on the sword doing the job. So we're probably, actually, definitely fucked. But I'll keep that to myself for now too."

Erin missed a step, she slapped her thigh. "Ah, Mum, do you realise you just said that out loud. Are things really that bad?"

Ryan halved his pace, he glanced behind him. "I've changed my mind. Send us home."

The Igigi walked close together, they lacked Izzy's pizazz.

Fate denied Shayne's request for a Mental Health Day. "Fuck. Sorry, no can do. I'll do everything I can to protect you all but I need your help too. Strap yourself in. It's gonna get rough like the pointy end of a pineapple shoved up your arse."

A mental cloud shifted across Shayne's third eye, images flashed, Zeke commanded a demon army from a fiery throne with a blazed crown on his head, Annu healed hurt light beings, dark creatures attacked beings in heaven, a doctor injected a substance into a frantic Enlil restrained to a hospital bed and Shayne nursed two babies alone, crying in their bedroom.

Shayne's mind calmed, reality reformed around her. "Holy fucking shit."

Chapter 49: Repent or die
Highest level of misery

In an abandoned building in a dead forest behind castle, this mission took the cake, shop, and whole bakery.

Frustrated pie tasted like arse, Annu juggled physical and mental demands. "Sit down and shut up. This is what's happening. Build a bridge and get over it."

"Shay, calm down. I'm not dying to even go to Heaven and I'll kill Ralf without the sword. Plus, I've got Enlil covered for the moment. Sometimes your visions are screwy and given where we are you're likely seeing the worst case scenario. Anyway, see you soon. All right?"

Enlil pouted on the opposite side to Izzy. "I'm an all mighty, powerful deity, not a child requiring babysitting. You're a cruel man. No one taught you any respect."

"That's easier said than done given the situation we're in. It's fucked. I'm ecstatic Izzy is okay but I'm pissed you don't even want the stupid, piece of shit sword anymore after the trouble its caused."

Izzy flounced into the middle of the room. "Not at the moment you're not. You're almost human and this is what you deserve. This is your recompense for all the suffering and pain you've inflicted."

She's a feisty one I'll give her that and it's a bonus.

"Yes, my love. It's very frustrating. Hang in there; all our problems are nearly over. Chat when you get here.

Enlil part climbed the wall, sores marked his arms. "Enki only created you to taunt me. You have no value of your own."

Izzy the mouse versus Enlil the elephant.

Annu soaked in discomfort. "Someone's getting testy. Is it nap time?"

Izzy's eyes blazed, she nibbled Enlil's cheese and her nails. "I swear I'll do all in my power to keep him in my sight. Be safe and please, please come get me if you need."

Enlil scratched scabs his arms, blood coloured his nails. "Wait, take me. I beg of you."

Perhaps the growing human side of him will allow a fresh perspective but it's possible I'm completely deluded.

Annu's skull tightened, reluctance plastered him to the door frame. "Ah, no. You're a persistent flark. Anyway, I'm off. Have fun."

"I'll believe that when I see it."

"It'll happen. It always does."

I can switch a communicator off when I've had enough of talking on it. What the flark do I do here? It's a lose-lose situation.

Annu slammed and welded the door. "All-righty then. Next flark up."

Light struck the penultimate planet, a hole in time's essence increased. Elders milled lined the outer walls, light focused on the castle's middle.

"I guess I know where the portal is without looking for it."

Annu across the forest and onto a tree top. "Another few of Izzy and some time would have been handy. How do I get in unseen?"

Enlil's creatures searched for something in the inner courtyard oblivious to all else.

On the next branch, leaves and sticks rained. "What are they—?"

Shayne buzzed like an alarm clock. *"Oh my fucking God. I just realised something. When you kill Ralf don't destroy his head."*

Two Elders removed the castle's roof and tossed it.

Nothing like a few renovations before a big event.

Annu wiped grit from his eyes. *"Why?"*

"Because we can use it to get out just like everyone else. There's nothing stopping us. Well actually there's a lot stopping us right now, but you know what I mean."

Renewed hope raised Annu, he banged his head. *"Holy shit woman. You're right. This is why I love you."*

"Really? I thought they'd be more reasons."

Here we go again. Another epic conversation.

"Of course there is."

A bump induced an epiphany. "I never actually have faith in us or anything else. When things go wrong I blame Enki, I don't thank him. Nor do I believe in myself. I haven't embraced any part of me or changes. Arrogance and self-obsession almost lost me the family I wanted. I have been foolish and there's no better time than now to change."

A female peered over a wall. "Have you found Ralf?"

Annu's verve swerved and crashed. "That sounds like another complication."

A bird creature flapped its beak. "We don't know where or when he's gone."

The elder snapped the creature's neck and yelled. "Keep looking until you find him."

Annu burned finger prints into the trunk. "No point panicking. This is good. Sort of. Maybe."

"Shay, Ralf's not here. We better find him before they do."

"Oh fuck it. All right."

Two male elders, one held a flaming sword; the other a mace patrolled the grounds.

I'm definitely, absolutely done with nasty surprises and dramatic flair.

Annu stepped along the limb, unease desecrated former peace of mind. "Where'd he go? Enlil can't be involved and we're not. So? Flark it. I can't be sure with him. Shit."

A red arm thumped the tree, flocks of birds swamped Annu.

The female elder popped between them. "You're nothing but trouble. Return Ralf and Enlil at once or you and yours shall to your last breaths."

I'm sick of hearing that. Can't people just be nice?

Annu flew backwards, extracted power from her and returned it tenfold. "Sorry, I don't have them."

Her head exploded and reformed. "I do not believe you. Where are they? You're not half the god your father is."

The two male elders destroyed the forest on route to him.

At tree height, Annu bulleted to tree height and unloaded. "Now that's where you're wrong."

The female's upper half melted, the males slowed.

Annu headed for the outbuilding. "Enki, if you're waiting for the last minute to right this sinking ship, it's now. I'm sorry I didn't understand your motives until now. But, I need you and I'm asking for your help. Thank you in advance."

Three orange weapons of destruction lumbered after him.

The door laid on the ground, three walls remained intact, the other blown out.

Time to move and get the lead out of my heels.

Annu burst into the room, desperation oozed between his butt cheeks. "Enlil? Izzy?"

A faint voice behind a fresh bricked enclave relieved some anxiety. "Annu? Is that you? I'm so sorry. He tricked me."

Annu crossed the room and lined up a strike point. "Izzy, it's okay. He's good at that and at least he didn't hurt you. Stand back. I'm taking down the wall."

Izzy's fear wavered his determination. "I'll make this up to you. It appears I too have much to learn."

Annu kicked out bricks for an opening. "It's not your fault. Seriously."

This is my fault whether I like it or not.

Izzy climbed onto the ground, claw scratches on her arms and face surpassed his limits. "Yes it is. I didn't see it coming and I should have. I hope the others get here soon."

"Situation update. There's another issue. Enlil's gone too. Shay, for the love of all things holy, please get up here and help me."

Another planet aligned, the male Elders gave up their pursuit and returned to the castle.

Annu calculated Enlil's overall capabilities. "Enlil, where the flark are you?"

Chapter 50: Shayne: Knicker Twisters
Third level of hell aka Divorce

"Enki, you said you heard if someone prayed down here so I am. First off, is there another, quicker way up to the next level? This is taking forever. Second, surely there's weed in this place and I'm entitled to a quick joint? Also, get us out of this. Please. Stat. Amen and that stuff."

Meters from an opening, Karma kicked arse. Hell hounds chased Rod in their direction. A bruised face, torn flesh, and the lumps Shayne left appeared the least of his problems.

Rod limped like Igor on speed for Shayne. "Help. Someone get them away from me. You've got to help me."

Shayne shifted out of the way. "Fuck no. Couldn't happen to a nicer person. That's poetic justice right there. It's great to know everyone gets what's coming to them. Deluded mother fucker. I should stick my leg out or freeze him in place. That'll teach him."

Fuzzy-Wuzzy's head and mood hung low. "You're so easily distracted."

Shayne gave him the bird and half jogged. "Well, get fucked. We can't all be perfect."

Ryan's high pitch reminded her of his presence. "Dad? Is that you? How did this happen?"

I forgot you guys were right there. I'm such an arsehole.

Guilt slit fun's throat with a razor blade.

Shayne mopped up the blood. "Ah, oh, fuck. Yeah, um. Hang on."

Erin sobbed on her knees and tugged Shayne's pants. "Why is he here? Mum, you have to help him. This is wrong."

Shayne battled right, just, and the desire for revelation of his true self. "He was…It's not. Shit."

Fuck. Give me a break. He deserves so much and then some. More suffering than he inflicted upon me. Argh. Why am I left looking like the bad guy?

A hound removed a chunk from Rod's heel, his screams tuned in her conscience.

Shayne flicked the do-gooder and froze the dogs. "There, he's fine now. It's okay."

A giant millipede burst from the ground, chomped Rod, swallowed and dove back in.

Shayne jabbed at the hole. "Fuck me and call me Dolly. You don't see that shit every day. I sure hope it counts that I did try helping him."

Erin screamed, Ryan wailed and Shayne's vindication dwindled.

Anti-arsehole alert. Come on, not right. I'll celebrate in private.

"Shay, now isn't the time for silence and taking your time."

Shayne patted her cheeks and lead her children around it. "I'm sorry, I temporarily blanked. What just happened to your father is pretty fucked up and I promise we'll deal with it later."

"Sorry, sorry, sorry. in the midst of a traumatising event but we're coming."

Erin plodded, her bottom lip quivered. "It, it, it, it ate him like a lolly. I don't understand why he's here in the first place?"

My spiritual progress apparently dictates I don't tell my kids what their father was truly like even though I want to scream it from the roof tops. My, my, haven't I grown?

Ryan tripped over his tongue, he shallow breathed. "I wish I'd never come. I should have stayed home. Dare I ask what happened to Sally?"

Liquid light from the Well spilt into Hell and disintegrated. The punishment for tardiness this time meant total destruction.

Shayne momentum quickened, her taste buds soured. "Son, I don't blame you and it's a fucked up, strange out of this planet story. In short she wasn't who she said she was."

I never have time for the long version. Not sure I'm sad about that.

Fuzzy-Wuzzy balanced on rocks and gestured up. "Hurry, innocents are being destroyed."

Shayne wrapped her happy in a big, red bow.

At the bottom she faced the kids. "You weren't at our last adventure Ryan so you don't have a comparison but this is bigger, badder, and tougher. It's real danger we may not survive from. In that regard, if something happens to me, promise me both of you will hide. You're smart enough to find a way out."

Erin's tears and hug unravelled Shayne. "Possibly, don't say that. We don't want you to die. Mum, what about the babies? It's not just you to worry about."

Shayne dismissed the fear quiet babies instilled. "You know the drill kids. I've a long way to go but I'm not who I used to be. But I bet you wish I still lay in bed feeling sorry for myself and dodging debt collectors than regularly saving the universe."

The babies are fine. They have to be. Especially if I don't think otherwise.

"Shay, hello? It's hard looking for three people alone and stopping an apocalypse. I'm good but not that good."

"Oh shit. Yes coming."

Sadness filled Ryan's expression, he stiffened. "Sometimes. It was much less stress. Find me a weapon and my powerless self with have a crack at this too."

Shayne wedged her foot in the next slot. "All right but stay towards the back. Trust me; you don't want to be too close to any of the enemy we're up against."

Ryan climbed adjacent and assisted Shayne's lift. "I'll learn fighting before the next mission. I'm sure Ang or someone will teach me. I'm in this for the long haul."

The distance to the top grew centimetre.

Shayne's arm muscles pulled. "You kids adaptability and resilience amazes me. If and that's a big if, there's another one, there'll be rules in place to ensure you're not hurt. With plenty of training in every regard."

Erin's tears dried, compassion softened her. "You're time to shine will come Ryan, no one decorates like you do."

While the location sucks, this time with my kids is amazing. They've shown me how amazing they are and I must give them credit for it.

Ryan embraced new purpose and smiled. "Smart arse. You can lose the bubble wrap now, Mum. I'm a man. Shove over I'll boost you two."

Shayne pushed off Ryan's knee and slotted her foot in. "I'm on the byway to hell, I'm on the byway to hell. That's all the words I know. I'm on the byway to hell."

Erin groaned beneath her. "Mum, we've got to talk about this bad singing you do when you're scared, nervous, um, let's face it any odd moment."

I love you guys so much. We're making real connections together. Although we may die. Let's skip that minor detail shall we?

Ryan's giggle trailed over the rocks. "Yeah, I'm in for that and a set of ear muffs."

Fuzzy-Wuzzy's paws disappeared over the ledge; they had several metres to climb.

Shayne swallowed the urge to die and continued. "Yeah, yeah, you're both hilarious. I know how good I am. You're all jealous."

Fuzzy-Wuzzy's yell killed all levity. "Shayne you better get up here."

Shayne's tongue stuck to the roof of her mouth, her breath caught. "Fucking fuck, what's wrong now?"

It's one thing after another and so on and so forth. And fifth.

Curiosity pushed the rest of the way and sideways over the ledge.

A tall, part decomposed man beat the shit out of Zeke.

Maternal instinct kicked in Shayne, she lunged with frozen hands. "Jesus, fucking Christ. You get off him. "

Chapter 51: Musings of a MadMan
Gamede

The search of castle grounds offered a small, short respite.

"Enlil, you mother flarking, cock sucking, tit licking, twat waffle. You better not do what I know you will."

Annu followed foot prints from the out building through the forest. "My woman's taking too long, da da di da da, I'm glad I'm strong, da da di da da, my father's a dick, we better end this quick, da da di da da."

Izzy weighed no more than a bag of potatoes. "You have a lovely voice much than, ah, never mind. Are you missing Shayne?"

Annu slowed past nooks and crannies, the footsteps got closer together. "If you value your friendship with her, never mention how bad her singing is. Yes, I miss her immensely. Look out for anything resembling a door in the ground or something out of place."

They'd be flark loads of hiding spots here making my task even harder.

Light directed onto the portal, it grew above the castle.

Annu wrote a mental resignation letter. "I hope Shay likes central heating with no thermostat."

As if she'd heard his thought, Shayne tickled his brain. *"I'm here but, well, I found Zeke and he's in quite a mood. No sign of the two fuckface's."*

"Thank flark. Is he okay?"

"Depends on your definition. I'll get back to you."

Annu edged closer to the forest's edge. "Come on. Give me a sign."

Izzy's soft tone didn't ease Annu's tension. "You seem to be somewhere else sometimes. Are you speaking to Shayne in your head?"

The foot prints stopped, Annu blasted clear the area around them. "Yes and occasionally others. It's kind of weird but I'm getting used to it. Most of the time."

No evidence suggested where Enlil or Ralf went.

Izzy encircled his hip, her feet clamped around his ankle. "That must be difficult when you're with other people."

Around and around, nothing stood out. "Yes and occasionally other times."

Like now.

Figures darted between bushes, Annu's senses prickled, and the hairs on his nape rose.

Annu flew around and landed meters away. "Please be someone I want to see."

Izzy dismounted, her hair stood on end. "The way things are going I'm not sure that'll happen."

Blue feathers and familiar faces alleviated concern, Elders within yelling distance redirected it.

Annu smacked himself in the forehead. "Not this time. They're on our side. How do I, oh yeah, duh. Use my brain. Literally."

"Ankor, I'm a few metres on your left on some rocks. Come my way as quiet as possible."

Izzy rested against rocks. "Maybe Enki heard our prayers after all. There's still time and extra man power."

Everything's a matter of perspective. They're all sacrifices in one respect.

Ankor crouched, waved and ushered the others over. "Annu, thank the Gods you're safe however I see it's almost too late."

The group consisted of a handful of lion beings, a few like Ankor, more Igigi and spider creatures.

They're strength is inspiring in light of their mortality is inspiring. They're more than worthy to fight aside me.

Annu gathered them out of antenna reach. "Not sure why you're here but I'm glad you are. Izzy, this is Ankor."

Izzy tipped her head. "Pleased to meet you," and rushed to an older woman. "Mother, you're all right."

Ankor's chest plume fluffed. "Likewise child. Annu, guilts wracked me since we left Enki Island. You're both right, it's easy to sit in a chair and make judgments about other people's lives in no danger yourself. It's also been several days and there's upheaval across the universes. How may we assist you?"

Shit. We've been much longer than we realised. This place screws with you. I better make the rest of my time here worth it.

A few guns remained in the hands of dead, Enlil's creatures.

Annu pointed, he loved delegation. "Gather those over there and anything capable of being a weapon. We're looking for Ralf and Enlil. Do not let either of them near the portal. The only things between us and our goal are massive lava beings, the elders. Do not engage with them. At this stage that's all we're left with."

Ankor removed a small gun from beneath feathers. "Of course. We've also brought some assistance of our own. Tell us where to go."

Ang stumbled from behind trees; deep cuts sliced his side and leg. "I've never been happier to see you, you ugly bastard. What's the plan boss?"

Annu placed Ang on a flat stone and healed the damage. "I'm not fond of seeing you get killed or hurt so knock it off."

Ang tucked his chin, it tripled. "What are you talking about? This is the first time. Well, except that bar fight in the badlands last month. Which was entirely your fault."

Oh yeah. My mistake. Unlike Ankor, he doesn't remember what happened on Earth.

Annu shifted aside and rose. "Yeah, that's what I meant. I didn't intend for he or his wife hearing what I'd said."

Ang bent his knee and patted the former wound. "Holy shit bloke. That's a heck of a trick. Next splinter I get I'm calling you."

Annu's cheeks warmed, he turned away. "Yeah, whatever. Now you can quit playing on it."

He's been a good friend; I hope he lives through this.

"Shay, your favourite feathered friend is here with Ang and more Igigi. Which doesn't mean I still don't need you."

Ankor clucked and pointed to the Castle. "Annu, I don't wish to criticise your time management skills but things are getting completely out of hand."

Annu stacked humility atop of heroism, contrition waited. "Oh, so you noticed all that? You're deceptively perceptive. There are a few other issues but we're on it. All in hand."

Someone's anyway, just not mine at this exact moment. Any second now. You don't need to know the details.

Doubt coveted Ankor's movements and disappeared. "I have faith and believe in you."

A male Elder boomed from the castle grounds. "Rejoice all. They've found Ralf in some tunnels but not the medallion. Our time has come. The portal is almost completely open, get the others ready."

For flark's sake. I knew that medallion was important for something. Flarking Enlil's a sneaky bastard.

The ground rumbled, the Elder's cheered, the sky split into half night, half day.

Ankor's voice raised two octaves. "Oh dear. I'm still having faith. Total faith. Stronger than ever before. Where do you want us to start?"

Annu cracked his knuckles and rolled his neck. "Pray, lots and find both of them. Keep on your toes because things change quick around here. It's a constant mind flark."

Shayne trickled into his brain. *"Annu, my darling and love, I'll be a little late."*

Annu dodged uprooted trees hurtled through the air; they impaled the ground around them. *"That's perfectly fine darling. Everything's peachy here. You take your time okay?"*

Why doesn't she do a bit of sightseeing while she's there. It's fine. Also meet some friends for coffee too.

"I'm going as quick as I can."

"Aha."

Chapter 52: Let's do the knicker-twist again
First level of hell

Shayne shattered the frozen man and checked Zeke. "Are you all right? Who was that arsehole? Thank fuck I found you. We've been so worried. Crap, I should bring a first aid kit with some band aids and shit in it."

Hatred darkened Zeke's eyes, plasma trickled down his arms. "I'm fine and I had everything under control. I don't and didn't need your help. You made me look like an idiot. I'm not a child; I'm a man capable of taking care of myself. It's worked so far."

Ryan joined Shayne's side and linked his arm in hers. "Mum, are you both all right?"

Shayne's goodwill bombed, she patted Ryan's hand. "Yes, it's fine. I'll handle this. Zeke, to me it didn't look like you had it under control and I didn't want to witness my soon-to-be stepson's death. So I stepped in. I'm sorry I ruined your machismo."

How'd I fuck up rescuing him? Ryan was never this irrational. That was always Erin and I.

Zeke winced, placed blue hand over injuries and lessened them. "That's not a surprise coming from a woman who thinks more than two thoughts is crowded. Back off and stay away from me. I already have a mother and I don't need someone who ruins everything she touches."

Oooh, ouch. He's got a smart mouth on him and we need less of those in this outfit.

Shayne stuck tape over the slice on her pride. "Right. I get it; you've had a shit time but don't get your knickers in a twist with me. I'm trying to be your friend not your mother. Come on, your dad's waiting, mate."

Zeke shrugged and snarled. "Do whatever you want and do it away from me."

Shayne's cheeks heated, she withdrew her hand. "Okay. I'm not stopping you. Go for it. Geez."

Erin strode the few steps over and crossed her arms. "Zeke, why are you so angry at us now? We're in this together and we all need help sometimes."

Light beings scooped souls back into heaven, demons did the same.

Fuck, fuck, fuck. Hurry up woman.

Zeke flung around and stomped to the well. "You work it out. Just, flark off leave me alone."

Erin flinched and leaned on Ryan. "If that's what you want. Fine."

Shayne's duties conflicted, she jogged and caught up. "You're going to rebel and chuck a wobbly now of all times? I'm sorry I killed him and you didn't. I know you're capable of doing it, but you should know when you do kill someone you don't feel good afterwards."

Save and except for a few people I've knocked off. They deserved it.

Fuzzy-Wuzzy groaned, he licked his paw and smoothed his muzzle. "Here you go again. You've got five minutes to sort this out and I'm gone."

Shayne's head thudded, her skull tightened. "Family first mother fucker. Jesus, I can't win a trick today."

At the Well, Zeke pushed souls towards light beings. "I said go away. I've got this."

Shayne hugged a stiff side and resisted freezing him. "I'm not giving up on you kid. We're all here for you."

I can't leave him to his own device; he's not in his right mind. Every time I think we understand each other I'm wrong. Is it me? Fuck. I'll consider taking parenting classes when I get home.

Ryan turned her by the shoulder. "Mum, maybe you should leave him alone. He's not listening and you know, remember the main objective."

Demons captured them mid route, their collection increased.

Shayne's cankles blended with her knees into knankles, the belly ache returned. "Perhaps your job is to keep me focused, son. All those mother fuckers will be dead soon anyway."

I can't deal with that too at the moment. I'm barely holding on as it is

A line of souls slipped from Zeke's grasp. "Yeah and what's the point of all this? Nothing we do makes any difference. It's pointless….," the next settled in his hands for a moment as if on purpose, "No. It's not, no. I messed everything up. It's all my fault."

Pain banded Shayne's waist, she ground her teeth. "Zeke, who is it? Talk to me."

He's not listening. What else do I try?

Blue plasma sparked from Zeke, an invisible string pulled the soul up. "No, no, no, no, no. Come back."

Shayne squinted against glare and plunged her upper half into the Well and scooped armfuls of warm liquid. "Who's is that? Help me here?"

An unseen vacuum sucked the souls towards the heavens. Demons stole more than light beings saved.

Zeke placed his palms on the wall, energy shattered the section. "Can't you see it's too late? I warned you all. Never come near me again."

Translucent fluid spilled onto the ground, the dirt bubbled and broke.

Shayne leapt back and lowered her hands. "Son, calm down and let's discuss what's going on. I can't help if you don't. Bring the crazy down a few levels. Your family needs you right now."

Fuzzy-Wuzzy thrust sword pieces at her and bounded off. "Take this and do what you like with it. If I don't see you again, I'm glad."

Oh of all the times to chuck a hissy fit.

Shayne put them in her pocket. "What the fuck am I meant to do with them? And right back at you, not so Fuzzy-Wuzzy."

Zeke's roar chilled her core. "I'm not your son and I never will be. Get out of my way."

Erin entered the Well and swam after the one he'd released. A light being met her part way and guided her.

Lightening cracked, thunder roared. Elders chanted from the portal, looked for Enlil or guarded exits.

Shayne backed up and lowered her hands. "Okay. Gotcha. Slow down before you do something you'll really regret."

Energy circled Zeke, his plasma increased. "I did that the day we met and I'm done."

Power surged from his feet into the ground; a shock wave cracked the ground and flung Shayne sideways.

Shayne landed butt first on Ryan. "Fucking fuck. Ouch. Jesus, God damn."

Ryan's breath whooshed up her shirt. "God damn, Mum. How much do you weigh?"

She rolled off and onto her knees. "I'm ignoring that for now."

Don't kill him. It's a reasonable question considering.

A blue blur zipped towards the castle faster than Shayne's lack of control.

"Ah my love, Zeke's coming in hot your way. Like mini chocolate hulk, tabasco sauce hot. I'm not sure what's happened to set him off. Oh and I am finally coming."

Ryan held his gut and rose. "You'll punch me for this but it might be time to lay off the chocolate for a while. Are you sure you're pregnant and it's not a giant, block of chocolate?"

Shayne followed Zeke's smoked path. "You're right I will punch you, later."

Zeke's mayhem in the distance encouraged swiftness.

Meters ahead fluffy legs protruded from bushes, her guts dropped, tears welled.

Shayne swallowed a breakdown; metal poles impaled Fuzzy-Wuzzy to a tree trunk. "That's totally fucked up. He didn't deserve that, especially because of a tantrum. It's not fair. If I'd said he wrote the Lexicon it might have made him realise he's important. We would have been great friends one day. I wanted to invite you to the wedding."

Why do people lie when someone they don't like is dead? I hate this part of it all.

Ryan stroked her neck and kissed her head. "I'm sorry, Mum. He seemed nice."

Shayne shook off despair, her fingers chilled. "Thanks. You're both staying right here. Well, not this exact spot because clearly it's not safe but somewhere else. I'm not losing my kids in this too. By the way Ryan, don't think I've forgotten about Joey or your crush on Izzy."

Ryan's bear hug calmed her. "Great. I'm up for living just for one of those conversations of yours I love so much. You know we're sticking with you anyway."

Erin rubbed her arms and shook her head. "Ditto despite wishing I'd never told anyone about my powers and stayed out of the whole lot."

I'm so blessed to have you guys. I never fully realised how much until now. I'm not sure I deserve you but you're mine.

Shayne squeezed Erin's hand. "My darling girl, I know I can't stop you but don't be foolish." She offered them to Ryan. "You look after this; I may turn it into a pair of earrings."

Ryan cupped his hands, his smirk contagious. "Sure. Do I look like a carry bag?"

Shayne tipped them in and said goodbye. "Yes but a cute one. You're a good kid."

In Ryan's hands, the pieces glowed, moved towards each other and reconstructed into a full sword. "Ah, will you look at that. What does that mean?"

Shayne blinked, blinked and blinked again. "Fucked if I know but it's gotta be good."

Ryan turned the hilt, jewels glimmered in divine light. "There you go hey. It's not as heavy as it looks."

Erin gasped, her stride slowed. "Wow. Wow. Wow. That's, wow."

Opportunity knocked and Shayne answered. "Holy fucking shit. Get the fuck out of here. Right when we need this baby again. Bring it on."

Chapter 53: Oh Enki where art thou?
First Level of Hell

Half of Annu's help dead on the ground, plus Zeke's ill timed flip-out edged him into a dark place. Tension and fear pushed him further in.

Holding onto faith is getting really, really hard. I'll lose it with my temper soon.

Annu split the group, his worry about their welfare refused to dissipate. "Okay, it suck's but grieving waits until later. Let's work on being as deadly and clever as them. You half follow me and cover my entry into the castle to kill Ralf; the others meet Shayne on route there. I'm sorry to say, at this stage it's likely none of us will get out via that flarking portal. If you want to run and hide, I won't blame you and now's the time."

Black bags under Izzy's eyes allowed compassion entry. "I knew from the beginning I wouldn't make it out and accepted it then. I didn't know about the possibility of getting out anyway. This is my destiny Annu. I'll never quit."

I'll cling to her and the other's hope; it's much stronger than mine.

Lack of chest feathers shrank Ankor; she resembled a plucked Earth fowl. "I'm ready too."

Annu longed for an Army, Navy or any other forces. "Izzy, apparently Ryan has a connection with the sword. It's giving us a big leg up so to speak."

Izzy's chin dropped, she clapped. "He must be related to Jazekial or someone similar. This is wonderful news."

Annu mentally weighed each person. "Who volunteers to fly on my feet as a shield?"

Matted hair flopped in Izzy's face. "I'm best served on the ground searching for Shayne given I know her and Ryan."

Elders blocked Zeke's entry in the castle grounds, his plasma bursts deflected.

I'll make use of his distraction, albeit at likely cost to him, but I'm not happy about this.

Annu pointed at two smaller Igigi. "Grab somewhere hard and hold on. We're finding Shayne first."

I hope I don't drop any on route. That'd be hard to deal with.

They each attached to a leg and Igigi invaded Annu's personal space.

Extra weight slowed their ascent a few metres. "No matter what do not let go."

Ankor, Izzy and the group spread into a V formation and trudged forwards.

Annu rose above the trees and removed angst hung from his ankles. "All right. Here we go."

The female Igigi mumbled; the male grunted.

He flew out of the woods adjacent to the castle. "What I wouldn't give for extra limbs."

In the periphery, Ryan ran with a glowing sword, Shayne waved beside Erin.

Annu exhaled forever, hope rekindled. "About damned time too."

Massive objects hurtled for them and struck the ground metres from Shayne.

A rusted, truck engine skimmed Annu, he spun like a top. "Shit, shit, shit."

The female slipped down his leg, she clutched his boot. "Oh gods, oh gods."

Annu righted and reached for her. "Quick, grab my hand."

The male stretched his arm. "Ellie, hold on."

Ellie climbed Annu's leg and dragged his pants. "I'm trying Davi."

Roots first, a whole tree flew in their direction.

Annu dipped sideways, branches gouged his back. "This is flarked up."

Davi lost grip and fell, Ellie wrapped her legs around his.

Annu descended upright after him, a headache thumped between his eyes. "This is not my idea of fun."

Debris hid Ankor and the others, Shayne's scream gave her location.

Davi thudded onto hard ground and crumbled.

Flarking shit, get it together.

Ellie's tears wet his pants, her fingernails dug into his leg. "Oh Gods. It's so far down. Please don't let me go."

Annu yanked her up against wind and hugged her waist. "I'm sorry. You're safe now."

Sections of brick walls went over their heads.

Ellie's presence deleted eruption. "Thank you, thank you, thank you."

For flark's sake. We're open targets.

Annu lowered beneath the onslaught. "Don't thank me yet."

Shayne, Ryan and Erin dodged equal sized obstacles.

Annu created a wall of fire around them and landed. "You've no idea how happy I am to see you guys."

Ellie jumped off, she kissed the dirt. "Poor Davi. Blessed by thy rest my friend."

Shayne launched—her arms and smile open. "I know this isn't the time but thank fuck. I've missed you so fucking much."

Inner peace put a lid on panic. "Ditto, my love. Ryan, I need you, your sword and an Igigi with me. Zeke's in trouble. Please keep him alive while we're otherwise occupied. Ankor, Izzy and a few more are on their way too."

Ryan's raised sword shimmered. "Oh, cool. I'm glad she's okay. This is baptism by fire for sure."

Shayne released the embrace and lagged. "Great. Can't wait. Erin and I will see you there with reinforcements."

Damned woman, you look good even half dead and in this place. You disrupt my focus.

Erin stayed time on the next barrage of crap. "You've got a few seconds max."

An Elder carried an inert Zeke towards the portal.

The lid blew off Annu's panic jar—the contents shredded him into pizza toppings. "No, no, no. Get on, Ryan. Ellie, now."

Ryan balanced with the sword on Annu's foot. "Up, up and away, Superman."

Annu lowered his arms and glanced at Ryan. "Huh?"

"Never mind."

Ellie dragged herself over. "This has been the strangest day of my life. I'm not looking forward to this."

Shayne clicked her tongue and stroked her belly. "You're not the only one. Babe, go, we're right behind you."

Erin's hold on time stopped, dirt billowed, sparks cracked. "Oh my cookies."

Shayne erected a wall of ice. "Hurry up."

Annu shot into the sky and flew to the Elder with Zeke. "Ryan, get ready. Stick it where I show you and put your back into it. We probably won't get another go."

Ryan raised the sword, sweat poured down his cheeks. "Okay."

At the Elder's nape, Annu pointed, heat seared his face. "Do it."

Ryan leaned and thrust the blade. "Ahhhhhh."

The male Elder turned his upper half and shifted their positions. "It's too late. You've lost. Give up and make it easier on yourself."

For flark's sake.

Ryan stabbed, the sword slipped. "Fuck it."

Annu drifted back again and hovered. "Come on, push it in harder."

Ryan's neck muscles tensed, he plunged, the end scraped across not in. "Why isn't it going in? What are we doing wrong?"

A bad feeling crept Annu's spine. "Try it again."

The Elder reached the outer wall of the portal room. "Your attempts are futile. There's no weapon that can harm us."

Annu reserved internal apocalypse for his father. "Flarking Enlil the lying, deceitful piece of shit. I bet the only thing that works is that flarking medallion."

Chapter 54: Liar, liar, your pants are on fire
First Level of Hell and Life

The end's in sight, hang in there I'm sure the babies are fine but I don't want more pain to hurry and worry me.

Shayne dismissed another contraction as extreme stress. "Fucking fucky, fuck, fuck. Now they've had a great idea they won't quit using it. They're worse than those shopping networks, the ones who include free steaks knives with every purchase."

Shit, please don't throw steak knives at us.

Erin diverted missiles Shayne missed; her swiftness saved their butts several times. "Yes I'm aware of them, Mum. I'm not sure it's relevant analogy in this situation however. Are we any closer? I'm terrified."

Shayne's lower back twinged, the next contraction intensified. "Yes baby, of course we are. I'm scared too and won't let anything happen to you."

Erin's fear nibbled Shayne's, doom rested upon their shoulders. "Me either, Mum."

Annu's timbered voice eased some tension. *"We're all right but we've been jibbed again. They've got Zeke near the portal, I don't know where Ralf or Enlil are and Enlil's wandering around possibly with the means to control the elders. Stay safe and if you see that bastard, tell me."*

"Yeah, great. *Just fucking great. You be careful too. I'm not having these babies without you or anything else for that matter."*

The only thing wrong with me and my babies are this begotten place.

Shayne pointed and headed towards a glimpse of orange skin. "Over there, I saw one."

The onslaught slowed, dust settled, their surrounds cleared.

Erin inhaled and held her breath. "Thank cookies. That was getting old real quick. I so can't wait to be home."

Fuck, fuck, fuck. I hate my big kids being in danger too. Damn me for allowing it to happen. Hang on a minute….

Shayne's anxiety level rivalled the National Debt, she clutched Erin's hand. "Oh my God, Erin. I just realised, I care what happens to you kids and how you feel. In fact, all you kids. I'm actually a proper, dopper mother who gives a shit. Look at me, I'm maternal as fuck."

I've come much further than I thought. I need to give myself some credit too.

Erin exhaled and coughed. "Yes, you are. You've become someone I aspire to being. Your strength and determination are incredible. Even though this is shitty I'm enjoying being with you and seeing what you come up with next."

Warm and gooey embraced Shayne, pride expanded her head. "Oh, ah, wow. Thank you my girl. Hey, there they are."

Two men and a woman huddled behind concrete blocks.

Shayne sped over, belly pain returned. "Fucking hell. You guys are giving me a heart attack. This isn't a great place to conduct a hugging convention."

Breathe, it'll pass. I'll head right to the hospital when I'm out. I swear. A lot.

The taller, bald man dipped his head and stood. "Thank you, thank you, thank you, our Goddess."

Shayne flushed, her chest heated. "No worries, it's what I do. Where's the others and Izzy?"

Erin assisted the woman to her feet. "Easy now, watch the rocks."

The other male flounced his hands. "We lost sight during that attack not long after finding them."

Fuck it. Izzy where are you kiddo?

Shayne's back pain upgraded, her breath dragged. "All right. Job's not done yet. Stay on your toes."

I've asked for the pain to go away nicely. That's about to change if it doesn't disappear.

The men walked one side of her, Erin and woman the other.

Erin whispered—brown spots now marked her arms. "Mum, everything tells me this is really, really bad."

Shayne ground her teeth, the ache dulled. "You and me both sweets."

Pressure induced silence amplified noise from the castle, the portal projected above its turret like a sore thumb.

Elders had returned to the castle and guarded the walls.

"Enki, please protect all those I love and all those who love me. Get me through this valley of death and I'll fear no evil any longer."

Shayne's confidence plunged into a pit of despair. "It's all a matter of perspective; we're just in the wrong one."

Beyond the rows of destroyed buildings, a dirt path led the way to the Castle.

What I wouldn't give for some fucking chocolate and a joint. Bad, I know.

Erin covered her mouth and matched Shayne's pace. "Oh my cookies. Nathaniel probably ever let me leave the house again. If we do get home."

The magnitude of their task swallowed Shayne and spat the bones. "Don't say that. It's not an option. Have faith, Enki will protect us."

Right Enki? You better my friend.

Shayne paused, caught her breath and continued. "What the fuck were we thinking? We're not prepared for this big a problem and enemy. Is there a degree for that too? Faith shmaith. I hope we aren't killed five minutes in. That's just embarrassing."

Erin smacked Shayne's arm. "Mum, you said that out loud, again. Are you serious?"

They crossed onto a lawn area before the castle grounds.

Shayne's energy drained, she surrendered to foot in mouth disease. "For fuck's sake. I really must watch myself doing that. I blame the pregnancy."

Erin walked around dead and icky things. "Mum, Mum, Mum, Mum. It's not touching me."

Shayne channelled courage for all and failed. "Keep walking, don't look, smell, or think. Pretend their slugs or something. Big, hairy, decomposing slugs."

Near the end of the lawn area an opened metal door opened onto the dirt, light illuminated a tunnel beneath.

Images of hallways, stone floors and a hidden doorway to the portal flashed into Shayne's mind.

Shayne tested the first step, it passed the heft test. "All-righty. That's our way in. I'll go last."

The woman gasped and took off for bushes. "My Lord, please don't be so."

Shayne stepped back and rushed after her. "Hey where are you going? What —"

Izzy rested against stone and held her side, blood pooled in grass. "You shouldn't be here. Go, it's more important."

Shayne sank to her knees. "Oh Izzy. I'm so sorry."

The woman removed her shirt and held it over the injury. "You hang on. We're not losing you my girl."

Izzy smiled and lit up the world "Stop him for good. I wish….I…I."

Shayne swallowed pre-grief, the amount of unfairness in goodness confounded her. "I promise we will. I know I'll kick arse. Lay there and rest. One of us will stay with you."

Beings chanted louder, the portal widened, time dissipated.

The woman beside Izzy's care allowed confidence in her absence. "I will."

Erin tapped Shayne's shoulder. "Mum, come on."

She hunched her back and waddled to the hutch. "We'll be back and you better be here."

Erin lead the two men inside, she offered her hand. "I'll help you down."

A contraction stole Shayne's breath and slowed her. "You go, I'm right behind you."

Okay, it still hurts. So much that I want to lie down, scream and die. Will I actually die from this? I will for sure if I stop now.

Wrinkles creased Erin's firm skin, she stayed put. "How does no sound? You're not fooling me. What's wrong?"

Shayne took Erin's hand, pain gnawed like a rotten tooth. "Geez you're stubborn. I have no idea where you get that from but I'm perfectly fine."

Erin walked two steps down. "Mum, I don't believe you. You suck at lying."

Each step increased the contraction's width, pain formed a band around her middle.

Breathe, breathe, breathe. It'll pass any minute. Or the next.

Shayne released Erin's hand at the bottom. "Yeah, yeah. All good chicken. I'm old, pregnant and over demanded. You scoot up ahead and keep them in the right direction. I just need to catch my breath for a bit."

Erin glanced at the Igigi and scowled. "Okay, but if you don't catch up in a literal minute I'm coming back. Got it?"

Shayne fake smiled, she dropped another step, and pain lapped itself. "See I'm fine, now go, please."

Erin's growl had less impact than Fuzzy-Wuzzy's. "All right, okay. Geez."

They turned a corner, Shayne hunched onto the bottom step.

Sweat poured down her back, her temperature soared, and nausea joined the party. "Don't do this. Of all the timed, it's…ooh…the worst, wrong ever. It's…too…soon."

A figure shifted in further along, shivers wracked Shayne.

"No, no, no, no, no. Someone help……"

Shayne slumped against the wall and lost consciousness.

Chapter 55: And the mighty doth fall
Hell

Spread eagle and chained near the portal, regret consumed the rest of Zeke's birthday.

Two spare posts either side of him uninvited hope to the party.

Zeke exhausted his escape options and rattled the restraints. "There are a number of things I'd do differently. First off, I'd have stayed with Ma and never found Annu as that lead to me failing her by being here when she died. Secondly, I'd gain better control of my emotions. They've done me no favours either."

An appointed demon waited to pierce Zeke's torso.

Ralf's shaven, bloodied, dirty head on the floor represented his failure.

I'm right; doing good gets your nowhere. Fatal error I won't get the chance to rectify.

Beside Zeke's heartbeat, the portal's whoosh dulled other sounds. "If Isaac killing me at the supposed party didn't result in Enlil getting out for sure earlier, I'd be out of my misery by now."

Fire lacked warmth, shame and disappointment prevented loneliness.

Zeke's weight tore his shoulder muscles, he straightened for relief. "Flark, flark, flark. Son's of bitches, bastards, shit suckers."

Beneath his feet light leaked through floor boards into an open space.

There's a room of some kind down there. If I get out of those ankle chains and kick the boards they should break. Which dismisses the ruining Ralf's head plan.

An Elder nodded, the demon sliced a dagger across Zeke's side, and blood trickled into a gold bowl.

The air electrified, energy drained from Zeke and circled the portal. "I wished I'd kissed at least one girl, eaten more of Shayne's chocolate, hugged her at least once and talked to my unborn sib—"

The chamber door banged open; several demons carried an unconscious Annu and Ryan inside.

Judging from the state he's in, he's put himself at risk again for me. He's no help to me out of it. Let's face it, or in it.

Ryan clutched a gold, encrusted sword. "Get off me you stinky arseholes. Zeke, mate, are you all right?"

Zeke's blood spilled over the bowl's edge, he winced. "Flarking fantastic. You?"

Demons dragged Annu to the pole on Zeke's left and restrained his arms.

Annu's head flopped, spit dribbled down his chin. "Bleke?"

Zeke's anger resurged; he popped a shoulder in and struggled. "Leave him alone or I'll rip you to shreds. Believe me, I've had a very bad day and I'm busting to take it out on someone. Let me out of here."

They secured Annu's legs; a demon sliced his other side and collected the blood. "Help me."

Red energy trailed from Annu into the portal.

The sky cracked open and revealed the heavens, space and beyond. Their ceremonious death replicated their action packed life.

Zeke focused on the chain links, a speck of plasma slipped across it. "So, this is what the end of the universe looks like. I wish I'd missed it."

The Elders combined yell rocked the foundations. An orange glow drifted from the portal and circled the room.

Annu grunted—his leg spasmed. "Zeke?"

Something or someone shifted in the space below, curiosity peaked.

Zeke shifted his feet, the thing moved. "Yeah, I'm right here."

An Elder punched the wall, rows of bricks crumbled. "Pick up the head and wipe it off. It's almost time. We have enough essence with those two but continue the search for Enlil."

A demon collected Ralf by the ears and wiped it off on his pants, the incantation cleared.

It doesn't look like I remember. Weren't there more words or another verse?

Zeke's stomach fluttered, his attention flipped. "Flarking heck. Da. Wake up."

Annu rolled his head and wriggled his eyebrows. "I'm fine. Back-up's coming."

The Elders blocked views outside the portal room.

Adrenaline strengthened Zeke's purpose. "Good. Nothing like waiting for the last minute. Listen, I think the incantations wrong but I can't be sure. What's your plan?"

Annu's pupils dilated, he clenched his fists. "Oh we should be so lucky. I know I took a while but you can't rush these things. We're left with destroying Ralf's head ASAP. There's no way around it."

A shadow from beneath shifted over Zeke's feet.

His internal thermostat cooled, his senses heightened. "Are your reinforcements down there?"

Annu shook his head and frowned. "Not as far as I'm aware. Unless it's flarking Enlil."

The demon read Ralf's head's with his fingers in the eye holes. "All hail the Guardians of Creation, cosmic energy, the Source, the Creator and elohim."

Zeke's drive escalated, he yanked the chains. "Ah, da, what do we do?"

Annu sounded like Zeke's butt hole felt. "Patience. Any second now. Come on."

The Head Elder's words filled the chamber. "Bestow upon us the universal knowledge of our forefathers —"

A group of orange skinned beings exploded from behind the portal and created a barrier around its entrance.

Zeke's tension reduced, his pulse slowed. "Thank flark for that and moments almost too late."

Demons paused, Elders grumbled and the portal grew.

The Head Elder's fist wiped out another wall section. "What are you waiting for? Get them now."

Demons remained in place, a sword preceded Ryan's appearance before them.

Someone else's face shifted across Ryan's. "It's all over. You're done. Untie them now."

The demon close jiggled a key and unlocked Annu's wrists. "I cannot keep up with this. Someone's in charge, then someone else is, then that changes again. Do this, no do that, not do this. I tell you, it's plain confusing."

Annu grabbed him, his hand a flame. "Hurry it up."

The demon one handed undid the other wrist and Annu ankle "All right, all right."

Head Elder's hand quivered. "Do not let them out you fool. It's a trick. They've no authority in this."

The demon paused over the last lock. "Here we go again."

Zeke's shoulders hurt in anticipation, unspent frustration bubbled. "Hurry up for flark's sake."

Ryan's skin turned orange, his eyes green and hair blonde. "It's no trick Artison. It is I, Jazeikal." Ryan touched his throat and cheeks. "What the fuck's happening to me?"

Zeke's patience climbed a hill and rolled down the other side. "You know what; I don't flarking care who any of you are just let me out."

The Head Elder's, Artison's loss of control stuttered his movements. "Jazeikal? Is it really you? How? This has been the worst day ever."

Ryan's other self went the other way, the sword lowered. "Um, this is just too fucking weird."

Great, so he's all big and important too now. We'll start a club. For flark's sake.

Annu grabbed the keys, shoved the demon back and unlocked himself. "Ryan, it's okay. Go with it. Keep calm. Don't lose it. This is your moment to show us what you've got."

Zeke rested against the pole. "Yeah, yeah, undo me."

Annu stepped across and unlocked a wrist. "You're as bad as I am."

Jazeikal ghosted Ryan and faced the demon with Ralf's head. "Yes it is I. Creature give me that thing."

Zeke rolled his shoulder, it clicked into place. "Thank flark for that."

The demon stared at it and shuffled. "Artison, do I?"

Artison hesitated, he oozed disbelief. "Ah no, you idiot."

Jazeikal-Ryan slipped behind the demon and held the sword to his throat. "Fine, then we'll do it this way. Carry it to the portal and toss it in."

Annu released Zeke's ankles and looked around. "Still no Enlil, Shayne or Erin."

Zeke stepped over the ledge. "Thank you. Don't think the worst yet. Ryan, where's your mother and sister?"

Ryan replaced Jazekial, he lowered the sword. "I, ah, I, they were meant to come with those guys."

Demons swamped Ryan, the portal area and Zeke. Ralf's head flew into Artison's hands.

Zeke summoned his remaining will power. "That's it. I'm over this and you're all flarked."

Chapter 56: All's well that ends well
The castle, Gamede

Annu's interference assisted not ended Enlil's comeback. The drama provided entertainment.

I've managed to keep my last resort for last, and thus it no longer matters I don't have the medallion. Artison and the others will obey me regardless. Ha. I made it, I'm here. It's almost done.

Righteousness blessed Enlil, breath requests slowed and hunger died.

The power blocker in his pocket moved, he pinched the woman's arm. "Wake you stupid mammal. The shows begun and you won't want to miss any."

Her squeal tingled his testicles, her stench cancelled lust. "You mother fucker, let me go. I'll claw your eyes out."

All ends met in the middle and peace from eternal damnation waited a floor above.

Enlil's slap to her cheek left a handprint. "That isn't part of my request so no. Damn you're annoying. Are you useful for anything other than talking?"

The woman didn't flinch, her eyes narrowed, her stomach contracted. "Fuck you arsehole. Ahhhh. Shit."

She's got courage but her labour complicates extraction.

Enlil injected healing via his finger on her gut and suppressed digging it in. "Be patient, your pain will cease forever soon. I must say, this turned out better than I imagined. The numerous deceptions built things up making the trouble worth it. Plus added to the overall ambiance. There hasn't been excitement like this around here for millennia. No one will ever doubt my power and strength again."

Boots stomped, people yelled, blood swished between the floorboards.

Her shoulders relaxed, she stared at her bump. "What did you do to me and my babies? I'll rip your fucking face off. You lying, evil, horrible, cruel beast."

Enlil pulled her off the chair and onto the stairs by an ear. "You're the feistiest, most determined but unskilled, moronic, female cunt I've encountered. Calm down, I've slowed things down. For my benefit of course. My one regret is not having the time to defile you before and after I rip your babies out."

The woman struggled, her skin heated. "You're the worst, shittiest, sickest, evilest future father-in-law ever to exist. Who the fuck thinks of that? Fuck it, I can't freeze you."

Enlil cracked her in the head and twisted the ear. "I guess I'm still not invited to the wedding? Luckily I made other plans. I had hoped we'd buck the trend of fighting in-laws."

Success tastes like sweet newborns.

Bodies crunched and beings, son included, yelled overhead.

She raised her chin, her bellow unnerved him. "I'm not scared of you. There's no way on this world or any other are you allowed near my family. Hey, hello. Annu, down here. Annu? Zeke? Elders?"

Removal of her mouth drained Enlil's stress, he tapped her skull. "They wouldn't have heard you anyway. Save your energy for suffering."

She kicked his shins, her determination almost inspired him. "Dhmipd."

Her daughter roused on the other chair, twisted and wriggled. "What the fuck did you do? Put her mouth back and get away from my mother. So, help me I'll kill you. Mum, I'm sorry my powers aren't working."

Her fear lifted a shroud from Enlil's shoulders, he held the woman at arm's length. "Yes of course they don't. Foolish girl, despite no need of you I'll make one. Perhaps I'll allow you to watch while I uncreate everything and everyone you've ever known. In the meantime if you don't shut up you'll lose your right to speak too."

She breathed hard and greyed. "Annu, Zeke, we're down here. Help, someone? We're down here. Hello? Hey, you guys."

Zap, zap.

The daughter's tongue pushed under her lip, tears streamed.

Her mother kicked regardless of distance. "Hmpphohh."

Enlil embraced mirth, and raised her higher. "Where were we up to? That's right, killing time and getting to know each other better. After I ascension I wonder if I'll still find time to torture beings or will I be too busy making my own? I'm sure I'll work it out eventually. By the way, are you aware the fuck word you use so often is a fairly universal term? You're not in any way original."

Her legs swung, her elbows jabbed. "Mdmdmdd."

Noise above ceased, Artison calmed remaining nerves. "Keep them in place and re-clean the head."

The woman's nostrils flared, her ears wiggled. *"I know you can hear me, you bastard. Put me down."*

For alhalso's sake. Does nothing stop her?

Discomfort ruined Enlil's good time, he blocked his mind. "Do shut up."

Hands tied and stuck to his side, she reached for her daughter. "Dhdhd."

For the love of everything unholy. What's with these people? There's no end to their escape efforts. They don't give up. It's really frustrating and time consuming. Will they get it already and learn their no match for me?

Artison's voice rumbled the roof, light brightened. "All hail the Guardians of Creation, cosmic energy, the Source, the Creator and elohim."

Enlil kneed the woman in the back. "Almost, are you excited? Either way doesn't matter." He faced the daughter. "Do exactly as I say or you're mother will suffer beyond your comprehension while you watch helpless. Get over here."

The girl nodded, his wave removed the chair ties.

She hobbled over and stood behind her mother. "Dhdhdhdmp."

Enlil tingled, lumps broke through skin. "Good."

Artison's voice rose above the portal. "We surrender freely to infinite knowledge, wisdom and power on the other side. Hear our words oh great ones."

Enlil climbed the bottom step, the rafters rattled, the ground rippled.

The blonde Igigi he'd disabled stumbled towards them and raised the medallion. "Let her go Enlil and back up."

Ah, not doing this interruption or any others. It's too late. It doesn't matter.

The daughter jumped and staggered. "Djdjdjd."

Enlil poised a blade to the woman's abdomen. "Both of you stop right there. Don't come any closer. Throw the medallion over to me."

A mother, daughter hug sickened him.

The Igigi girl raised the golden icon. "I call upon—"

Enlil likewise erased the verbal problem and levitated it to him. "Finally, back where you belong."

Artison's recitation triggered the next stage of evolution. "Bestow upon us the universal knowledge and experience of our forefathers."

The Igigi girl ran to the daughter, they embraced.

Enlil's energy soared, his powers returned in fractions. "I don't understand why your kind feels the need to hug and touch each other all the time. It's disgusting and spreads germs. Plus you smell rancid." He wrenched the woman up the stairs. "So long sad times, so long bad times, we are rid of you at last. Howdy gay times, cloudy grey times, you are now a thing of the past. Everybody, happy days are here again. The skies above are clear again, so let's sing a song of cheer again."

Chapter 57: Not my Just desserts
The portal room, Gamede

Annu's efforts drained into a bowl a good kick's distance away. "Well that was a total waste of time."

Their return to the posts and chains soured him.

All right, time for the next bright idea.

Aside from his pregnant woman, no more rabbits hid in their magic hat.

"Shay, where are you? Why aren't you here? Are you all right?"

Annu worked at the chains, they didn't budge. "There's nothing like making life more interesting is there? Noooooo. I didn't have anything better to do like get married and be normal. Noooooooo. I had to find out who my father was at any cost, and boy did I get what I wanted."

Artison pursued his own freedom with the vigour of one long imprisoned. "We give ourselves freely to the Source's greater design."

Swirl, swirl, swish, swish,

The creature held Ralf's head less than two meters from Zeke, so close and so far.

Which leaves me with, what to work with except full panic? Breath, it won't help if I pass out. Maybe. I'm considering it.

Annu dismissed a mental eulogy and clung to life. "Hey, Zeke, wake up. I really need your input here."

"Shay, you're really stressing me out, woman. Give me a sign you're okay."

Corralled by creatures in a corner, Ryan's persistence enthused Annu. "Hey, you big red dudes, you won't succeed. Give up now. My mum's coming and she'll tear you a new one."

Annu tapped the boards with a toe, it echoed. "And the rest of us too. I hope and pray."

"Shay? I'll buy you that chocolate factory if you answer me."

Tap, tap, tap, thud.

"Of all the flarking times for her to shut up and not answer straight away. Where the flark are she, Erin, Izzy and Ankor? There's one reason I can think of why they wouldn't be here and I don't want to go there."

Tap, tap, tap, thud.

The plank under the blood filled bowls shook. "Zeke, Zeke, Zeke. Kid, for the love of Enki, wake up."

Zeke turned and groaned. "My head hurts. Da, are we still trapped or am I dreaming?"

The air cooled, lightening cracked in geometric shapes above the portal.

Annu's mortality drifted out of his reach. "My boy this is no dream. Snap out of it and embrace your angry side. It's finally got a place. Ryan, please bring Jazekial back."

Ryan bobbed up and down, his arms flailed. "I can't. Without the sword I'm just me. You've got another plan right?"

No pressure, it's fine. Of course I do. Like a million just sitting there waiting for their turn.

"*Dear Uncle Enki, it is with great distress I ask you to please flarking help us or have an incredible excuse not to. Unkind regards for now, me.*"

Annu held a panic attack at bay. "Sorry son, not yet but working on it. If I see it I'll let you know. Is there anything else requiring my immediate attention that I can't do."

Bruises covered Zeke's cheeks; he looked around and rattled his chains. "Shit, shit, shit. We're flarked. Get me out of here."

Annu added another problem to the list and tossed it. "My sentiments exactly but not at the moment. We both must have faith, lots and lots of it. They're strong and so are we. Think of something son, I'm out of ideas and everyone's relying on me, us."

Okay, I'm rethinking this sober deal. You can keep it, stick it, and wallpaper with it. I'm out first chance I get.

Artison raised his voice, the other elders copied. "We shed our former selves and embrace the new to come. Mighty ones hear our words."

Zeke's sobs undid Annu's wits. "I can't do this anymore. It's too hard. No matter what we end up flarked. It's our time to die."

Annu's mercury burst out of the thermometer. "You're not going anywhere before I kick your arse for leaving home and stealing a ship without permission. So snap out of it. We're going out fighting."

Tap, tap, tap, the bowls jiggled.

"Shay, know I love you and always will. More than I ever imagined I'd love another, much deeper and truer than Jaid. I'm truly blessed. We would have been great parents together. I know you'll raise all our kids right. I'll find a way back to you somehow, someday."

The castle creaked and crunched. The portal sucked up lose objects, they circled around it.

If that doesn't get her talking nothing will.

Zeke tapped one foot after the other. "I can't get any oomph into it."

Pride illuminated Artison, he quickened his words. "Pex, pex, cousin, kussun, elrah."

Annu mustered strength into his boot and fractured the board. "It's a start. Son, have another go. You can do it."

Zeke arched his back, he stretched his leg. "Is this going to work? Seems kinda basic."

Thud, thud, crack, the bowls shifted.

Artison frowned at the portal and swiped the head. "That's the last line. Why isn't it opening? Ah, of course," he spoke to the bowl creature, "pour the blood in."

The suspense is literally killing me.

The creature reached and touched the bowls.

Anticipation forced Annu into action; his boot heel thumped the board. "Ah, flark no."

Zeke stomped his section over and over. "Yeah, I second that."

The board split, flipped and tipped the bowls over.

"Shay, Shay? Shay? Where are you?"

Blood covered the bowl creature and the one with Ralf, his head dropped.

Weight on Annu's back lessened. "Yes. Now for the next bright idea."

Artison's eye and hand twitched. "Pick it all up and stop messing around. It's so hard to find good help these days."

The creatures followed orders, hopelessness returned.

Artison raised his palms, "Tip it in," and roared. "Pex, pex, cousin, kussun, elrah."

Annu questioned his entire existence and received no answers. "Here we go. Goodbye cruel worlds, it's been emotional."

I hope oblivion is better fun than this.

Nothing changed, the Elders mumbled.

Artison frowned and yelled. "Pex, pex, cousin, kussun, elrah."

Zip, zilch, the status quo endured.

Grateful rested upon Annu's shoulders. "I don't care why but it sure as flark helps."

Zeke jiggled his leg and huffed. "Yeah me too but how do we get these chains off this time?"

Annu checked his power tank; he drove on an oily rag. "Another thing I'll work out shortly."

Tap, tap, tap, crack.

The creatures shuffled and mumbled to each other.

Artison's growl buzzed Annu's ears. "Why isn't it open? I've completed the incantation a number of times. What's wrong with it? I demand to know what's—"

The air crackled and the portal ebbed.

"Dare I ask?" Annu's foot dangled into the room below. "Hey Artison, everything okay over there?"

"Shay, is it you stopping the portal?"

Artison stared at the opposite wall. "Mmmmmmmm."

A trap door in the corner flipped open, all heads turned in its direction. Creatures moved back, the bowls and chain keys hit the ledge.

The sword clunked to the ground in the middle of the room.

Annu pointed and pulled against the chains. "Hey Ryan, it's over there."

Ryan skidded towards it, feet blocked the way. "For fuck's sake."

Out of the hole, Enlil raised a mouthless Shayne and the medallion. "The reason it won't work my old foe is I have the final part of the incantation memorised for such occasions. As if I'd ever let any of you get that far."

No, no, no, no, no, no. I'll kill him regardless. Son of a bitch.

Annu's ire focused on his father. "You flarking bastard. I'm so over playing your games."

Enlil lost his human features in quick transition. "Good. Strap yourself in because I'm just getting started."

A blur of blue feathers flashed past, Ankor landed on Enlil's head and clawed. "Let her go you beast."

Annu embraced the darkness within, his blood heated. "You're so flarked now."

Chapter 58: Everybody do the Hokie Pokie
Portal room, The Castle, Hell

If wishes were valium I'd be in a massive coma right now. I want my fucking mouth back and it's such a fucked up thing to wish for.

Birdy's onslaught instilled Shayne's auto-pilot.

Shayne leapt and hooked the medallion over her finger. *Yes. Move fast.*

Elders against the outer wall followed their movements. Demons formed groups and watched.

Enlil struck Birdy and bumped into Shayne. "For heck's sake, get off me."

Shayne stumbled, the medallion slipped into the trap. *Oh fuck, I can't go get it. Shit, come on woman. Keep your shit together.*

The Elders's daze broke and they milled along the wall.

One in the middle spoke through pursed lips. "No, not yet. We need them to finish this. Enlil, I should have known the depths of your deception. She's dropped the medallion; you've no control over us, give me the last line."

Shayne jumped the hole and further into the room. *This is now between them and not my problem. Geez I dread what I look like. Here comes pregnant Witchypoo.*

Before the portal, a chained up Chocolate Hulk and Zeke rained relief.

Annu rattled his bonds, he lacked his usual flare. "Thank flark woman. What kept you? Where is your mouth? Never mind, pick up the keys off over there. They're for the chains but unlock yourself first of course."

"And he stopped you talking mentally too?"

Shayne gave thumbs up and waddled to the spot. *Great idea. Does Annu look relieved?*

Zeke bounced, the chains tightened his ankles. "Hoo-flarking-rah. I don't know how to fix that, but it's first time ever I've been happy to see you stepmother."

Shayne rolled her eyes and opened the locks. *Smart arse. Look what imminent death does to one's family attitude. I'll take it for now. Later though, he's in deep shit.*

The trap door snapped shut on Erin and Izzy.

Shit, maybe they're safest down there.

Enlil strangled Birdy, she scratched his chest. "I've killed many of your kind." Feathers dulled his growl. "Attention idiots. If you want to live get the woman and the medallion she lost."

Shayne massaged her wrists on route to Annu. *Fuck, fuck, fuck, fuck.*

Ankor oozed pain and strength. "Then you're aware of our tenacity. You'll not leave this place alive fallen one."

Fuck. I'm liking her again and she's re-invited to the wedding. Hah, yeah like we're getting out of here for that to happen.

Demons shunted Shayne onto her knees, she dropped the keys. *Fucking hell.*

Enlil stomped and wrenched Ankor from his head. "I said get her not play football."

Demons snapped to attention, the chances of failure amplified.

Shayne raked dirt, touched the keys and lost them again. *No, no, no, no, no. Now isn't the time for lack of coordination.*

Artisan's voice preceded movement in all directions. "Do not listen to him, bring the woman and head to me fast."

Feet and legs came at Shayne, she hunched her back. *I'm very over this. I admit I don't have the not giving up thing worked out yet.*

For once in her life and albeit close to death, a diminutive stature worked in her favour.

Enlil shivered her timbers, he wrestled Ankor. "For fuck's sake. This is your creator speaking. You will obey me or suffer grave consequences."

Shayne combed the dirt; three attempts pushed the keys further along. *Okay, so can this get any harder and fucked up? How did it all come down to a set of fucking keys? We'd suck at a swinger's party.*

Frustration bridled; she tried again and succeeded. *Fuck yeah. All right.*

Demons moved closer and further away.

Annu opened the front door to overwhelmed. "Shay, if nothing else gets Ralf's head and toss it this way. The rest we'll do after I'm free. Keep going straight and it's a few meters away."

On her feet, Shayne slammed it, the head, headed the other way. *Yep. Like I need more exercise at the moment either. The universe does hate me.*

Ryan appeared between demons on her left. "Mum, when you're close to it, grab the sword and bring it to me. I know what it's for now. Trust me, it will help."

Annu's clipped tone dragged across Shayne's nerves. "Thanks Ryan, hang tight for a moment. Shay, quick run down, Ryan's the reincarnated Igigi leader Jazekial. But, Ralf's head is the number one priority. I can't stress that enough."

Shayne ducked, crawled and popped up. *That's great and all but really? Am I going to the supermarket and you're adding shit to the list or saving the world? Why do I get to touch the funky head? Fuck me. Later.*

The demon turned Ralf's head not far from Annu and the portal. The sword laid unprotected meters away.

Shayne ran two steps, someone raised her by the jacket, and she kicked. *Cut me some slack here. For fuck's sake.*

A demon walked her to Enlil. "Quit it."

Annu banged and thudded the floor. "Put her down. Shay, hang in there. Shit, Ryan where are you?"

Shayne's skull compressed, her brain hurt, she swung. *This is humiliating. It's happening way too often.*

Enlil flung Birdy across the room. "Die already."

Oh gods no. That's sickening. Please someone save her.

Ankor smacked into shelves and collapsed, blood stained her torso. "Annu, you must stop him."

Shayne's soul wept, grief reached new depths. *Oh fuck. The innocent volunteers are suffering the most. It should be me and Annu not her or anyone else. This is completely out of control.*

Annu's pained wail raised it further. "Ankor? Shit, please be okay. I'll heal you if you hang in there."

Artison spat lava, a patch of floor ignited. "Bring me the head, damned you."

Enlil's roar commanded attention, he doubled in size. "You still don't have the last part Artison."

The demon dropped Shayne at Enlil's feet. "Here. This is the last time so finish this. By the way, if you fail, we're starting a Union."

Shayne scooted on her butt and reconvened. *Fuck. I actually achieved nothing from escaping.*

Artison hesitated, he slammed a fist. "You still can't control us."

Enlil yanked Shayne's hair and pulled her back. "True, however, if you kill me you'll never get out. Stop your protesting and you will." He kicked Shayne in the hip and faced the demon. "Collect more blood."

Annu drooped, anguish contorted his expression. "Leave her alone. For flark's sake. Let me at him."

Shayne's scalp burned, she clutched his wrist. *This is not how it all ends. It can't be. It's too smelly, loud and in the wrong place. I'm too young. Hell, we're all too young to die.*

Zeke tugged his chains, the pole moved. "Shayne, don't give up. Sing or something. Please. Oh wait, flark."

The anti-power box fell and slid across the floor.

Shayne reached, it ended at the trap. *All is not lost yet. We're nearly there. Don't give up remember.*

The portal slowed and shrank, divine light dulled.

Enlil clipped her upside the head. "Get back here."

Shit. One more hit to the head and I'll get dementia mother fuckers.

Pain pounded Shayne's brain, her Shayne blood pressure rose.

Izzy entered via the trap and stayed the civil war. Blood trickled down the medallion in her hand.

Erin followed two steps behind and crushed the box, her mouth reappeared. "Thank cookies for that. Mum, are you all right?"

Shayne's energy, power and own mouth returned, she replaced Izzy's. "I am now. Thank fuck and all things holy for that."

Artison stepped back from the wall. "One of these days I'll get that damned that necklace and stick it right up your anus, Enlil."

Shayne sent ice through her head. "Now it's your turn, you son of a bitch."

Enlil's arm froze to the shoulder, it broke at the wrist. "No it's not. Stop it you wretched creature."

Izzy walked over and waved the medallion. "This time, you're definitely wrong. It's all over."

Erin paused the demons, she ran to Shayne. "Mum, I'm so glad you're okay. I heard it all and could do nothing."

Shayne rose and lead Erin across the room. "Me too but this isn't over yet. We better untie Annu before he implodes."

Enlil's smile revealed sharp teeth, fear flickered in his eyes. "On the contrary, this is a minor challenge."

Izzy swung the medallion to the wall. "Artison, I command you to destroy Enlil."

Part way to Annu, Shayne's memory triggered. "Izzy for the love of god don't kill him."

Not that I want to care.

Izzy squished her nose and frowned. "All right. No killing Enlil yet. All Elders shift away from the wall."

Shayne shuffled faster, the keys jingled. "Okay so faith does pay off but it pisses you off until it does."

Artison's puckered mouth indicated annoyance. "I make no guarantees for later."

The sword rested on the ground meters ahead.

Ryan edged out from demons sideways. "Mum, Erin, pick it up quick, before it's too late to use it."

Shayne deviated towards it, her ankles swelled. "Oh yeah, now it's useful. Stupid thing."

Erin picked it up, ran and placed it in Ryan's hand. "Do your thing, brother."

A different face replaced Ryan's, he glowed. "Jazekial has returned."

Enlil's smile widened despite Izzy's closeness. "Cocama, cocama, veristat."

The portal widened, divine light brightened.

Despair crashed Shayne's hope plane. "Someone shut that mother fucker up."

Chapter 59: The Prodigal son betrays
Portal Room, Castle, Gamede

Annu's frustration surpassed crucial mass. "Izzy slap a hand over his mouth."

Main problems temporarily stayed and we've got this. Humanity and togetherness will best him, not godliness.

Izzy smacked the problem shut. "Great idea. I hope it hurts."

Enlil backed into a wall, his progression reversed. "Mph."

Mayhem slowed, the portal steadied.

Metal stood between Annu and freedom. "Ah, Shay, any closer? I'm starting to think you want me like this."

Zeke slumped against the pole. "You might be right."

Artison ambled after the others, his footsteps echoed. "Well, that's it then. It's outrageous. I did not see this coming. How did a bunch of unworthy, inexperienced clods best us?"

Shayne slipped under a demon's legs. "Get fucked, arsehole. I'm coming but the head keeps rolling away. I'll never get this sticky stuff off."

Izzy's arm shook, she pushed harder. "I can't hold him like this much long."

Erin paused. "Ditto."

Annu tugged, pulled and yanked. "Okay. Not much I can flarking do like this."

Jazekial-Ryan approached Enlil, the sword sung. "It's all right. He won't go anywhere."

Shayne popped up in the middle of a pack with the head, she grimaced. "For fuck's sake. I've got it."

Ralf's head's current state befitted its former host.

Darn right you do. You're beautiful even covered in goop and dirty.

Annu mentally clapped, chain links creaked. "Yes. Hurry up woman. We're almost out of time."

What I'd give to be on the other side of all this now but we're close. Flark yeah.

Enlil struggled, twisted and glared hatred. "Djdjdjjd."

Shayne waddled with the head at arm's length. "Izzy, pray, he fucking hates it. Our father who art in heaven, helloed be thy name, oh holy of holy's, Jesus Christ, Enki blah, blah, blah, that sort of shit."

Zeke banged and clanged. "This is taking too long. Hurry up."

Enlil flinched and flailed. "Fhdidd."

Annu dropped his weight forwards, a link broke and freed his left arm, and power tingled along it."

The portal maintained a medium speed, volume and hypnotic rhythm.

We've got a really small window of getting out of here.

Izzy's voice rang around the room. "Enki, the Source, the Older's and all that is holy, please bless us in our divine mission. Have faith in us as we have in you, oh holy, blessed beings."

Jazekial-Ryan and Erin joined in.

Annu streamed flames up the chain, it glowed red. "Come on, you bastard."

Enlil shrank, human skin reformed, sweat drowned his forehead.

One tug and the lynch pin snapped, Annu swung the chain. "Now we're talking."

Zeke's chin dropped, he nodded. "I don't think we're meant to be able to do that."

Annu focused on the other, the metal melted into liquid. "Impending death's an incredible innovator."

His leg chains released from the main lock, full power surged through him.

Thank flark for that. Now let's end this.

Shayne cradled the head under her arm and approached the ledge. "Are you kidding me? You don't even need the keys anymore? I wish you'd stop doing that to me."

Plasma trickled from Zeke and fizzled. "Ah no. Apparently one of us still does. Undo me please. I just realized it appears I didn't need to hide the book after all. It's funny how things turn out. I almost got all bitter and twisted."

Izzy's scream diverted Annu, her hand slipped from Enlil's mouth. "Oh Gods, oh Gods. He's biting me. Holy creator, bless thee on our divine mission in your name."

Annu ignited, he faced Shayne. "Shay, finish up here, this I have to do on my own."

Enlil clawed at the medallion and gouged Izzy's arm. "Dweidids."

Erin paused time, he bucked against it. "Fuckkkkkkk."

Shayne clutched his forearm, her touch cooled. "Honey, are you sure? It might be the best idea given how he manipulates you. Wait a second."

Jazekial-Ryan stabbed Enlil, the sword slipped. "For the love of Enki, our creator in the heavens."

Enlil grabbed the hilt and chomped Izzy. "Mmmm. You little bitch."

Everyone and thing else faded, stored frustration centred on Enlil.

Annu soared across the room. "We're done here. He's toast."

Shayne's yell followed. "Hey, you don't have to do this alone. Shit."

Annu punched Enlil downwards in the mouth, he stumbled. "That flarked you didn't it."

Izzy, Erin and Jazekial-Ryan stepped out of the way.

Blood poured down Enlil's chin, his chest heaved. "Faddd."

Annu cracked his neck, rolled his shoulders and followed up to the gut. "That one's for all the bullshit. The next is for hurting my family."

Enlil hunched, he dry wretched. "You bastard child. You'll rue the day of your birth."

The darkness re-emerged, Annu embraced it. "Yeah and so will you, mother flarker."

Enlil scoffed, the monster beneath twinkled. "I already do and you don't have what it takes to bring me down or stop me. You're a pathetic excuse for a son and father."

Annu's grabbed him around the throat. "You're one to talk. I don't care if I'm stuck here. The universe is better off without both of us."

Enlil kicked and scratched Annu's arm, blood vessels in his eyes burst.

I need this release; you deserve all you get and then some.

Engulfed in plasma, Zeke nudged him. "Da, listen to me not him. We're right beside you. You're a good father and you know how much Shayne loves you. Focus, if we all hold him off and retrain him; I'll get the book and we're out."

That's it, stupid man. It's our togetherness that will save us and stop him. Not our godliness.

Shayne brushed his lower back, darkness abated. "Shit aside honey, this is family affair."

Annu loosened his grip for Enlil to breathe not talk. "You're right. Do it fast."

Enlil gasped air, his kicks slowed, colour drained from his face.

Izzy shuffled closer and sighed. "Thank you, Gods in Heaven."

Erin cleared a path to the portal. "We're not there yet, kiddo."

Jazekial-Ryan held the sword against Enlil's throat. "We've got your back."

Annu expected an inner struggle at the loss of control, peace arrived instead. "Thank you, all. I best keep remembering that."

Zeke clicked his fingers and the book appeared, he opened it. "I've missed you. Oh shit. What the flark?"

A chip devalued the diamond plan; Annu tightened his grip on Enlil. "What's wrong?"

Zeke flipped pages and fluffed. "It's flarking blank. There's nothing in it. No incantation. Nothing at all. Enlil's still the only way we'll get out."

Shayne combed fingers through her hair and tossed her head back. "How could that happen when you wrote the thing?"

Zeke whipped in her direction. "Say what? I wrote this? How do you know?"

Annu reconciled disappointment and acceptance. "Oh okay. We'll, look, talk about that later. Unless someone comes up with a way of extracting the lines from his brain we're back to stuck here."

Enlil slipped from his grasp and transformed into a twenty foot horned beast, a tail whipped Jazekial-Ryan across the floor. "We've got at least a few minutes before the last words must be recited and I'd hate to waste it."

The group's combined enthusiasm crashed into a brick wall.

Erin and Izzy tripped over each other's feet.

Shayne hugged her belly and drew a cross on her chest. "Oh fuckity, fuck, fuck. The power of Christ compels you; the power of Christ compels you. Someone hand me some holy water. Stat."

Back to me fighting him alone again. I'll do what I have to even if I don't like me after.

Annu brushed her cheek and kissed her forehead. "It will be okay. I promise you that. You might want to move back out of the way."

Shayne blinked and shuffled back. "All-righty then."

Inside the dark laid the light, Annu channeled it from the core outwards.

Annu's muscles increased and bulged a million fold, he matched Enlil's height. "Bring it on, cock sucker. "Everyone hide, it's going to get messy."

Chapter 60: We are not Family
Portal Room, the Castle, Hell

All powered up and nowhere to go, Shayne paced. "I should totally watch more horror movies involving possessions. I'm all out of ideas, though Annu has it all taken care of. He doesn't need me, us, whatever."

Does staying here mean I'm forever pregnant but don't have the babies? Annu might be resigned to staying here but I'm sure as fuck not.

Their situation sucked, unshaved monkey balls.

Shayne circled Zeke, fluid in her ankles drained. "Okay, so this is stupid. Utterly stupid. There's another way, there must be. What does the book say now? Where's fucking Thor or even Loki when you want them huh?"

Her-Chocolate-Hulk and Monster-in-Law smashed through another wall.

Zeke clicked his tongue, he tapped a page. "Still nothing and your ranting isn't helping."

Jacekial-Ryan caught his breath and rested the sword against his leg. "I'm sorry what did she say?"

Izzy's healed injuries returned her pep and vigour. "Don't worry, Grandpa, she speaks a different kind of language."

Erin's giggle lightened the collective mood. "Ryan, Nan always said you were old before your time. Grandpa suits you."

I can't even being to understand that. It's blowing my mind.

Shayne brushed off the heebie jeebies. "Ah, old man, may I have my son back, please?"

Jazekial-Ryan lifted the sword and clucked. "If I understand you correctly, he shall return when Enlil's contained."

Izzy tugged his sleeve, the medallion jiggled. "Let's help in that regard. The bind on his mouth is wearing off and there's minutes left before ascension passes. I guess we should consider where we'll live in this place. Do we share a home or build somewhere new?"

I'm glad she's adapted but does she need to be happy about it. Who makes plans this early in the relationship?

On his feet, Monster-in-Law threw Her-Chocolate-Hulk back into the chamber.

Erin jittered, she bit her nails. "Mum, how much longer will you let this go on? When are we talking about the staying here situation? I'm about to lose the plot."

"You're right kiddo but their fighting keeps Enlil away from the portal. I better be doubly sure it stays that way and join in." Shayne rode a board to the main wall. "Hey, Izzy, I'm coming behind you. By the way, I'm not fucking living or visiting you guys here. You get that out of your pretty, little head thanks."

From my mouth to Enki's ears.

Zeke provided a ready, protective arm. "Take it slow and careful. I want to see my siblings soon."

Shayne choked on cold, bold panic. "Fucking shit. Yeah of course. Not too soon okay. I'm not ready for this at all."

Erin rubbed Shayne's back. "If you can deal with all this, pushing out babies will be easy in comparison."

If they come back and we're out of here, I'll have to push those suckers out. There's labour and if memory serves me correctly it hurts. A lot and this is twice that. Shit. Though, since Enlil stopped it early, I'll have time to get used to the idea again. Not, not, not.

Shayne hyperventilated, her head buzzed. "Ah no. Just no. I'm definitely not ready. This is bull shit."

Zeke's sigh brushed her hair, he pushed her. "Yeah you are. You're not half as bad as I make out. I'll give you a hand here and there. Just don't take advantage of my generosity."

Aw, he's not such a bastard child after all.

Erin gasped and clutched her chest. "Oh, oh, I've got a good idea. I'll get the medallion off Izzy and make the Elders fix the Well of Souls."

Shayne's heart warmed, pride filled her chest. "Aw, good one, sweets. I'm so proud of you."

Zeke huffed, his confidence dipped. "Wish I'd thought of that."

A demolished turret and castle demanded renovation. Tile and colour selections stormed Shayne's brain.

Shayne faced Zeke akimbo. "Is the book still blank?"

Zeke shuffled her forwards. "Yes for now and yes for later."

The floor cracked beneath collective monster weight and created a hole into the floors below.

Shayne wrote a mental list of repairs. "Okay okay, just checking. Listen, about all the stuff around the Well before, let's forget it ever happened."

Why did I say that when I can't forget Fuzzy-Wuzzy died because of his temper? Is his death considered a casualty of war or a life lesson?

Zeke drifted away mentally, he stiffened. "I saw my mother, it, well, you know."

Humiliation stung Shayne, non-realisation roiled her guts. "Oh Jesus fucking Christ Zeke. That's fucked. I should have realised. I'm so sorry. God I'm an arsehole."

Enlil wailed and shrieked. "Stop saying that."

Shayne slid along the bloody floor. "Jesus Christ, Jesus Christ, Jesus Christ fuck arse."

Her Chocolate-Hulk twisted Monster-In-Law's head three sixty degrees. "Don't talk to her."

Zeke's hand stayed on her back. "Jesus Christ, Jesus Christ, Jesus Christ. Hey, who the flark is Jesus Christ and why does he hate him so much?"

Shayne foot slipped, her knees creaked. "Some nice guy everyone wanted to kill and did. He's meant to be God's son and look, the details are hotly debated and I don't care right now. Anyway his name shits Enlil."

Monster-In-Law repositioned his head and slashed Her-Chocolate-Hulk across the face.

Shayne's gut lurched, bile burned her throat. "Oh shit. Honey, are you okay?"

That's such a stupid thing to say but so's most of the stuff out of my mouth.

A dishevelled Ang clambered through the main doorway. "Where the flark did you all disappear to? I can't fly remember," he watched Annu and Enlil, "Ah, what's going on?"

I totally fucking forgot about him. That's it, next time everyone gets name tags and gets ticked off attendance lists.

Shayne motioned towards them. "I'll explain later when we're all sitting around a nice fire. In the middle of the room and everywhere else."

Ang hesitated and pushed off the doorway, he reached them in seconds. "What do you want me to do?"

Zeke removed his hand and slapped his thigh. "Shit, hang on a minute. I'd forgotten all about it."

Shayne stepped over demon chunks. "Same thing we are, backing up the Hulk, and making sure Fuck-Face doesn't get near the swishy thing in the corner. If Annu loses hold of him, you step in. Who knows how long he can Hulk out for? He must be exhausted."

Zeke removed a folded piece of paper from his jacket pocket and shook it. "Holy shit. Shit."

Her-Chocolate-Hulk kicked Monster-in-Law in the demonic balls and upended him. The portal shrank another metre, its flow reversed, objects dropped to the ground.

On an upside if we fail I probably won't get mail down here so no more bills to ignore.

The board beneath Shayne's feet flung up, she banged into Ang. "Shit, sorry."

Ang steadied her by the arm and stomped on the board. "You're all right. I got you."

Zeke flapped the page under Shayne's nose. "I've got our way out."

Shayne squinted and leaned. "Ah, hello. Stepson, what are you doing? We're not playing rock, paper, scissors here."

Zeke stretched out the page and pointed. "I have the full incantation right here. We can go home."

Say what? Is he kidding me?

Erin ran over, dangled the medallion and took off. "I'll be back soon."

Shayne slapped his hand, the paper dropped. "No fucking way. Are you serious?"

Oh my God, oh my God, oh my God.

Zeke picked it up, his eyes blazed. "Yes, I am. Come on."

A monster bundle headed their way, tumbled and changed directions.

Enlil's determination never waned. "Dhmmm."

Shayne tripped on her tongue and feet. "We don't have much time. And we'll have to restrain Enlil without killing him. Shit, shit, shit."

Another wall destroyed, a future DIY project—for someone else.

Yes, yes, yes. Here's that faith shit working again.

Erin returned to Shayne's side. "Done. All sorted. At least someone is."

Shayne kissed Zeke's cheek and hugged Erin. "You fucking kids have earned the biggest Christmas and Birthday presents for the next hundred years. Erin, get a few Elders back to retrain Enlil, I'll round up Izzy and Ryan. Zeke, you hold onto that page for dear, literal life. We'll form a line behind Annu in front of the portal. Yeah, yippee, woohoo. Oh and Ang, you, you be you. We're going home baby."

Zeke's cheek, he blushed. "Aw, oh, yeah, okay. Enough of that."

Erin's inhale staggered, her eyes brightened. "Hell yes. Thank God. I'm in."

Shayne's brain wheels turned, "We'll have to get him close enough to the wall which risks Enlil being close enough to jump in the portal. But," the axles greased, she bounced towards Izzy, "together we've got all bases covered. Let's Kumbaya this shit up."

Enlil's monster resurged; he tossed Her-Chocolate-Hulk aside and stormed for the portal. "Hedydydh."

Shayne's belly jiggled, her boobs jumped. "Honey, shit. Guess what, new plan."

Thank you, thank you, thank you, thank you.

Chocolate-Hulk rolled to his side and shrank two feet. "Hurry, stop him. I'm fine."

Shayne slid around yuck, her socks red. "Now isn't the time to be stoic. Shit. Hey—"

Don't say it out loud, dickhead.

"Zeke has the Lexicon's incantation. We must bring Enlil to the wall so the Elders hold him while we get out."

Her-Chocolate-Hulk expanded, he barrelled for Enlil. *"Flarking all right. That's my boy."*

Ah, I'm the one who got all excited about it and told you but anyway.

Zeke scooped up Shayne. "I look forward to being home where you can drive me crazy all over again."

Shayne waved at Izzy, her back ached. "Sounds good to me. Oye, bring him over this way."

Jacekial-Ryan plunged the sword into Enlil's gut and twisted. "There's more suffering for you yet."

Take that you bastard.

Enlil surrendered to the human side, his scream shattered the one remaining window. "Will you all just die and leave me in peace?"

Izzy raised her hands, her voice steady. "I bind him from speaking, close his mouth and mind."

Enlil slapped at his mouth and pulled out the sword.

He's as frustrating and annoying just like other in laws. Except we can't usually trap them in hell.

The babies wriggled and released the last of Shayne's stress, her soul freed. "Thank the fucking Gods your back and I don't have to redecorate."

Chapter 61: The Devil's in the details
The Portal Room, the castle, Gamede

Renewed purpose, validation and support invigorated Annu. The plague of inner darkness died, goodness took its place.

Annu coat-hangered Enlil and pulled him by the collar. "I stand correctly. Good things do come to those who wait. Even though it might take a really long time."

The portals high levels no longer induced heart attacks, divine light flooded the room.

Jazekial-Ryan and Izzy maintained his position near Enlil, they repeated a prayer.

Annu faced Zeke and lined Enlil's head up with rocks. "I'm really proud of you son. You've shown your true self as a great man. It's thanks to you we're going home. I promise I'll make this all up to you and we'll have a birthday party. A fun one. But if it's all the same to you, no Isaac."

Enlil's head clunked, his blood eased the drag. "Hdmdpd."

Erin yelled from the outer wall. "They're in place and I've paused the portal until you get over here."

Annu shifted over a few planks, he quickened. "Great. Thanks love."

"Shay, hold off on saying the first line right up until the very moment we have to."

Thud, thud, clunk.

Enlil's claws on the floor boards slowed him.

Annu pulled and flung him forwards. "Quit while you're ahead, like Ralf."

Izzy ran after him, licked her lips and massaged her throat. "Bind him, bind him, bind him."

Enlil hit the outer wall sideways, red arms reached for him.

Jazeikal-Ryan caught up with Annu. "You lose control of him again and not matter what he's dead. I understand your issue but I have no such emotional attachments."

Shayne lifted Annu's annoyance. *"Yep. Thought of that. By the way once we've assessed the damage and taken care of the immediate stuff, you and I are locking the doors and spending time together. Quality time, with baths, chocolate and you're cute brown bum."*

All manner of ideas enticed Annu, he cleared his throat. "Yeah, all right. I'm so there."

The Elders mumbles had the converse effect to earlier.

Zeke hovered in a blue aura before the portal. "Hurry up people."

Annu downsized and double timed it, he patted Zeke. "Yeah, yeah, yeah. Just because you solved this doesn't mean you're boss."

Izzy's lips moved, no sound came out.

She's praying mentally. Good idea.

Kick, scratch, claw, claw.

Artison wailed, Enlil escaped and ran for the portal.

Annu caught him by the leg. "Flark no."

Enlil touched Annu's shin, the portal room disappeared.

Images of Jaid, Junior, Shayne, the babies, Zeke dead and dismembered infiltrated his mind. "No. It's not real."

In a dank place, blood covered their dead bodies and stuck to Annu's boots, the air chilled, faith stuttered.

Shayne's screech transcended the lies and woke him. "Honey, snap out of it."

Enlil's hand shifted, the room reappeared.

That's the worst thing I've ever experienced. He's using my true weakness against me, because he can't beat me physically.

Jazekial-Ryan sliced Enlil's side. "Cut it out. You know you're done. Don't make it worse."

Annu stuck a Band-Aid over pride and delivered him to Artison. "Don't flarking lose him this time."

Artison drooped like wet noodles, he dangled Enlil. "You know, we are not gophers at your beck and call."

Izzy prayed with renewed vigour, her chest out, her faith the glory.

Enlil flailed—his expression panic stricken.

While I feel mostly sated, part of me wishes it didn't end this way with him. Like I don't completely want to give up on my father but not at the cost of my loved ones.

Ryan-Jazekial impaled Enlil's thigh. "I pray you suffer for eternity as one of the beings you despised so much you threw it all away. On behalf of all creation, fuck you."

Enlil lagged, Artison flicked him. "Feels good doesn't it?"

Jazekial-Ryan withdrew and backed up to the ledge.

Shayne wiggled her eyebrows, she tickled his ribs. "Just wait until we get home."

Zeke clicked his fingers and flounced. "Hello people. Are you ready yet? I realise the portal's paused but that doesn't mean we take all day."

Annu turned; his arm around Shay. "Yes, we are. Geez, your patience needs some work."

Ang limped up the stairs. "Thank flark. You guys took forever."

I'll admit I'm wrong, good things happen to good people. I must remember that.

Annu pulled him onto the ledge. "How about next time I send you in first and see how quick you are?"

Ang's silence escalated his happiness.

Thought so. Everyone's a smart arse around here.

Shayne's tears cleaned streaks along her cheeks. "Finally. This has been a doozy of a mission. Fuck, I just realised Orion lost another Grand Counsellor. And, the UPA will be all over us when we arrive home. Well screw them. They can get fucked."

Political aftermath soured Annu's taste; his memory muddied the experience further. "Great, I forgot about those guys and Ankor. We have to take her body back with us. Sorry, Zeke, give me a minute to get her. I won't leave her here."

Ankor deserved so much more than she got.

Shayne released her hold. "That's the least we can do."

Artison tapped his fingers on the wall. "Hurry up, seeing you all go is the only part I'm looking forward to. How about you Enlil?"

Enlil's expression suggested he'd rather a hot stake shoved up his arse.

Annu jumped off the ledge. "This isn't for fun, son."

Zeke dropped his arms. "Fine, for flark's sake, make it quick then. I'm bringing a timer next time."

Artison bounced Enlil on his palm. "So, how does it feel to fail again and to your own kin?"

Enlil's hair and skin greyed, he trembled.

Annu rounded the corner and stopped. "Ankor, you're alive."

Ankor dragged herself in a trail of blood. "Thank the Gods. I knew you'd stop him."

Annu picked her up and carried her over the ledge. He healed through his palms. "Lady, you've got great timing. For a minute there I thought you were ah, not all right." He climbed up. "Anyway. Bye, father. It's been horrible meeting you and I hope we never see each other again. I won't say thanks for the memories because I don't flarking mean it."

Zeke raised the paper. "Yes, now everyone hold hands and concentrate. Repeat the incarnation after me. Erin, please let it go."

The portal roared and widened.

Erin held Izzy's hand. "Yay. I cannot wait."

Annu's pulse quickened. "Me too kid. Me too."

Zeke held the page, the portal roared and opened. "Repeat after me, Cocama, cocama, veristat, retsuan, retsuan."

Divine light flooded the room, the Elders gasped and turned away.

Enlil clawed, scratched and bit Artison.

Annu faced the light and squeezed Shayne's hand. "Cocama, cocama, veristat, retsuan, retsuan."

Life is good once more.

Chapter 62: I'm leaving on a jet plane and will not be back again
Portal Room and Marduk

Shayne ushered Ankor into the portal. "I'm leaving on a jet portal and I won't be coming back again," flash, flash. "See you soon Birdy. Bye, bye, Birdy, Birdy bye, bye......"

Calm hugged and peace elated her. No amazement or wonder in the world's distracted Shayne from her recompense.

"Hey Enki, we're getting good at this shit aren't we? I'm even signing better than before."

Yeah, we're getting it. We've got our groove on.

"I know it's a yes, you just can't hear me yet."

Annu's glances, smiles and kisses made up for the nightmare. "I love you. I should tell and show you more often. Starting from the moment we get home."

Izzy and Ryan stepped inside together.

Flash.

The babies gained weight each second, Shayne shuffled between feet. "Among other things you better. Maybe there's something in the Lexicon about, oh yeah. Shit. Zeke, you better start writing that thing first chance you get."

The couch, bed, pantry and supermarket missed Shayne, she reciprocated their feelings.

Has Annu considered how much money I've saved him on groceries since we've been gone? I shall remind him before he restocks.

Zeke puffed his chest and jutted his chin. "I intend to. How cool is it that I created the book and sent it back from the future to help us. Except, when I get home I'll have to deal with Ma's death."

It's not fair he lost a mother who cared and I lost one who might have.

Shayne nudged Zeke's waist. "We're here for you and we'll help you get through this. You don't have to do anything alone, okay? I never doubted you had great power inside of you whether you believe me or not. I'm looking forward to getting to know you better."

I better come up with some ideas of what we'll do together and how we'll make him feel important aside from training or babysitting.

Annu did a double take and wiped his forehead. "Flark, Zeke. That's why you went nuts. I had no idea. I'm so sorry."

Erin paused with one foot over the ledge. "Geez, Zeke. That's awful. I'm sorry too. You better take care of this." She handed Zeke the medallion and kissed his cheek. "I'll see you on the other side."

Flash.

That's my girl. I wonder if I'll have another? If we do, I'll call her Irica so she'll always be with us. I guess the original Irica was right about her coming back. It seems my vision was twisted by being here and nothing to worry about.

Zeke's Adam's apple jiggled, he shifted. "Ah yeah. All right. Later. Much later."

Shayne's heart cracked, she hugged Zeke. "You're a good egg and don't forget that."

Most of the Elders dispersed around the castle grounds.

Artison squeezed and unsqueezed Enlil, his eyes popped. "This may be more fun than I thought."

A female Elder on his left bopped Enlil's head. "You're right."

Ang hesitated on the precipice and peered in. "I'm not so sure about this."

Annu shoved him in, he chuckled. "You can complain about it later."

A laugh caught in Shayne's throat, she kissed Annu. "Fair enough. All right, I'm next. You better be right behind me and not do anything silly okay?"

Enlil climbed between two fingers, Artison poked him back in. Enlil's legs wriggled out the bottom of his fist, an iota of fear paused her.

Annu glanced at the wall and waved her off. "Of course. It's fine, go."

One foot in and light bombarded Shayne, she transferred into energy. *Who needs LSD I ask you? Taking a trip without leaving the farm. That's what I call fun.*

In the middle of the universe, pink light encircled Shayne.

A familiar voice projected from unseen places. "Are you ready, Ashera?"

Surge of power, knowledge, wisdom and energy hit her like a brick shit-house. "Yes, my creator." Shayne mentally pressed pause. "Oh, wait. There's something I must know."

"What troubles thee child?"

"Enki didn't really answer my question, why do men have nipples?"

Whoosh, billions of planets, people's, races, flora, fauna, sacred geometry, wormholes and the combined godly experience instilled itself into her consciousness.

Shayne's godliness raised a few levels, a deeper wisdom accompanied it. "Now you're talking and fair enough."

A parade of stars picked her up; she travelled a tunnel to its end.

Shayne appeared outside the caves she'd originally entered, she inhaled decomposition and terror. "I haven't missed this place at all."

Erin did star jumps and cartwheels. "I feel fantastic even though I really want to go home."

Ryan walked over to Shayne. Jazekial's reflection shimmered in the sword by his leg. "So, it appears I do have some powers. Well, Jaz does but I feel pretty good about the whole deal."

Ang vomited on his side and spat. "Screw you guys. I'm waiting for a ship to come get me."

Izzy stretched and exhaled. "I feel amazing too. Shayne, are you able to send me straight to my home planet?"

Pain swept across Shayne's pelvis, she hissed. "Yep, sure can. Just give me a second."

Where is he? He's taking a while and it seems I still need a fucking hospital.

Ryan frowned, and examined Shayne. "What's wrong? Where are you hurting? Is it the babies or the autoimmune?"

The pain subsided, Shayne faked smiled. "Neither. Just a cramp that's all. I'm guessing you want home too or Enki?"

Erin stopped gymnastics and hustled over. "I saw you wince, are you okay?"

"Aha. Sounds good. Really, ready to go home." Shayne peeked into the cave. "Annu? Zeke?"

Birdy spoke to her wrist metres away. "Thank you. Yes, I'll see you soon."

I'm glad she's going home to her family. I will make time to get to know her too.

Worry curdled her relief. The pain intensified, her stomach contracted.

I'm trying very hard not to stress but it's impossible. What's holding him back? I can't keep doing this without medical help.

A well timed volcano eruption in the distance provided the perfect cover to get herself together.

Shayne clenched her inner thighs and opened a wormhole. "All right everyone going home, now's your chance."

Please be me and my man leaving soon too.

Ryan held the sword and oozed concern. "To Izzy's planet please Mum. I don't like leaving you alone. "

A minutes reprieve relieved Shayne, she held her breath. "It's fine. It's only until Annu and Zeke come. I am not going anywhere else without them.

Ankor's calm demeanour didn't alleviate panic. "Shayne, thank you for your offer, I won't require you're assistance and will be collected shortly."

Shayne gritted her teeth through another contraction. "Okay. No worries."

Ang waited behind Ankor. "Yeah, ditto. I'm out."

Fuck I need to keep hiding my pain a bit longer.

Shayne's pelvis hurt, her stomach lowered. "Yep. Gotcha."

Izzy stayed inches close to Ryan. "Shayne, are you really all right?"

Another contraction tore down her sides. "Will everyone quit asking me that. I'm fine all right. Stress less. Get your own shit sorted."

For fuck's sake will everyone and everything just shut up for a minute.

Ryan linked his arm in Izzys. "I'll take that for now but if you aren't home soon, we're coming back for you. Ah, somehow."

Flash, flash, goodbye.

Erin's chewed nails affected Shayne's confidence. "Mum, you're doing it again. What's wrong?"

Absence of Annu and Zeke increased concern to distraught, the pain eased.

Shayne swept aside reservations and unloaded. "I'm worried they aren't back yet and I'm having semi regular, okay totally regular pains. I might be in labour."

Erin rubbed Shayne's upper back. "Hey, they might have landed at Enki. Things go a little messed up when we play with big powers. Remember, the receptions all screwy here? Chances are that's where they are and you're worrying about them for nothing. As for the babies, it's even more important for you to be on Enki and at the hospital."

Shayne hunched—her back spasmed. "But what if they come here soon and I've missed them?"

The volcano spewed lava, trees burned, the air thickened.

Erin looked around and sucked her lip. "Ang will be here for a little while. When you're settled, open a wormhole and check with him if he's still not back."

Agony surrendered Shayne to her daughter's arms. "All right. I'm sold. Let's go."

Among the stars, silent space released Annu, his minute status in comparison to the planets opened fresh perspectives.

After Zeke pushed me out of the way to stop Zeke did he make it out? I hope so.

Annu absorbed ascensions gifts, his concerns lowered. "I must accept it's over and we're done. We covered our bases, acted with love and compassion. I'm in a good place and prepared to protection creation at all costs. We'll gain as much from mortal beings as the other gods and demigods. There's so many and much to learn from each other and dangers to go along with it. And, I'm also ready to be a father from the beginning. "

A meteor shower illuminated and coloured its way across space. Craft flew between planets or hovered in outer atmospheres.

Orion glimmered in the distance and Marduk several planets to the left of it.

True, deep, real peace enveloped Annu. He veered towards a cluster of stars. "Man, I'll smash the heck out of Shayne for the next month. She's never leaving my side again and we're getting married tomorrow. Everything from here on in is together, we're a unit. Warts and all. I've finally let Jaid and Junior go and moved on. I'm not holding myself back in the past or anywhere but the present anymore."

Space crackled, sparks formed a light tunnel.

Annu careened into it. "This is always such a strange and exciting experience. Especially from one who used to balk at using PFD's. I must make time to take Johnny for a ride. I wonder how Shayne feels about him living in the front garden?"

The tunnel twisted, turned, and looped.

Anticipation cushioned Annu's journey out. "Yes, yes, yes, yes."

He stood on a golden path edged by flowers and bushes—birds chirped. "I don't remember seeing this on Marduk and it's sure as flick not on Orion. So, where'd I land?"

Huh? I didn't mean to say flick, I meant flick. Why can't I curse? Well that's really flicked up.

The path continued in either direction surrounded by orchards full of ripe fruit.

Annu wore white, gold trimmed robes and sandals. "Ah, who changed my clothes and when?"

A group of small, furry creatures scampered across and into bushes.

Beautiful surrounds aside, curiosity drove Annu ahead.

One step and clouds puffed under his feet, he floated along the path. "Mmmm. Yeah, okay. Kinda weird but beats being shot at. I still have no flicking idea where I am? Shayne will not be happy about making another trip."

Past the orchards, dead trees, burnt ground, dead bodies and terse atmosphere interrupted the peaceful surrounds.

A golden castle glowed further along; a fracture to the Well of Souls tarnished the place's shine.

Annu's feet clouds beneath greyed and halved. "What the flick's going on here? Am I still in Gamede?"

Light beings, Well and other castle eliminated the consideration.

I'm heaven? Did I die? Or screw up without realising? Shay, the babies, Zeke. Why am I sad but not angry or scared. I understand there's a reason for this if I'm right.

Annu drifted to three light beings over a dead body. "Hello. I'm sorry to interrupt. I'm Annu and I may seem dense but I'm not sure where I am or why."

They extracted a soul, it flew to the castle.

A female turned, rose and bowed. "My Grace, I'm glad you made it. I'm Alyce," she pointed to the male on her right, "this is Elijah," to the left one, "and Grayeeme. Normally, there's usually an orientation and light beings assigned to assist your integration. However, given the situation you experience as well, we're otherwise occupied."

Mmmm, that's not telling me much or confirming I'm dead.

Elijah stood a foot taller than Alyce. "My Grace, if Alyce allows, I'll show you the ropes so to speak. Or do you wish to visit deceased family and friends first?"

Patience lay where frustration once resided, Annu calmed. "Okay. Listen, you've jumped a few steps. Catch me up. First of all why am I here? Nothing killed me on route, what did I miss and how do I get home?"

Groups of Light beings attended to the Well, others regenerated flora, fauna and clusters of cabin homes.

In normal circumstances I'd be in flames and angry. Another big clue I'm probably in heaven. Can Shayne open wormholes here?"

Grayeeme raised his hand. "Ah, I see. Our apologies. We didn't realise you didn't know. In the moments before and during your ascension, Enki went missing or more aptly disappeared from Heaven. As genetically next in line, you're his replacement. This will shock you, you cannot leave unless Enki is returned, returns or your son swaps positions with you."

I'd never considered that would mean here too.

Annu gasped un-needed air. "This is, I, well, flick. Shay, the babies, the universal clean up. The wedding, the sex. All of it. Flicking heck. Did Zeke at least make it home?"

I say what? What? What? Again, what?

Dark clouds shifted across the sun, the air chilled, rain sprinkled.

Alyce's aura widened and covered Annu. "Only Enki the creator, now you, sees all from his chambers. We are privy only to what he discloses. It's a lot to take in. Come, we'll guide you."

Annu's mind boggled yet his head didn't thump. "Oh crip, ship, flick. I'm not missing my babies being born."

Lightening cracked, thunder grumbled, rain hardened.

Grayeeme motioned toward the castle. "Not to alarm you but your moods effect the weather here and it may concern the residents."

Annu shook himself and gathered his ship. "Who last saw Enki and when?"

Elijah's words danced, he glided along the path. "No one's seen him for some time, though the concept of such is rather different here. When the levels opened it was the perfect opportunity."

"No offence but I'm launching an immediate investigation." Closeness amplified the castle's magnificence; a chill ran up Annu's spine. "It's incredulous."

Alyce paused and faced. "Grayeeme, Elijah, I'll take over from here, you help the others."

Grayeeme's smile brightened the sky. "Yes, of course. Call me if you need me, my Grace."

Elijah tipped his head, he bowed. "We'll visit you soon My Grace and give you a damage summary."

Annu relaxed and continued forwards. "Thank you. I appreciate it."

Can I govern creation? Me? Is there alcohol here to soften the blow? If not I'm sure I can muster some up. I've got two months before Shay has the babies to get out of here. She won't be happy with the situation but it beats me being dead.

A rainbow lit the castle grounds.

Alyce touched his sleeve. "I thought it might make things easier if you saw someone familiar. Irica is waiting for you."

Gratitude filled Annu's heart and stung his eyes. "I'm glad. We've got lots of catching up to do. As soon as I ensure my son is safe."

Colour everywhere else paled in comparison to heaven.

Alyce sagged when they passed bodies. "Of course. You'll also be able to see and speak telepathically to Ashera anytime you wish. I'm sorry you being here is under such extreme purposes."

Annu steeled himself for the onslaught. "Yeah. That will be interesting. Is there a first aid station in the castle?"

Alice shook her head and faded. "I'm sure you'll be fine."

"Shay, I love you and was right behind you until Enlil struggled. Zeke push me in and well, Enki's gone and I'm in Heaven in his place. But, don't stress we've got time to figure it out. I'm sorry; I'll help you from here as much as I can. Is Zeke with you?"

Shayne rattled through his head. *"What? Where? You're flicking kidding me. Hey, don't freak out, if you can but you don't have two months. Maybe two hours and Zeke isn't with me."*

Dread re-clouded the sky, Annu's calm deteriorated. "Flick. Flick, flick."

Chapter 64: The Reluctant Heir
The Castle, Gamede

DNA kicked Zeke in the teeth, an inert portal and no divine light darkened his soul. "I'm getting out somehow. I'm not staying here. It's unfair and cruel. How did I end up getting punished? I've been slapped in the face, treated like a second grade citizen, or worse one of the bad guys. After all I sacrificed for the others. Flark, I held Enlil back to save Annu. Except the flarker got out anyway and I'm stuck here. Everybody else got what they wanted except me. Flark. Flark. Flark."

Perpetual night cloaked Zeke's hope and faith in goodness.

The Elders awaited their own fates subject to Zeke in the castle grounds, another burden to bear.

I've been tossed like part of the trashed castle. I hate, hate, hate, this flarking place. Why me? Why?

Zeke twirled the medallion, anger and hatred tainted him. "Flarking bastards. Flark Enki, flark all of them. Like I said, I'm controlling my life from here on. I got caught up in the whole family duty shit and I lost sight of me. Now look at where I am? Good got me trapped anyway. I'll never forgive myself or them for this."

Artison's scare factor had dwindled to zero. "It's their loss and my gain. Notice how they all went before you? They tricked you so they'd escape safely and you'd stay here. "

Plasma burned holes in the floor, Zeke sweated ire. "You're right. They'd probably planned it all along via telepathy. The whole forgetting about my birthday and tearing me from the party was part of it too. To wear me down, make me vulnerable and willing to do what they wanted when the time came."

Artison shifted his weight. "On the contrary here. Zeke, you're destined to rule this realm not your father or grandfather. Your power and intelligence deserve recognition, nurturing. Enlil's self-serving desires ruined many opportunities which prevented him and this place achieving its full potential. You're young and your power is limitless, there's no boundaries stopping you."

Between the devil and the deep blue sea, Zeke drowned in waves of acceptance. "Because, I'm smart for starters. If Annu hadn't lied as much as Enlil, I'd be home a little drunk and a lot happy. Don't even get me started on Shayne."

Gamede, Zeke's new home, required serious work and devotion.

Do I burn it all and start again or just burn it? Why am I even thinking about staying here long enough to burn it? Because they left me here.

Artison's tone transfixed Zeke. "Here's an opportunity to exact your revenge, design your own place and beings with us at your side. Together we'll achieve great things and you'll find a way to re-create your mother."

Dammit. He's got valid points and I don't want to be alone.

Zeke paced away unspent adrenaline. "Humph. You don't care about me at all. You just don't want to be stuck back in a hole so why should I listen to you?"

Artison shifted closer, the half wall crumbled. "Of course that's a huge factor but I'm inspired by your bravery, courage and strength to teach you. I provide secret, ancient knowledge to take you to the next level."

He conjured a floor and a large, leather, cushioned chair.

Zeke plonked and slung his legs over the arm. "Well, it makes sense. Not that I'm saying yes or anything at the moment, I'm considering it. Shayne told me I wrote the Lexicon and there's incredible information in it. I'm the one who told them about the time jump from it that saved everyone in last mission. So, I'm incredibly powerful some point in the future. Now too but more later. All without Annu and Shayne. They needed me and the book, not the other way around. That tells you something right there."

But the darkness, it's evil and I'm not. What does that mean for me?

Artison's tone softened. "Zeke, don't fear the dark power. It's not bad and evil. The good believes thus as it's more powerful than they are. They're scared of it and cannot control it. No one thus far has been strong or brave enough to fully harness its capabilities."

I can't ever show him I'm scared or unsure. I'll allow him to stay around but only has I say. It's my only shot at making this shit situation work for me.

Zeke focused on the Lexicon in a corner and floated it over. "Yeah, I'm still not rushing into anything. So quit pushing me. It only ticks me off."

Blank pages begged for his knowledge and experience, a fresh slate to showcase his power.

I need to create someone to protect and look after it when I'm not around. Like who? That guy Jacob maybe? He did take good care of it.

Artison's gaze bored into Zeke's soul. "If you command it, I'll shrink to your size to help you adjust and not feel so alone. It's a big place, souls will start coming in again and you need someone on your side."

The expanse beyond the castle instilled panic, Zeke swung his legs. "All right, but only because I don't know where stuff is."

Artison leaned onto the wall and shrank to eight feet.

He walked to Zeke and extended his hand. "I'm pleased to formally meet you, Zeke. You've made a wise choice. The first of many, I'm sure. You may call me Art if you desire."

This place is feeling comfortable to me and I'm not sure I hate that idea anymore.

Zeke wedged the book into the chair. "All right, Art. Why didn't you make yourselves smaller earlier? Hey, what's there to do around here when everyone's not killing each other?"

Art swept an arm and bowed. "That would have been less successful, My Grace. Whatever you wish to fill your infinite time with is at your finger tips, at your beck and call. All your desires will come true." A fiery crown appeared in his left hand. "I believe this now belongs to you."

Pride fluffed Zeke's feathers. "I could get used to all that."

Chapter 65: Lick your wounds
Australia, Earth

Heat hotter than Gamede on a good day crackled across red, hard dirt. The sun fried the landscaped and all within its reach.

In the middle of somewhere Enlil's bald head burned. "Where the hell am I? Could have given me some directions or a map book, something."

Trees covered each direction; unseen creatures cackled, cawed and shrieked. Giant dirt mounds and mountains provided the sole incongruence.

The Source's mark over Enlil's breast burned as a permanent reminder of his transgressions. "You didn't hear my side, no. It's all about Enki and the others. How does anything live in this place? Where do I go? Surely this isn't where I'm staying? It must another dimension."

"You'll hear me now, brother; I'm still coming for you. No matter what it takes or costs me."

A brown snake longer than Enlil's resentment hissed and slithered.

Sweat poured from his scalp to his arse crack, he backed away. "Easy, I don't want to," *oh yeah*, "for you to hurt me."

Stripped of power, a shorter height and wider girth topped off the punishment.

Annu's voice rattled Enlil's nerves. *"Enlil, where are you? Where's Enki? What have you done with he and Zeke? Where are they?"*

The snake flicked and whipped, venom dripped from its fangs.

Madness danced across Enlil's mind, he skidded in soft dirt. "I don't know what you're talking about. Help me and get me out of where ever I am."

Shadows stretched and licked his toes. Tree's clawed arms reached for him.

Enlil's human, mortal form laboured, his chest tightened. "I'm not staying. There's no way I am. Perhaps Annu knows where this place is? Hang on, why did Annu answer me when I spoke to Enlil and why's Annu looking for him?

The snake struck, its fangs lodged in his boot and scratched his toe.

Annu jabbed Enlil's thoughts. *"Answer me. Where are you? Where's Enki, you flarking bastard?"*

Or not.

A light brown, two legged, two armed, long tailed creature jumped from trees. A smaller version poked its head from a pouch on its stomach.

Enlil used his other boot to squish the snake's head. "That's just all kinds of wrong. Was Enki smoking something when he designed this place or what? And he judges me. Typical."

The animal twitched and sized him up.

Poke, poke, stab, stab, ouch, ouch. *"Enki, don't avoid me. I have the means to find you and I will. You're not getting away with what you've done."*

Enlil's heart pounded, dizziness overwhelmed him. He tugged his collar. "I can't take this, something's wrong with me. When I felt like this on Gamede Annu called it fear. Does it kill you? Is this my end? Oh, oh, no, I can't breathe properly."

Jab, jab, jab. Ouch. *"Enlil, it's only a matter of time."*

Enlil strode backwards on short legs. "Yeah, yeah, yeah. Look unless you're helping me, I've got bigger problems."

"Good."

If Annu wasn't so determined he'd be better company and worth talking to.

The animal bounced across the road and back into trees, three more followed it. A tree sized lizard scampered up a trunk and hissed.

Enlil's pulse rose, fell, rose, fell, rose and fell. "Everything here wants to kill me. What the hell is that thing?"

The sun rose higher and the heat intensified, it hurt to breathe.

Enlil fanned his face and blew. *"I don't know where they are, all right. It's got nothing to do with me. When would I have had time? Look, I'm sorry. I was under a lot of stress. Get me out and I'll do whatever you want. I'll help you find the useless bastard."*

Annu's tone lightened. *"I will, but not yet. You'll suffer until Enki's returned. If you're lying this time there's no, no kill order. So, ah, have fun with that."*

Crunch, crack, groan, snap.

The top of a tree broke and thunked to the ground.

Dirt sullied vision and the air Enlil breathed. *"Screw you. Have pity on—"*

A dark skinned man picked up another snake by the end and whipped it. "You right there, bloke?"

What the heck? He's insane. It'll kill him.

Enlil's blood pressure dropped, he swayed. "Why are you touching it? It's dangerous. Get rid of it."

Everything blurred, he overheated, his gut churned.

The man's short pants revealed muscled legs. He threw the snake into bushes. "Steady on there, mate. You're a big fella and shouldn't be out here without water. Hope under in the shade for a bit. Have you had a prang or break down? "

I don't understand what he's talking about. Are we speaking the same language? Or is my brain completely fried from the heat?

Enlil's mouth dried, his tongue stuck. "Who are you? Where did you come from? What realm or planet is this? Where are the portals located?"

Massive birds circled, insects attacked him, and his skin itched.

The man held a flask to Enlil's lips. "You can call me Kev. Me and mine live in this area not far away. You're on Earth and any portals I know about are secret ones. Hey, did ya crash your car? Are you from Darwin?"

Enlil gulped water, his throat moistened, his tongue unglued. "I'm Enlil. I don't have a car or know what one is. Where in the universe is Earth? I, I don't belong here. I'm a God not human and belong in the Heavens instead of this forsaken place. I demand you show me these portals you speak of."

How do I get it through his head? He's not capable of understanding the enormity of my position.

The man ushered Enlil to a boulder and sat him down. "Aha, of course you are. Don't feel bad about being a little nutty. It happens a bit to people from the heat. The effects will wear off as you cool down. Don't worry about it. Some people just can't take it. I'm guessing you aren't from around here."

Enlil held the rock and caught his breath. "No I'm from Gamede. What's an NT? Cease speaking in riddles man. What clan are you from? Take me to your leader immediately."

If I stay any longer this strange land will kill me.

The man removed a device from a pocket, tapped and held it to his ear. "Good morning. I need an ambulance to Jabbaroo Caravan Park."

Enlil pushed onto his feet, the world spun. "Listen to me or die, damn you. I'm the dark lord, the fallen one. Capable of destroying you and everyone you know."

"Annu, are you there? Help me, please, I beg you, son."

The man turned the other way and lowered his voice. "No, I don't think he's had an accident and he's not looking for a lost passenger. But he's crazy as a box of bats. Talking about being a God and stuff. I bet he's a lost tourist caught up in Demigoddess fever. Anyways, I found him a few K's into the state park. He's decently fucked in the head."

Ribs dug into Enlil's side, life sucked. "Someone respect my authority. This is an outrage. I demand to go home. You're holding me against my will and torturing me with this environment."

The man sighed and nodded. "Make that two boxes of bats. All right, see ya's at the park soon. The fellas aren't going to believe this one later."

Wasps buzzed, bugs bored into Enlil's brain and crawled under his skin. "Something's terribly wrong with me. I don't feel right."

The man raised Enlil under the shoulder. "Yeah mate, I know and I'm working on getting you some help."

Enlil's legs refused cooperation, they dragged. "Stop. Where are you taking me?"

The man took three steps to Enlil's twelve. "Ah, to my Leader, remember. All good. Calm down."

Enlil relaxed and stumbled along. "Oh well, that's fine then. It's a start."

They'll take one look at me and know how important I am. This isn't such a loss after all.

Chapter 66: Don't wear white after labour day
Enki Island, Orion

Shayne gripped the bed rails, pressure and pain in her down-under fought denial. "I don't care what anyone says, I'm not praying to my fiancé and I'm not doing this without him. Let me out, I'm going home. It's too soon. They're not ready, I'm not ready. Fuck, no one's ready."

Sam changed shades in the corner, and dry wretched. "That's not right and cannot be normal. I've never seen it so mad. It's really angry. I'll never look at another one again."

The next contraction lifted Shayne off the bed. "Will you please stop looking and talking about my whooha. This isn't about you. Someone let me out of this bed."

Sam settled on a green pallor and faced the windows. "You've broken me. My sex life will never recover and screw having kids."

I'll fucking kill him in a minute too. Giant pussy. Not so tough now is he? Actually neither am I but anyway.

Doctor Ruc pushed her down. "As the babies are concerned they're not only ready but eager. These are the first recorded, almost full God babies born in recorded history. There's bound to be surprises."

Shayne pulled him by the beard and glared. "Like I give a fuck and you'll get fucking surprises in a minute if you don't make the pain stop. Give me whatever drugs you've got or I'll punch your lights out."

Rosie detached the doctor. Her patient tone sent Shayne psycho. "Now Shay, calm down. Breathe, in and out. You can do this without pain killers. You've done it before. You know, I cannot get over what that fake Sally did to you nor your real mother sacrificing herself in the midst of all that other stuff. It's incredible. I wish I was there with you. I'm sorry you went through it all alone. Not anymore, I'm here now."

Is everyone around here oblivious to the horrific suffering I'm enduring? What's wrong with them? Maybe I'm not loud enough.

"Fucking Annu should fucking be here so I can yell at him instead of you. It's not fair." Shayne clenched Rosie's hand, pain annihilated her. "I beg you as my oldest and dearest friend, make this all go away and take me home. I'll buy you whatever you want. Name your price. If it helps, I'm hungry, gassy, tired and emotional. I need sleep and food not babies."

Doctor Ruc shifted from harm's way to the other end. "It's way too late for that. However, I'll definitely make note of your pain tolerance for next time."

There's will never be a next time. Mark my words. Oh gods, I'm dying, this hurts so fucking much. How did I do it twice before? I hate Annu, he sucks. It's all his fault. I'll kick him in the.......oh gods, oh shit.

The urge to push over rode everything else, Shayne bit her lip and twisted Rosie's hand. "Fuck, fuck, fuck. You fucking maniac. I'll kill you. Every. Single. One of you. Ouch."

This level of pain cannot be normal. It must be worse than other women.

The overhead light burned her eyes; the whale background music infuriated her above all else.

Shayne's body took over, a baby created the burning ring of fire. "Turn that shit off. Crap, I'm pushing whether you want me to or not."

Rosie squealed and prided off her fingers. "Jesus, woman. Maybe I should have gone home instead. I'll getting Erin to take over."

Shayne's whooha burst forth a head. "No. No. No. It's your job. She's not seeing this and neither is Ryan. Except Sam, he should suffer more. Oh Gods, why won't you help me? Ahhh, get it out of me."

The head popped and shoulders slipped, Doctor Ruc cradled a baby. "It's a girl. A perfectly healthy baby girl."

Sam clunked to the floor.

Shayne's brain swished, pain and relief mixed into delusion. "Shit, who's kid is that?"

Rosie rubbed her arm, she clicked her tongue. "Ah, yours darling. Switch on."

Doctor Ruc handed the baby between Shayne's legs. "Congratulations. She's a beauty."

The overhead light flickered, machines beeped, instruments jiggled and fell off a tray.

Shayne held the child at her side. "You sure she's mine? She's too perfect. Shit, we didn't agree on names. Another thing left up to me." Her stomach contracted and whooha stretched. "Oh, not again. Fuck. I forgot there's another one. This is cruel and unusual torture. Worse than hell even."

Sam levitated off the ground a few centimetres and fell, he groaned. "What the fuck happened?"

A nurse reached over Shayne for the baby. "I'll weigh and check her and bring her back in a few minutes."

The door whooshed open and closed, everything jingled.

That's annoying as fuck.

Shayne slapped the nurse's hand and snuggled the baby into her side. Another whooha explosion loomed. "No fuck off. She's mine. Oh, oh, oh, oh. Shit, shit, shit, fuck, fuck, fuck."

Rosie wiped sweat from Shayne's eyes. "You're nearly nearly there. One more time and you're done. Breathe, in and out. Why is your hair standing on end?"

Shayne's breasts heaved. "Like I care right now. Oooohhhh. Only a man came up with such a painful way of giving birth."

Burn, burn, burn, push, push, push, pop.

Sam lay back on the floor and curled into a ball. "Why did I look at it again?"

Rose peeked over Shayne's legs. "One more push and you're a mum again."

Shayne mustered her reserves and pushed. "Ahhhhhhhh."

Shoulders emerged, the rest slipped out. The baby wailed and pain ceased.

Doctor Ruc raised another bundle. "It's a boy and he's got some heft to him. Another good looking kid, Shayne."

The bed shook, the floor vibrated, alarms sounded and staff scattered.

Rosie slid and gripped the bed rail. "Shay, are you doing this?"

"Not as far as I know." Tears wet Shayne's cheeks; she rested her daughter on the bed and retrieved her son. "Oh my precious, precious babies. You're better than okay. You're amazing. All the smoking, chocolate and universal mix ups had no effect on you. You're safe. Mum's got you now."

The alarms stopped, floor stilled and door stayed shut.

Doctor Ruc changed his gloves. "That's weird. You're lucky and haven't torn much. Plus, you can heal yourself anyway."

Everything will be all right. I'll never let anyone hurt you. The only thing that would make this moment better is your dad beside us.

Shayne lay back with one baby under each arm. "Whatever you say, Doc. It's all good. I'm fine. We're fine."

Rosie's tears dripped on Shayne's bed. "Shay, they're beautiful. What an amazing, incredible second chance. You'll be great a fantastic mum. I just know it."

Lack of Annu threatened Shayne's afterglow. "Thanks, sweet, and I'm sorry about your hand."

Rosie rubbed bruised knuckles. "Yeah, me too."

Doctor Ruc sorted instruments and finished at the business end. "In a few minutes once you're all cleaned up we'll move you three to a private room. I'd like to keep an eye on you here for a few days, make sure everyone's on track. Given you'll be on your own somewhat."

The remark ripped the Band-Aid off anguish and poured salt on it.

Shayne choked a sob, the babies wiggled. "Thanks for reminding me. I'm trying not to focus on it. It's his first time doing the baby scenario and he's missing it all. Nothing I can do about it at this moment in time."

Rosie hugged Shayne's neck. "Aw hon. I'll stay with you as long as I can and when I have to go home, Sam and I will do shifts or something. Right, Sam?"

Sam vomited into the bin. "Not until this has been wiped from my brain forever more."

Doctor Ruc removed his gloves and tossed them in a bin. "I know it's hard but I'm here anytime you need me. You're stronger than you think and despite recent events you're here."

A nurse tidied the bed and supplies, Shayne's single parent status echoed around the room.

She gathered the scattered straws of her prior life. "Yeah, but that doesn't mean I want to do this alone or like it."

The lights brightened and buzzed.

Rosie's undying love blew the straws closer together. "My sweet friend, since we met for sure but after you entered the wormhole in your pantry, you haven't been alone. I more than anyone know where you once were and what you've overcome to get here. You've got this and when you don't, we're all here for you. No matter what. I also know you'll find a way to bring Annu and Zeke back home soon."

Shayne's confidence increased with fatigue. "Thank you. I wouldn't be here without you. I am blessed. I do know that."

The babies fell asleep, a pink aura covered her daughter, a blue one her son.

I wonder what other powers will come out of you?

Leah knocked on the door. She clutched a bunch of flowers. "Hi, is it too soon to visit?"

Her tight body killed and buried Shayne's ego. "Kinda. Yeah."

Bitch, fucking bitch. I'm lying her all fat and shit and in she strolls like a model.

Leah eyed Sam and rushed to his side. "Oh dear Sam. Are you okay? You look awful."

Sam sprung onto his feet, he wiped his mouth. "Ah, wow. You look, ah, amazing. I didn't realised you'd be here. I'm fine just something I ate."

The urge to kick Sam in the testicles overcame Shayne. "For fuck's sake. Really? Really? You're killing my baby buzz."

Rosie rolled her eyes and grinned. "Well, look at that. A miraculous recovery. You've finally got some competition, Shay."

Not after I slit her throat and toss her body in the ocean. Bitch could have least have the decency to be an arsehole and make it possible for me to hate her.

A headache pulsed Shayne's temple and intensified. "All right. I need some time alone. Everyone please leave. I'll let you know when we've rested enough for visitors."

Sam slung his arm around Leah's waist. "Sure thing. You got it. Catch you later."

Leah allowed him to lead her out of the room. "Sorry I didn't stay long. You make beautiful babies from what I saw."

Rosie cocked her head and raised her eyebrows. "You sure you don't want me to stay longer?"

Shayne's nod compounded the pain. "Yeah, I just need to absorb all this for a while."

Rosie patted the bed frame. "Of course. Let me know anytime you change your mind and are feeling down."

"I will. Love you lots."

"Love you too."

The vacant room allowed a chance to absorb the last few minutes, hours, days and months.

Shayne lifted her knees and rested the babies on her lap. "Hey you two. I've got one name picked but any suggestions for the other?"

A screen in the corner turned on and off, the lights copied.

"Mmm, clever but not helpful, my sweets."

Irica ethereal self appeared beside the bed. "I'm most proud of you Ashera. What beautiful babies and the perfect mother to teach them about all manner of things."

She touched Irica's hand, it hit the hand rail. "Thank you. That means so much to me. It's good to see you again. I appreciate the visit."

Irica brushed each baby's forehead. "Likewise, precious. I haven't just come to see the babies, there's something else I must speak to you about."

Shayne deflated, anxiety picked her bones. "Of course there is. What is it? Break it to me gently. I'm fragile."

Irica's patient smile achieved the opposite. "Besides Enki missing, demigods and gods in other universes are systematically being killed. You must be careful as they're coming for you and the babies too."

Shayne's marrow cooled. "Great, just fucking great. When? Do I at least get a nap first?"

Irica faded, her concern lasted longer. "Soon child, soon."

Shayne swiped at empty space and laid back. "It's the end of the world as we know it, it's the end of the world as we know it. It's the end of the world as I know it and I'm not fine."

The babies cried and wiggled, the lights exploded, the door splintered.

"Fine. All right. I finally get the hint. Now what do we do about this problem?"

The End

Stay tuned for Shayne and Annu's next complete disaster in A Goddess's Guide to Intergalactic Warfare.

R.L. Andrew

R.L Andrew is a former Legal Executive, chronically ill Australian writer and Movie Reviewer. Along with many short stories published in International Anthologies R.L. is also a regular, long term contributor to the CrypticRock.com Website based in New York.

This is R.L's third book in the series. You can find all her books in the locations below.

Purchase Books from: Signed paperbacks $25 plus postage (dependant on location)
www.jacolpublishing.com
 or Amazon

https://www.amazon.com/dp/B074YCZDK5

Social Media/ Website/ Blog Links:

Social Media links:

Amazon Author Page - includes short stories in anthologies

http://www.amazon.com/-/e/B00R0OY14A

Facebook Page:

https://www.facebook.com/robyn.andrew.9

Blog:

rlandrewauthor.wordpress.com

Twitter:

https://twitter.com/RAndrewAuthor

Website

https://rlandrew.com

Good Reads:

https://www.goodreads.com/user/show/46603326-robyn-andrew

Genre: Science Fiction/Romance (albeit unconventional)